THE
COMPACT

BOOK 3
OF BATTLE OF WILLS SERIES

MAROLYN CALDWELL

NEWMAN SPRINGS PUBLISHING
320 Broad Street
Red Bank, NJ 07701

First originally published by Newman Springs Publishing 2024

ISBN 978-1-68498-901-0 (Paperback)
ISBN 978-1-68498-902-7 (Digital)

Printed in the United States of America

CHAPTER 1

Early morning, Monday, April 11, 2017,
in the mountains of northern Georgia

It wasn't the patter of raindrops that jarred Lorie Maratti awake that morning. She was getting accustomed to them lulling her to sleep at night or, more perversely, keeping her peacefully snoozing far beyond her normal wake-up time. Nor was it the rumble of thunder…more like the thrum of a small plane engine.

Way too low! Someone trying for a landing? Where?

She pushed herself quickly out of the big bed, where a moment before she had been snuggled comfortably next to her sleeping husband, and reached the window in time to catch only a glimpse of the small high-winged aircraft.

It skimmed across the stables of the elegant horse farm where she and her little family were sheltering and dipped out of sight behind the largest barn. With a roar of acceleration, it rose abruptly into view again above the meadow, scattering several horses peacefully grazing a moment before in the soft rain. Something bright suddenly arced into a pile of wet straw, momentarily bursting it into flame!

Continuing its trajectory, the plane briefly banked sideways—only barely avoiding a disastrous collision with one

1

of the tall pines rimming the pasture—then roared upward, disappearing into layers of low-hanging clouds.

A sharp ring! Jeff levered himself to his elbow as Lorie grabbed for the phone. Sam Mitchell, the ranch supervisor, was at the other end.

"Someone dropped an incendiary." Sam's voice was terse. "The straw was too damp to sustain a fire, thank goodness!"

"Did you get registration numbers?"

"It happened too fast, but I'm betting this is Compact-related."

Lorie sighed. "That would explain a lot."

"What are they targeting?" Jeff put in. Lorie passed the question to Sam.

"Trying to see if the big black is here, I expect. He was standing just outside the barn. I moved him inside quick as I could."

"Get ahold of Ewen," Lorie told Sam. "Ravenwing needs another place to hide."

"Already on it!" Sam disconnected.

Her husband grabbed for his clothes. "And we should go with him!"

Lorie's gut twisted. She had never been as content as she was in this wonderful place. But he was right!

The flowering bushes and trees of the southern forests were reaching their glorious spring peak. Although the brilliance had been somewhat diminished by persistent cold weather and showers, life was finally renewing itself after a puzzling winter, and she couldn't even tell Jeff—her beloved husband, her soul mate—how very much she wanted to stay here. But they had already begun to suspect that the security of their refuge at Ewen Taylor's secluded horse farm had been compromised.

"Why is The Compact rearing its ugly head again?" Lorie grumbled as Jeff emerged from the bathroom clad for action in jeans, a plaid wool shirt, and barn boots. "Those people can't still be looking for Moses's diamond."

"Revenge!" The word resonated. "We keep defeating them at their own games, and they're becoming fearful they can't hide any longer. This may be the first strike in a new strategy—keeping us on the run. Or if they actually don't know we're here, they might be trying to disrupt our good host's life. Ewen is still testifying in a number of trials. So is Emily Wallace, more to the point. She thinks she's been followed several times—although Ewen's guards have been very helpful at keeping her out of harm's way. She must remain hidden. And well protected."

"As must you!"

Jeff headed toward the kitchen. Lorie hurried to dress: grubby jeans, the first long-sleeved shirt she could find in the closet, wool socks, boots. She checked Sara Maria's small bed in the next room. Saree, as they had taken to calling her, was still asleep, her sweet chubby cheeks a prime target for spontaneous kisses. In view of a late teething disturbance during the previous night, since resolved, Lorie figured she had at least a short window of time to join her husband and the outside crew without her small child's vigorous assistance.

When they located Sam in the pasture, he was crouched down, inspecting something he was holding in his hand. A deep frown added even more creases to his weathered face.

"What is it?" Lorie said.

Rising to his full height, Sam gingerly held up a heat-distorted plastic water bottle. "I can't get it open, Mrs. Maratti. The lid melted down in the flame. It came from the plane, though. I saw it bounce high when it hit. There's something in it. See that?"

He handed it to her. It seemed to be a small piece of paper, folded at least once.

Jeff took the bottle, drew out his pocketknife, and began to worry away at the plastic. At last, a large enough hole was driven through. Jeff carefully worked his longest blade into the container, hooked a corner of the paper, and, with great care, maneuvered it to a place where he could retrieve it with his fingertip.

It wasn't large—half the size of an open hand. A page torn from a small notepad.

Jeff unfolded it. "My god!"

"What?" Simultaneous voices.

"'Help us,'" he read aloud and added in a low ominous voice, "It's signed 'the Searchers.'"

"What does that mean?" Sam asked.

"Big trouble. For us." Jeff glanced at Lorie and then quickly scanned the area around them. "I'll update you just as soon as I find Jeb. He might have different thoughts."

He didn't have far to look. Lorie turned, too, at the sound of hurrying feet and saw Jebediah Wallace, shirt tail flying, fingers reaching for buttons, coming at a brisk trot toward the barn from the direction of the small farmhouse he shared with his wife, Emily, and their infant son, Todd.

"You folks gotta git outa here," he called out, "and we're goin' too, Sam. We gotta keep Em safe. We'll take the black with us. Ewen says there's a nice apartment in the bunkhouse at Guy's new place and lots of stable room for Ravenwing." To Lorie he said, "They're offerin' you folks the guesthouse. Plenty of room there, he says."

Guy Taylor was Ewen's youngest son, still in his early thirties. An avid horseman. He and his young family had just moved back to the States from the extended Taylor family's retreat in Switzerland, settling themselves into a prosperous little horse farm in the mountain country of Virginia so Guy could raise Thoroughbreds and, when needed, work within his father's electronics empire. Lorie had been looking forward to meeting Ewen Taylor's family.

Not quite this precipitously!

"I know that flyboy that just went overhead." Excitement resonated in Jeb's voice. Jeff's eyebrows shot up. "Davy Simeon," Jeb went on. "He'd just got outa the military when The Compact pulled him in to be a Searcher. A real hotshot. Could've been an airline pilot somewhere down the line, I reckon, but he was called out by The Compact first. Scotched that notion."

Jeff's response was abrupt. "What makes you think...?"

"That thing he did. Tippin' the plane and then shootin' up like a rocket. He used to practice it in the big back field we farmed one summer for one of The Compact honchos. He knew I'd recognize it, which means he's figured out that I'm here, and they don't know what he knows, but they're on him hard to find out. What's the message?"

Jeff handed him the paper.

"Shoot!" Jeb said with feeling. "Damn it all! Shoot! They wouldn't of called old Davy out to search again. He's got bad knees and ever'one knows it. And he's too damn old. They must've called out his son—that's why he's askin' for our help. They've tried for years—the Searchers—to avoid the most dangerous parts of the mountains when they was first called out to find the remains of that old bi-wing plane Randolph Junior went down in. They've covered most everyplace they figured it could've cracked up in Maryland and the Virginias. I reckon the trouble spots is all they got left. The high ridges and cliffs.

"That flyer," Jeb went on, "Davy Simeon. His boy, Thad, just got back from the Middle East in one piece. And now the kid's bein' called out to do somethin' way more dangerous!"

"How do you figure it?" Jeff asked. Lorie could tell he was clearly unsettled by Jeb's explanation.

Because Jeff's responses to Jeb's suggestion of under-cover work among his old Compact associates had always been uncompromisingly negative, Jeb's answer took on a tone of defiance. "Okay, I've been lookin' up some of my old buddies—doin' spy work for the lot of us." He glared hard at Jeff, whose expression remained stern. "They pass over to me lots of things The Compact don't want anyone to know. I ain't never let on where we live nor what we're doin'. But we can't stay this close to 'em without someone pickin' up somethin' along the way—you know I've always been fearful of it. And everyone knows about Ewen Taylor's involvement! It's in the papers all the time."

"It's those drones," Sam put in. "I've seen several in the last couple of weeks. One of the boys shot one down that was bothering the horses the other day. They thought it was a kid's toy until they picked it up and found the high-res camera. If whoever's spying didn't lock in Ravenwing then, they're for sure getting too close for comfort now."

"That's what brought out the unsupervised visit from Davy then," Jeb said firmly. "Come on, folks. Let's git this show on the road. Out by dark and no one'll know where we went or why."

"Good work, Jeb," Jeff said—a bit grudgingly, Lorie thought, hating to criticize her husband but seeing an honest difference with him on this point. She thought they were mighty lucky to have a former Searcher like Jeb guarding their flanks. Strangely enough—given her jarring introduction to Jebediah Wallace, whose aborted attempt to kidnap her had almost resulted in his own death at the hands of his Compact masters—it was she who knew him well enough by now to trust him implicitly, even if Jeff sometimes had lingering doubts.

But to move right now when she was feeling so warm and comfortable… "Do we have to leave right this minute?"

"If Jeb thinks we must, we will."

The older man's face reflected relief at knowing he had been heard and his advice taken seriously. "And this is the way we'll do it," her husband continued. "Jeb, you folks get yourselves packed up into one of the small horse vans. Sam, do you have one that's suitable?" At Sam's quick nod, Jeff continued, "Load Ravenwing and his favorite mare while you're still inside the barn so no one knows he's going with you. Once you drive out, be casual—stopping here, stopping there—like you're shopping for the farm or grabbing some grub. Don't let anyone suspect you're doing anything but routine errands. Take woodland roads. Pause under cover of trees occasionally and check to see if you're still being spied on. If you're not, full speed ahead. If I know how to gauge the mileage, it'll be an all-nighter and some more for you folks. We'll follow tomorrow." He looked long at Lorie, his expression one of determination tinged with regret.

"After one last assignment," he added then. "I need to see Riverside Plantation again, honey, before we leave Georgia. There's a notion that's been gnawing at me lately that there's something else to be found over there and I want to explore the grounds. One more time. Just a quick look-over before we go."

Intrigued by her husband's request, Lorie was also grateful to glean a little more time to get herself organized.

The minute she got back to the house, she started an inventory. They had very little of their own to transport from Ewen's beautiful mountain hideaway/laboratory in northern Georgia. There were a few small pieces of furniture, some personal linens, clothing and bathroom incidentals, written expense records and a few books—including Jeff's journals, into which he wrote a little something each day. An interesting occupation, Lorie mused, left over from an earlier time when people did not have access to typewriters, computers, or recording devices.

All of the baby furniture and toys would go, of course. Saree's possessions, in fact, would probably take up more of the van's space than both of theirs combined.

Ravenwing's security was prime. The sooner the big stallion was moved, the better. It was also imperative that the Wallace family leave as quickly as possible. Jeb's beautiful mulatto wife was directly related—several generations back—to Jeff's half sister, Rosette, only child of the beautiful Celé...last name unknown, and Jeff's father, Isaac Preston—a fact that had to be kept even more secret than Jeff's presence at Ewen's horse farm because of potential retaliation by The Compact hierarchy.

Emily walked over to the house late that afternoon to announce that they were almost ready to head north. She was carrying her son, Todd, a darling child of eighteen months, plump and healthy, with bronze skin, intelligent green-blue eyes, and thick russet curls unlike either of his parents. *No,* Lorie corrected her thoughts. *We really can't pin that down, can we?* Emily had been repeatedly raped during her time with The Compact's previous version of the Inner Circle as an unwilling "maidservant," and to date, the genetic father's DNA was an unknown quantity. It would take some time, Lorie knew. She also knew the truth would eventually be revealed—and that his father's genetic heritage wouldn't matter any more than Celé's, as Todd was so well loved by his current family that he would never be abandoned either in body or spirit.

She reached for the smiling youngster. "He gets cuter every day." He was already heavier than Saree, who was rapidly approaching her first birthday. Todd was a happy child and Emily a happy mother. Lorie grinned at her friend.

"He's so strong," Em said warmly. "Jeb dotes on him. He loves this baby as much as he ever loved our Celeste. I'm proud of Jeb for taking in a little stray. He says the baby reminds him of himself, and in that way, if no other, Todd is his true son."

"Is Celeste still loving school?" Lorie asked. When somebody risks their own life to save yours, you don't ever forget! An unbreakable bond had grown between Lorie and Emily's brave daughter. But Lorie hadn't seen Celly since Christmas, and emails were no substitute for the chatter they always shared when they were together.

"She's loving everything," her mother replied with warmth, "and doing quite well scholastically, as you predicted she would. What a difference these two years have made in the life of a young person out on her own in a great big world. She is blossoming nicely, Lorie. Both her grammar and spelling are perfect now. And I've been told she's very popular on campus."

Lorie grinned. Jeff's wonderful grandfather, Rolf Maratti, had facilitated Celeste's acceptance to one of the finest small colleges in the country. She was well protected there. And what she was learning in her chosen fields of the physical sciences and education would be invaluable in any aspect of future employment. Lorie's smile faded as she thought about it. The practicality of what that young lady had learned through her nomadic existence—her parents' continuing efforts to escape notice by The Compact's Inner Circle—was far more valuable in terms of the reality she would be facing the rest of her life...unless The Compact could be destroyed!

Lorie sighed. Was that even possible? Twice they had thought they had the problem licked. Twice a new Inner Circle had popped up, each one more determined than the one before to find Jeff and his compatriots and put them out of business.

Very soon their friends left the compound. She and Jeff stayed undercover while the Wallace's truck got underway, hopefully indicating to potential watchers that its venture into the outside world was of no great consequence—just another housekeeping chore.

The back doorbell rang. Lorie ran to the door and opened it to Sam. "Ready to get packed up yet?"

"Here's what we have right now." She pointed to a small stack of boxes. "And these pieces of furniture are ours." She handed him a list. "Early tomorrow, Jeff and I will take my Escort down to Riverside Plantation to have another look-see. We plan to be back around noon to trade my Escort for the van. That's when we'll head north."

"We sure hate to see you go," he told her, and then to Jeff, who had just walked in directly from the horse barn, he said, "You were right to be cautious, Mr. Maratti. When Jeb turned the horse van onto the state road, we spotted another drone circling overhead. We haven't had any reason to look for them before—and now I'm seeing one every time I look around. I wish I'd had a rifle to shoot it down." He paused and, in a grim voice, added, "Unfortunately, we can't draw that kind of attention right now."

Jeff nodded. "Understood! I've talked with Ewen, and he says his son's staff will be ready for us. Sam, my gratitude to you and the staff—and to Ewen—is more than I can ever express."

"We're going to miss you folks around here. I've got to say that you're the most interesting people I think I've ever met."

Once the door closed behind Sam, Jeff began to chuckle under his breath, as did Lorie. "Interesting people" was probably an accurate description. Sam just didn't know the half of it. "When will he get past calling us 'mister' and 'missus'?" Lorie said. "Everyone else calls us by our first names."

"No one's ever formally explained our presence here—I think he probably suspects that we are not exactly who we say we are!" Jeff chuckled.

"And this sudden move proves all his suspicions correct!" She laughed. "Nevertheless, I expect Sam would place himself in front of a speeding bullet for either one of us. He's a true friend."

"And that," Jeff said gently, "is exactly why we have to leave. These people don't need the trouble we seem to generate."

Lorie's reply was thoughtful silence. Once again flooded with regrets at having to leave a place where she had been content and useful, she finally said softly, "Husband, we either need to come to terms with this way of life—or make some major changes!"

He nodded, understanding! All levity ceased.

The remainder of the day, she worked hard at organizing and packing the remainder of their limited possessions, continually interrupted, of course, by her ongoing motherly duties. But even after all the last-minute errands had been checked off her chore list, even though she was completely exhausted, she still had trouble falling asleep—until Jeff took her into his strong warm arms and soothed away her lingering doubts.

CHAPTER 2

Tuesday morning, April 12

She woke early, invigorated and eager to face all the uncertain but no doubt interesting adventures coming around the corner. As she showered and donned fresh farm clothing, she mused on the fact that her life had never taken a smooth path. Indeed, she seemed rather often to have sought out the "road less traveled." Adventure was beckoning once again. Smiling when she heard Saree chattering to herself in the next room, content within her own little world, Lorie returned to reality.

Jeff had already risen, the fragrance of freshly brewed coffee indicating that he had deliberately let her sleep in. He knew it wouldn't take her that long to prepare their child for travel, and in any case, Saree's parents were already packed and ready to go. Sam had seen to it. Under cover of darkness, Lorie discovered he and the other hands had loaded their meager belongings into one of the farm's oldest but most reliable utility vans. Even more warming, the farm wives had provided them with not only several substantial picnic lunches to feed them all the way to Virginia but also boxes of kitchen supplies and enough provisions to see them through their first week, if not their second. Lorie was forever being reminded of the great kindness of good people.

What, then, was lacking in the makeup of The Compact leaders that seemed so apparent and fruitful to most of the rest of the human race? Lorie shook her head, still unwilling to concede that the corrosive power of selfishness might often be stronger than a basic human instinct of man to help his fellow man—or woman—to help women, truth be told.

The faithful little Escort, Lorie driving, got them to the Riverside estate property in less than an hour. Spring was creating a fairyland in the surrounding woodlands, azaleas, and rhododendrons either in full bloom or, thinking about it, fragrant lilacs just beginning to display to a wondering world what spring is all about. The weather was beautiful, luminous blue skies dotted with fluffy little white clouds, brilliant sunshine creating shadows that brought into sharp relief all the glistening shapes, angles, and colors found with profuse new growth.

Although a great deal of grading had been done during the fall on the gravel access road to Riverside, the winter's snow and rain runoff seemed to have had other ideas. The roadbed was uneven and bouncy. Saree giggled every time the car hit another bump. "She's in a really good mood," Jeff said.

"She's a good little trooper," Lorie agreed warmly. "She takes after her daddy."

"Which one?" Jeff said, grinning at her, and startled, it took her a moment to sort out what he was referring to.

"Ah," she finally answered, "the gene donor—or the handsome dashing father who will raise her? Both, I suspect. Jeffrey Maratti—body—Jefferson Preston—soul. They fit together hand in glove."

"Body and soul—both troublemakers, as you well know. Jeff Maratti's awareness is serving Saree brightly, but I think in truth she is more like her dear adventurous mama.

This child is totally fearless, walking at nine months and now trying really hard to converse."

"Well, she's sure trying to do that." Lorie laughed. "Give her a few more months and we might actually know enough about what she's saying to answer her coherently."

"She'll either learn our language or we'll have to learn hers." Chuckling, Jeff turned to check on his little daughter, who was sitting alert in the car seat gazing around. When she realized they were talking about her, she laughed, bright blue eyes sparkling, her nose and cheeks wrinkling endearingly, showing off two rows of tiny perfect teeth.

They came out of the woods at last. Lorie parked the car beside the overgrown laurel hedge surrounding the grounds of the melancholy ruin that had once served as a plantation home. This had been Riverside, Jeff's childhood Eden in those pre-Civil War years. The long avenue that accessed the house across a wide acreage that had once been its lawn was almost impossibly rutted. Lorie didn't want to put her precious car to the test.

Jeff retrieved the stroller from the car. But when tall grass proved too daunting even for that, he put the stroller back into its place and took a willing Saree into his arms.

"Where will you be searching this time?" Lorie asked.

He looked around, thoughtful. "I haven't tried the Quarters yet. There's a possibility Moses gave something to conceal to one of the staff. Lorie, I don't know why I have this feeling that we have an important object to find, but it's almost overpowering. Surely my 'ancestor sense,' as you have deemed it, is working overtime. I just wish it would speak more plainly!"

"Sara?" Lorie called out. She looked around, hoping to see the golden sparkle of light she associated with Jeff's beloved youngest sister. She'd seen the light several times, generally at moments of crisis. Nothing was apparent on this beautiful warm morning, with everything bathed in golden sunlight.

"Saree?" her little girl said inquisitively, holding out her hand.

"Not you, honeybunch," Lorie said to her daughter. "I'm calling Auntie Sara this time."

"I don't think she's here." Jeff also was searching for something recognizable. "But there's a strong pull, love."

"Hand the youngster over, Jeff. Go and do your thing." She took a compliant Saree into her arms and made her way through the deep grassy lawn to an area that at one time might have been a flourishing garden. Vast beds of wildflowers spoke of kitchen herbs, others of cultivated flowers gone rogue after almost two centuries of neglect. Not far away, corsages of tough little lavender irises splashed with gold were beginning to emerge from the damp earth.

Lorie drew in all the scents and senses of the beautiful day and turned several times, trying to find just the right spot before selecting a place to settle. She had brought her workaday red sweater with her, and now she spread it open across a lush plot of grass, placed Saree into the cushiony center, and sat down beside her. "Okay, kiddo," she said. "Let's see what Daddy can come up with. See him over there?" She pointed toward Jeff's retreating figure. "Daddy's trying to find something very important."

Saree looked up into her mother's face. Her dear little face crinkled into a big smile. She pointed toward the house. "Daddy?"

"I do believe," Lorie exclaimed, "you've finally said that crucial word. Your daddy will be so pleased!"

"Daddy," Saree said, beaming and pointing again. "Daddy. Daddy. Mommy. Doggy." She threw in a few unde-

cipherable words and looked around, her bright eyes sparkling with curiosity. "Doggy?"

"No doggies," Lorie answered, grinning. "Just Mommy
and Daddy."

"Doggy!" Saree repeated, sounding quite pleased.

Gazing around herself, seeing a multicolored patch of
wildflowers blazing out from deep foliage a few steps away,
Lorie said, "Flowers. They're some beauties. Now you stay
right here, honey, and I'll get them for you."

It hasn't been more than a minute, she thought with
shock when she turned back to her baby, bright corsage in
hand. *Not more than a minute.* And yet the red sweater she
had spread out across the grass was empty!

She looked toward the cavernous ruin of the plantation
house, looked toward the hedge beside which she had parked
the car. No little blond head, no toddling infant, nothing
moving! She raced across the lawn, to the front of the house,
to the back, pushing through the deep grass, stumbling,
catching herself on prickly foliage. No sign of Saree. No sign
at all.

She didn't even realize that a wild scream had issued
from her throat until she saw Jeff running across the back
lawn toward her. She could hardly speak when he grabbed
her, held her tight, and asked her in a stern voice what had
happened.

"Saree's gone! She's disappeared! Jeff!?"

He looked toward the house—toward the hedge. He
turned, taking in all the aspects of the area where Lorie and
Saree had been sitting, where the red sweater still lay.

Lorie saw his face go white.

"The well," he said in a strangled voice. "This is where
the well used to be! Where did the well house go?"

"Saree!" Lorie screamed.

"Mommy." A tiny voice. Far away. "Mommy. Daddy." A pause. "Doggy...?"

"I'll find it," Jeff said, his voice cracking. "I'll find it." Carefully he strode foot by foot across the ground, tearing up turf, looking around, calculating, trying to gauge in his own mind where the well house had been in relation to the big house, the house that had been burned to ragged ruins by Compact murderers more than a hundred and fifty years before. Suddenly, his foot slipped on debris. He pulled up some rotten wood. More. Another handful. "Here." He stepped backward. "Lorie, do you have your light? The little flashlight?"

She grabbed up her purse, scrabbled through it until she found the tiny LED light she always kept with her, and brought it to Jeff. He was still tearing away at grass, dirt, and rubble. Saree?" he was saying over and over. "Saree, baby, are you there?"

"Daddy?" The voice seemed so far away.

"Daddy's coming, honey. Just stay still. Lorie, the flashlight, please." He grabbed it from her hand and pointed the narrow stream of light into the depths of a looming hole, one that had been concealed only by tall tangled weeds, most now bent and broken. Lorie leaned over his shoulder as light flickered across dark earth and broken wood and finally found its target. A fuzzy little head was down there in the darkness. Far down. Ten feet? Fifteen? The baby turned her face toward the light above. "Doggy," she said. Lorie saw blue eyes looking upward at them and the other eyes, bright eyes, also looking up. "Doggy," Saree said again.

"What is it?" Lorie whispered.

Jeff laughed shakily. "A little fox, I think."

"Doggy," Saree said stoutly, meaning it. "Mine!" She tightened her arms around the wild creature.

17

"How do we get her out?" Lorie couldn't hold her voice steady.

Silence for a very long moment. "Go get the car," Jeff finally said. "There are ropes in the back. I'll rig a harness and go down to get her. I have to be very sharp, Lorie. I can't make even one mistake."

"Should we call for help, Jeff?"

Silence again. When he spoke, it was with hesitation. "I realize people can listen in on cell phone calls, and I certainly don't want to raise any outside interest in what's happening here. But I think we do have to chance it." He hesitated. "I'm bringing Saree up first, but I will need help bringing up the object she is sitting on. I just hope to heaven it doesn't slip downward with her pressure on it." Noticing Lorie's suddenly arched eyebrows, he continued in a calm voice, "The deep water down there, love, is still far below her. As far as our baby girl is concerned, at this moment, she is quite dry."

Lorie gasped, panic returning, knowing how very active their daughter could be.

"Did you make it out?" Jeff seemed to be speaking in a strange tone.

A quick shake of her head. What was he getting at?

"It's the end of a dark wooden trunk with brass trim. It looks to me to be the same size as my father's document safe." He stared at her, words unspoken. She stood speechless as well, her heart throbbing wildly, recalling the tragedies she had been told of. This clearly was the artifact Jeff had been summoned to retrieve.

Jeff spoke again softly. "We can't make any mistakes now, Lorie. We must bring Sara Maria up first and quickly with her 'doggy,' if that is possible, without putting any pressure on that sea chest. We can't chance it sliding beyond the point where it's resting. If it shifts and drops, we may never retrieve it. If it goes with her sitting on it…" His voice broke. She saw tears slipping across his cheeks.

"Keep Saree from moving, Jeff. I'll call Ewen. I'll talk in generalities. He always seems to understand what I'm asking for."

"We must get our baby girl out of that dark hole, Lorie, before she tries to climb out by herself. Remind me what she's wearing today, please? My mind isn't working too well right now."

"Blue denim bib overalls. Straps over her shoulders. Pink baby shirt underneath. A little sweater overall. White baby shoes."

"Of course! That's good." He turned back to the hole as somewhere below the face of the earth a cry of mild discontent began. "Stay very still, Saree darlin'. Daddy's coming in a minute. We'll bring your doggy up too, honey."

As Jeff tried to sooth his increasingly frustrated daughter, Lorie made a frantic call to their friend's private line. When Ewen answered, she talked in measured nonspecifics—"We've got a…well…problem…with Saree…out at the plantation. We could use some muscle." He understood immediately. She got his shocked and hurried promise to bring help.

That task done, she raced to the car. Undercarriage be damned, no car could ever mean more than her Saree! The Escort gamely humped across the rough yard and in minutes was backed up to the hole, brakes pulled tight. Lorie opened the trunk, grabbed out Jeff's ropes, and handed them to him. He started configuring the ropes, quickly making knots while still talking to Saree in a calm deep voice.

"We need something to assure the car won't slide backward with my weight hanging from it," Jeff said to her softly. "Find a downed branch to wedge under the back wheels."

In debris scattered by winter storms, she found exactly what she needed—a wide, decently stout branch with a few stubs still attached as solid anchors. With Jeff's quick help, she shoved it under the rear bumper until it hit the back tires. She rotated it until the stubs dug into dirt and then stamped it down firmly at both sides with both feet. That car was going nowhere!

By the time she was done, Jeff was rigged, roped to the trailer hitch, and ready to go. Using the small shovel that had found a permanent place in the trunk, he was carefully enlarging the opening, pushing away pieces of rotten boards, widening the gap enough to allow him free access, even with a bundle in his arms.

"She seems to have quieted down," Jeff said softly. "Stay very still, baby," he repeated to Saree as he lowered himself carefully into the darkness. Lorie held her breath and heard far in the distance but growing louder the sound of a helicopter's rotors.

CHAPTER 3

She scanned the sky until she saw it—a small copter, a two-seater. Moments later, it put down in the matted grass covering the side lawn, and two men burst from the cabin—Ewen Taylor from the pilot's side, his spiky white hair riffling in the wind, and sandy-haired Randy Ross from the other, both suitably clad in work clothes and leather flight jackets.

"Randy?" Lorie felt a wash of relief that two of their most reliable friends were with them now. "Ewen. That was fast! Thank you."

Their voices were subdued. "We were at Randolph House planning the next equine event in Randolph City," Randy said. "I'm glad I was there when your call came in, Lorie. How's Jeff doing?"

She directed the beam of light into the hole. Ewen whistled softly through his teeth. "Pretty far down," he said softly. "Twenty feet at least. I'll get my light and some of the equipment we've brought."

The light was welcome. There had been no way for Jeff to use the flashlight as he worked his way down the lines. He had almost reached Saree when the wide bright beam went on.

"Thanks," he called up. "Much better. The trunk is caught on a pipe and some old wood that's stuck along the side of the shaft. It's mired in mud on the other side of the hole. Saree's right in the middle, not hurt, behaving herself admirably, hugging her new friend. She's a scared little girl but she's being really good, aren't you, darlin'?"

There was a long break, ominous to Lorie when she heard an annoyed cry issuing from Saree's throat. But to Randy, looking downward, events seemed very encouraging. "You've almost got her, Jeff. One more foot...there, you've got her straps. Oh, the fuzzy thing. Put it inside your shirt and button up. It's probably too scared to bite. There you go, got her." Randy looked up at Lorie and Ewen, a smile of triumph creasing his face. "Let's start pulling, people. We'll have them out in no time. Even Fuzzy Big Eyes!"

Things happened very quickly after that. First the little fox was handed out. Lorie carefully took the scraggly little creature into her hands, patted its head a bit, removed some mud from its fur, gave it a cautious kiss, and placed it in the garden, hoping it might find its family.

Next, Saree was handed over. Her cries were fitful as she snuggled into Lorie's arms. "You're safe now, baby girl," Lorie said to her, lulling, soothing, relieved beyond measure to once more be holding her child. Saree's clothing seemed to feel wet against her arm, causing Lorie to wonder at Jeff's assessment of the water level in the well—until she smelled a familiar odor. She spoke to the gentlemen around her.

"Time for a change. I'm going to get a fresh diaper and take care of it. Thank you one and all." She managed it neatly on her red sweater, still spread wide across the grass near where the men were working.

Doing the necessary business brought her quickly back to a kind of normalcy. By the time she returned to the well, Saree once more fresh and sweet, Jeff was also back on solid ground. He, Randy, and Ewen were discussing how best to retrieve an old trunk tenuously balanced twenty feet below the earth's surface, deep dark water yawning an unknown distance below, waiting greedily for the wrong move.

"Could you get a couple of ropes around it?" Ewen asked. "We brought some with us."

"I could give it a try," Jeff answered with a question in his voice, leaving Lorie also to wonder just exactly how that could be done.

"I've got something better," Randy said. He trotted back to the helicopter and pulled out a bundle of ropes. "Climbing ropes with grappling hooks. There are four here. I didn't know exactly what we were facing, so I brought one for each of us. Think you can hook one on each corner underneath the trunk, Jeff? Weave the ropes together and fasten them to this big old rusty pulley I just stumbled over, which we will secure to that nice piece of tree you have stuck under the car and—let's get the car out of here, Lorie, we need that tree branch you're using. I bet we can do this ourselves, guys. Three's plenty enough manpower for this job."

Lorie saw her husband's broad grin and knew that for all practical purposes, the problem was solved.

Saree's initial whimper had by now turned into a fretful cry, so while the men planned and plotted, Lorie placed her in the car seat, where she would be safe, dry, and warm, and moved the car out of the way of progress.

"Doggy," her little girl was saying frantically, now reaching toward the window. "Doggy."

Lorie turned back toward the garden. She braked and stepped out of the car. The little fox was still there, sitting in a dispirited slump and looking as forlorn as any creature ever could. Lorie thought about it. Perhaps with luck she could catch the kit, and Saree could at least give it a goodbye hug.

She walked slowly toward the animal. It didn't move, just looked woefully up at her.

Then Lorie saw the second kit. It was nearby, probably the same age, lying motionless on its side.

Lorie carefully reached out to touch it. It didn't move, and she realized with a bit of a shock that it was quite cold. Long dead. Either the mother had abandoned the kits or, more likely, couldn't get back to them for some more disastrous reason. Perhaps she had fallen down the well herself. It was clear the kits would have still been too young to care for themselves. She looked back at Saree's "doggy." Streaming through tree foliage above, a shaft of sunlight surrounded it in a soft glow. It gazed up into her face. "Okay, it's not quite Sara's trick," Lorie said softly, "but I'm not going to argue with sunlight either. Doggy's got a home." She shucked off her utilitarian red sweater once again, wrapped the kit carefully within its folds, and brought the whole package back to the car.

"Doggy?" Saree said, grinning at her mother.

"You've got a doggy, my darling," Lorie said softly. "A gift from…well, the earth, I suppose. No instructions with this package. Probably a lot of fleas." She shook her head, grinned back at her daughter, and said softly, "We'll have to do a little research on how to care for it." She placed it on the car seat where Saree could see but not touch. Saree looked up at her, giggled, and reached unsuccessfully toward the sweater. The little fox examined Saree and then Lorie. Surrounded by red wool, unable to escape even if it wanted to, it decided to make the best of things by huddling into a little bundle and closing its eyes.

Two babies to care for now, Lorie thought warmly. Both safe, thanks to the three men now clustered around the helicopter. She turned back to see what progress had been made.

Much had happened. They were loading what seemed to be an obviously heavy antique trunk into a space they had created behind the copter's seats. Once it was in place, ropes went quickly back and forth, efficiently securing precious new cargo.

From the conversation she was overhearing, Lorie realized the team was once again plotting a strategy of simple misdirection in case The Compact was watching the horse farm, which by now it undoubtedly was. Of greatest importance, the trunk would be taken immediately to Ewen's so-called hunting lodge to await their arrival later in the day.

The boxes and tools Ewen and Randy had removed from the copter to make room for the trunk were already being transferred to the Escort. Lorie would drive the Escort back to the horse farm to be stored in the barn. She and Jeff could reclaim the car sometime later, hopefully unnoticed by prying eyes.

The utility "moving van" they were borrowing from the farm was currently hidden inside the largest barn, almost but not quite ready to go. Jeff would do much of the driving, finally getting the open road driving practice he so sorely needed. They would do a couple of ordinary shopping chores for the horse farm first. Once certain they were not being followed, they would join Ewen and Randy at Ewen's "hunting lodge" to reconnoiter and do a quick survey of the old trunk's contents before heading north into a long evening and night.

The helicopter took off shortly thereafter. Lorie waved as it lifted across the lawn, rose high over the old ruin, and turned toward mountain country.

Jeff was silent as she guided the car, much more carefully this time, across the rutted lawn, eased it past the surrounding hedge row, and maneuvered it back onto the bouncy gravel road. "Will we ever see this place again?" he said softly as they reentered the leafy wilderness that concealed the ruins from casual passersby.

"We'll beat the hell out of those Compact people," Lorie said fiercely, "and after that, we'll see anything we damn like anytime we damn want to."

Jeff turned to her, chuckling. "You did it again."

"Did what?"

"Showed me why I adore you so much!"

She grinned at him. How could she not love this wonderful unpredictable man who showered her with compliments every time she turned around?

Saree was babbling tiredly. "Hi, Mommy," she said. "Hi, Daddy. Hi, Doggy. Hi, Papa."

"Papa?" Lorie laughed. "Where did she get that one? We've always called you Daddy." Jeff didn't answer. As the silence continued, she turned toward him.

Her husband was looking straight ahead with a peculiar expression on his face. There were tears slipping across his cheeks. His hands were limp on his lap, as if he couldn't feel them.

"Jeff? Jeff, talk to me!"

He spoke very softly. "'Papa.' That is what we called our father when we were very small. How could she know that?" His voice broke. He bent his face into his suddenly lifted hands and began to weep. The floodgates of emotion had finally shattered for him.

Now it was Lorie's turn for silence. She braked the car abruptly in the middle of the forest road and killed the engine. Finally, tentatively, she said, "The reason she was sitting there so quietly that whole time? Being so good...?"

Still weeping, Jeff reached for her hand.

Behind them, Saree said softly, "Mommy. Daddy. Doggy. Papa." She giggled again, a sleepy giggle. "Night

night, Papa." A few moments later, her eyes closed, her head rolled sideways, and her cheek sank into the small pillow that had been placed behind her head.

"He wanted me to find the trunk," Jeff whispered. "Did he put our little daughter into danger just so we would find it? Would my father have been so callous...?"

Lorie didn't think so. Not for a moment. She wiped at her eyes. She was convinced it was the other way around. From sheer gratitude, she burst into tears too.

Rats! She wouldn't be able to drive if she kept this up. Her purse was on the back seat next to Doggy. Hiccupping from attempts to squelch her emotions, she got out of the car, opened the back door, helped herself to a handful of tissues from the cavernous depths of her purse, and handed several to Jeff. She didn't see anything that didn't belong, but something was there—she could feel it. Very quietly she bent across the little fox to kiss her sleeping child.

It wasn't until she tried to straighten up that she realized she was trembling. She couldn't move, or her legs would turn to rubber. She couldn't see...colors, lights were just a blur... couldn't speak, not even to ask for help...and she wondered if she might simply collapse onto the seat or the rough road. A moment later, she felt warm arms about her.

Jeff was there. She buried her face into his shirt, clinging to the sheer physical strength of him, inhaling the scent of him, letting the emotions she had held back for too long finally sweep across her. "Cry, love," he whispered. "Scream. Do what it takes. Brain and body. Both have their needs, and we must heed what they are telling us." She cried hard now, letting the emotions flow. What if she had lost Saree simply because she had turned around to pick a flower? What if Jeff hadn't been able to find the well until it was too late? What if Ewen hadn't been in Randolph City with the helicopter and Randy—and Randy's ropes? What if? What if? What if...!

Jeff held her tightly, soothing her, kissing her face, her hair. Very slowly a quiet calm began to quench the anguish. None of those things had happened. They were all fine—all three of them. Even the funny little stranger in their midst was fine, more or less. They would care well for the baby fox. He would be okay, too, eventually.

When she finally knew she was able, she leaned her forehead against Jeff's shoulder and nodded into the cloth of his shirt. "We can go," she said, still having to clear her throat several times before she spoke. "I'm okay. I'm okay now."

He helped her back into the car and resettled himself in the passenger seat. He turned toward her and kissed both of her hands and then her lips very gently before refastening his safety belt. He remained as quiet as she was. No need for words.

Once again on course to the farm, she realized that beyond any rational reason for it to be so, her small vulnerable family was still intact. For that, she was filled with gratitude encompassing the entire universe.

CHAPTER 4

It was early afternoon by the time his brave wife was able to park the Escort beside the farmhouse. Jeff gathered up their now alert child, leaving Doggy to Lorie's care. Depositing his squirming youngster into her playpen, he ran a washcloth across his face to dispense with his lingering tears and returned to the car. Saree's car seat was quickly folded, along with the stroller, and Jeff brought both inside to be repurposed in the farm van. He walked into Ewen's spacious office where he knew the remainder of their luggage was being stacked. There was no time now to question what had just happened at Riverside Plantation, no time to worry about what his father might or might not have intended—if, indeed, it was his father who had summoned him back to Riverside and made sure, one way or another, that he found the trunk. Maybe it was his sister Sara trying to warn him about the kind of person his father had really been...

To his surprise, he found every member of Ewen's farm staff waiting there, everyone wanting a chance to say goodbye and good luck by throwing an impromptu birthday party for his little girl. In view of what had just happened at Riverside, Jeff was nearly overwhelmed. When Lorie walked into the room, she burst into tears again, but by her wide-open arms, Jeff knew they were tears of gratitude. It was an unplanned celebration, an expression of concern, friendship, and loyalty. Many, if not most, of these people had become their good friends during the time he and Lorie had been residing at the horse farm.

Every bit of food was gobbled up, stories were shared, tears were shed—and the new toys were packed into carrying bags. When Saree's first birthday party—only three days in advance of the real thing—ended an hour later with the birthday girl by now completely exhausted, the same number of good people who had entered the house emerged. To satisfy the curiosity of any hidden spy drones, the family of three who returned to the house after goodbye waves had subsided were not the same people who had so many months ago taken up residence at Ewen Taylor's beautiful farm home. For future drones, hopefully the similarities would be far more prominent than the differences.

Jeff was wearing overalls now, as well as a farm cap. Lorie had disguised herself by donning a shapeless work dress. It was she this time who was carrying the sleeping Saree, very carefully so as not to wake her. The utility van was ready to go, having been quietly packed during the time of the party. The back seat would be Saree's haven. Her car seat was already in place, and thanks to someone who knew a great deal about pet foxes, Doggy was kenneled in the back end inside a large dog carrier complete with a hanging water bottle and a bowl of softened kibble. Lorie placed Saree into the deep basket that would serve as her comfortable bed on the back seat, secured her with a baby harness, put a security strap across the whole package, and gently tumbled into the basket many little items that might interest her daughter when she woke.

This was to be a long trip. Saree had never before made such a journey. Jeff knew that Lorie was concerned as to how their daughter would behave. But it would not be for lack of foresight or advice from many parents who had been at the party—a heartwarming affair that both he and Lorie would treasure in their memories, even if their little one didn't remember a thing about it.

Jeff couldn't believe how rapidly the plans had come together, but he had known for some time how remarkable Ewen's staff was. Many had come from prior service in clandestine branches of the government and, within their midst, much had been garnered about secrecy and misdirection.

His family got on the road by midafternoon. This time, he was driving. Lorie had insisted on it. A couple of stops at farm stores were listed on the direction sheets that had been handed to him. Products were ordered at both stores to be delivered to the horse farm on the following day. No one in the designated business places seemed to care who was ordering supplies for the farm. And, of course, if any inquiries were made, there would be no ready memory of which staff member had appeared at the counter. Potential questioners would discover only that one of the usual employees was simply doing routine weekly purchases.

Following the printed map and the odometer and with Lorie's invaluable assistance as timekeeper and guide, Jeff turned the van off the highway onto an unmarked dirt road traversing forested land many miles away from where they had begun their journey. Half an hour and many twists and turns later, Lorie pointed out the second, even more unlikely graveled road. That road terminated several miles past its turnoff within a large parking lot adjacent to a multicar garage constructed of logs. An arbor-covered walkway rimmed by tamed wildflowers led from the garage to a large handsome lodge, similarly constructed but cut through by many glass windows.

"We got here in one piece," he said, grinning proudly.

"Good job," Lorie replied proudly as she unlocked her seatbelt. She leaned over to give him a big kiss. "We'll make a driver of you yet."

Jeff stepped out of the truck and came around to retrieve his child, still sleeping quite peacefully after a full day of Saree-focused excitement.

Jeff knew that this house, with its high-peaked roof, while quite ordinary on the outside—if one could deem a log house ordinary in this new century—was on the inside not ordinary at all. While Ewen liked to call it his hunting lodge, it was in fact a fully functional modern office building in disguise.

Ewen Taylor, entrepreneur extraordinary, encouraged his staff to greater heights by letting them reside and work in beautiful woodland settings while they were immersed in creating experimental devices either for his own far-flung companies or for the United States government.

Three of his most trusted research engineers were highly educated, intense young men who knew computers from the inside out. Jeff liked them, even if he didn't exactly understand how their minds worked. The names they went by were Ivan, Bill, and Jared. Although they had homes of their own, and in Ivan's case a wife, they spent a good part of their time either in the many-windowed research section of the hunting lodge overlooking a small lake or in the cave-based laboratories that lay beneath Ewen's two contiguous properties.

As he carried his now sleeping daughter toward the front door, Jeff became aware that today things were to be different. The genius trio was not in evidence. Only two cars were present: Ewen's blue Tesla, tethered to a charging device planted beside the walkway, and Randy's red Ford truck. This was to be a very private gathering. He was grateful to Ewen.

He had not been certain how he would react when he opened his father's trunk.

Their exuberant host, his white hair as tossed as usual, met them at the door. "I'm burning up with curiosity," he boomed and then softened his tone when he saw the sleeping child. He nodded toward the trunk. "Do we get to poke our noses in there too?"

Jeff suppressed the laugh that had bubbled up in his throat. He had to admit it—his own curiosity was strained to the limit. "As soon as possible!" he whispered.

"Put her on the couch in my office," Ewen whispered back. "We'll check in on her now and then."

"Give her to me, guys," Lorie breathed, coming through the door with baby paraphernalia. "I'll settle her properly and join you after you've opened that thing."

Ewen and Randy, they told Jeff, had with some considerable effort manhandled the trunk from the copter to the lodge and, with further effort, into one of the conference rooms, moving tables and chairs to one side to make room for it. Now the men gathered to one side, examining it critically. Standing thigh high, it was nearly four feet wide across the front and roughly three feet from front to back.

"Whew," Randy said. "That's one heavy trunk. What's it full of? Gold bars?"

"I don't know!" After having read something of the past history of the man as recorded in his mother's journals, he wasn't certain now that he wanted to know anything more about the early life of the father he had all his life loved and respected—the father about whom he now held very ambivalent feelings. Only recently had he been informed that Isaac Preston was one of the signers of the Blackheart Compact's bloody document and, as a verified pirate, had sailed on a ship called *The Black Rose*. Jeff cleared his throat and then looked up at his two friends. Both of them were viewing the trunk with increasing frustration. "Any suggestions?" he asked.

Ewen was staring at a formidable latch that seemed to be welded shut. "No keyhole." He looked up at Jeff. "But I'm guessing you don't have a key, anyway."

He shook his head.

"I used to try my hand at lock picking," Randy offered, "when I was twelve and studying to be a magician instead of policeman."

Ewen grinned up at him. "Did it ever work?"

"Seldom, if ever." Randy chuckled. "That's why I'm just the rooky police chief in a small, outa-the-way Georgia hamlet and not a big-city PI. Well, let's take a look. Can we locate anything that looks remotely like a keyhole? Something in disguise." He knelt to examine the latch with a magnifying glass. "I expect it's a trick lock. I can't see any way to open it even if we had a key. Maybe a small stick of dynamite." He turned to Jeff. "What's in this, anyway?"

"It was a sea chest. I've always thought this fancy stuff was just someone's attempt to keep water from blowing through the keyhole. See this little Greek temple welded into the center of the hasp?" Jeff ran his hand lightly across the worked metal. "Perhaps one of the pillars…"

Randy moved his fingers curiously across each of the ten pillars, jabbing at them as he went. The next to last one flopped open. "A keyhole!" he crowed. "I saw that once on the internet."

Ewen looked at Jeff again. "We still need a key."

"Maybe I can find one." As Randy had done, Jeff traced the top of the trunk with his fingertips, examined the heavy metal straps that bound the leatherwork, and especially the brads securing the straps. Not yet finding what he had expected, he continued his examination, running his fingers across the leather itself, the sides, the front, the back, as well as midpoint construction and each of the elaborate corners. No luck.

Then he found it—an anomalous lump under the leather, scarcely noticeable unless one expected it to be there. It was located on the center back strap not far below the hinged lid. He pressed on the lump. Nothing happened. Again, he ran his hands over the metal. Moses's signature, of course—a second anomaly—was found several inches below the first. Jeff pressed both lumps at the same time. A portion of strap that lay between them burst open, side to side, revealing beneath a solid iron key.

"Got it!"

Cheers arose.

"Shhh!" Lorie said, coming back into the room.

"You're just in time!" Randy was scarcely able to contain his excitement. He turned back to Jeff. "Who's the genius who thought this stuff up? Our redoubtable Major Preston?"

Jeff rose to his feet, glanced at Lorie. Her face remained impassive. He looked at Ewen. Ewen's eyebrows were slightly raised. His gaze shifted back to their good friend, Randy Ross, whose expressive freckled face and intelligent gray eyes now held many more questions than the simple one he had just asked.

Randy was one of the three people who had buried Moses's priceless South African blue diamond cluster—the ransom that was to be paid to pirates by a Zulu king for the safe return of his brilliant first son whom he thought had been pressed into slavery. For his own protection, even Ewen was not privy to any information about the diamond cluster. Jeff had not a doubt as to Randy's complete discretion. Much more had to be accomplished before this campaign was over.

It was time Randy, at the very least, knew the truth. "It was my father's trunk. He'd been a sailor when he was young."

Randy's mouth dropped open. Then shut. He was quiet for a time. "Your father Carl lives in New Jersey," he finally growled. "He's a great guy, smart as a whip. I've had lots of chats with him. Besides being a high school history teacher, he owns a jewelry store. Same as Rolf, his dad. Your grand-father. Your father told me flat out one time that he's never been a sailor in his life. He told me he gets seasick when he sees a rowboat. Why would he have a sea chest?"

When Jeff didn't respond, Randy looked around and noted Ewen's bland expression. Lorie's as well. He found a chair. Sat down. He looked up at Jeff again. "I thought so!" He stood up, reached out his hand to Jeff. "By god, you really are Major Preston, aren't you? I've always thought so, felt it deep in my gut, but I figured that if I said it out loud, every-one would think I was nuts!"

Jeff took his hand, grinning, and then clasped his hands across his friend's shoulders. "It's a little hard to explain," he said, "even to me, but it will be easier to deal with the con-tents of this trunk if everyone here is, as they now express it, 'on the same page.'"

"Welcome to the deepest layer of the counterconspir-acy," Ewen said to Randy, also reaching for his hand. "The only other people who know about this strange business are Rolf and my twin brother, Bob."

"Don't forget Rolf's lawyer, Arthur Ehrlich," Lorie put in while giving Randy a hug. "But he has decided there has to be another explanation, so we don't push it. Emily knows, too, but she's related to Jeff and she senses these things."

"She's related?" Randy echoed softly. "And the young man we call Jeff, Carl Maratti's son? The soldier whose brain was so badly damaged he shouldn't have recovered. Where is he? Is he dead?"

"An even stranger arrangement," Lorie said.

"He is right here," Jeff said softly. He touched his chest and then his head. "Flesh and blood. Here remains the corporeal part of his body. I can access his memories, sweet or tortured, at any time if I so wish. I will carry them until this body has lived out its full life, and his parents will never know of my part in their son's existence. But of the more elusive essence of life that animated him, the consciousness you might call it—the raw awareness that realizes the world in its fullness—our little daughter now carries that precious gift, and will never know who she was in a past life."

"Wow!" Randy sat down again, put his head into his hands, and sat silent for fully five minutes before lifting his face to them again. "That's kind of hard to get my brain around! It's like a…a transfer of a soul, right? It ties in to the mystique associated with the Blackheart Compact, doesn't it?"

"I am beginning to wonder," Jeff replied quietly, "if that Compact document has a blood component to it that somehow transcends time. My mission—our mission—is to annihilate that document, bloody signatures and all, so that no one is further harmed. Apparently, my father was one of its original signers. This is his trunk. We hope it might hold some clues as to how we can locate The Compact itself. The original document."

"This trunk…" Randy pointed, his eyes widening. "Isaac Preston—former pirate. This is his sea chest?"

Jeff nodded. "He was a young man who seems to have grown up very fast during that time. More importantly, later in his life, this trunk served as his document safe. When he realized raiders were on their way to Riverside Plantation during what you now call the Civil War, he must have asked his men to drop it into the well so it couldn't be found. Apparently, he then directed them to destroy the well house so no one would think to look there."

"How did you know the trunk was there?" Randy asked.

Jeff answered slowly, "I didn't. I woke up several days ago aware that there was something yet at Riverside I needed to find. Unfortunately," he gave a short wry laugh, "Saree got there first. But thanks to you folks…" For the moment, he was unable to continue speaking. A large lump had come into his throat. Understanding, Randy placed a comforting hand on his arm.

"Do you think The Compact document is in this trunk?"

Jeff shook his head, finally taming his emotions. "We've been told that the Inner Circle has continual access to the original Compact, with enough documentation, highly computerized…"

"As we have discovered to our occasional advantage," Ewen put in, a sly smile creasing his face, "since we have very good code breakers working for us."

Jeff continued in a grim voice, "Unfortunately, that's how they locate the descendants of the original signers so they can 'call somebody out' to do what they consider 'a necessary task,' on pain of a loved one's torture or death if the task is not completed quickly and correctly. My simple duty—our duty, if you choose to join us—is to destroy the original document, all copies and all the accompanying research. Break the traces to family lines. In sum, obliterate The Compact!"

Without comment, Randy held out his hand.

Jeff took it, as did Ewen, who then said impatiently, "Well, are we going to open this trunk or not?"

Jeff grinned. "This key is burning my fingers!" He brought it back to the keyhole, slipped it into place, and heard the latch move smoothly backward into its shaft. He returned the key to its hiding place. "Done! Let's get our marching orders!"

CHAPTER 5

The huge dirty white canvas, weathered and torn, had been folded many times over, its bulk concealing everything below. When Jeff began to draw it out of the trunk, a gasp escaped him. Still unknowing, Randy took a corner to give an assist. Also trying to be helpful, Ewen took the other corner. As they lifted and unfolded the first section, a black symbol seemed to leap from the cloth.

"Damn!" Ewen exclaimed, dropping his end.

"Skull and crossbones!" Randy whispered with distaste as the flag slipped from his hand to the floor with a thump. "Holy shit!"

Lorie gave a cry of alarm and backed off—almost as if she had been pressed!

"It's only a piece of canvas cloth," Jeff said sharply. "Woven cotton. And black paint—simple black paint!" Again, he wrapped his hands around the huge bundle, jerked it intact from the trunk, pressed the loosened sections deep into the canvas folds from which they had appeared, and shoved the artifact under the nearby table.

But he, too, had felt the power of it—a slash across his chest. This dreaded symbol of fear, of torture, of the frantic grasp for an elusive death. This flag—almost a living organism!

"I bet," Ewen said rather too lightly, still trying hard to regain his own composure, "that some museum might welcome an authentic pirate flag."

Lorie answered definitively. "Not this one!"

"It must be destroyed," Jeff said quietly, "along with the original Blackheart documents."

Ewen cleared his throat. "I stand corrected. It won't go back into that trunk either." He left for not more than a moment and returned with a thick black plastic bag meant for holding yard waste. The flag was handled as little as possible, simply shoved into the bag. Randy folded over the top of the bag several times and finally sealed the opening with wide reinforced tape.

Jeff nodded his gratitude. He took a couple of deep breaths. "Ready for more?"

An obviously shaken Randy said, "Couldn't be worse! Bring it on!"

The next several layers consisted of accumulated journals, all carefully scripted in black ink. Jeff handed them out to Ewen and Randy two or three at a time. "It might be easier to document them if we can get them into chronological order. Are they dated?"

"Inside the front cover of each," Randy said. He had been scanning some of the pages. "From the date of the first entry to the date of the last. Very organized, your father. He had fine handwriting. Some of the spelling seems a little strange, though."

"He told me," Jeff said, "that his mother taught him how to write when he was a small child. Anything else he knew about writing, my mother taught him, and that was well after these books were written. She was a practicing teacher when Father married her."

Ewen had also been taking brief forays into some of the journals handed to him. "When did he learn Zulu?"

Jeff raised his head. "Sorry?"

"Zulu." He looked up at Jeff. "This whole book is written in Zulu. It's a bit different from the journals your mother left but not that much. Possibly I can do a little reprogramming and get the computer to read them."

"What's the date?" This was something totally unexpected.

Ewen turned back to the inside cover. "July 1830."

"My god! Are you sure?" His mother had not met Moses until she arrived at Riverside Plantation as a new bride. "The way I understood it," he said a bit tentatively, "my mother devised the Zulu code with Moses a couple of years after she got to Georgia, 1832 would be the earliest. Maybe '33."

"I've got one, too," Randy said, holding it up. "This is dated August 1828."

Jeff was perplexed. "May I see it?"

"Sure." Randy handed it to him.

He leafed through it. "It's definitely Zulu." He looked up at his companions. "That's my father's handwriting. And you're right. The words don't seem to be quite the same, although I expect if we knew the correct pronunciation, perhaps they would be."

"So you read Zulu, but you don't know how to say it out loud?" Randy glanced at him with renewed appreciation.

He smiled. "I wish I did. I heard it often enough in the markets. It's an interesting language, and even though I couldn't speak it properly, I could understand it pretty well. When it came to conversation, I listened and didn't let on unless I needed to." No one answered him. Lorie and Ewen were sitting very quiet watching Randy, who was staring at him with a strange expression on his face.

"What's the matter?"

"Markets?" Randy said hesitantly. "Dare I ask what markets you were you speaking of?"

"Probably the ones—the ones you think I'm talking about."

"Where people were bought and sold as slaves?" Randy said softly. "I can't imagine…"

"It was heartbreaking—an infuriatingly helpless experience for those of us who knew black people to be flesh-and-blood human beings as closely connected to friends and family as we ourselves. What's more, they were all alone, defenseless in a world where they understood nothing, not even the language—and most especially *why them*!" He cleared his throat and then said briskly, "Okay, how many journals do we have?"

Ewen had been jotting down a quick log, including dates. He started to count. "A lot. I've got fifty-one recorded so far." He peered back into the trunk. "Four left in there."

"Fifty-five." Jeff repeated the total and then made his decision. "Can you pull out all of the journals written in English, please. Lorie and I can take them with us. The rest, Ewen, can remain here for further examination, if it's okay with you,"

"I'm honored!" the big man said briskly. "This is fascinating! I'll get my experts on it, and we'll keep in close touch."

The books were sorted quickly. As they had just discovered, twenty of the books seemed to comprise a young man's journal written in some version of English, with accompanying illustrations. They fit easily into the leather mailbag Ewen pulled from his office closet and handed to Jeff.

The remainder were packed into cardboard file boxes and taken to a walk-in safe in one of the back rooms of the log house. "Safe from predators of all kinds," Ewen said.

"Okay," Jeff said as the boxes were stacked. "Let's see what the next layer holds."

A carefully cut piece of canvas had been laid down in the bed of the trunk prior to the books being placed inside. This canvas had been secured by metal brads hammered firmly into a form of substructure beneath. Clearly, something was there.

Ewen went away to find a solution. He came back with several hefty screwdrivers and a couple of prying tools, and the three men went to work. It took half an hour to remove the many nails. Starting at one corner, Jeff lifted the canvas—very carefully.

His first view was of soft velvet bags of many sizes and colors sealed by encased cords tied tightly at the top. He picked up a relatively heavy bag, pulled it out for all to see, and started working at its cords. "Bring something for me to pour this into," he said as the bindings loosened. Ewen brought a large ceramic bowl from the kitchen.

"Will this do?"

"We'll see." He tipped up the bag. A torrent of various-sized coins tumbled out, filling the bowl with liquid sunshine that settled a moment later into luminous metal.

Like a gust of wind, a wordless sigh whistled through the room.

Head filled with confusion, heart with revulsion, Jeff looked desperately from Lorie to Ewen to Randy. "We will leave these till another day," he finally said in a very deep voice. "Are you willing to store this trunk, Ewen? I can't think of a safer place to leave it. We must get back on the road. We have many miles to travel yet."

"Consider it done!"

"Thank you again for everything." Struck nearly numb with the unwelcome discovery, Jeff reached out hand. "Please feel free to examine the pirate gold if you wish. It would be prudent to have an accounting. If museums or private collections were raided sometime in the past, pieces must be returned."

"Jeff," Ewen said softly, seeming to understand quite clearly his good friend's aversion even to putting his hands on potential evidence of his father's misdeeds, "please defer your judgment to another day. We'll do some investigation. Your father's written accounts may well explain what lies here."

"It can't possibly be good." He turned to Lorie. "Ready to go, honey?"

"I'll get Saree." Lorie, too, seemed disturbed by what she had seen. They would figure it out together, he and his excellent wife. It would all come clear given time.

But Ewen was not all that eager to have them leave. "Whoa, partners," he said, and with Randy's help, a quick meal was pulled together. Thus, they were able to sit down for a time with good friends while a feeling of "normalcy" slowly returned.

Lorie also had time to phone her parents and her aunt Carol in Marietta on what was designated a "safe" phone to let her family know what was happening—and to reassure Carol and Carol's doctor husband, Phil, that they would call as soon as they were resettled. It also gave Saree a chance to eat new food, explore exciting territory, discover amazing new objects, cuddle with all her admirers, and build up a comfortable tiredness that would assist in her sound sleep during the remainder of their journey. A decided plus!

In addition, they were able to tend to their new little pet, Doggy, who seemed to crave the warmth of their welcoming arms as they offered him tidbits of food.

As a result, in the short time before they had to be on the road, much of the intense emotion that might well have crippled Jeff had been released.

Good friends, he mused with a cleansed sense of normalcy and well-being, are a far better treasure than gold.

CHAPTER 6

Tuesday evening, April 12–
Wednesday morning, April 13

Daylight was fading as Jeff finally turned the van north onto the interstate. He had wanted to stay on country lanes, not looking forward to tackling crowded highways. But by now, he figured that time might pose a problem. They had stayed a little too long at Ewen's log cabin—even though he was happy they had done so. Yes, it had freshened the air, he thought. He had been far luckier in his friendships, it seemed, than his father ever had.

The monotony of driving was good right now. He didn't want to have to think about what had happened that morning: Saree's tumble into the well, the discovery of the terrible trunk, the realization that they were now genuine fugitives! Not important right now. None of it. All he needed to do was to concentrate on keeping the van headed north while trying to avoid travelers who seemed to think he was driving too slowly in what Lorie called the passing lane and let him know it by blinking their lights or using their annoying horns. He experimented with the gas pedal, finally found a good speed—much the same as the car ahead of him, which had just moved back to the driving lane—and followed that blessed car for mile after mile after mile. Lorie had been asleep for some time when he began to hear chirping sounds coming from the back seat.

"Honey," he said gently, "I think somebody's awake." In retrospect, he was beginning to feel pretty tired. Perhaps it was time for a couple of changes.

Lorie's head rose reluctantly from the cradling pillow. "Good timing, love," she said sleepily. "There's a rest area ahead. Pull in when you get to it. We'll see what the children need and then switch drivers."

Now comfortably settled in the van's passenger seat, content, he snuggled his tired head into Lorie's pillow and, surrounded by the essence of her, fell into dreamless sleep. The roads rolled smoothly beneath the van's tires, and when he was nudged awake for Lorie's coffee break and "potty stop," he realized with amazement that they were somewhere deep in the heart of North Carolina. This whole thing—night driving on a huge roadway—was mindless, soothing, like a kind of dream. All you had to do when you were in charge was to sit on a comfortable couch propped into position by a rotating wheel, set the computer device that told the car how fast its tires needed to turn, and let the road move effortlessly beneath. The only major problem, as he could see it, was having to keep your eyes open and your mind sharp. Big signs loomed out of the darkness to tell you where you were. Small lists of towns posted alongside the road informed you how far you had to travel to get to a branching destination. There were many comfortable inns to offer private beds if you wished, as well as more than decent food. And of greatest importance, toilet facilities were superb, and there was always warm running water available to cleanse your hands, face, and more intimate parts of your body.

It was a quite a difference from the conditions he had been accustomed to during his first life. Even the brand-new locomotives put into service in the Southern states during that time to transport carloads of passengers along iron tracks had not seemed as comfortable as this mode of transportation. He was pleased. This was quite a good thing!

Twice more during the night, he and Lorie changed places. He thought she didn't want to leave him too long at the wheel in the dark of night when, with fog rising, oncoming headlights occasionally seemed to hang in midair bereft of a road. "Too confusing," she had said. Sometimes it was surely that. But now that he was beginning to get the hang of it, he sensed that night driving was something that Jeff Maratti, his alter ego, had truly enjoyed.

As a golden glow began its spread across the eastern sky, he realized with delight that they were occasionally passing through clouds, that the roadside vistas at each side were grand, sweeping, and excruciatingly beautiful. "We're on the Skyline Drive in Virginia," Lorie said, pleasure singing in her sweet voice. She sat up and inspected the big map book, which she kept in the door pocket. "And we're within striking distance of Guy's place now. Would you like me to take over so you can see the sights and mind the map? There's this wonderful place I want you to see!"

And so he became navigator through a portion of Shenandoah National Park—the only part of the road he had to pay for and not much at that—and by the time dawn broke in its full radiance and they left the park to descend into the Shenandoah Valley, it was as if they were flowing along with the river itself between two mountain ranges. Shortly, Lorie turned the van off the main highway onto a country road and, at last, into the driveway of a sprawling twenty-first-century, two-story home nestled behind white fences, gates, and concealing trees.

A tall good-looking young man, clean-shaven, blond, muscular, hurried from the house to meet them. "Hi. I'm Guy Taylor," he called out. "You can park your van in the first barn." He walked beside them to show the way, opening all the appropriate gates and doors.

"You do look so much like your father," Lorie told him as she finally opened the car door. "Except for the hair!" Smiling, she took his hand in a firm shake. "Thank you for taking us in on such short notice."

Grinning broadly, Guy said, "Anyone with Ewen Taylor for a father is used to emergencies like this." His smile faded, and his face became serious. "Let me caution you right now—we don't use his last name here. We're using my wife's last name. Striker."

"Your father is a very wise man," Jeff responded solemnly.

Guy grinned and went on. "He's waiting for you in our big study, the one he uses as his Virginia office. I guess he'll have to tell you why." He then focused on Lorie, leaving Jeff alone to absorb the shock of his announcement.

Ewen was there? They had just left him in Georgia!

Guy went on, as if what he had said hadn't hit like a thunderclap. "We have a small but very nice guesthouse ready for you folks, Mrs. Maratti. You might like to take your little girl over there and get her settled right away. We've got a great nanny on call who's volunteered to help you get your personal things unpacked, and she can babysit for a time. Come on up to the big house when you're ready for some breakfast."

Later, Jeff realized how smoothly that task had been done—in a flash—separating himself from Lorie and giving her a few small tasks to keep her busy for a crucial half hour.

Ewen was here? Why? How had he got here? Jeff looked across the horse pasture and saw the Robinson R-44 sitting on a pad in front of a decent-sized hangar. "Come," Guy said to him softly, urgency in his tone.

Ewen met him at the doorway and ushered him into a pleasant office area complete with a large desk, a bank of computers, a couch, and a very welcome coffee maker. "I had to speak with you privately," he said to Jeff, closing the wooden double doors even against his own son.

Dread crept across him. "What's happened? The farm? Randy?"

"No no no!" Ewen said. "The pirate flag."

"The flag?" He was confused. They had bagged it to be burned.

"We took it out of the bag, Randy and I, to get a second look. When we opened it, this spilled out, along with a note." Ewen held out something wrapped in a towel.

Very carefully, Jeff pulled it open and then recoiled. "Scalps?"

The first had long black hair attached, ending in a pigtail bound with a bloodstained ribbon. The second was blond and sparse with a bit more dried skin clinging to it. The third was a full scalp, skin and hair. The color was russet, and it hung in tight curls.

The dream quality of the trip that had been clinging to him shattered. Once more, he felt the nightmare!

Ewen cleared his throat. "So they are human scalps. I wasn't sure."

"No doubt about it. What did the note say?"

"Now I don't know what this means—I hope you'll want to tell me, but I won't force you to say anything."

"Just read the note, man!"

Ewen looked directly into his eyes and then down at the paper. He read very softly, pausing at the end of each sentence. "'Revenge for Talisa. My son can burn these with the flag. The score is even. The pain lingers.'"

"Oh, dear god!" Not touching the scalps, he rewrapped them with Ewen's towel and sat still for a long moment. He didn't move until he heard Lorie speaking to someone outside.

"I'm going to be here for a day or two, Jeff," Ewen said, "helping you with your move. If you want to tell me anything, you may. Or not. It's for you to decide."

"Let's try to keep it from Lorie. Please!"

"Your call, Jeff."

Jeff looked up at this man who had become such a good friend to him that he thought of him as an uncle—perhaps even an older brother. "Thank you for your discretion. When we have a moment, I will tell you all I know. Perhaps the rest can be found in my father's journals."

"Good enough." Ewen took back the wrapped package and placed it into a deep drawer in his desk. He closed the drawer, locked it, and handed the key to Jeff. Then striding to the doors of his study, he threw them open and welcomed Lorie and Saree warmly into his son's home.

They had arrived in time for breakfast. Guy's four-year-old twins, Tony and Jack, were just rising from their beds, wondering what new exciting thing Grandpa had just brought to their house. Guy's wife, Alexi, showed no sign of surprise or annoyance. She was beautiful, calm, and efficient all at the same time. The first time Jeff saw her, she was barefoot and wrapped in a long robe. Thirty minutes later, her feet were clad in moccasins, and she was wearing jeans and a red sweat shirt with the words "Mountain Magic Farm" written across it in a graceful white script. Her long brown hair was pulled back into a loose braid. She looked to be quite at home in this country environment. "I grew up on a horse farm in Kentucky," she told him. "This is heaven to me, looking around and seeing mountains, green fields, white fences, and lots and lots of horses." Without seeming to put any effort to it, she produced, as he told her, a breakfast worthy of some of the greatest cooks who had ever fed him…with the notable exception of his own wife, Jeff thought privately, reaching for Lorie's hand under the table and grinning at her.

She squeezed his hand. He could tell she was wondering what Ewen was doing here but wasn't going to ask. He squeezed back, raising his eyebrows, indicating that everything was okay and she would find out sooner or later. She gave him a wink. They never seemed to need words to communicate.

Saree, wide awake by now, was having a delightful time sitting in her high chair at the table, banging with a fork for attention, asking for pancakes and bacon by pointing at them, and turning her most beseeching gaze toward her father until he caved. Unmoved, the little boys bolted their food and then headed toward more promising territory—their toy baskets in the next room, packed this morning with small gifts from Grandpa!

"Quite an appetite," Guy said, laughing as he watched Saree. "Our guys have got to the point that they're picky as can be. Every couple of weeks they switch off on what they don't or do like—and of course, it's never the same for both of them."

"They look so much alike," Lorie said, "but I can see that Tony's forehead is a little higher and his cowlick more pronounced. And Jack's face is a little rounder."

"Well done," Guy exclaimed. "But if you don't have them both right in front of you for comparison, can you still tell?"

"You mean like Ewen and his twin, the redoubtable Bob? Absolutely!"

"You are very discerning, my dear Lorie," Ewen said, smiling at her. "And empathetic to a fault. With what you have had to deal, it's good to have those traits among your genetic characteristics. They have gotten you into a lot of trouble…but," he paused for effect, "they have got you out as well!"

"I have my moments." Lorie laughed.

Jeff let his eyes linger on his wife. She was everything to him, everything he had ever wanted. Would what he might have to tell her now make any difference in their relationship? Would she be angry at him for concealing something so important to his history?

She had never been demanding. She had not asked him anything about his past life that he was reluctant to tell her. And she never asked him about Jeff Maratti's past memories. He thought she would always try to keep him as far away from those dark thoughts as she could.

In their own way, he thought, many of his memories of Georgia were as grim as some of Jeff Maratti's memories of Afghanistan. He had tried to keep that part of his life separated from the rest. He would talk with Ewen first. Then he would decide how much he could tell this brave beloved woman sitting beside him, smiling into his eyes.

The doorbell rang. Alexi hurried to the door. Voices could be heard, happy laughter. Jeb's voice and Emily's. Lorie got up to greet them as they came into the kitchen.

"You made it okay then?" she said to Emily, who was first through the doorway, beaming with delight. "How's Todd doing?"

"He's doing great," his mother said, looking behind her as her husband came through carrying the lovely child he had encouraged his traumatized wife to bear and rear—the little boy whose russet mop of curls, Jeff realized with a refreshed sense of shock, were the exact shade and consistency of the curls on that gruesome artifact now lying concealed in the big drawer in Ewen's desk. How had he not made the connection at once?

Jeff turned to Ewen, whose quick understanding glance held a clear message. It was time for a conference. Now!

"Are you ready for a short update?" Jeff asked him, keeping his voice neutral. Lorie glanced at him, curious but in no way alarmed. He looked up at Jeb. "Care to join us?"

"Good," Emily said. "Let's get the guys out of the way and talk babies."

"What fun," Lorie agreed, grinning. "We've been so busy I haven't had a chance to just chat in months."

"Let's go into the sunroom," Alexi said, leading the way. "All the kids' toys are in there." As the ladies moved off with the children, the men adjourned, with coffee, into Ewen's office.

Jeff had come to a decision. Since Emily was a descendant of his biracial half sister, Rosette, Jeb's family, maybe even the little redheaded newcomer, was his genetic family as well. Emily already knew him for who he was. Randy now knew. It was time Em's husband was told.

They seated themselves in comfortable wing chairs placed in front of an unlit gas fireplace. "Who talks first?" Ewen said.

"What's this all about?" Jeb said, looking from one to the other of his companions as if they had suddenly lost their minds.

"It's time for you to know who I am," Jeff said, and Jeb grinned at him and saluted.

"Yo, Major Preston. I've always knowed it. I just wondered if you'd ever git around to levelin' with me. Thank you for unloadin'! I take it as a compliment."

Jeff laughed, relieved. "Emily told you. I wondered if she had."

"Our marriage is rock solid. Don't you be worryin' about me spillin' any beans, Major, and causing more worry to my wife! Nobody would believe me, anyway!"

Jeff was surprised and, he had to admit, impressed. "Okay, here it is. Jeb, we found something at Riverside Plantation that you should be privy to as well as the rest of us." Jeb's silence, and Ewen's, told Jeff he could proceed. "It's an old trunk. It was in the well."

"The well." Jeb's voice was soft. "When we was searchin' there, we didn't see a well."

Ewen gave him a curious glance. "You searched Riverside too?"

"When they tell you what they want, you don't question. But you don't work too hard at it either."

"My father was a cautious man," Jeff said softly. "It's obvious now that when he learned raiders were headed for Riverside, he had the trunk dropped down the well. The well house was then torn apart and disposed of piece by piece. He had obviously planned for that eventuality. The trunk was waterproofed. Among other things, it was packed with his journals."

"Journals?"

"Diaries," Ewen put in. "Notes made practically every day by Isaac Preston for most of the years of his life. There are exactly fifty-five books available for us to translate and study."

Jeff added for Jeb's benefit, "Many are written in code. It's a little different code from the books we used a year ago to gather information on Em's family—but the same general idea applies. Translating them will take some time, but we hope finally we'll get enough information that we'll be able to locate the Blackheart Compact document itself. Our aim is to destroy it!"

A quick soft sound issued from Jeb's mouth. Almost like a "hallelujah."

"But…" Jeff was looking into Ewen's face as he spoke even more slowly, "after we left the farm, Ewen found something else in that trunk, something other than diaries. That's why he's here. We're trying to make sense of it." He removed the key from his pocket and handed it back to Ewen. "If you would, please wait for my story to be told before we show Jeb what you found."

"Lead on, Major Preston," Ewen said.

The room became quiet. Two sets of eyes focused on him. "When I first came into this new world, Ewen, two years ago," he was finally able to say, "I was, to my way of thinking, twenty-seven years old."

"What are you now?" Jeb's eyebrows had raised.

"Jeff Maratti Randolph is twenty-seven this year. A two-year difference. It seems rather a complicated way to regain two years of life." A rueful laugh issued from his throat. "But the point is, I had never married, not in my earlier life. That was unusual for a person of my standing, and there were a number of young women who seemed to find me attractive."

"No comment," Ewen said under his breath, and Jeb chuckled.

"In any case," Jeff went on, trying to ignore extraneous comments, "when I graduated from West Point, to all intents and purposes, I was given a compassionate discharge from the army so I could care for my family's businesses and look after my mentally impaired father.

"But in fact, I was never officially discharged from the army. There were people in the War Department who could envision what finally came to a head at Fort Sumpter. Several of them were aware that I had been active for many years on what we called the Freedom Road—and they asked me how I would feel about doing intelligence work for them. I agreed, of course, and my life was turned rather into chaos. I traveled across the country many times in many disguises."

"Disguise? With those eyes?" Ewen said, waving a hand. "Back in those days, it'd be pretty damn hard to disguise your baby blues."

Jeff laughed. "You'd be surprised how off-putting a pair of thick darkened glasses can be." He continued more solemnly, "At any rate, how could I ask any naïve young woman to marry someone like me, whose life might be taken at any time leaving her a widow, possibly with multiple children. While I was traveling on the plains, I met many such army widows and their children. I vowed never to leave a family in such a sorry state of affairs."

"Understandable," Ewen said gently. "I faced the same dilemma myself. It's why I married somewhat later in life than most of my friends."

Jeff looked away into one corner of the room, for the moment seeing nothing. No one spoke. Minutes later, he shook himself and began again. "This is not to excuse what I did but to explain."

There was a scrape of chair legs on the floor as once more he took up his story. "While we were working on the Freedom Road, my mother introduced me and my older brother Will to a young Creek brave just about our age. His name was Chitto. We were then in our adolescent years.

"To go back just a bit in case no one mentioned it in your history classes, in 1838, when I was a small child, the

Creeks were forcibly moved out of Georgia by President Andrew Jackson—some in chains. Chitto and his older sister Talisa, the only remaining members of their immediate family, went into hiding. They were living in a small shallow cave deep in the forest, trying to make do on very little.

"If you had known my mother, you would not question why she took them in. She let them live on a remote portion of our plantation land and even had a small cozy house built for them, fireplace and all. They brought us fresh game and herbs they cultivated, and we gave them stews and baked goods and my mother's woolen cloth to make their clothing. They had to be very careful not to be recognized as locals, as there was much animosity toward the native tribes even then.

"From necessity, they had already become superb trackers and hunters. They knew all the game trails and how they intersected, and when we needed to take someone north, they were our guides until we learned the trails ourselves. Virtually everything Will and I knew about tracking and hunting we learned from them. What surprised me was that Talisa was far better at it than her brother. We spent much time together, the two of us, and had, you might say, a mutual admiration of each other. But she was quite a bit older than I, ten years, maybe twelve, and I didn't see her as a companion or…"

"A bed partner, in other words," Ewen said softly, not letting him dangle over the explanation of a delicate topic.

Grateful, Jeff nodded. "But when I returned from West Point all grown up to take over the management of Riverside from my very ill father, Chitto asked me if I would consider taking his sister as a wife. I told him that I was not going to get married, as my work was too dangerous, and besides, she was his sister and she was far too old for me. That's when he told me her story.

"Before the Indian wars and the forced march, Talisa had been the wife of one of the chiefs of their tribe. She had been quite young at the time of her marriage, and she was showing signs of becoming a great beauty. He fully expected her to give him strong beautiful children. It became apparent within the first few years, though, that those children would never appear. She had been no more than a young teenager— as you currently express age—when she went through that marriage ceremony. Her ability to conceive was impaired, that fact alone had already destroyed my father's friendship with the chief. He was even more furious when Talisa was put aside so the chief could take another wife. She was then shunned by the rest of the men of the tribe except as a potential plaything, one of the primary reasons she and her brother had left the community."

"But she admired you," Jeb said, his voice resonant with understanding. "You are a kind person. I kin understand that."

"She needed the warmth of a loving relationship," Jeff answered softly. "At the time, so did I. My mother was gone and all my siblings but Sara. And now my father was sinking into a state in which I was never sure if he knew I was there."

Quiet for a time, he finally admitted, "It was a good match, Talisa and myself. Chitto, Moses, my father, and undoubtedly Sara knew of our intimate friendship. I'm not sure I was in love with her, not in the same way I love Lorie, but I admired her enormously and was proud of everything she accomplished. Unfortunately, we could not be seen together, as there was still much prejudice against the Indians, and for the same reason, there was no way I could legally marry her. But despite his other shortcomings, my father was delighted at the match. She was a brilliant young woman, and he had always admired her, as had my mother—

my mother's approval still played a very important part in his opinions."

"What happened to Talisa, Jeff?" That grim question came from Ewen.

Between those words and Jeff's answer lay the three scalps.

"I'm not sure." He sat quiet for a moment, searching for memories. Then nodding gravely, he began again. "A few weeks before the war started, I left on a mission of most urgent importance. I had no way to stay in touch with home and had to hope that Sara and Moses were looking after everything in my absence. When I returned, I found them both in tears and Chitto in a terrible state—angry all the time, unwilling to talk with me, in fact. Sara told me it was a fever that took Talisa, something that needed a more powerful medicine than could be obtained. Chitto backed up her story. Moses wouldn't even talk about it. When they showed me her grave, I cried more tears than I knew I had in me." Ewen handed him a tissue, and he blew his nose. "I'm sorry. This is one of the parts of my life I have tried to put behind me!"

"So you really don't know what happened?" It was Ewen's soft voice.

Jeff pushed himself to his feet and began to pace. "Nor have I told Lorie about any of this! Please show the artifacts to Jeb, Ewen, and the note, but no one else!"

"Great God Almighty!" Jeb said under his breath when he saw them.

"The note that was left with the scalps…'The score is even'…that's my father's handwriting for a fact." Jeff paused. "Could it really be, as Lorie has long suspected, that he was feigning his illness during that time to give me cover for the important work I was doing? There is so much I still don't know about my father!"

"What dates are we speaking of here?" Ewen asked.

"Just before the war. Before the attack on Fort Sumter."

"So you think April 1861, maybe?"

"The journals," Jeff said. "Would you be willing to translate the books written in Zulu with your supercomputer, Ewen, and tell me if you find anything we need to know?"

Jeb had been listening intently to Jeff's story. "I can read an awful lot into those scalps and your father's note," he said grimly. "They say 'rape and murder'! They say 'revenge'! Case made and closed."

"But who are the rapists?" Ewen asked.

"I don't know about the other two," Jeb growled. "But the curly-haired redhead? I've got a take on him! I saw a painting of him when I was called to the head honcho's house to do a bit of rebuilding a few years ago. They told me that red-haired guy in the picture, a relative of The Compact's head honcho, had died just around the time the Civil War started! So the timing's right. The bullies at that house acted like the guy in the painting was God Almighty and could of won that war single-handed if he hadn't been murdered by Indians! If I could remember whose house it was, I'd know which of the bastards at the top of this heap of manure is the spawn of that man, but I've been to so many houses… Those lowlives never have to pay for work that gets done on their properties, they got slave labor, and they never introduce themselves neither.

"Anyhow, the guy who owns that house, he's the big muckamuck of this bunch right now. He didn't have a beard nor any hair at all when I worked for him, clean-shaven even back then! But they sure showed him a passel of respect because of that red-haired relative!"

Ewen's response was instantaneous. "A take on the Mediterranean pirate, Barbarossa. But Barbarossa way predates anything we've been talking about. Redbeard? A fictional character. Much more recent than Civil War times. An old comic book hero—hero only because no one in today's world comprehends how heartless those brigands were."

"No hero at that house," Jeb said firmly. "Not judgin' by the people around him! His kids was scared to death of him. And their mother too! She was nursing a black eye the time I saw her!"

"Okay," Ewen said firmly. "I've got to remember we're dealing with the Blackhearts!"

"Mean as junkyard dogs," Jeb growled. "Once we find the evil spawn, we'll know who hurt my Emily too."

"Obviously not anyone we've rubbed elbows with yet," Ewen added. "Obviously higher up the ladder than the people we've been battling with to this point. Jeff, I'll search out any references to 'Redbeard' in the journals as well and let you know what we've found."

"I'll tell you one thing for sure," Jeb said sharply, "Whoever the bastard is, he'll lay claim to my Todd only over my dead body!"

"And that, brother," Jeff said, reaching for Jeb's hand, recognizing him fully as a solid compatriot, "is something we will not allow to happen."

CHAPTER 7

Wednesday evening, April 13

Lorie sensed that something very important had transpired that day, but she had been too busy moving in and unpacking supplies to deal with it. If she needed to know anything, Jeff would inform her when the time was right. Until then, there was the unpacking and there was Saree—and Doggy, who simply refused to leave Saree's side. Quite enough for one tired housewife/mother/fugitive to deal with. One thing at a time. Just one…then another… then another!

"Something else we must not forget," she said wearily to the little band of fugitives late that evening after an exhausting day involving readjustment of luggage and lives, "is that along with a warning, we received a cry for help. What are we going to do about that?"

She and Jeff, Jeb and Emily, and Ewen—who, with his wife's enthusiastic approval, had remained at their son's house to lend a hand with any remaining chores—were assembled in the now darkened sunroom. They were settled on comfortable couches arranged around a gas fireplace that put off just enough warmth and light to make them feel comfortable and cared for. Wine, beer, and soft drinks were available to those who so desired, and the quiet contentment that comes from feeling safe had at last enveloped the company.

Guy joined the party bearing another tray of delicious finger food. "Alexi has some work to do tonight," he said apologetically, "and says she'll see you in the morning. However, if you're willing to let me sign up with this association of conspirators, I'd like to be able to help you do, well, whatever it is that y'all seem to be doing!"

"Bravo!" Jeff said cautiously. "But I feel you should reexamine that notion, sir."

"Listen to Jeff, son," Ewen concurred, deadly serious. "We're going to be facing some really bad dudes. There is a good chance of getting hurt."

"Did that ever stop you?" Guy said to him, a strong flavor of pride in his voice.

"Oops! Maybe I've been giving you wrong messages all these years."

Lorie heard Jeff's quiet laugh. "The fruit does not fall far from the tree, sir." It was obvious that pride went both ways in Ewen's family.

Ewen smiled broadly at his youngest child. "I'm thinking you should wait a bit longer to enter the fray, son, at least until we know what we're facing. More importantly, we need someone on call here at all times."

Guy looked hard at his father. Finally, he nodded. "Part of the team, but you're putting me in a place of safety. I bow to your assessment, sir, and I won't push it!"

"You understand fully," Ewen said, obviously relieved. "Thank you, Guy."

"Okay," Lorie said with a sense now of calling a vital meeting to order, "we have been loosely labeling ourselves Justice Seekers, whose mission roughly is to find the embedded Compact members in our midst and recruit them"—she grinned at Jeb—"or redeploy them to places where they can't cause any more trouble. We've had some minor successes.

"But have we made any kind of strategic impact against The Compact itself?" she went on. "Or have we just been stepping on some outliers? Aside from several dozen indictments and a few bad dudes behind bars, we don't have any insight right now as to how to gauge the depth of this conspiracy arrayed against us. However, we have now been handed a more-or-less formal request to intervene by a number of its members who seem to have noticed our occasional interferences." She paused and then continued a bit more reflectively, "At least a few people appreciate our presence, even though we're not sure exactly who they are, presumably some of the Searchers who feel they are being exploited. Is this a trick to draw us out? Or do we believe it's a genuine cry for help? Jeb? You're the only former Searcher here. Suggestions?"

After a moment's reflection, Jeb responded, "I've been thinkin' on it, and my conclusion is that it's a genuine request from the Searchers their own selves. It appears to me that someone from the outside is tellin' the boys they have to pick up the search again for that bi-wing airplane that went down close to a century ago—1918, if I recall rightly. Someone still wants to find it. They never said to us why. What I suspect is that the night Jon Randolph Junior died in that crash, he was takin' away somethin' real special, and they don't want nobody else to find it but them. I think The Compact muckamucks are fearful that we're gonna find it first and there'll be hell to pay! It might open up a big new can of worms for 'em!"

"Rather like finding your father's trunk, Jeff," Ewen said softly.

"I agree, Jeb," Jeff answered. "That is the situation in a nutshell. But in order to offer help to our reluctant Searchers, which I'm sure we all would like to do, we need certain information. Can any of them tell us where the searches have been focused during all these years? Has anything of value been found so far? If not, why not? And do they know any Compact names we might recognize?"

"There are lots of planes that have never been found," Emily said in a rather offhand voice. "Amelia Earhart's. On the bottom of the ocean, probably. That might be a little harder." She had been very quiet, and now Lorie sensed that Em was approaching a tipping point. Her words had been a bit too flippant, very unlike Emily. "Just a thought," Em said again, reaching for another sandwich.

Lorie noted the swift tentative glance Em gave to Jeb. If the remark was supposed to have evoked a comment from her husband, it didn't. The words had passed over his head without notice. "Em," Lorie said quietly, "please tell us what you know."

Surprised, Jeb turned to his wife. "Em?"

She looked at him for a long pregnant moment. Then calling upon the personal courage with which Lorie knew Emily had long faced her private terrors and humiliations, she said very softly, "If you folks want to know where the Searchers have been surveying and mapping since 1918, please help me to find my family. They've been keeping track ever since the night of the crash. Probably still are."

Jeb's mouth dropped open.

Jeff chuckled. "Lorie told me you'd open up when the time came, Em."

Emily reached for her husband's hand. He seemed confused. His mouth was still open, but no words were issuing from them. "Honey," she said to him softly, "I couldn't tell you. I've seen them whip people, smash their faces, break their fingers, do what they did to our daughter, for god's sake. To me! I never wanted anybody in my own family hurt—

not you, most of all you! If you don't know anything to tell, you can't slip, even if they beat you." In the grim silence, she turned back to Jeff and said staunchly, "Everybody associated with the Blackheart Compact needs to be taken down! If we can find my family, we've got a good chance to clear all the vermin out of the woodpile at one blow."

Lorie smiled. Those were the same words Emily's daughter, Celeste, had used in describing members of The Compact. "Vermin!" They had probably spoken of it often. Emily had just been biding her time.

Jeb was looking at his wife as if she were suddenly a stranger. She gave him a little slap on the wrist. "Come on," she said. "You've got secrets too! Lots of 'em." She leaned across the brief space between her chair and his, pulled his face toward hers, and kissed him warmly.

"Your family?" he said when he came up for air. "They're working against The Compact too?"

"You never noticed only because they didn't let you."

"How do we start tracking them down, Em?" Ewen Taylor asked, obviously trying to defuse a situation he appeared to think could have a very awkward ending. "How long has it been since you've been in touch with them?"

"Too long." The words were softly said. "My sister called me eight or nine years ago while we were living in Atlanta to warn us that Searchers had come asking about us. She told me then that my little brother had moved, along with our parents, and said that her family was moving too. She couldn't say where they were going. I haven't heard from any of them since. There's only one place I know…but they couldn't be there. They would have found a way to let me know…" She went silent for a time, and Lorie recognized a sparkle of tears in her eyes. When she realized everyone was waiting for her, Em added, "I expect my sister is still okay, or

I would have heard from someone. But even if she isn't, they couldn't have found everyone. I have many cousins."

"How many know about The Compact?"

"I don't think that word ever came up in our description of those people. We just called them the Searchers."

"They're all involved?" Jeff was impressed. "Your whole family?"

"It's their lifework," she said softly. "Aside from learning how to stay out of the Searchers' way, my family is trying to take the whole system down when they have all the damning information they need to take to the authorities…if they find any authorities they feel they can trust!"

"What do they do for a living?" Ewen asked. "Maybe we can find them that way."

"They pretend to be coal miners if they're in Pennsylvania or Kentucky," Emily said softly. "Sometimes clerks, waiters, streetcleaners, the list goes on."

Lorie was intrigued. "Pretend? What are they really?"

"Accountants, lawyers, computer programmers, miners, many miners. Engineers as well. Very good at many things."

"Eureka!" Ewen breathed, obviously impressed, and added, "Do you still have addresses for any of your cousins? We could start there."

"I was afraid that if I got in touch with them, they'd have to move too. I burned all my address books when I was called out to be a 'maidservant,' so if anything happened to me and they came to search the house, there wouldn't be anything to find."

Lorie noted the expression of pain that instantly distorted Jeb's strong features.

"Then we'll do it the hard way," Ewen said grimly. "We'll go to the places you last saw your closest relatives and ask people if anyone has a forwarding address."

"No one will tell."

"You never know, Em. We might be able to convince someone otherwise."

Before she went to bed that night, Lorie mentally reviewed the plans that had been sketched out. When the sun came up, she would be taking care not only of her Saree but also of Em's Todd, while Jeff drove Emily to the last place she had remembered some of her relatives living, a small town in the Allegheny mountains of southern Pennsylvania. "An old unincorporated mining town," Em had told them. "Kind of hidden. Everyone who lives there is related to me. If the town is still there."

"I was there," Jeb had added, obviously stunned by what he was hearing, "when I was with the Searchers. That's when I first saw Emily. We searched that whole area and didn't find a thing...," he was looking at Em as if seeing her again for the very first time, "except for the love of my life." Shortly they left for their quarters hand in hand.

With a big yawn, Ewen excused himself not much later, smiling gently at Lorie. "Save everything till morning," he said. "Answers will come while you sleep. They always do."

Lorie sighed. She hadn't realized how tired she was. When she glanced up at Jeff, she saw the longing in his expression. "Saree is fast asleep," he said with a smile. He held out his hand. "Em and I have to be up and out early. I think it's time for us to try out our new bed. What about it?"

She smiled, thinking how wonderful it would feel to lie in his arms. "Yes," she said.

CHAPTER 8

Thursday morning, April 14

Jeff and Emily left early in the morning, dressed as if they were going to church. At least that was the way Jeff thought of it—they were all "dolled up." His face was smoothly shaven, his hair had been neatly trimmed, and he was wearing a sparkling white shirt with a dark blue suit—something Lorie had insisted that he purchase, although he'd not had an occasion to wear either garment yet. Lorie had adorned the shirt with a tie—another embellishment with which he was not entirely familiar but had noted men wearing in this new age when they wanted to be more formally dressed. *Appropriate for this morning's meeting*, he thought.

Em's shining black hair had been woven by Lorie and Alexi into an elaborate braid and then wrapped around her head as if she were wearing a crown. She was wearing a fitted woolen pantsuit made of a soft brown plaid and low-heeled but very attractive shoes. Her long-sleeved shirt was white. He thought the total effect, with her own lovely coloring, was stunning even though, strictly speaking, she was wearing trousers to a formal meeting. Well, fashion was what it was no matter the century!

Lorie had laughingly complimented the two adventurers on their "disguises" and assured him she didn't mind being left behind. It was a great opportunity, she had told Jeff privately, not only for him to practice driving but also for him to get better acquainted with his sister Rosette's many-great-granddaughter.

He had selected one of Guy's farm cars for the trip, an old but sturdy blue Ford "minivan," which he had found easy to drive, and Lorie had assured him that the car would attract no particular attention. Emily would function as navigator with computer printouts and a regional map she could fold to whatever area they wished to explore. In addition, Emily was also the keeper of the cell phone, and she was the backup driver if that became necessary.

"The town where I met Jeb is a good place to start," Em told Jeff as they turned from the barnyard onto the long driveway rimmed by white rail fences. "It won't be on any map, but I know how to get there."

"Why is it not on any map?"

"Never formally incorporated as a town. We called it Home Place, but you won't find it by doing computer searches."

Jeff chuckled. "You do have clever relatives!"

"After Isaac Preston brought Grandmother Rosette back to her mother, the beautiful Celé, last name unknown," Em continued, "the reunited family moved lock, stock, and barrel to Pennsylvania—a free state. Grandfather Isaac not only gave them the funds to help them relocate but also provided an Indian guide to get them there. He told them he would have done it himself, but he didn't want to be gone so long that people would notice something irregular and come to check up on him."

Jeff smiled to himself, thinking he could probably put a name to the Indian guide.

Emily went on. "It was still pretty wild back then. Not so hard if you didn't mind traveling on Indian or game trails. According to the written accounts, the hardest parts were the rivers. Ferries weren't always available, and ferrymen whose attitudes toward escaping slaves were questionable were too often the rule rather than the exception. Boats were rare, available only if you knew the right people or had enough cash, which we did. Every month like clockwork, even during the Civil War, an allotment came into our secret bank account doled out by a northern bank from someone named P. Isaac."

Jeff was quiet for a time, thinking, wondering. "My father was a very smart man," he said to Emily. "He was strict with his children. I always thought of him as a kind and understanding person. But I was never aware of this level of involvement in the Underground movement. I suspect our mother didn't know he was involved at all. Is it possible he never told her?"

"He told our family," Emily went on as the miles to the north rolled smoothly away, "that he was living two lives—the one he had to live and, at rare wonderful times, the one he wanted to live."

"Trapped by The Compact. Why did he ever sign the damned thing?"

"He never said anything about The Compact to my family members, but he did warn them to be very careful of his neighbors and their friends, especially the ones who had threatened to hurt Grandmother Celé. Perhaps one of his journals will explain."

As navigator, Emily selected byways that flowed serenely through the valley of the Shenandoah River. Lovely mountain vistas displayed spring's finery at either side. Interesting old towns offered food and fuel. Neither was needed, as he and Em had feasted well before they left Guy's farm, and they had a full tank of gas, also courtesy of Guy. In another context, it could have been a joyous outing.

They eventually crossed the Virginia state line into a jagged outlier of West Virginia's eastern real estate, and not too many miles later through a slim splinter of Maryland where all roads funneled together and he no longer had the option of ignoring the interstate system. The town of Breezewood lay northward in Pennsylvania. It was an anomalous hub in the interstate web, Lorie had told him, the only place where cross-country interstate travelers actually had to negotiate traffic lights in the heart of a small crowded town.

Jeff had to agree it was quite unlike most of the towns he had encountered in this new world. Service stations displayed their wares everywhere he looked—every brand of gasoline he had noted to date—and more—could be purchased. There were fast-food restaurants as well. Anything a hungry stranger desired was offered for sale in letters too large to ignore. Chicken was frying somewhere. It smelled so good his stomach growled, but he had sampled that fast-food kind of fried chicken before. It was nothing like the fried chicken his mother had prepared for Sunday dinners. He had a fleeting regret that they had not stopped at one of the old-timey restaurants they had bypassed in those sleepy small towns through which they had just driven.

Emily seemed to have been bitten by the same hunger bug. "I'm hungry as a horse," she said. "How about searching out some fancy local establishment?"

He laughed. "Just what I was thinking. Keep your eyes open, Em."

They were moving at a snail's pace through an extraordinarily congested area of town when Emily said to him urgently, "There, go there!" She pointed ahead to the next intersection. "See that old-fashioned sign with an arrow on it? It says, 'Tired of eating the same ol' fast food? Join us for a home-cooked meal at...'" her words sank to almost a whisper, "the New Home Place."

Could it be this easy to find her family? Maybe! He made the required turn. Even if it weren't her family, he was willing to brave any alternative to fast food!

The establishment lay a few miles north of town on an unnumbered but well-marked two-lane road. The restaurant had been created from a beautiful gray mansion—Lorie would have called it Victorian—embellished by intricate white trim. An elegant place. A far cry from "usual." Many cars were parked in its generous-sized lot. He hid the blue van between two huge farm trucks. Tempting odors wafting on soft breezes brought the growl back to his stomach.

"Could it be?" Emily whispered.

"Don't get your hopes up too much, Em. Coincidences do happen. At the very least, we'll eat!" Many people were congregated on the porch, sitting on the swings, lounging on rocking chairs, and chatting happily. "We may have a long wait, though," he added, chuckling.

"At least we can get our names on the list." Grinning, Emily opened the door into a large entry hall.

The interior was as tastefully polished as the outside. To the left of the entry hall, two large rooms, both with stately mantled fireplaces, had been opened into one, allowing space for many tables and chairs. Tall windows offered views into exquisite flower gardens. Azaleas in many colors blazed along the rear parameter of a neatly trimmed lawn, and beds of other colorful plantings rimmed clusters of tables and lawn chairs. Indoors, seated diners shared quiet conversations while waitresses in white shirtsleeve blouses, their long black skirts shielded by white aprons, moved with professional dispatch throughout. Business seemed to be excellent, the work-force efficient.

A dark-haired, coffee-complexioned woman at the res-ervations desk glanced up, said, "How many?" and noted the time they had arrived. "If you don't mind," she added, "we have somewhat of a backup right now. Find a seat some-where, and we'll be with you very shortly." She pressed a but-ton on the top of her high desk and wrote the name Jeff gave her, something he made up on the spot. He devoutly hoped he would remember it when it was called out!

Jeff turned back to Emily. She had become very quiet, her attention caught by a patchwork quilt hanging on the wall alongside a staircase that rose into a dimly lit stairwell just behind the desk. "Jeff," she whispered, "I can read this old quilt."

"Read it?"

"The North Star. At the top. See that?" She moved closer to the quilt and raised her hand, just avoiding touch-ing the ancient fabric. "The points of the star are worked in shades of red and orange."

The quilt was a beautiful piece of art, many fabric pic-ture blocks stitched together. They seemed to be telling a story, although he thought he would need a guide to under-stand what the colorful narrative depicted. "What does it say to you, Em?"

"It says very simply," Emily answered in a quiet but excited voice, "that someone here is related to my family. Someone who moved to the North before the Civil War. All the children in my family, way before I was born, learned how to make that North Star so they could recognize each other if they ever got separated and found themselves trapped into slavery! I made one of those myself when I was a child. Also, Jeff," she went on, almost breathless, "see that log cabin?"

Her excitement was contagious. He nodded, hunger now forgotten.

"Grandma Rosette made up this pattern, Jeff! Her oldest daughter would have inherited the quilt. In fact, this may be it! This may be the original! The Gathering Quilt!" She was becoming more animated by the moment. "This would have been Grandma Rosette's interpretation of the first Home Place in Pennsylvania. The house our family owned looked exactly like that when the family first moved there, although it's been added to many times since. It's much larger now."

He had known his half sister Rosette was a talented artist. He had seen her pencil sketches, her exquisite watercolors. He had never seen what she could do with colored fabric and a needle. "We must ask someone." His interest in food had completely disappeared.

Behind him, a woman's voice said, "Please come along. Your table is ready."

"So quickly?" Em whispered.

Puzzled but pleased, they followed the waitress past a gaggle of people still waiting to be seated, through the two joined parlor-dining rooms, and at last around a corner into a smaller private room. The waitress closed the door behind them and then turned around.

A soft cry of surprise issued from Emily's throat. "Bernice!" She flung herself into the older woman's open arms. "Bernice, I'm here!"

The woman was as beautiful as Emily, if a little heavier, and perhaps a slight shade darker in complexion. But their faces were remarkably alike. Still embraced by the waitress, who was mopping at her eyes with one hand, Emily turned back to Jeff and said through her own tears, "It's my sister, Jeff. It's Bernice. We've found her."

"Why did it take you so long?" Bernice said crossly.

It took a few moments for the sisters to reconnect. Tears were even rolling across Jeff's cheeks. With hugs and tears done, words could again flow freely.

First, Jeff was formally introduced to Bernice Thomas Richards, Emily's oldest sibling. "This blue-eyed young man is closely related to us, sis," Emily went on. "He's Jeffrey Randolph Maratti. We call him Jeff."

"Jon Randolph Third's great-grandson." Bernice held out her hands to him, her face glowing. "I'd know you anywhere, Jeff Maratti. You have the family look, much like our joint ancestor, Major Preston. Except that the major's hair was jet-black and his eyes were a beautiful brown. I'd say right now that you're the spitting image of his second son, Jefferson, with those blue eyes of yours. I expect you would be mighty interested in seeing the paintings we have of them both. Welcome to your extended family. Now you sit yourselves right down and let's get you something to eat. I'm going to bring you our 'special,' Em. Remember Sunday dinners?"

Too hungry to focus on the many anomalies he had just been hit with, he sat. It was a meal that included everything his own mother had served her lively family on many a Sunday when they were hungry enough to root out tree bark: a big slice of honey-baked ham, baked sweet potatoes dripping with home-churned butter, snap-fresh green peas, okra relish, home-made corn bread—all the savories his mother had favored him with when he was feeling poorly or down-in-the-mouth depressed. He felt almost as if he, too, had come back home. How had he forgotten any of those good-for-the-soul foods he had taken so much for granted during his growing-up years?

Rosette must have remembered also. Even if they weren't aware she was their sister, she had always sat at the table with them as if she were family, learning table manners along with the others, joking and teasing, always as an equal when she was with them. What fun she had always brought to the table. Jeff found tears welling as memories slipped by one after the other.

Finally, Bernice seated herself at the table with them, almost as if Rosette had just joined them. "Now tell me what brought you here?"

"The same thing that made you unfurl the Gathering Quilt, I expect," Emily answered. "We just received notice that the Searchers are at it again."

"And who did you hear this from?"

"A couple of days ago, someone in an airplane dropped an incendiary device into the pasture of the farm where we were hiding. Besides lighting a fire, the pilot also dropped an empty water bottle containing a request for help."

"There is nothing about that whole narrative that leads me to believe you are doing well!" Bernice said crossly. "Do you know who dropped the bottle? How do you know it wasn't a trick to ferret you out?"

Emily laughed. "One question at a time, sis. Jeb thought the pilot was a man named Davy Simeon. His son, Thad, just got back from Afghanistan in a chancy state—on the edge of a major breakdown—and Jeb thinks the young man is being called out to search."

"Very likely," Bernice replied, backing off a bit. "We heard from one of our regular watchers that they are on the move. That's why we're gathering. This time, they seem to be focusing on the section we've been successful in keeping them away from for the past hundred or so years. Somebody probably began to wonder why it was they had never searched that particular piece of real estate. Got any ideas on how to maneuver them somewhere else?"

A sketchy liaison had just been offered. Jeff was elated. "I'm assuming then that you know where the plane is."

Bernice looked hard at Emily, who nodded. "No one safer," Em said quietly to her sister.

"It's never been touched," Bernice said evasively. "Not from the time Junior radioed the family for help. Tragically, even his family couldn't do anything when the time came. But as a memorial, the family has kept everything just the way they found it. Jon Randolph Jr. was by all accounts a worthwhile citizen, and every honest person who met him was his friend. Unfortunately, we had no way to notify his family as to what had happened as they also seemed to be living in hiding, a caution that did not go unnoticed by our side of the family."

Jeff frowned. "Did no one search the crash site to see if anything valuable remained?"

"The area in the mountains where he died," Bernice said quietly, "is almost inaccessible. It is very dangerous to explore."

"Can you tell me, Bernice," Jeff asked, feeling there was a great deal of unnecessary evasiveness going on here, "exactly what happened to Jon Randolph Jr. that night?"

She closed her eyes for a few moments and then looked at Emily, who nodded eagerly. "Okay, Em, if you say so. It's hard to do this after all these years of silence. Well," she looked straight into Jeff's eyes and spoke very softly, "most of the family stayed in Pennsylvania after the war—it's the Civil War I'm talking about here! A few of our lighter-skinned folk had returned to West Virginia because they had established businesses and never had to deal with the slavery issue except in passing. Junior Randolph knew the whole family. I suspect some of them were working for him, as they always seemed to have a little extra cash on hand after he left.

"In any case, he was in Maryland that dark night, probably on government business because that's what he did, when he radioed to say he would need his gas tank filled when he got to our airfield. Someone had tried to siphon his fuel, but he'd caught them at it and chased them away. He was in a big hurry, there were people right behind him, and he was going to have to pray hard that the few gallons he always carried with him as emergency backup would make up for what he'd just lost. He sounded hopeful about still having enough to get to our field. If the weather had cooperated, he probably would have made it. But he met strong headwinds. If he'd had that last little chance, our people said later, he would have made a safe landing.

"Our men had created the landing strip," Bernice went on, "out of the top of a relatively smooth wooded plateau high in the mountains. There was a cave of sorts in the rocks just below the edge of the landing field, and if Junior was doing night traveling, he'd radio ahead and someone would go down on a rope and set a lantern in the cave so he could aim toward the light.

"The men who were on-site that night heard a sputtering engine. They saw a bright light coming toward the field, but at the last minute, they realized he was coming in too low to clear the cliff. They signaled him to pull up. He tried his best, but it was no use. He went straight into the cave." She was using her hands now to illustrate. "He hit the lantern before he hit the wall. The flame went out, and that's when our fellows realized Junior's gas tank had gone empty and he was just floating on air. If it hadn't been, the whole place would have blown up. The crash itself knocked a lot of the ceiling down, and a portion of the cliff came along with it.

"One brave soul went down on ropes to see if Junior had survived. He dug his way far enough inside to confirm that there was no use doing any more. The poor man was gone. So the family rolled rocks down into the rubble to try to close up what openings were left and encouraged vegetation to cover the whole site. We were always afraid, though, that if someone was hiking in the area they might spot signs of the old field. When the Searchers started to get close so many years ago, the family replanted the whole mountain top with fast-growing pines.

"But there are still indicators that could be a dead giveaway if anyone knew what they were looking for. The pines themselves, now that they're fully grown, don't appear natural for that area, especially if you see them from above. Wrong species for that area and a little too regular in spacing, I'm told."

"If we can get there first," Jeff said quietly, "we will carefully remove whatever it is that Jon Junior took from The Compact—if it's still there and intact. We will allow them to discover only a grave with moldering bones and, if possible, the remains of a broken machine. Hopefully, at that point, they will decide that after all these years, it's time to pull up their stakes and fold their tents…and free the Searchers once and for all."

Silence. Bernice's eyes had narrowed once again. She seemed to be considering him a little more critically. "We have maintained that area for almost a century as a memorial. We do not want it desecrated. For whatever reason."

Jeff gave Bernice what he hoped was his most winning smile. "We would never desecrate his grave, and I can assure you that he won't mind a bit if we play a few tricks on these fellows. Whatever Junior was bringing back with him must have been vitally important. If The Compact is still searching for it after all these years, it's imperative that we find it first."

"Jeff is very good at tricks," Emily said with an impish grin.

Bernice sat silent for a time. Finally, she said, "May I consult with a few people?" She seemed to have withdrawn significantly.

"Anyone you like." He pulled a small notepad from his jacket pocket, wrote his cell phone number on a page, tore it off, and handed it to her. "I also wish to consult with a few people. Call when you are ready. If everyone is in agreement, it's high time for your group and ours to meet. We can negotiate the place."

"We've been at this for a very long time," she said firmly. And then a bit defensively, she continued, "Junior's wife never tried to find us. His son never tried to find us. The only things we ever knew about Jon Randolph Third was what we saw in the newspapers. What's the difference now? Why exactly do we need you?"

"We are as determined as you are to destroy the Blackhearts and their Compact," he said with equal fervor. "If we combine our knowledge with the secrets you have been guarding so well all these years, I suspect we will finally have the means to do so."

Bernice looked up, a puzzled frown creasing her face. "Blackhearts?" she said. "Their Compact? What the hell are you talking about?"

Silence. A very long silence.

Jeff finally asked what had become to him the most obvious question, "What did you think we were talking about?"

"The Searchers," she answered in somewhat of a huff. "Capital S. Searchers. We've been on guard against them ever since that night. We've never quite known why they were targeting our family, especially after slavery was abolished and it wouldn't pay them peanuts to haul fugitives back down to the South.

"But we finally figured out it was in our best interest to identify them. We know who most of them are now. A very diverse group, all men. Mostly in their late teens and early twenties with armed guards to keep them on task. We think they might be hostages or reluctant recruits of some kind. We check out all the newcomers we see, and we've managed to identify most of them. We have many resources. We still haven't discovered what it is they want with us…or from us! But we don't think they mean to be friendly."

Frowning, Emily asked softly, "Who do you think they are?"

"Let's put it this way," Bernice answered. "When Grandfather Isaac left his daughter Rosette in western Virginia with her mother Celé, he said, 'Never tell anyone you're part of my family.' He told us there'd be hell to pay if we did. He warned us specifically to always keep a sharp eye out for what he called the Searchers. I thought they were slave catchers. But if they're still doing searching for this group of yours, I'm beginning to gather that it's something way beyond finding escaped slaves." She looked hard at Emily. "Your husband Jeb is one of the Searchers, isn't he?"

"He was a Searcher for the people of the Blackheart Compact at one time," Em said softly. "He isn't a part of that group anymore. We're hiding from them, Jeb and I. We know too much about them to let down our guard. They have every reason to want both of us dead."

Bernice recoiled at the bluntness of her sister's statement. A moment later, she asked, "Hasn't he ever told you what he was supposed to be searching for? If not, why not? What makes you think we can trust your husband?" The tone was subtly hostile.

"They never told him what they were looking for." Emily looked around desperately at Jeff, her eyes pleading. "Except that it was an old bi-wing airplane."

Jeff could answer now without hesitation. "After a good deal of provocation, Bernice, this part of your family has begun to fight back. That includes myself and a select group of people who have also been targeted by this group. Jeb Wallace has successfully escaped his former masters and is now one of our most trusted associates. His word is gold."

"We've been collecting names and faces for a long time," Bernice said, clearly still not convinced. "If you can prove to our satisfaction that you will not betray us, we can share with you what we have. But if you don't..."

"Good enough," Jeff said. And then silently, *First test of many*. He couldn't really blame her. For all Bernice knew, they could be working at cross-purposes. She needed to know he could be trusted. He gave her his phone number and then shook her hand warmly. Thanks and hugs were renewed— and he and Emily left with as little fanfare as any other diner to retrace their long journey back to Virginia.

They had not gone far before Emily said softly, "Thank you for standing up for Jeb."

"My pleasure," he said solemnly. "He has passed many tests under fire."

Her gratitude was reflected both in her silence and in the glow that came across her lovely face. "He's the dearest person in the world. And he's as committed as we are to taking out The Compact. I don't care what the rest of my family might think about him."

He squeezed her hand. She was a relative to be proud of.

The rest might be a little chancy.

Everything now was dependent on a phone call.

CHAPTER 9

W hen they arrived home late in the afternoon, Lorie caught up with him almost immediately. "I've got something to read to you," she said excitedly. "You need to hear it."

He couldn't help but laugh. The topic was so different from that which he had been working his head around. "Honey, don't you even want to know what happened today?"

"Yes, yes, I do, but this is far more important! This will definitely change the way you're looking at things about your father! Saree and Doggy are asleep right now. So give me these few minutes, please, Jeff, while it's quiet."

He turned briefly to Emily, who was grinning at Lorie's excitement. "Grab your little son, Em, and go update Jeb on what's happening. And by the way, cousin, get some rest! We'll talk later."

"Will do. Get some rest yourself, Jeff." She blew him a kiss as she moved off with her sleeping child in her arms toward the spacious bunkhouse apartment where she and Jeb were staying.

The "quarters" he and Lorie had been offered for the duration of their exile was an attractive mid-twentieth-century five-room farmhouse, quite likely the original house on the property. Now called the Guest House, Ewen had described it as "modest," but Jeff saw nothing modest about anything in this house. In his first lifetime, he had slept in huts, in tepees, in one-room apartments in drafty city buildings, in soddies on the high plains, even in grand places with hanging chandeliers and fancy drapes—all created without the benefit of running water or private bathrooms. If windows had been cut through the walls, they had certainly not been covered by double-paned window glass nor sealed in any way against cold breezes.

This was a home his friends and relatives would have given up everything they owned to possess. The living room and kitchen were both brightened by large windows displaying the surrounding Shenandoah mountains. A television set located in the far front corner of the living room, easily viewed from the comfortable couch and its matching reclining chair, would satisfy every need for entertainment and current news.

At the back, three bedrooms and a bathroom were conveniently accessed from a central hallway. In the largest bedroom, with private access to a smaller but still adequate bathroom, the closet and the dresser easily accommodated the few belongings he and Lorie had, and Jeff had already found the wide bed to be extraordinarily comfortable.

His wife had been her usual productive self during the time he and Emily had spent journeying. Besides her baby-tending duties, she had unpacked the lot of their meager personal belongings, including their daughter's, and tucked away all the pots, pans, and dishes they had brought with them from Georgia. The packing boxes themselves had mysteriously disappeared, undoubtedly whisked away by attentive farm staff members.

Now Lorie seated herself on the living room couch and patted the pillow beside her. As he lowered himself into the cushion, she said, "I've been reading journals, love."

His rosy cloud suddenly evaporated. He was back in the hard world, the one where people got hurt! He began to push himself to his feet.

She pulled him back. "Nope!" she said. "You've got to hear this!"

Again he tried to pull away, saying, "I'm too tired, honey. Tomorrow will be better. It was a long trip."

Her grip was strong. "Not on your life, Jefferson Richard Preston Maratti Randolph. You are going to listen!" The last sentence was said with an emphasis on each word.

Knowing her as well as he did, he finally took a deep breath and conceded. She would not relent! And he owed her so much.

She pulled the book from beneath the couch and opened it. It was about the size of one of the novels she sometimes left on the bed table, but the paper on which the words were printed was quite different. It seemed to be more the consistency of fine parchment. On the cover, he saw the legend "Marseille, France, 1808" written in black ink. It startled him. "This is what you need to hear," she said firmly, opening the book to the first page. Inside the cover, he caught a glimpse of words printed in a childish hand.

She started to read aloud, "France. April two in the year of one thousand eight hundred and ten. My first name is Isaac. My last name is Preston. I think I am seven years old."

It took a minute for his mind to connect. Then the utter shock of it caused Jeff to close his eyes. This wasn't his father. It was a little boy, a child who wasn't even sure how old he was.

A wave of emotion swept over him. "Go on," he said, slumping into the couch. She was correct—he did need to hear.

Lorie began, "'My new friend Lak gave me this book and told me that since my mother taught me to spell and write when I was a child, I should set down all that has happened to me so I do not forget. I do not know why I would ever forget, but he says that I will forget much as I reach manhood. I told him I would like to forget all of it. But he says that I should not forget my mother and my father because I will want to remember them when I am old and gray. I told him I will never be old and gray because I will be killed first. But he said I will not be killed if I keep my wits about me as I have been doing these last two years.'" She looked up into his eyes. A world of emotion lay in her expression.

Again, he was swept with a sense of shock. Two years? Without comment, she turned back to the book. "'Lak saved me from being killed yesterday. He told me I forgot to do what I have been doing, and I should never forget until I am at a place where I can escape to an American warship and tell the officers what happened to me.'" She turned to him again and added, "I'm reading what I think he's saying, honey. His spelling isn't perfect, and his punctuation is nonexistent. But the sense of it is pretty clear. Jeff, have you ever heard the name Lak?"

"Dear god!" he said softly, suddenly recalling. "That is what he used to call Moses when he wasn't thinking about it. It's a very shortened version of Moses' real name. Ukuhlakanipho. Seven years old? Just a little boy, Lorie! I thought he met Moses in this country when he was a grown man, purchased him as a slave!"

"Apparently not! Jeff, do you realize this means your father was only five years old when his parents' ship was taken?"]

"He never talked of it! Never! This is very hard to absorb all at once. How much more...?"

"Much more, my love!" she said firmly but with unusual tenderness. "You can read it yourself later, but right now, this is specifically what I want you to hear." She turned back to the book and began to read once again, her voice rising as he tried to interrupt. "'When Lak saw me first at the docks, two sailors had caught me and were beating on me, calling me 'the dumb boy.' It was nighttime. He came toward us through a dark alley like a storm at sea, with lots of strange noises and sparks coming off him everywhere. The long sleeves on his black robes were whipping around like angel wings. He carried a big staff. I thought he was a great black god coming to kill me, but he hit those two sailors instead. He cracked their heads open, and blood ran out, and they fell down dead right by the gaslight on the dock. He threw them into the sea. Then he picked me up and carried me to a warm dry place. He gave me a bath and put me in dry clothes. Then he said to me in plain English spoken like an Englishman, 'Little man, you are the boy they call deaf-dumb. Those men do not like to pick on people their own size, so they pick on you. They will never do that again. But you must be more careful. When I first saw you, I knew you were a very wily little fox and neither deaf nor dumb. Someone else may think the same thing, and then you will be in big trouble.'"

If Jeff had wanted to speak, he couldn't. Words would not come. He was stunned by what she was reading, so stunned that for that moment, he couldn't even remember his father's face.

Lorie glanced up at him, paused only a moment, and then continued in a soft voice, "'I asked him, "Why did you not think I was deaf and dumb?" I had not really talked for a long time, and the words felt scratchy in my throat. He said, "You thought you were alone, but you were not because I was there in the black shadows, and I am black, so you did not see me. You heard a kitten give a little cry and you turned your head. Then you crouched down and started talking to the kitten. Never do either of these things again. Even when you think you are alone." My friend Lak is very intelligent, and I will do what he says.'"

He was stunned. "Deaf and dumb? That's exactly the way he was acting those years after Mother's death when I thought he was becoming senile."

"Earliest lessons learned, hardest to forget. Maybe he thought someone in his household was a spy."

"I don't believe that anyone on his staff were spies. But there were always the near neighbors and their slaves who came by frequently as acquaintances do. We children suspected some of those slaves were spying on us for their masters, but we couldn't prove anything."

"Will you read the books, Jeff?"

He looked at her and then took her hands into his. "I will read them, love. Thank you for giving me this new picture of my father. It has already softened my judgment of his behavior after the rest of our family was murdered." Gathering her into his arms, he gently pulled her down beside him into the embrace of the couch and held her close against his chest. He felt her breath on his cheek, the softness of her lips against his skin.

He hadn't meant to fall asleep—evening was not yet upon them—but bone-tired as he was now both physically and mentally, he sank into deep slumber.

He woke sometime later, disoriented, realizing the house was now wrapped in the soft darkness of night. He heard Lorie in the baby's room, her crooning voice accompanied by the creaking of the old rocking chair they had brought with them. He then realized that what had been nudged off-center about the newly revealed events of his past had quietly shifted and stabilized and taken on new meaning.

Wordless in the wonder of it, he rose to extinguish the remaining room light. He pulled off his outer clothing and hung it across a chair. Exhausted as he had ever been, he fell back again into the pillowy cushions of the couch.

When later he again emerged from deep slumber, she was beside him, clad in her nightgown, breathing deeply in sleep. Her arm was spread across his chest as if she meant to guard him from everything menacing. He reached for the couch coverlet, pulled it across the two of them, turned toward her, and slipped comfortably back into sleep, his lips just brushing her forehead. He thought that he had never needed the touch of her so much as he did that night.

CHAPTER 10

Friday, April 15

The call came at seven in the morning. Lorie was no longer beside him, but her fragrance and the warmth of her still surrounded him. She came quickly from the small bedroom they had delegated to Saree and grabbed for the cell phone. She said hello, listened, and spoke for a moment, and then handed it to him.

"We're willing to talk," Bernice said bluntly. "In person. When and where?"

He shook his head, still somewhat disoriented. "Good morning," he mumbled.

"Sorry to wake you, Jeff Maratti. Who was the lady?"

"My wife, Lorie."

"We'd like to get together," Bernice said, all business, "to talk about what's going on. When and where?"

"When is the New Home Place least likely to have customers?"

"We're not open on Mondays, but we've got to talk sooner than that. Saturday morning. Tomorrow. We don't open until noon, so we have some time. Vince is flying in. He wants to meet with you."

"Who is Vince?"

"Our younger brother. He's in California right now. He thinks this is far too important to let it wait even an extra day."

"He is correct, Bernice. We must talk as soon as possible."

"Tomorrow then, 10:00 a.m., the New Home Place. There'll only be the two of us. Bring Emily and whoever your counterparts are. I need names."

She was pushing him. He had to think fast. He wanted to take Lorie, but because of the logistics of their sudden move and the impact it might be having on Saree, there was still too much needing to be handled here in Virginia. Lorie could be dealt with later. She wouldn't complain.

Not Jeb. His time would come.

Randy Ross, Ewen Taylor, Rolf Maratti. "There will be three others besides Emily and myself." He gave the names, business addresses, and phone numbers.

"We will vet them thoroughly." Her voice was brisk and businesslike.

"Wow," he said softly to himself as he hung up, echoing one of Randy's favorite expressions. "What are we in for?" He made the calls.

*****

It wasn't until midafternoon that Lorie noted activity at the big house. Carrying Saree, she walked over to see what was happening.

She found that the guest facilities at Guy's farm were going to be stretched even thinner this evening. Ewen Taylor already had a designated bedroom in his son's house, a Spartan room just off the large office area allocated to his use. The only furniture within was a fold-out couch and a bed table with a lamp.

Jeff's present-day grandfather, Rolf Maratti, currently én *route* by private plane from Princeton, New Jersey, was to be granted the elegant guest room at the big house.

Randy Ross would be arriving by truck after a very long drive from Randolph City. He had accepted Lorie's offer of the spare bedroom in the modest house she and Jeff were occupying.

Because Jeff would be closeted with Ewen and Emily for most of the remainder of the day, Lorie took the job of point person when it came to Randy's arrival. She spoke with him several times during his journey, giving him specific directions, and late in the afternoon when he let her know that he was at the big gate, she directed him by phone through the maze of parking lots and driveways that served the guest house. She knew there was no need to interrupt what was currently going on elsewhere.

Although the tie was missing and his shirt unbuttoned at the collar, he was still wearing the dark business suit and white shirt newly required by his position as chief of police in Randolph City. He pulled his bag from the back end of the truck and followed her across the lawn and into the little house.

"Are you kidding me?" he said when she apologized for the size of the bedroom and the fact that the mattress was a single. "I'd sleep on the hard floor just to have the privilege of sharing your wild adventures and to get a cuddle from your sweet baby child." He told her that when Jeff had called to ask if he was available, he had simply made a few calls from his office, retrieved his gym duffel bag, and headed north.

Now settled into his temporary quarters, wearing jeans and a khaki pullover, he was once again the sandy-haired young man she was beginning to think of as a second brother. Slumped comfortably in the front room recliner, sipping a big glass of iced tea while intermittently playing peek-a-boo with a giggling Saree, he turned to Lorie to answer all her questions: "Who's guarding the fortress back in Randolph City? What's happening with Sue and Sid? How's the new job going?" Randy had only recently accepted the position of chief of police. It was a demanding job when tourists were in town, but Randy had grown up there and knew most of the people and all the ropes. Lorie thought the job was a perfect fit for him, at least during this stage of his law-enforcement career.

"Sue and Sid Bailey are doing great," he told her. "Making money hand over fist with the ice cream parlor they opened in the drugstore. Great ice cream, by the way! Their own recipe. Not sure what the secret ingredient is, but it may be rum. Sid's innovation," he added when she started to giggle. "Sue probably doesn't have a clue, and she really likes it.

"In regard to your first question, though, we've got some good cops in Randolph City now. People with level heads and honest resumes. I pulled in a couple of retired Marietta cops I trust with my life to cover while I'm gone, since I don't know how long you'll need me here. The stalwarts are on watch," he said decisively. "That's important for everyone in Randolph City. I've never seen a town so protective of its citizens at this point. Even if they're split on everything else, politics, religions, beer brands, since they went through that Compact siege at Randolph House, they know what's really important. None of the above!"

"Friendship and a safe community." Lorie smiled. "I have only good feelings about that town. We may end up there someday when we're not so toxic."

"Might be a good place for you guys, after all. You could move into Randolph House."

"Too many ghosts!" Lorie caught herself and burst into laughter. "What can I say…?"

"I'm honored to be let in on all the family secrets," Randy said, grinning. "I can hardly wait to talk with Jeff about the history he's seen."

"Right now," she responded, "he's learning some new history." She stopped, grimacing. "Or 'old' history, you might say. It's the journals his father wrote."

"About being a pirate?"

"Can a five-year-old be considered a real pirate?"

"Geez! That's starting pretty early." Randy was instantly serious. "How did a five-year-old become a pirate?"

"Very tragic story," Lorie answered, now solemn herself. "Isaac's father, Gerard Preston, had business in Europe buying Egyptian cotton for a different kind of market—consumers who didn't want products made with slave-picked cotton."

"Sounds like our kind of dude. An abolitionist?"

"Without question. And a very brave soul. I'm assuming that he felt our marines had finally taken care of the piracy thing in the Mediterranean, so he brought his family with him on this trip—his wife, Elisa, and their little son. You've heard about the shores of Tripoli, I assume?"

"Sure, who hasn't? Our marines stormed Algeria and took Tripoli and put a stop to a lot of piracy on the Mediterranean."

Lorie nodded and continued, "That episode happened during Jefferson's term. 1805. But piracy didn't stop in the Med just because the US Marines made a stand. Some people who weren't quite as intimidated by Yankee ships as the Algerians were doing a little freelancing on the side. Add to that the Embargo the United States imposed in December of 1807, something that Jefferson and the new Congress devised, among other things, to try to avoid involvement in the Napoleonic wars. Unfortunately, it trapped American trading ships away from home, so *The Red Rose* was stuck in the Med for the duration." Lorie saw the look on Randy's face and grinned. "You're hooked now, aren't you?"

"Keep goin', babe."

She sat back, thinking how to summarize the many tragedies she had so far encountered in Isaac's journals. "Okay. Through the eyes of a very small boy, as translated by a person—me—who knows zip about sailing vessels!" She took a deep breath. "Since the Preston's ship was not a warship, it had only minimum gun power. A group of pirates saw it as easy pickings and boarded after a very short scuffle.

"Isaac was only five—this was in 1808—and he was very scared. His mother put him under an empty crate that was sitting on deck and told him to be silent no matter what happened. But one of the pirates, a quiet-spoken man named Will Deerfield, confronted her. Isaac's mother pleaded with pirate Will to spare her baby. He surprised her by telling her very quietly that several years ago he had lost a son about Isaac's age, and he still cried for his boy every night. She was touched and she asked Deerfield if he would care for her son if anything happened to her. She also told him that Isaac had long ago put one of his favorite things, a blue diamond necklace, inside a Chinese puzzle box that he had been playing with, and that if Isaac were asked politely, she was confident that he would give it up. Isaac, writing about it later, says that he was a lot less confident that he would give it up than his mother was, but he was smart enough not to say so out loud."

When she heard the deep chuckle, she grinned and continued, "The passengers and crew were rounded up by the pirates and told that those who didn't pay a ransom would be sold into slavery. Gerard told the pirates they could have all the goods he had purchased and all the cash he had on board, but he didn't have anything else to give them.

"One of the paying passengers, however, lacking the funds to buy his way out, ratted out to the pirates that he'd seen Gerard's wife wearing a shiny necklace. When the pirate captain demanded it, Elisa informed him, truthfully, that all her jewelry had been stolen."

"Truthfully?" Randy asked, eyebrows raised.

"Except for the blue diamonds Isaac had in his little chest, she was telling the truth. Isaac knew for a fact that her jewelry had been taken by a crew member who decamped somewhere along the journey. She wrote off the loss as 'lessons learned,' but she wasn't going to give up the blue diamonds if they could save her little son. The pirate captain didn't believe her in any case. A little too coincidental, he thought. When he threatened to do a body search on Elisa to find her jewels—in public—her husband came to her defense. Gerard was immediately eviscerated with a cutlass, and his bloody body was tossed overboard to the sharks.

"I'm radically condensing the story here, Randy," she explained, finally coming up for air. "Given that it was written by a seven-year-old over a period of time, it's pretty hard to read. But he was really taking to heart the compulsion he must have felt to write everything down on paper so he wouldn't forget anything about his parents. Nor the bloody cutlass, which he saw up close when the pirate captain grabbed his mother's arm a few moments later! The blade had a symbol engraved upon it—an ugly black skull and crossbones inside the crude symbol of a heart!"

"The Blackhearts! Geez, that poor kid!"

Lorie nodded. "It's heart-wrenching to read, Randy. Besides Elisa's grief and fear, realizing the humiliation facing her in front of everyone, including her son, and being hopelessly aware that she was destined for a lifetime of slavery in a very foreign country without her little boy, Elisa jerked away from the pirate who was holding her, blew a farewell kiss to Isaac, and jumped over the rail into the ocean—joining her husband in death. When someone finally discovered Isaac inside the box, he was so traumatized by what he had witnessed that he couldn't speak even if he'd wanted to. Nor did they think he could hear them. Deaf and dumb. That's what they called him."

Randy was sitting up straight, motionless. "How come he wasn't killed outright?"

"Because Deerfield said the boy was his and drew his own cutlass to press his claim. He pointed out that because of the nature of Isaac's infirmities, the little boy wouldn't be a bother to anyone. Obviously, Deerfield won the argument. As of the time period I'm now reading, he hasn't even asked Isaac about the necklace. It seems Pirate Will was determined to do right by Isaac after what had happened to his parents."

"What it doesn't explain," Randy said softly, "is why the poor kid would sign that damned Compact later on."

"Don't know the answer to that yet," Lorie said. "I haven't gotten that far. It's tough reading, as you can imagine, but I did find out that Isaac met Moses—he calls him Lak—somewhere on the docks in Marseille, France, when he was seven. According to my calculation, that's around 1808."

"Go on," Randy said grimly.

"Well," Lorie put in, "I've got to back up a bit to fit some more history in here." She thought for a time, flipped open a reference book, and, a short time later, turned back to Randy. "In 1808, Napoleon seized all the American ships that entered French ports, claiming that since they couldn't go back to the US because the ports there were blockaded, it was obvious they were British ships carrying false papers—and those two countries were at war, so fair game! The pirates on the *Red Rose* then claimed they were American ex-patriots—

loyal to no country. The French didn't buy that argument either and took the boat. The pirates were really pissed!"

Randy chuckled. "Serves 'em right! What did they do next?"

"It seems they hung together and finally decided that if they couldn't get it 'legally,' they'd take it the same way they did the first time."

"They stole it back?"

"Slit a few throats and took it out in the middle of the night," Lorie said, grimacing. "Right under the Frenchies' noses. They 'appropriated' the necessary provisions and water, repainted it black, changed its name to *Black Rose*, and, thumbing their noses at everyone, went unofficially legal with counterfeit French papers."

Randy laughed out loud. "Crooked down to the last detail!"

"It was about that time Isaac met Moses," Lorie went on, unable to keep the wry grin from her own face. "Moses, aka Lak, had spotted Isaac on the docks several times and knew he wasn't deaf—nor dumb in any sense of the word. He told Isaac to keep up the game he was playing and to stay with the ship and his friend Will until he got all the way back home where he could understand what people were saying to him. Then he was to turn himself in to the captain of the first American warship he recognized as soon as he reached an American port. He was to tell that person everything that had happened to him, his family, and his family's ship. But it didn't turn out to be that easy."

"How's that?" Randy asked eagerly.

"The pirates didn't go back home! They spent a number of years pretending to be an American trading vessel in distress. They stayed in the Med, hoisting the skull and crossbones at the last minute to prey on would-be rescuers! Fortunately, warships from a number of Mediterranean countries finally made it extremely unhealthy for them. It was blasted out of the water by an American warship. That was in 1814."

"Standard Compact incompetence, I suspect," Randy said, laughing.

"Now that I know something about them," Lorie said, chuckling, "I agree wholeheartedly! Some of the pirates escaped, however, taking Isaac and Will with them. Isaac is eleven years old in the journal I'm reading now. The date is 1814. They're still in France, and Madison is the president. I had to do some boning up on the history of the era to get this into context, so it's been kind of slow reading."

"Did Isaac stop being a pirate then?"

"Haven't got that far yet."

"Can I read them?" Randy asked, almost wistfully. "The journals, I mean."

"Don't know why not!" Another thought occurred to her. "Let's both do some serious skimming and then share notes. If Isaac wanted us to have these books, then there's something in them we have to find, something pertinent to what's going on right now. It's pretty slow going for just one person. And very depressing."

"I'm with you, babe," Randy said to Lorie, saluting. "I can't think of anything more interesting."

"But right this minute," she said, hauling herself to her feet, "I hear the clanging of a bell. That means Grandfather Rolf has finally arrived, and dinner is being served over at the big house. Jeff and Ewen have been locked away all day plotting, and I bet they're as eager to check in with Rolf as we are. Let's go!" Hoisting her daughter into her arms, she and Randy hastened to join a party already in progress.

Wonderful odors were drifting through the lush sunlit air of early evening.

"I've been doing some close-up examinations of satellite photos…" Lorie heard Ewen's voice booming out as she and Randy approached the patio doorway opening into the dining room area, "and I have at least two sites that could be the acreage Bernice was talking about. Maybe three. You'd have to do an in-person walk-through of the areas to confirm that any of the locations ever served as a runway, though." Lorie saw now that he was talking with Emily Wallace. Both were bent over a table, looking at the huge map spread out across it.

"If our qualifications satisfy sister Bernice and brother Vince," Jeff answered from across the room, "they'll let us know exactly where the location is. A lot depends on what happens tomorrow morning."

"It's not us I'm worried about." It was Ewen again. "It's those other folks. They may have found the same indicators with their drones, and that's why they're swarming."

"Good point." This time, it was Rolf Maratti's softly accented voice. "I expect if we go exploring, we should be armed."

Now Emily's husband spoke up—sharply. "The Searchers have never been armed. It's The Compact drivers that carry the guns. Pistols and rifles both. I'd hate for someone like my friend's son, Thad, to git accidentally shot by one of us when our goal is to break him free of his so-called obligation."

Lorie saw Jeff turn to Jeb. He asked quietly, "Have any of the Searchers ever rebelled when they're asked to do this kind of thing?"

"When they ain't allowed the tools they need, they sometimes put up quite a clamor."

"So if their tools somehow go missing, they wouldn't get into serious trouble by being grumpy and just sitting down until everything is returned to them?"

"Kind of pushin' it, maybe." But both men grinned, obviously on the same page. "It's fair to say," Jeb went on, "that no one's gonna ask a fellow to climb down a steep cliff without the proper ropes. They don't mind punishing really valuable assets, but they don't much favor killin' 'em. Leave too much trouble behind and people come lookin' for you, wonderin' why you're there, especially in a National Forest, where Forest Service Rangers can pop up when you're least expectin' 'em."

When the plotters looked up and saw Lorie standing in the doorway with Saree and Randy, all talk of mayhem came to an end, and smiles and welcomes began. Randy was introduced to Ewen's son and daughter-in-law, and warm handshakes were exchanged with all his old friends. Jeff got a brotherly hug from Randy as well.

Rolf Maratti Randolph also embraced Lorie and gave Saree the biggest hug of all. Excited to see him, she called him Grandpapa without prompting. He was extraordinarily pleased, as was Lorie, as she hadn't been certain her daughter would remember Rolf. It had been a couple of months since they had been with this-century-Jeff's birth family—parents as well as grandparents. It was something they tried to do as often as they could.

"Food is ready. Line up at the kitchen counter," Alexi said cheerfully, "and fill your plates to the brim. Drinks will be brought to the table. Go to it, folks!"

The food was too good to ignore, Lorie thought happily, even for people so intent on thwarting a grave robbery that they were plotting the most effective way to pull it off first. A chicken casserole, as lovely to look at as it was delicious; a crusty seafood dish, bubbling hot around the edges; a colorful vegetable salad; fresh rolls still oven-warm with plenty of butter to melt inside. "Bravo," Lorie said quietly to Guy's wife. "I don't think you'll ever be able to top this meal."

"A challenge! It's a good thing I like to cook." Alexi grinned and lifted her wineglass. "I'm a farm girl at heart, a gourmet cook by choice."

"I'm inclined to stay here when everyone else goes away," Lorie laughed, "just to inhale the odors." But not long after the remainder of the dinner dishes were cleaned up, home she went with her daughter, her husband, and their very welcome guest. Lorie busied herself taking care of a hungry Saree and an equally hungry fox kit named Doggy, putting them both to bed, temporarily at least, in the same room.

Rolf showed up at their doorway shortly thereafter as darkness settled in. Emily and Jeb arrived only moments later. Jeff had not specifically asked them to come, nor had Lorie, as the morning wake-up call was scheduled for well before sunup.

But such a gathering was perhaps inevitable on an evening this momentous—the inception of a new and hazardous venture for a family perpetually under siege by relentless forces, which, after more than two centuries, were still looking for revenge.

From her seat on the couch, Jeff's hand clasping hers, Lorie examined the faces one by one of these treasured people as they spoke so companionably with one another. For many years feeling himself the ultimate outsider, Rolf Maratti Randolph had finally discovered that he was the genetic son and rightful heir of the man he had known all his life only as his Italian mother's rather standoffish American husband. Now seated in the recliner at Lorie's right side, a contented smile gently creasing his aristocratic features, he was gazing with great pride into the face of his beloved grandson, Jeff, whom he once thought had been lost to him forever.

Emily Thomas Wallace sat relaxed on the couch at Jeff's other side, holding hands with her husband. Jeb had melded into the comfort of the small wing chair borrowed from the bedroom, and he and Em were grinning happily at each other, all tension forgotten.

Leaning back on one of the sturdy kitchen chairs, one long leg folded across the opposite knee, Randy was another part of what was right about this association of souls: an engagement announcement between Jeb and Em's beautiful daughter Celeste and himself lying not too far in the future. His sweetheart was saving the news to break it to her parents in person, so Lorie could only wink at Randy and smile.

Such a marriage would bring Randy officially into the family. But then he had always been there when he was needed! He would never betray a trust. He would lay his life on the line for any one of them. He was a true and unassuming hero, as were they all!

And then it struck Lorie like a spark! She knew little yet of Isaac Preston. But surrounding her in this small room were the two disparate parts of his family. Had Isaac played any role in arranging this meeting? The two parts of his family had not had contact for a century and a half, not until Jefferson Richard Preston Maratti reentered the scene. It was clear there had been strong bonds in the past—the letters between Sara and Rosette was graphic proof of that! Was one of Jeff's many tasks that of repairing broken bonds?

Rolf was currently the elder of one of Isaac's family lines, comprising some of the most ethical people she had ever met. At her other side were the descendants of Isaac's other family, the part she was already calling "Em's line" in her own mind.

Em's husband, Jeb, didn't know where his own ancestors had come from, as his mother had "served" The Compact bigwigs just as Em had more recently. But he and Emily were both inherently dignified people who never gave up under siege, determined to maintain their integrity in the face of unspeakable evil.

Lorie felt movement against the back of her legs and looked down. The little fox had just trotted into the room and was pushing his way into the small space between her feet and the couch. How had he managed to escape from his cage? He looked up at her with what seemed almost a smile on his funny little face as she gave him the room he needed and then nestled down and curled up quite contentedly.

With a start, she recalled the passage she had just read to Jeff from his father's journal, something his friend Moses had told Isaac when he was very small: "When I first saw you, I knew you were a wily little fox and neither deaf nor dumb."

For a blinding moment, Lorie went numb. Another element had joined their small determined band, something more powerful even than Sara's protective presence. A decisive battle was looming. The Compact was a sinister foe with deeply concealed roots—roots that needed to be ripped out and dispensed with in the clean light of the sun, a momentous task bristling with unseen hazards.

Perhaps at last they could confront The Compact on equal terms.

Isaac was with them, Lorie now knew for certain, and, strangely enough, demanding neither hate nor revenge. The power he brought was love.

CHAPTER 11

Well before dawn, Saturday morning, April 16

Jeff felt they were quite prepared to present an unambiguous face to the people they hoped to claim as allies. But he also knew that the simple questions which most needed answers probably didn't have answers yet—at least nothing Emily's family would be privy to.

According to Jebediah Wallace, former Searcher, it was either a notebook or a briefcase. What could it contain? A list of members' names? After a century and a half, everyone on such a list would be long dead and buried. Even if names were revealed, what difference would it make? Political families ensnared enough to be embarrassed? Captains of industry? The way Compact names seemed to be haphazardly disremembered and shifted, it would be easy to claim mistakes had been made. Nothing quite made sense about the guesses that were being bandied about.

At Jeff's request, Emily briefed the men on what she remembered of her brother, still a child the last time she had seen him but intelligent and creative, and her long-widowed sister, who was older by two years and determined to maintain the superiority she felt by reason of age. The group quickly agreed that Emily should take the lead. She knew both worlds, and her sister Bernice was definitely a force to be reckoned with!

There was plenty of leg-and-elbow room for five adults in the farm's large SUV. Once their quick breakfast was done, eaten in the darkness of early morning, Ewen claimed the steering wheel, much to Jeff's relief.

Emily was "riding shotgun," as Lorie always called it, in the front passenger's seat, recalling the guard position on what Jeff used to know as a mail coach. She would be the person in charge of navigation. Rolf and Randy flanked Jeff in the back seat, strapped into place and, at least to Jeff's way of thinking, reveling with him in the supreme comfort of the ride. Stray complaints were met by his terse comments on the sheer hell of traversing by horseback the distance they were going today. The journey itself might consume more than a week, he told them—if the horse were a good one and care was taken of it—to say nothing of the primary needs of its passenger during that time such as food, privies, and night-time accommodations that allowed for a private bed and a roof over one's head!

"You win," Randy said to him, laughing heartily as they all were. "I will complain no more about driving a few hours early in the morning after a warm shower, a hot breakfast, and a potty break!"

The remainder of the trip was livened in like manner, high good humor, and camaraderie masking a grim under-standing of the vital nature of the liaison they were preparing to forge with all its possible repercussions, including, if they were not careful, serious injury or death.

They reached Breezewood, turned onto the country lane when they spotted the sign, and pulled into the park-ing lot of the New Home Place at 9:45 a.m., well ahead of schedule.

Bernice Thomas Richards was sitting on one of the big porch swings waiting for them. She rose to her feet as Ewen turned the car into the parking lot. After giving Emily a big hug, she shook hands formally with the new players. Jeff introduced each man in turn and gave a brief summary of how each fit into the picture.

"Now," Emily said eagerly to her sister when preliminary courtesies were concluded, "let's see my baby brother. I haven't put eyes on him in at least fifteen years."

"He's all grown up," Bernice said. "And you just may be surprised at the way he turned out." She called to her brother to come out to the porch.

Jeff was dumbstruck when Vince Thomas came through the doorway. He was quite tall, probably three or four inches more than six feet. His skin was a rich tan, his eyes a beautiful brown with luxuriant eyelashes and brows. His black hair was tightly curled against a well-shaped head, and his voice had the deep-throated mellowness that Jeff had always associated with Moses. But Vince's many-great-grandfather, Isaac Preston, had, through a young girl named Cosette, handed down to this portion of his line a strong genetic resemblance. Very strong! Except for the skin color, it could have been Jeff's own father standing there!

Jeff strode forward, reached for Vince's hand, which was a shade darker than his, and gripped it tightly. Now it was Vince's turn for surprise. "My god, I'm seeing my white double. How often does this happen to someone?" He let out a roar of laughter and wrapped Jeff in a tight embrace. Both laughing, they stood back from each other, taking in the remarkable resemblance.

"I have more scars than you do, I bet," Jeff said.

"I'm not taking you up on that bet," Vince said. "Looks like you've seen some action."

"Afghanistan, among other places." He could not express the pleasure he took in meeting this man. What's more, when Vince smiled at him, he could clearly see an echo of his beloved half sister, Rosette. His relationship to this man was transparently obvious!

As Rolf shook Vince's hand, he said with a grin, "As an only child, I'm pleased to meet a new relative but sorry to tell you about the hazards of looking as much like my grandson as you do."

"There's a family resemblance for sure," Randy said, adding with a chuckle, "but I don't think you'll have to wear a disguise anytime soon."

"The way I see it," Vince said, laughing with no sign of cynicism, "a black face is about as good a disguise as it gets, since most people don't look any farther!"

In the short time he had been alive in the new century, Jeff thought he had to agree that what Vince was saying was unfortunately true. Not enough had changed in all the years since Mr. Lincoln had told the slaves they were free.

"Nice to meet you, Vince," Ewen said, holding out his hand. "Haven't I seen you on television now and again?"

Again, Jeff was surprised. But then he hadn't been watching a lot of television. He was not used to being that sedentary.

"You made me in one," Vince Thomas said to Ewen, his face lighting up. "Yes, sir! Commercials put a lot of shekels into our family coffers."

"And the big screen too," Ewen went on enthusiastically. Jeff was trying with difficulty to keep up with the incomprehensible dialog that was spilling out. Big screen? But Ewen's next words made everything fit. "Action movies," Ewen went on. "Spy stuff. I've seen all your features. Not very realistic—now mind you, I'm only saying that because I'm in the spy business myself. But they're terrific entertainment, Vince. A lot of fun to watch!"

Vince grinned at the effusive compliments as he shook Ewen's hand, acknowledging with laughter that the action he portrayed was certainly not autobiographical and that maybe he should start taking notes now that he was standing next to the real thing!

"Come on in," Bernice said. "Let's get something to eat, and then I think we have a lot to talk about."

In the intimate dining room where Bernice had brought Jeff and Emily two days before, she and her brother had set out a variety of hot and cold drinks and laid out plates of doughnuts, breakfast rolls and breads, along with a basket of fruit. "Please help yourselves," Bernice said in a businesslike voice, "and then we can go upstairs to the meeting room."

They took the staircase that rose alongside the heirloom quilt that had earlier drawn Emily's attention and entered a dimly lit room. Bernice touched a switch, and bright fluorescent overhead lights illuminated seven chairs set around an oblong table over which a small ceiling fan began to pulse. Pads of paper and sharpened pencils had been furnished at each seat. Along the back wall, a bank of glowing computers was doing something internal, lights flashing in seemingly random patterns.

"We are connected to our home base from this equipment," Vince said.

"Very impressive," Ewen said. "And I won't ask where home base is located, as I presume it is somewhere safe and inaccessible except for the chosen few. I see that you are quite knowledgeable about what computers can do in this day and age." He seated himself at the table.

"We boast many university degrees in the various computer languages," Vince stated and then chuckled. "We are connected to the world, my friends."

"And you folks," Bernice said, settling herself beside the white-haired entrepreneur, "are also well connected. We have been doing our homework." She opened a notebook and turned to an indexed printout. "I am impressed, Mr. Taylor. You have many very important companies to manage, and yet you have carved time out to involve yourself in a family battle quite unrelated to your line of work or to you personally. Why?"

"This is much more than a family matter, Mrs. Richards," he answered. "Our attention has become focused on what we are learning is a national conspiracy. It affects many hundreds of people, if not thousands, and may have worked its way into various branches of the government, including the judiciary. We are trying to determine how to strike at its heart—to destroy it, if that is possible."

"The name is Bernice, please," she said quietly, "and I will be interested to learn how you—who are not family—became involved and why we should listen to you and buy into this national conspiracy theory!"

Ewen gave her one of his most charismatic smiles. "I was a longtime friend of Jon Randolph III, Bernice. I was his protégée within several clandestine government services and served with him overseas as many times as I could manage. As one of his closest friends, I was a witness to his last will and testament. Because of that, I was marked for assassination."

Her eyebrows raised. "But it seems you survived."

"Not without scars. I am sorry to tell you that none of the other witnesses survived and their deaths are all suspect."

She paused. "My word!" After another pause, she said, "Were you CIA agents together? You and Jon Randolph III?"

Bernice still seemed a little nonplussed by the stark revelation of her relative's secret life, about which she obviously knew very little—if nothing! It was a wake-up call!

"Our branch of government service does not have initials that people recognize."

"My goodness." Considerably subdued, Bernice then turned to Rolf, who had settled himself into a comfortable position at the table across from her. "I'm extrapolating from fairly extensive notes here," she said, looking up at him. "Dr. Rolf Maratti. BS, MS, PhD in geology. Professor of mineralogy at one of the best Ivy League schools in the country, now retired. Certified gemologist. Specialist on rare gemstones. Lecturer at many universities on the nature and complexity of minerals and gemstones. Consultant for numerous museums."

Jeff had heard very little of his current grandfather's background before this moment, and he was more than impressed—he was overwhelmed. Bernice went on, "Owner of several high-end stores selling precious stones set in exquisite settings. *Etcetera, etcetera, etcetera.* How do you figure into this mix, Mr. Maratti?"

"Make that 'Rolf Maratti Randolph,' Mrs. Richards. Natural son of Jon Randolph III. I became aware of that genetic relationship only recently, thanks to some very good friends of mine." He glanced at Jeff, a half smile on his face. "Only a few people are aware of the relationship, and I am told I should keep it that way."

"I do understand," she said very softly. "Please call me Bernice, Rolf. It seems we are closely related after all. We have been equally vigilant at hiding our relationship."

"After he died," Rolf said quietly, "a letter written to me by my father came into my possession. He explained his unwillingness to reveal our relationship and strongly suggested that I continue isolating myself from his legacy. I have found that to be a helpful suggestion and have found that I can be far more valuable if I am less visible."

Bernice gazed at him for a time and then turned her attention to Jeff. "And this handsome young man sitting beside you who so resembles my brother...who is he? I have found nothing in the computer to validate his presence here, although the fact that you are blood kin offers many explanations."

Rolf took a deep breath as he turned once more to face Bernice. "This young man is my grandson, Major Jeffrey Maratti, former US Army Ranger, now retired due to PTSD acquired on the front lines in Afghanistan. He is currently in hiding due to his involvement in two major tactical strikes against The Compact. Because of Jeff, any number of Compact members are now in jail or under indictment for criminal activity. They are not happy with him nor with me."

Bernice's response was muted, Jeff noted. She looked from Rolf's face to his and back again several times. It wasn't surprising that she could not find the appropriate words. It wasn't clear either if she wanted to continue reading from a notebook which had suddenly become irrelevant.

"I'd also like you to meet Randy Ross," Emily finally said. Jeff thanked her with a grin for moving the conversation along. Em's bright smile was directed toward the lithe young man leaning against the wall next to the door. "At the grand old age of twenty-six and a half, Randy is currently the youngest police chief in the history of Randolph City, Georgia. He got the job when the chief there was killed by a member of The Compact. Turns out the chief and several policemen had also been corrupted by this group, which has spies and assassins in many unlikely places."

"Why," Bernice said quietly to Rolf, "aside from this recent activity you speak of, is this Blackheart Compact group targeting your family?"

"Our family!" Emily said firmly. "Our family, Bernice. You must keep that firmly in mind! The Blackheart people were pirates in years past. They claim our joint ancestor, Isaac Preston, was one of the original signers of their Compact. Apparently, it included a blood oath that they and all their descendants would be faithful to the Blackhearts and do what they were told to do until the end of time.

"Isaac Preston just said no. Not many people said no to the Blackhearts. When they finally caught up with him, they killed him."

"But," Rolf put in, "there was one survivor the Blackhearts missed. Isaac's youngest daughter, Sara. Wife and then war widow of the first Jon Randolph."

Emily once more took over the narrative. Her voice softened. "It's a long sad story, Bernice, Vince. The upshot of Sara's story is that after everyone in her family was killed, including her first husband, Jonny Randolph—a Confederate conscript who died in the Wilderness of Virginia—she remarried and moved north with her new child, unaware that most of her troubles had not been caused by the war but by a mysterious group bound together by something called the Blackheart Compact. Sara's last name changed to Manning. Her second husband was a Yankee officer. Both were alumni of West Point. The Compact lost track of her—and her children.

"But eventually her first son, Jon Randolph Junior— your friend and mine according to family legend—went into his family's real business, espionage, and that's when The Compact members finally caught up with him. As family historian, Bernice, you probably know more about John Junior than anyone else. I've brought the other side of our family here so we can compare notes. It could be very helpful.

"The third Jon Randolph—Junior's son—came back to Georgia from suburban Chicago completely unaware of his family legacy. When he started restoring Randolph City, The Compact picked up the scent again and came sniffing 'round, trying to take back what they thought they were owed. Without Mr. Jon's knowledge, they surrounded him with spies and traitors and would have taken over the entire town, including Jon's entire legacy, except for this young man"—she indicated Jeff—"who waltzed into town without a by-your-leave, straightened everyone out as to the past history of the Prestons and the Randolphs and the town itself. He also drove a deep wedge into The Compact. Not a fatal blow but a quite noticeable dent. Now, Bernice, please tell me, if our folks had no knowledge of the Blackhearts, why are we are still dodging around and hiding here and there?"

"It's because of the Searchers," Vince said a bit defiantly, now standing straight, his feet firmly apart. "If this cocka-mamie Compact stuff and all these Jon Randolphs you're telling us about is why they're targeting us, it's news to us. We have never known who these jerks were, except that for the most part the leaders of the pack are thugs. We've never known exactly why they were targeting us or even what brought them our way. But what they've always wanted to find out is where Jon Randolph Junior's old bi-wing plane went down.

"Well, Jon Randolph Jr. was Family, even though we're honor-bound not to reveal that relationship. We honored him and we honor his resting place. We aren't going to give that up nor whatever treasure they think he had with him. Not to thugs. Period!"

"I know exactly who the Searchers are," Em said with deep feeling. "My husband Jeb was one of them. Do you want to know why they do what they do?"

Her siblings stood motionless, neither speaking nor nodding, devoid of emotion, Jeff thought, and almost hostile, as if they were trying to prevent their sister from telling them something they sensed but really did not want to confront. Perhaps they were still hoping to wish away what they were beginning to discover was the most troublesome part of their already troubled legacy.

Emily was not to be denied. She continued with passion, "It seems that someone way back in Jeb's family tree was a pirate, part of the crew of a ship called *The Black Rose*. At some time in the past, that person, probably with a knife to his throat, signed a document they called The Blackheart Compact. We're assuming it was something like the Mayflower Compact but evil! Unlike the Mayflower Compact, however, the Blackheart crew members had to sign in their own blood. Pirate blood. Legend says that the document declares that its signers are bound to it for eternity—till the end of the world."

As Jeff watched carefully, a multitude of emotions—from distrust to distress—began to reflect in Bernice's face.

"We tried to escape them, Jeb and I," Emily went on softly, "but they have spies everywhere. They found Jeb first. When they wanted him to do their dirty work, they took me hostage and held me as a house slave. Jeb was forced to spy on Jon Randolph III. They do not know, thank goodness, that I am related to Isaac Presto or that you are either. If they did…"

Vince's mouth tightened. Jeff could see the anger rising inside him.

Emily continued with even more passion. "But they were sure aware of the Thomas family of West Virginia and its business association with Mr. Jon Randolph Jr. They grilled me about Junior's plane every single day. Hard as they tried to break me," Emily said with an icy passion, "I never told." Now she had to stop. Her voice had finally broken. She pulled out a tissue and wiped at the corners of her eyes.

When there was still no response, she resumed her narrative, her voice becoming even more determined. "They want that plane, folks. They're sure we know where it is. They want it so bad it hurts. Bern, Vince, if our family can work together with Grandfather Isaac's other family, we can rid the world of the Blackhearts not only for our own extended families but for many, many other families who have been caught up in its evil web over too many years."

The answer was still silence.

The meeting room remained quiet for some time. Jeff waited, wondering which way the coin would drop. Finally, Bernice stood up. "What do you need?" The tone was low, icy.

Jeff took a deep breath. He answered in a very calm voice, "The first step is easy. Take us to the burial site. We need to retrieve whatever it was that Jon Junior took from The Compact so we can add it to our database. That being done, we can subtly direct Compact Searchers to the airplane. After their own inspection, when they see there is nothing of relevance within the wreckage, harassment of your family should end. You will finally be free to live your lives without their interference. We will take it from there."

Neither Bernice nor Vince responded for several long minutes.

Finally, Vince said, "The plane isn't easy to get to."

"Would a helicopter help?" Ewen asked.

"Wouldn't hurt," Vince answered. And then with a sense of urgency, "Better yet, though, do you have someone who's comfortable on ropes?"

Ewen answered quickly, "Yes."

"Then let's do it!" he said in a voice rife with impassioned anger. "They can't hurt my big sister and get away with it!"

"Vince." A word of warning from Bernice.

He turned to her abruptly. "These people are family!" he said firmly. "They've come a long way to help us, Bern. Me. You. All of us. They look more or less like us. They talk like us. They're sure as hell not after our cash…"

"Okay, okay, okay. I get it!" she said, her voice modified, softened. She looked at Jeff and smiled—this time with something akin to friendship. "I've got to check with a few other people first, if that's okay with you folks."

"Check with whomever it takes," Ewen said. "However, it seems The Compact is closing in on what they seem to think is a legitimate target, so it would help if you made it sooner rather than later. If we're going to get this expedition on the road, we have to put people in place. Our attack plan is always to be two to five steps ahead of The Compact at any time. Our primary strategy is to be…"

"Yes?" Bernice's eyebrows rose.

"Sneaky!" Randy finished Ewen's sentence with a sly grin.

"That does it," Vince said with enthusiasm. "I'm with these folks, Bern. Let's get active. I'm on contract and I have to get back to the coast as soon as I can. But this is something we have to do first. *Have to*! Bern, let's make plans!"

Bernice turned to Ewen and thought about it, turned to Rolf and then thought about it, and then turned to Jeff and looked at Randy. "Who's in charge here?"

The question was so unexpected Jeff couldn't help but chuckle. "I never thought about it before." This time, he did think about it. "Ewen? Rolf? Randy? How do we work out our plans?"

Rolf shrugged. "Things just start to seem obvious, and then everything falls into place—until something goes wrong—and then we work out another scenario."

Ewen seconded that thought. "It is a little *ad hoc*," he agreed. He was quiet for a time and then said, "We do a lot of preplanning, researching, thinking through all the obvious strategies. Suddenly, something seems to jell right in front of us. If contingencies come up, we roll with them. Jeff arranges neat zingers all the time like poison darts. I really liked that one."

"Poison darts?" Vince's eyes widened.

"It worked really well," Randy said. "We had a lot of zombies on our hands for a while. They all recovered, but they were sure mad."

"Zombies? You've gotta be kidding me!" Vince started laughing. "Are you serious?"

"There's always the faithful bullwhip," Rolf put in, his eyes twinkling now.

"My question is," Bernice said, hands on hips, "which one of you do I call when I get an answer from my own troops?"

"Jeff," everyone but Jeff called out.

"That's all I needed to know," she said. "Now let's get you folk some food before you go back home and start strategizing. We can show you some maps and give you some basics right here. Our next meeting will have to be on-site. Tomorrow noon or as close to it as you can get there. Do not be late! At that time, we'll introduce you to this month's guards. They can tell you as much as we know about the grave and what it contains."

"Good to go!" Randy said enthusiastically. "Let's eat!"

CHAPTER 12

Saturday afternoon, April 16, 2016

For Lorie, the day had seemed endless. She had to restrain herself from calling Jeff on the cell phone to see if everyone was okay—or to find out if Emily's family was receptive to joint plans. It was hard to be away from the center of activity. She busied herself by sprucing up the house—washing a growing pile of clothing and bed linens, making cookies, playing with Saree—and when her daughter went down for a much-needed nap, she found herself gravitating once again to Isaac Preston's journals.

There was something she needed to find in one of the early books. The partial date, noted in a childish scrawl at the top of the first page of the third book, was April 1809. It wouldn't hurt to read this book again much more carefully.

"I have a good friend in Marseilles," Isaac had written. Lorie's mind automatically corrected many unusual spellings as her attention skimmed the pages and finally caught again the word she had been seeking. "His name is Ukuhlakanipho." Yes, she had not mistaken this word. This time, she was not surprised. And this was the part she needed to read again. "He spelled it for me," Isaac had written. "The way he says it is hard for me to get my tongue around. Maybe someday I will be able to because he is teaching me his language and even how to do clicky African things with my tongue. He is the person who gave me the journal to write in. I did not know what to do with it then, but now I do. I want to remember Lak, so I will write about him in order to remember him at all times. He is an interesting person. Will told me I would meet interesting people in Marseilles and I have. Many of them are Lak's friends. They are all free people even if their faces are black as can be. Just like Lak's.

"Lak knows I can hear things. He said it was easy for him to see that I could hear and talk when he first met me. But he is teaching me how to hide these things from other people. He also has taught me many other things, including something he calls necessary stealth. And he also has introduced me to many people of different colors from Africa and from different parts of Europe and is helping me to learn other languages besides his Zulu.

"I would rather stay with Lak than with my friend Will when the boat goes out on the water to kill sailors on other boats. I hate the blood and the gore I have to clean up. But Lak told me not to let on about being friends with him because he knows the crew will not like it, and he does not want to take the chance of not seeing me again. He told me I should not even tell Will.

"I had to tell Will about Lak last week, though, when I got sick with a strange disease that made me very hot and shaky with funny dreams. I kept saying 'Lak, Lak,' and finally Will asked someone on the dock who Lak was. When Will found him, Lak told him he had some medicine that would help me to get better. He had the disease in Africa once, so he cannot get it again. I was afraid Will would get it, but he told me he had the disease, too, one time and lived only because he also had a black friend who liked him and gave him medicine."

Whatever disease it was, Lorie thought sadly, it was the same vicious organism that in the end had destroyed Isaac's family. All the grown-up Isaac could do was watch in despair as his wife and children perished in his arms one after the other. The medicine Lak had given him in France was not so readily available in the New World.

She turned back to the small book. "My friend Will likes Lak a lot, and he will not tell anyone that when I am gone from the boat, I am with Lak because I feel safe with him. I am glad that Will knows about him now because I do not like to keep secrets from my good friend."

Sighing deeply, she slipped that journal back into the trunk and picked up the next.

This book was dated 1810. Isaac would have been seven years old by then. It contained many pictures of ships under sail, pictures of knots, pictures—fully realized by a talented young artist—of ports of call. "We were in a terrible battle again today. The captain told Will I had to stay on the ship when it left port as I know too much, and even if I cannot talk or hear, he saw me sketching on paper one day. I have to be very careful that he does not see me doing that again or find my books. I am hiding them in the bottom part of a new sea chest Lak made for me. I am the only one who knows where the chest is. It is getting very heavy, as Will gives me part of what he calls his wages every time he is paid. He says these heavy shiny coins will take care of me very nicely after we sail home to America, and I am not to touch them until then. My little Chinese chest is in there, too, with my mother's pretty blue stones hidden in it. I wish sometimes that I had given them to the Blackhearts so they would not have hurt my mother. But then I remember that it would not have made any difference. She would have been hurt first and then killed, anyway. I have seen it done too many times since then.

So I keep them to remember her. They are the color of her eyes, which were beautiful like the sky."

Tears came to Lorie's eyes. She had found a picture of a pretty blue-eyed young woman in the same journal—a small watercolor painted by her very talented child.

Isaac had probably never been aware how much his eyes were like his mother's—genetic duplicates of the eyes that brightened Jeff Preston's own scarred face.

Lorie put the book down for a time until the tears stopped flowing. The little fox came to keep her company. She gave him a careful hug. And then again, hoping that what Jeff was finding out was as interesting as what she was learning, she again picked up the books.

Saturday evening, April 16

The Justice Seekers turned for home triumphant, bearing maps and suggestions as to what equipment might have to be brought in.

"Let's take a look at our satellite photos again," Ewen said as he turned the SUV south at the Breezewood intersection and reentered the Interstate system. "I think I was looking at an entirely different section of the mountains. They obviously have been very resourceful in their own planning and deceptive abilities. I'm impressed by your relatives, Jeff."

Jeff was still glowing from his first contact with blood kin, who to this point had been completely unknown to him. "Delightful but devious," he said, grinning. "That trait seems to be part of my father's inheritance."

"You mean deviousness is inherited?" Ewen asked with a huge laugh. "I learned it from Jon Third! He was the Master at Deviousness!"

"I also inherited The Compact," Jeff said, his grin changing to a grimace. "I am discovering that my father was a much more complex human being than I ever gave him credit for."

"That's something everyone has to figure out for themselves." This time, Ewen's voice was solemn. "Parents are every bit as complicated beings as their children are—even if their children worship them as gods." He chuckled at the varied reactions of his fellow passengers on that description of parents. "A very rare condition, I admit. But more to the point, every human is a contradictory, unpredictable, often ornery piece of work—always quite different from what their children believe them to be."

"Amen to that," Rolf said quietly.

The joking continued, and everyone was almost unreasonably hyped by the time they reached the horse farm in the Shenandoah Valley late in the afternoon. With an excited smile on her face, Em gathered up her son, thanked Lorie profusely for babysitting, and headed for her quarters.

"We did it!" Jeff said to Lorie. He grabbed her into a big hug and then rained kisses on his little daughter, who giggled and hugged back. "We have a good idea where Junior is buried!"

"Wonderful," Lorie said. "I'm relieved that everything went so well. What's next?"

"Examining maps. Finding ways to get to the places we need to go. Making plans to get there."

"And reading your father's journals," Lorie said with a beguiling grin.

"Can it wait?"

"No."

"After dinner, my dear one. Right now, I've got to get a short nap."

"Saree's ready for a nap too," she said to him gently. "Get some sleep while you can, and then I've got a few things to show you."

Half an hour later, much refreshed, he joined her at the kitchen table. The first item she brought out was his father's third journal.

"I'm sorry I haven't been able to keep up with you, honey," he said to her, "but we've been so involved... Is reading the first two journals necessary for me to understand what you're showing me now?"

"The first two journals were horrifying, illuminating, and fascinating." Her words were very gentle. "And you must read them to get an understanding of the inner workings of the child who became the man who was your father. Quick summary—the death of his parents, his adoption by Will Deerfield—master seaman and apparently an unwilling member of the pirate crew—possibly a prisoner himself. Your father learned a great deal by following Pirate Will around like a shadow and doing exactly what he did, all the while pretending to be deaf and dumb. Will eventually figured out what was going on, though, and didn't tell."

"But in the meantime, your father learned a lot about ropes and knots, far more than he already knew from growing up on a ship. He put it all into the book in little pictures. Also, he knew which sail was best for what kind of weather. He put a lot in the book about Moses too, Jeff. Lak is still what he calls him at this point.

"There's much here about Lak's friends. Isaac was invited to gala parties in Marseilles with African ex-patriots, many of whom were students in European universities. Wealthy blacks with a few whites thrown in. Isaac seems to have learned a lot of African languages that way—at parties.

He says he listened and later asked Lak/Moses what those different words meant."

"I saw some of that already as I was skimming through it," Jeff said reflectively. "It's a little hard to believe that boy was my father. What's the time frame on the first book?"

"The *Red Rose* was taken in 1808 when Isaac was five years old. He drew some pictures of it in the books. He was a pretty good artist even when he was young. The second book is much like the first, with more pictures than words. He didn't begin chronicling with real sentences and paragraphs until he was seven, which was in 1810. That's the third book. He started writing when he was sick in bed from a disease that was going around the docks. Will thought he might die, so he was waiting on him hand and foot. Jeff, this is the part I especially want to show you. I'm guessing it was the same disease that killed the rest of your family later on. If so, it's no wonder your father was immune when it hit the plantation so hard."

"Did he say there was a lot of coughing?"

"Coughing up yellow phlegm, he said, or words to that effect. Nose and throat so full that he couldn't breathe. Sounds like either a bad case of pneumonia or a flu of some kind. Even now there's not a lot to be done about flu but wait it out. It's a viral infection. Our current antibiotics don't touch it."

Jeff said very softly, "It sounds exactly like the disease that took away my mother and Will and the babies." He looked up at Lorie, at her concerned expression, "I almost hated him for keeping Sara and me from coming home, from saying goodbye to everyone..."

She came around the table with open arms. He rose to her embrace. "He did the right thing, love. He kept you away until the epidemic had run its course."

"Then he will always be my hero," Jeff said softly.

"And mine," Lorie answered, lifting her lips to his. He longed to go to bed with her now, feel her arms about him, immerse himself in the love that now enveloped them both.

But now, unfortunately, was not the time. He was expected momentarily at the big house. "Tonight," he said softly. And Lorie, understanding as always, took both his hands in hers and brought them to her lips.

*****

"Where do you think The Compact database might be located?" Ewen asked again while they were discussing the prospect.

Jeff's immediate answer: "The same place The Compact is kept."

He, Rolf, and Ewen were in the study discussing options. They were soon joined by Randy and Jeb, who had been checking out the horses Guy was training. Guy was with them. Rolf looked around the room. "Where are the ladies?"

Jeff said, "Lorie's catching up on bills and babysitting until Saree wakes up. She'll be here."

Jeb chuckled. "Emily is helping Alexi prepare dinner for tonight. She's havin' a great time. Thank you, good folks, for takin' us in, Guy. This is my idea of a dream come true." He nodded toward Ewen. "Not to disrespect you, my friend, for your hospitality, but this valley between the mountains seems to open up to the sky a lot more regular."

"It does," Ewen answered warmly. "The Georgia mountain retreat is meant to be a place of solitude, study, and creativity. This is a real home."

Then began the retrospective of the day's meeting and much discussion of what needed to be taken care of before the next stage of their quest began. Dinner, when it finally appeared, was tasty and filling, and conversation began in a lighthearted manner.

But before long, topics morphed into the inescapable. "We're meeting our counterparts tomorrow as close to noon as we can make it," Jeff finally said to the gathered plotters. "Who's going?"

"I'm the designated point person," Guy said. "On the phones here. But you can use my R-22 copter if you need it."

"Only two seats," Ewen noted. "How about the R-44? Room for four."

"Jeb needs to go," Jeff said, looking up at his friend. "He knows how the Justice Seekers work. Randy's a climber as well."

Ewen said, "I've done a lot of climbing in the Alps."

Rolf Maratti held up his hand. "I'm not much of a climber, but you'll undoubtedly need people on the ground."

Ewen concurred. "Okay. Five. We'll really have to take the SUV. Any other takers?" He glanced at Lorie.

"It's a guy thing," she said with a feigned sigh. "So much as I would like to join you, practicality wins out this time. We gals will do what gals have done from time immemorial. Hold heart and hearth together. And mind the babies."

Emily concurred. "We're going to try not to be terribly hurt by your abandoning us in this virtual paradise."

"If anybody is interested," Alexi said, laughing once again, "coffee is being served in the sunroom. And cookies. Along with lots of little kids who are probably overwhelming our nanny right about now."

Ewen grinned. A bell chimed, and he rose, walked to his fax machine, and came back with a piece of paper. "In addition to what they've already given me, they've just sent specific directions to cut our travel time in half. We're to follow their list of GPS directives. They want us at this location"—he jabbed at the large geologic survey map he had laid out on the table—"at twelve noon tomorrow. They say it's urgent that we be there on time." The men gathered around him. He consulted the new information and pulled his finger along the route lines. "It looks like they're putting us directly across several mountain ranges on, well, roads that look pretty dicey until we get way over here in the westernmost part of the state. What the hell is going on here?"

"We ladies are leaving now," Lorie said softly to Jeff. "Taking care of babies. I'll see you at the house later tonight."

"Journal time, I expect," he said, giving her a broad smile as he turned back to the map. "I promise to read them, honey."

CHAPTER 13

Sunday morning, April 17, 2016

The bright stars of very early morning promised a clear dawn. As Jeff rose after a satisfying night with his sweet wife snuggled beside him, a rush of anticipation tinged with sadness hit him in the stomach. His good mood flattened. Today, if all went well, they would stand at the spot where Jon Randolph Jr. had so tragically perished on the same night his child had come into the world.

But even if his sister's son had survived the crash, Jeff mused as he pulled on his jeans, would he have been able to destroy on his own the Blackhearts? It might by that time have already become too formidable an organization to eliminate single-handed.

Had he and Lorie discovered the existence of The Compact and its signers by sheer luck? If Jon Third's traitorous lawyer had not finally opened up to his part in the conspiracy, would the organization's long-running private vendetta against the Randolph family ever have come to light? Jon Third's survivors might still be wondering why they were experiencing such incredibly bad luck.

On the other hand, he mused, he had awakened into this new century with enough vital information in his bag of tricks to start the search, which was finally unmasking their adversaries. Maybe sheer luck wasn't as much luck as everyone had thought!

There was no point speculating. It was what it was and it was up to the Justice Seekers to finish the job. Failure was not an option.

It would be a relatively long ride—four to five hours, he had gauged—over roads that seemed to be barely navigable. It was possible that the amenities they had previously enjoyed during their travels would not be so easily available. Well, they would take the cards as dealt. They had all seen combat of one kind or another in places where amenities were nonexistent.

"We'll hold the fort till you get back," he heard Lorie say softly.

"A warrior, bold and true!" Smiling, he leaned over the bed to give her another kiss.

*****

A faint light in the eastern sky was just beginning to press at the rim of the world as they left the farm. Ewen was driving, grumbling at the thought of being ordered around by Bernice. Why did she need them on-site at noon sharp? Peculiar, he thought. Jeff had to admit that he concurred. But Bernice didn't seem a rash person. She must have a reason.

They were all dressed for hiking and/or climbing. The cargo space of the SUV was filled with appropriate gear, and Jeff thought there might be a gun or two stashed there, too, in inconspicuous places—although he had frowned at it.

The roads Bernice's directions had put them on, he soon discovered, were generally high-speed pavements constructed at the lowest point of mountain-rimmed valleys. Those were the easy roads. Deviations from numbered highways led onto what at first seemed simple cross-country byways. But more often than not, those roads devolved into difficult uphill/ heart-stoppingly steep downhill graveled tracks heading roughly west through rugged mountainous terrain.

As a matter of fact, the directions were pretty straight-forward: set the fastest course that you can find across the mountains and don't let anything, either ordinary or unusual, interrupt you because we need you at high noon, thank you very much!

The trip itself wasn't helpful toward soothing Jeff's grow-ing fears that he might have to do some climbing. A successful spy operation the previous year, which found him dangling ten stories over the cement sidewalks of Washington, DC, did not make this current expedition any less terrifying. He still held that ingrained fear of heights. He hoped he would be able to conquer it again if he were called upon. He hadn't encountered his sister Sara's presence for some time—she who had brought him the courage he needed when he required it the most. Maybe now that the body of her first son was being unearthed and his accomplishments acknowledged, she might be able to find the rest she so blessedly deserved.

Conversation was sparse during this journey. "Are we still on course?" Ewen asked now and again, often request-ing global positioning numbers determined by satellites far overhead to make certain they were where they were sup-posed to be on earth. Randy had been designated the num-bers person. He read them aloud, and Rolf double-checked them against the notes handed to them by Vince or Bernice. So far, everything fit the preprinted directions, and they were still on schedule.

And then at half past 11:00 a.m., as they were making a hair-raising turn on a dirt road around the sharp side of a steep mountain on one of the most hazardous roads they had yet encountered, they were halted by a tall muscular black man dressed in dark clothing and carrying a rifle. He was standing in the middle of the road where it disappeared upward to the left around the edge of a steep hillside. "This is personal property," he growled. "What's your business here?"

"Bernice sent us," Ewen said. She had instructed them to say no more than those three words—in that order!

"Give me your names, all of you."

This was not a surprise. Bernice had requested a print-out of each of their names, addresses, and phone numbers. Ewen handed the paper to the rifleman.

"I want you to repeat this information one at a time," the man said. "In person." A hijacker to their party would not be able to give quick answers. Good defense.

Everyone emerged carefully from the car. Located on the passenger side, Jeff devoutly hoped not to make a misstep on the raw edge of what he perceived as a stomach-churning drop-off but which, he finally had to admit, would have been a manageably recoverable slope had he somehow slipped. As quickly as he could, he relocated to the "safe" side of the car.

He now recognized the drill: each passenger was to be taken separately around the turn in the road for interrogation. Jeb was selected first, much to his consternation. Upon his return, the expression on his rugged features was of extreme relief.

Ewen was next. "My god," he said when he came back, shaken. "They really are suspicious. This has to be handled with kid gloves, people. Do exactly as they say. Do not try to be assholes. No joking around. Period!"

"They have pictures of all of us," Jeb whispered. "How did they get a picture of me?"

"Good question," Randy said softly. He had just rejoined their group. "They had a photo of me wearing my Marietta police uniform and another of me wearing my new Randolph City police chief getup. Their network is better than ours. We don't know anything about them, and they seem to know everything about us—that's a little intimidating!"

Rolf finally came back in one piece, obviously relieved, and the guard beckoned for Jeff to come forward. As he turned the corner, he spotted Vince emerging from the doorway of a small shack fitted into a crack on the upward side of the cliff. Taking a chance, he waved. Vince waved back as he approached and smiled. Thank goodness! They truly were with friends here. He had begun to wonder.

"Yo," Vince called. "It's good, bro! We do this occasionally. It throws people off, and they get out of here like bats out of hell!" He added, laughing, "As soon as they can figure out how to back down that road." He waved toward their armed guard. "Meet my cousin, Cletus Thomas. Our Chief Intimidator. These other big burly guys are cousins too. Ras, for Erasmus. Demetrius—we call him Dee." They clustered around Vince. Good looks inherited from Isaac, and/or Rosette were apparent in all their faces no matter what shade. What an attractive family, Jeff thought, awed by the stark awareness that these big burly fellows were his blood cousins!

Three of the men were grinning now, including Vince. With a humorous laugh, Cletus's stern face finally broke into a wide grin, strong white teeth showing brightly in a face turned surprisingly friendly. "Nice to meet you, Jeff Maratti. No question of your relationship with cousin Vince here. You guys look almost enough alike to be brothers, except for the skin pigment thing." He waved his hand in the direction of Vince and then reached for Jeff's hand.

All of the men were grinning now. Jeff took the hand Cletus offered, now laughing out loud. "Well done, cousins!" Jeff said. "Our own intimidators couldn't have pulled it off better, and we're pretty damned good!"

Cletus said somewhat apologetically, "We wanted to demonstrate to you our methods of keeping the site sterile. Well, it's about time to get your travel mates over here so we can soothe some feathers and explain why we needed you so quickly."

He walked back to the car with Jeff and, much to everyone's relief, cordially invited the newcomers into the narrow headquarters building of the Thomas Family Guard Station No. 1, seemingly carved right out of the cliff that rose above them. Jeff had not expected to see a large interior, but there it was, cleverly carved out from the side of the mountain. He smelled coffee brewing and saw a plate full of breakfast goodies on a table in a far dark corner.

When nobody invited the newcomers, however, to help themselves, questions annoyingly reemerged about the hospitality quotient of these folks. Jeff was just about ready to tear off some tree bark to chew, and he hoped there was an answer somewhere down the line, as his stomach was beginning to growl.

"Hate to hurry us along," Vince then said urgently, "but if we don't get going right now, we'll miss the 'ghost light.' Bernice is sure it will show up this year with you folk appearing on our doorsteps so conveniently! She thinks it's a miracle! I think it's a natural phenomenon. I don't know what Cletus thinks because he doesn't want to tell me." He grinned at his cousin. "He's probably scared of it."

Ghost light? Not something that had been mentioned in their briefing about the hidden grave. Jeff's thoughts swirled.

It was not the way Sara would present herself. As much as he had tried to will it, he didn't sense her presence here at all!

With a loud snort of amused derision, Cletus pushed forward, leading the way. They walked silently through a pathless forest in what Jeff felt to be a westerly direction. Their guide made a sudden turn to the north. Jeff checked the compass he had attached to his belt and found that his sense of direction was still on point. Now he looked around more carefully and spotted what before he had taken to be random markings slashed into several of the older trees. He had seen those markings before. Very cagy, these people. They had been taught to blaze trail by someone close to his family, and he felt sure he could put a name to that person!

A ten-minute walk brought them within a long stone's throw of an abrupt drop-off. "It's under this cliff," Cletus said bluntly. "See our marker there? Skull and crossbones— just like pirates would use! We don't go nearer the edge than this unless we have proper climbing gear on. We've got good sunlight today, so I expect we'll get the light! Bernice figured you'd want to be here if it happens. If she's right, we'll hook you up to the special harness that was made many years ago for rescue work, and we'll lower you down with our block and tackle. Also old but very efficient. Built by an old sailor, I've been told. Someone who knew all about pulleys and ropes and the Pythagorean Theorem, thereby proving he was a genuine engineer.

"But all you can do is look, friends, even if we let you down there. There's no good place to stand. We've been told that eons ago, the rocks on this ledge were the base of a riverbed, a series of thin layers of sandstone that have a tendency to slide across each other if someone steps on them. Unfortunately, they're kind of standing on end. Tread carefully! We've got flashlights if you need them."

"You have climbing equipment here?" Ewen asked in an excited voice.

"For rescue work only. It's quite old but very solidly made, and we keep it in good shape in case we have cause to use it. Are you willing to take the chance?"

"Of course!"

"I'll grab the harness," Cletus answered. "It's stashed in a hidey-hole not too far away." He disappeared into the woods, likely following a different blaze.

"Who wants to go down?" Vince asked. "To be frank, except for the first guy who dropped down there to find out if Junior was still alive—great-great-great-uncle Wade Thomas—we've never tried to get into the cave. Uncle Wade was a mountaineer born and bred, and he told our people it was far too dangerous. But our family owed Junior everything, so Uncle Wade took it upon himself to find out what he could.

"When he came back up top, he said that everything inside the 'cave' was so linked together that when one rock shifted, everything else shifted—like a booby trap. He went in just far enough to confirm that Junior was dead. He couldn't get close to the plane itself, but he said from what he saw, Junior was just as broken up as his plane was. His neck was obviously broken, his face was smashed in and covered with blood! There was no doubt in Uncle Wade's mind that he'd died instantly. Uncle Wade also said it would be too hazardous to retrieve the body. He declared this shallow scooped-out opening to be a proper and fitting burial place accessible only by birds, and we've kept it as a memorial ever since!"

Ewen spoke up. "Thank you, Vince. I'm the one who's going to be putting together what we need to retrieve the alleged briefcase, so—keeping Uncle Wade's cautions in mind—I'll do a quick descent just to see what's causing the legendary flash."

"I've seen the flash myself!" Vince said, a bit defensively. "It's not fiction. And if it's going to show, this is the date, and five minutes from now is the time!"

Rolf turned to him. "We don't disbelieve you, Vince. What we need is for you to tell us all you know about the light before Ewen steps out into space."

Cletus gave a low whistle, and Vince got serious. "It's not just a flash *per se*. It's a fairly strong beam that lights up the underside of wind-blown leaves above the cave one day each summer—always on the anniversary of the day Junior Randolph was killed. That's today! We've never found its origin. The light also shows up in early autumn."

Rolf frowned. "A flashing light? Some kind of code?"

Vince explained once again patiently. "On the rare occasions it's visible, it sometimes flashes but not in a regular pattern. In my opinion, the so-called flash is simply caused by leaves being blown by a breeze. People in the valley below began to notice it years ago, and now they set out a watch for it this time of year. Full sun is essential. If it's going to show, this is the ideal day!"

"Have you searched the area to see if there's a crack in the cave ceiling?" Rolf asked. "I'm a mineralogist by profession. I've done a lot of cave exploring in my time. Caves sometimes have openings in unusual places, and I know sunlight has a way of bouncing around. Sightings noticed twice a year at regular intervals…sounds to me like what sunlight might do."

Vince's reply was wary. "Sounds logical, but no looking for us. We don't trust the cave roof for a minute. Anytime we've had to make trips out there, rare occasions only, we put climbing harnesses on."

Cletus reappeared, carrying a contraption constructed of sturdy leather and attached to two very long businesslike ropes. He secured the ends of each of the ropes firmly to metal rings, which seemed to be extruded from a wooden case half buried in the forest floor far back from the rim. He held the harness out to Ewen, who took it, and, with Jeb's help, quickly pulled the leather leggings up his legs and fastened the leather belt around his waist.

With Jeff, Randy, and Vince controlling the ropes from a safe distance, Ewen was lowered slowly over the edge of the cliff. "Just a little farther, gents," he called out a few minutes later. "I can almost see into the cave."

Jeff heard Cletus say excitedly, "There's the light, Vince. See it?"

Vince pulled out a phone and punch-dialed Ewen. "Do you see a light source?" He switched the phone to speaker mode.

"I sure do," Ewen replied, his voice faint and eerily resonant below the edge of the cliff. "And now that I've had a chance to push some of these hanging vines back, I've solved your riddle to boot. The light is a bounce-back from a big piece of metal. In the dust that was disturbed into action by my movements, I see both a sunbeam coming down and a sunbeam going up or vice versa. Can't tell which is which. Let me get a bunch of pictures." A pause. "There! Okay, folks, I think we've got the location of one of the old propeller blades. It's pretty badly twisted, but that's what the sunlight is hitting right now. It reflects sunlight upward to hit the underside of the trees up there, which are shimmering in the wind that always comes up from these cliffs. I'll order up some high-tech gadgets from my labs, and we can proceed with all due haste."

"Do you need to see anything more?" Jeff called down.

"Negative. Like the man says, it won't be easy to do anything in here. I concur with Uncle Wade. I put my foot down for only a second, and everything began to shift. This is a good place to get injured. Everything's at odds with everything else. These persistent vines—blast them—they're in the way anywhere you turn! But we don't want anyone to know we're here, so we'll just have to deal with them."

Once Ewen was pulled back to the top of the ledge, he worked his way carefully across the outward area toward a large crumbling rock structure of some kind, taller and wider than a man and partially enveloped within the embrace of an ancient long-dead tree. "Can I give you a boost, Randy?" Ewen asked. "We've got to see what's on top of this thing."

With Jeb's assistance as well, Randy scrambled up. "Hollow," the young man said, looking down at Ewen. "Definitely the source of your light stream. It seems to be a natural rock formation shaped kind of like a chimney. Probably would have crumbled away years ago except for a tree that grew around it and rooted it to solid ground. On two specific days during the year, I expect, sunshine comes down through the rock chimney, hits the metal under it at an angle, and bounces upward, out of the cave!"

Vince said, "You gotta be kidding! Why didn't we ever think to look there?"

"Why would you?" Randy asked. "It's in a dangerous location!"

Jeff could tell Ewen was burning up with ideas now. "I've got some operatives," Ewen said enthusiastically, "who can give us just what we need to search the interior and do the retrieval without anyone touching either the ceiling or the floor of the cave. Or the chimney. I'm calling right now." A few moments later, he called out, "Done. They're on it. Okay, pull me back out there, folks. I'm going to take pictures of the entire area with a long focus lens. Keep hanging on to those lines, guys. We've got this baby corralled."

Jeff chuckled. He knew who Ewen had just called: Ivan, Bill, and Jared—the genius trio. If anyone could extract a briefcase from an inaccessible cave with a heretofore unknown remote device, they would be the ones. He was willing to bet that, ironically, drones might prove to be the solution here. He grinned. It was Compact drones, he recalled, that had frightened them into leaving the horse farm in Georgia and set off this whole search. Revenge could sometimes be very sweet!

"I think," Ewen called up a short time later from below the cliff, "we have it solved, folks. Let me check to make sure I have all the cave photos I need, and then we'll put a few people to work."

Twenty tense silent minutes later, he asked to be brought back to the heights. He was ecstatic. "I've got measurements for everything, including the exact latitude and longitude of those light beams and the angles they are taking in relation to the propeller and the rock chimney. If our guys can't think of some brilliant way to retrieve this proverbial briefcase from a cave without disturbing anything else, nobody can. Let's roll, people. We have lots of work to do."

CHAPTER 14

The back wall of the guard shack, Jeff discovered, once they were allowed past the front steps, concealed the entryway to a sizeable natural cave. On this day, it was brightly lit and bustling with activity. One side of the cave was lined top to bottom with computer monitors and all the portable electrical equipment necessary to keep everything working. Five young men with bright inquisitive faces were on duty at the monitors, and an equal number of older fellows were handling printouts and plotting maps at large tables.

"What or whom are you tracking?" Ewen asked Vince. The entrepreneur's eyes, his whole body, showed excitement at this unexpected information center. Jeff chuckled. Ewen lived for moments like this.

"Searchers," Vince told him. "We've all done this duty at one time or another. We're taught computer programming the same time we learn to read. In previous generations, we all knew the radio codes and Ham radio language, and before that, Morse Code, and before that..."

"Semaphore, I expect," Ewen said softly, pleasure in his voice.

Vince chuckled. "Wig wag, they sometimes call it. How'd you guess?"

"Because it's something I learned as a Boy Scout many years ago, and it helped me to decide what I wanted to do with my life."

"Sneaky stuff," Vince said with a laugh, mimicking Randy's turn of phrase. "Well, we've concluded that you're a lot more up-to-date than the Searchers we're tracking. About the best they can do is punch-dial a cell phone."

"Don't underrate their corporate masters," Ewen said solemnly. "They are far more sophisticated than you suppose. We've been keeping tabs on as many of The Compact's internet interactions as we can locate on a twenty-four-hour basis. Sometimes they're a little too smart for their own good, however. If they were still using telephones—not smart phones but the ones connected to phone lines—they would be a lot harder to track. We'd have to know exactly which phones we wanted to tap and then get permission. It's a whole lot easier right now, sad to say, in a world where protocols and regulations are seen to be words with no substance. Now everyone's life is streaming along in midair, ripe for the plucking."

"Except for you folks," Cletus said. "We know nothing about you."

"You knew an awful lot about us," Randy put in, his voice rising.

"Only you," Cletus replied, turning to the young policeman with a twinkle in his eye. "Heroes are hard to hide. We have it on good authority that you helped rescue a group of kids who had been kidnapped. And your name came up in a rescue recorded earlier in the police activity section of another paper. A young woman and her father were being held hostage by a gang of thugs. You got yourself shot up, if I recall."

"Those things were reported in newspapers? They shouldn't have been. Ewen, did you know...? And besides, it was Jeff..."

Ewen's face clouded. "No one I know would touch those stories with a ten-foot pole!"

"There was a reporter at the hospital when you brought people in. Helicopters are hard to hide." Cletus grinned and hastened to add, "Don't get your panties in a bunch, folks. Here's the rest of the story—some of our people just 'happened' to be on staff at the hospitals where your victims were brought in. And in the newspaper offices also.

"We managed to get both stories squelched before they reached the outside public. In fact, we bought up every copy of the first printed edition of the newspaper that reported the child kidnappings in Georgia. We'd been monitoring that particular gang of Searchers for a long time. This was the first time they had done anything that caused them to be noticed. And before you ask, those who haven't yet gone to jail still remain under close surveillance by our family."

"The *zombies*," Randy said quietly to Jeff, a chuckle in his throat, and Jeff grinned too.

"We wondered where you folks had come from," Cletus went on. "We wanted to welcome you to our association. But needless to say, you have till now avoided all attempts to be found. Well, here you are at last! Welcome to our humble mountain headquarters!"

Jeff saw Randy take several deep breaths as again he warmly shook Cletus's hand and then Vince's. Newspaper accounts, Jeff knew, would bring the wrath of The Compact down upon Randy's head from directions heretofore unknown. Any record of the earlier event would also target Tim Murphy, his partner on the Marietta police force. Tim had shot and killed one of The Compact members. Both Tim's and Randy's names had been wiped from police reports, and after the investigation cleared Tim of doing anything more than protecting a fellow officer under fire, the matter had been quietly dropped. "Thank you," Randy finally said. "I probably owe you my life." Tim had quit the police force, and he and his young sons had taken possession of the country store previously owned by Jeb Wallace. They were all doing well at the moment.

"I was the hospital patient in that shooting scuffle," Jeb said softly.

Now, Jeff noted, it was Vince's turn to be surprised. His demeanor suddenly shifted to high alert. "I heard that the man who was shot was a member of the gang. Bernice is now talking about something she says is called The Compact. Are you a part of that group?"

"Aren't we all?" Jeb replied wearily. "The way I hear it, all of Isaac Preston's children and grandchildren are members of The Compact because he's the one that signed the book or whatever it is! And if I wasn't a member on my own hook, owin' to someone in my mother's family, I'd be a member through my wife's family."

Vince relaxed quite as rapidly as he had bristled. "You're Emily's husband, aren't you, Jeb? I'm sorry. Sometimes I let myself get a little too judgmental. This lifestyle is somewhat exhausting." He held out his hand. "Welcome again, Jeb Wallace, to Em's family. I'm relieved you survived the ordeal. And I'm more than happy you're on our side. I understand you and Em have a daughter. How is she holding up?"

Jeb accepted the handshake with a smile. "Apology noted and accepted. And I'm happy to say that our daughter, Celeste, is farin' quite well, thanks to some very good friends of mine. We have a baby son as well. Em's a great mother!" He said the words proudly.

Rolf Maratti Randolph was standing to one side, uncommonly silent. Jeff turned to him. "How are you doing?" he asked softly, concerned.

"This man whom everyone calls Junior," Rolf murmured, the faint Italian accent that still remained in his voice sounding somewhat jarring in this association of American back-country patriots, "was my paternal grandfather. They talk about him as if their family knew him well. I was never allowed that privilege. If we can bring his murderers to justice, I will feel we have given him at least some of the honor he deserves for the services he performed for this country—and for his own family."

"We'll do it," Vince answered gently as Jeff put a reassuring hand on Rolf's shoulder. For much of his life, Rolf had thought he was the son of an Italian traitor working hand in glove with the Nazis during World War II. When he discovered that his genetic father was Jon Randolph Third, his entire outlook on life was transformed. This expedition was, for him, very personal.

It was then Jeff realized that his search for his own father, Isaac, was taking a similar path. He and Rolf, an intensely proud and intelligent man, were journeying together, trying to discover for better or worse the legacies their ancestors had left for them. Interesting legacies, he was now beginning to realize. Parallel legacies in many ways. The search was worthwhile, he thought, even if it was exhausting. And dangerous!

"Come with me," Vince said. "I will show you where the airfield lay on that fateful day."

He took the newcomers deep into the pine forest on an almost hidden trail that bypassed the guard cabin. The remains of the landing field lay on a sizeable plateau. "This is where it was," he said, speaking very quietly, "this whole area around us. See how still and beautiful it is now that the trees are so tall. But in the beginning days of flight, this was a pretty lively place. Junior would bring his flying friends here. Sometimes they'd climb into big-winged gliders and launch themselves out into space. They would circle over the valley for a while, soar with the eagles and buzzards, and land way down there on that long strip you can still make out alongside the river. Then they'd get lifts from a couple of bi-wing planes based down there and come back to leave the gliders in a safe place where no one could paw over them and throw their precious instruments out of kilter.

"I used to hear tales of Junior Randolph visiting our family now and then. In his own plane, of course. He liked to give the young people rides, some of the old-timers too. Those times were so exciting for the family. He'd stop by for long catching-up-with-family visits. And then if he had business in Washington, DC, he'd fly off to a private field near there. He kept a car hidden close by—in a barn, I think. If it still exists, it would probably be worth a fortune." He laughed. "And if I knew more about Junior, I could write a movie script and probably get paid a lot of bucks. Until then, it's action movies up one side and down the other. Not much glory in it but pretty good pay."

"Pretty good movies too," Ewen said, grinning at him. "Don't knock 'em!"

"You're my kind of guy!" Vince said, still chuckling. "Now let's get some food. My big sister has spent a lot of time preparing something special for you folks, and I have this nagging feeling you're going to begin searching out tree bark to gnaw on if you don't get some decent food in you pretty damn soon."

Jeff grinned. Thanks to Rosette, his mother's little saying was still alive and well on both sides of the family divide. It warmed his heart to hear it echoing still.

Trading humorous jibes now, they joined a reunion party being put together in the brightly lit cave/office. Bernice had arrived all the way from Breezewood with food fit for royalty: a superb mix of old-timey soul food and gourmet seafood dishes served with wine and laid out on fine linen tablecloths. The service was made on rough-hewn log tables in a rugged cave setting, and Jeff chuckled, thinking how Lorie would envy him.

Once the men had finished eating and after a rousing shoutout of thanks had been directed at Bernice, she pushed herself to her feet, held up both her hands, and demanded quiet. "Okay, guys," she said, "we've gotta get serious here. I hate to tell you, but there's a reason I've been so bossy and unreasonable with all you outsiders these last few days. I'm gonna lay it on you fast and hard.

"First off, I want to thank all our new relatives for following my difficult travel instructions and getting here on time. As you can probably see now, if you were to understand what the ghost lights were, you would have to see them for yourselves. I didn't expect a scientific explanation, but while I am pleased to have it, it has come just a little too late, and the mischief is already done." She looked around the large table, surrounded by kin.

All extraneous sound ceased. Smiles disappeared. Bernice's pleasant face took on an expression of deep concern as she continued, "Off and on over the years, there's been a lot of hubbub in the surrounding towns about ghost lights up here in the mountains. We try to cool the topic by making fun of it. But about a year ago, a writer came sniffing around, looking once again for Appalachian legends to write about. His primary topic was, what else, ghost lights. He went around the community asking if any lights had been seen in this area."

A groan went up. "Don't tell me!" Vince spat out.

"Unfortunately," Bernice countered, "we've been outed." She looked at Rolf and then at Jeff. "In case you're wondering, it wasn't anyone known to us who blabbed about the ghost lights and their tenuous connection to someone who, by local legend, crashed into a mountain back in the beginning days of flight. It was someone new to this area—a middle-aged lady, if you wish to call her that—who buys worn-out furniture, embellishes pieces with primitive artwork, and sells them as antiques in an old store she acquired in one of the neighboring towns.

"She also collects local ghost stories. We have discovered that no story—semifactual, fiction, or outright made-up—escapes her notice. And now she and the ghost light hunter, having gleaned all the garbage they could from people around the valleys, have published a book about our local ghosts. The two of them are thick as thieves. They have their own website, offering the new book at the grand price of ten dollars per copy to anybody who wants it.

"Concurrent with that, we have just received notice from well-placed relatives that the Searchers have zeroed in on this area, and this time, there is no escape."

A loud groan arose, along with a few words Jeff knew his mother would certainly not have allowed at the table!

"Is the gathering quilt still out?" Cletus asked.

"Still hanging at Breezewood," Bernice answered, "drawing in a goodly number of kin who are willing to join us. A notice about the New Home Place has opened on our secure family website, and we're passing the word there too.

"We have heard reports from several people that Searchers are assembling in Front Royal already, and they'll be working their way this direction as soon as they have sufficient manpower. In a day or two, they'll be all over this territory. We'll have to seal this place up during that time and hope no one tumbles to the fact that some of our rocks are hollow."

"Seal the firewall and lock the cabin door!" Cletus asked, eyebrows raised. "Our usual drill?"

Bernice sighed. "Because we haven't done this for a while, I'll repeat the checklist—if any of you haven't already committed it to memory. Turn off everything electrical as soon as you've tucked away all the important files and put the computers to bed. Remember to put lots of insulation behind the walls so the weaker areas don't sound hollow in case anyone thinks to check. Push the rock door closed as tightly as you can, seal up the visible cracks, and eliminate all floor scratches that might lead excited explorers to wonder what's hidden behind the walls. Make sure all footprints are wiped out and use the leaf blower to distribute loose dirt across the cabin floor." She turned to Ewen. "How soon can you be finished with the Memorial Cave?"

Ewen pulled his phone from his pocket. Facing Bernice, he put up a finger, indicating a brief wait. "Is it ready?" he asked into his phone. He nodded. "Bring it," he said. "It's an overnight trip but not that bad." A pause. "Hold on." He looked at Vince and then at Cletus. "They say we can do this by late afternoon if there's any place to land a helicopter."

Jeff saw eyebrows go up all around the room. It didn't take long for someone to speak.

"We've got a heliport nearby," the man named Demetrius said. "We keep it clear for our own chopper."

"Terrific! Enough room there for an R-44?"

"Absolutely!"

"That's good," Ewen said, nodding. "Get me the GPS numbers, will you, so I can brief my guys?" And into the phone, he said, "Will the largest drone fit into the R-44? Great! Notify us when you're on your way. We'll see you when you get here." He turned toward the assembled kin and said, "They are doing a few more quick modifications for us, and three of my best men will be underway within the hour. We should be ready to go on-site by early evening."

"There's no light in the cave," Cletus reminded him.

"We're self-contained," Ewen said with a smile. "Just wait till you see what they've cooked up."

Grins returned to faces all around.

It was finally time to let tension go, to get better acquainted, and to catch up on many years of family history. Jeff had not felt so comfortable in a very long time, and when he glanced at the man who was his grandfather in this century, he could see years melting away from that wonderful face. As for himself, he sensed this must be something akin to what a family reunion would have been like with the brothers he had lost so early in their own years. Through a mist of tears, he chuckled silently at the realization that the all-too-familiar faces he saw here came in so many different colors—from black to brown to golden to white—a marvelous justification for every sacrifice his family had made during those long years of strife. Freedom. Equality. Personal responsibility. The last of these three aspirations, his father had always said, was the most important gift they had been granted by the people who had founded their country, and they should mind it most particularly or lose all else.

He suddenly felt a strong sense of Sara's presence and another loving presence as well, one even more encompassing. He wasn't sure who it might be. Rosette? How wonderful that would be—to have his beloved older sister present, even silently, at this reunion. His father, Isaac? He thought he would know if his father's presence was nearby, and this didn't seem quite the same. Once he returned to Guy's horse farm, he would ask his dear wife who she thought might have joined the reunion. She was so often right. One thing he knew for certain: he could hardly wait to introduce Lorie to his living, breathing twenty-first-century family.

CHAPTER 15

Sunday evening, April 17, 2016

Jeff was on the front row as the R-44 helicopter arrived at the Thomas mountaintop heliport around seven that evening, an hour before nightfall. Three young men wearing dark jumpsuits worked and wormed their way out of the craft. They were all carrying huge bundles. Jeff recognized all of them. As they passed by, they all gave him the thumbs-up symbol he had come to recognize as "all is good."

"Thanks for making the trip so quickly," Ewen said to them. "I didn't realize you'd been putting so much of your time on drones. I'm delighted that you took the initiative, guys! I'm really proud of you."

Jeff chuckled. He knew how deeply Ewen cared for these young men. Ivan, the oldest of the three, the baldest, the tallest—thereby the head man—answered for them all with feeling in his voice. "When you, your family, and our joint friends are being threatened by *those people*," he said, spitting out the last two words, "we are willing to put in whatever time it takes to set countermeasures into place. In this case, we are arranging for your enemies to be hoist on their own petards."

As if on cue, Bill said, "We have brought two drones." He was the red-haired genius who wore dark-rimmed glasses most of the time, and Jeff knew he was trying to grow a neat beard. But Bill was genetically built to focus specifically on problems at hand, and while growing the beard was not a problem, *neat* took a little more thought. *Conventional* was not a word that could be used with Bill. Jeff grinned. *Conventional* was not what was required in any part of this enterprise.

"It's hand-operated," Bill went on, handing the control stick to Ewen for inspection, "although the robot could go remote if you program it right. All the GPS measurements you gave us are programmed in right now. This one lights up the entire area, if you like, or just specific objects and captures images from micro to macro. Also, it takes 360-degree pictures on demand."

"This larger drone," Jared put in, nodding at the craft he was now reassembling on a smooth flat spot he had claimed on the former landing field, "is a retrieval tool. If we find the object you're looking for in the wreckage, this baby is capable of dislodging practically anything to access its target. It then picks up the item and brings it directly to us. That's depending on the size, of course, or if the object is pinned down by something too heavy for its load limit, we've got other theories." He cleared his throat, as if not really wanting to discuss the other theories. "We haven't tested it on everything, but we have picked up a briefcase holding two moderately heavy dictionaries. It worked. Once we scope out the area you're talking about, we'll know how to better configure its capabilities. We may need to do some probing or pushing."

"How do you feel," Ewen asked a bit reluctantly, "about mountain climbing? In case something goes wrong."

"Do it all the time on my days off," Jared said dismissively, and Jeff now understood why that attractive young man was so physically fit and often sunburned. "But I've studied the pictures you sent. I think we can get our drones past that field of vines. Large openings there toward the far end. You can't see them against the cave's darkness. We enhanced your preliminary photos to discover the most likely entry points. We don't want propellers to get tangled up with vines. This is a great chance to field-test the equipment, boss. Let's get going!"

Obviously relieved, Ewen turned to Vince, who was standing by almost dumbstruck. Jeff suppressed a chuckle. "How quickly can we transfer this gear to the ledge?" Ewen said. "I don't want to add to the ghost light phenomenon by turning lights on in the cave once it gets dark. A glow of that nature could be seen for miles. Even now, that kind of light in the cave might be chancy. If we time it right, people might just mistake it for reflected light from a setting sun."

Vince looked up at the sky. "I hear you. It will take about fifteen minutes to walk to the ledge from here." He summoned his kin. "Everybody grab some of this gear and let's get this show on the road." The parade began in good humor and at top speed, and in even less time than Vince had estimated, all the equipment had been transferred to a staging area above the cave—safely back from the hazardous rim and its many skull and crossbones warning signs. Interesting things were about to happen.

Jeff grinned at Rolf, who had been watching the procedures with a half-smile of anticipation on his face.

From a safe location away from the top rim, now hunkered down in a forest glen beside Ivan, they both viewed the preparation process with quiet fascination. The wizards of Ewen's companies had outdone themselves. Final assembly was made on their complex machines, controls were tested and retested. Powerful batteries, necessary for silent power, were inserted in appropriate places and activated. Keypads were brought out. The smallest drone, Bill at the controls, was being prepped by letting it rise silently far above the trees that made up the peaceful woodland. A moment later, it turned in lazy circles just above the watchers and then slipped casually through smooth air toward the abyss below the cliff. When its capabilities were verified by its ability to meet and conquer winds coming up from the valley, Bill moved it farther out across the vastness of that magnificent space. Its abilities were thoroughly probed: the drone swooped and turned just as it was meant to do. Jeff was enthralled—and not at all surprised. Nothing the genius trio had invented to date had misbehaved.

The drone approached the rim of the cliff, made a quick turn, and dropped from sight. Jeff's attention now focused on the large monitor perched atop a nearby tree stump. It came to life on command, and the fascinating pictures he was now watching proved conclusively that Jared's small craft had made a successful transit to the interior of the cave. Rolf, close beside him, let his breath out in a long whisper. "Terrific!"

The view from the craft was remarkable. When the camera was pointed outward, the whole spectacular valley could be seen on the screen as if from the eye of an eagle—as viewed through a gentle curtain of swaying greenery. Mountains angled across the continent from northeast to southwest in varied hues of blue and gray, one range following after another as far as the eye could see. As the sun moved lower in that vast blue sky, sparkles of gold played across a bank of clouds building at the western edge of the world. The eye of the spycraft turned slowly, and closer views showing the open mouth of the cave moved across the television monitor, succeeded at last by a panorama of tumbled rocks crowding against wall and floor. Illumination at this point came only from the brilliant light of a lowering sun, filtered through interlaced curtains of foliage.

As the craft made its slow turn into darkness, Bill switched on the lights. The first quick sweep of the cave's interior was with the wide beam for a general examination. Then while holding the craft in place over a section of torn metal, Bill focused the camera lens much more discreetly around the cramped inside space. Broken struts and loose canvas lying close beside the drone could be easily identified. "That's the wing," Jeff heard Bill say softly. The camera turned even more slowly now until the side of the aircraft became visible. The lens began to rise across the side, and a portion of the shattered glass windshield suddenly appeared, then a sprung half door. Bill moved the lens upward very slowly.

The top of an ancient leather pilot's cap rested against the edge of the open cockpit as if its owner had reclined his head for a short nap. The shoulder of a leather jacket could be seen trapped just below. The camera's eye turned again, following the shadowy contour of the pilot's remains. Slowly it entered the cockpit area. At that point, the drone moved slightly, its eye focusing on a downward track.

There it was—exactly what the Searchers had long been told was there to find. Behind him, Jeff heard a rush of breath emanating from his good friend and former Searcher, Jebediah Wallace, who must have been holding it for some time. On the floor of the plane, atop parts of a broken landing gear and a crushed rubber tire, was a large leather case, grounded by two aviator boots and several bones.

He heard a soft exclamation from Rolf and realized the wrench to his own gut shouldn't have surprised him, as he had never been able to view human remains without emotion. But more to the point, these bones were a tangible reminder of his sister's first child, someone she had reared and loved and, even knowing the risks, had encouraged to enter into the service of his country. She had done it probably with strong misgivings but with a patriot's sense of duty.

"This is not the time for emotion," he reminded himself, but it was with some difficulty that he put those sudden dark sad thoughts aside. They would be dealt with later.

"It's not a briefcase at all," he heard Rolf say softly and realized now that his grandfather had moved up close beside him to whisper into his ear. "It's more like a portfolio. The kind architectural drawings are carried in."

Ivan spoke once again to his fellow wizards. "The case seems to be in the clear for the most part, except for the pilot's legs and feet. Let's get the other drone in to move those boots from the area temporarily. If that's all, we've got a quick job. We can grab and go."

Now it was the mountain climber's turn. Jared was not only a genius at making drones, but he was brilliant at flying them. His larger craft had already taken measurements of the cave opening and knew which section of the vine wall was the easiest to breach. It slipped beneath the vines with no apparent problem and moved directly across the cave toward the wreckage.

Bill raised the smaller craft to give wide illumination to their salvage operation.

Jeff was fascinated by what was happening on the screen in front of them. Ewen had asked before they left for an agreement that all the proper protocols would be followed if a body was involved even if this operation were being done by stealth. In addition, it was vital to keep the site as undisturbed as possible so their Compact counterparts, if they ever got to this point, would never suspect that someone else had been there first.

Jared had apparently moved the large craft carefully into position above the cockpit of the ancient airplane. Jeff watched as a grappling tool was lowered into the plane, and after several quick photographs were made, the same tool reached into the cockpit with slender metal fingers to move the bones to a safe place. The shoes were quickly placed beside the bones. The portfolio was now fully revealed. Very slowly now, Jared worked the fingers of his tool around a woven rope handle attached to the top of the leather case. He gave a tentative pull.

Jeff heard a sharp expletive. "Damn!"

The clamp had pulled right through the handle.

"Rotten!" Bill said softly to his coworker. "Let's try another technique." Jared selected a different tool, something that looked to Jeff like a pair of large spatulas joined together by a flexible hinge.

Jared shoved the bottom half of the tool under one side of the case and then used his controls to lock the face of the other spatula tightly against the top. He gave a pull. The case moved, slowly and then faster. Working very precisely now, Jared raised it inch by inch from its long rest under the feet of Jon Randolph II.

A great sense of accomplishment grew within Jeff's soul. These remains were all that was left of his sister's son, an extraordinarily brave man who had found what he felt might be vital evidence to help his family—and his country— escape the corrosive power of The Compact. And his half sister, Rosette's kin, in honoring their good friend, had for most of a century guarded and preserved that for which Jon Junior had given his last full measure until a method could be devised to retrieve it without disturbing his remains. Now working as one after so many years of separation, both parts of his family were helping to complete his mission.

The large leather case was carefully lifted from the cockpit and carried out of the cave.

A few moments later, Jeff heard behind him the muffled whirring of powerful little blades. When he turned, he saw Ewen releasing the portfolio from the arm of the drone. White hair churning in the cyclone caused by the powerful rotor, Ewen was grinning with triumph at the amazing accomplishment of his three most trusted researchers.

It was not over yet. Once he knew the portfolio had been secured and placed into a large new cardboard carrying case, Jared returned the retrieval drone to the interior of the cave. Jeff turned back to the monitor and saw how carefully the young man was working his drone once again within the cave, returning Junior's shoes and his leg and a multitude of foot bones one at a time to their original position inside the wreckage, double-checking their placement with the photographs that had been taken. When he was done, the lights in the cave blinked out. The drone turned. Their view disappeared.

Jeff rose to his feet and held out his hand to help Rolf rise as well. Through the silent rows of trees, a magnificent sunset was spreading its glorious color across all the surrounding mountains.

"Job well done, Jon Randolph Jr.," Jeff said softly. "We will take it from here, sir."

"Amen," Rolf echoed quietly.

There was in the forest above the cave an extraordinary moment of stillness, something more than the great peace of nature. Many people stood silent as sunrays blazed once more, and the glow sank slowly below the horizon, leaving behind for a moment a distinctive green flash. No words were spoken. None needed.

"I think," Jeff heard Rolf say quietly behind him many long minutes later, "that he knows his mission has been accomplished. Am I wrong?"

"You are not wrong, Grandfather," Jeff said softly. "It now appears our family's many sacrifices will not have been in vain."

Rolf went on, still in a quiet voice, "Freedom. Equality. Personal responsibility. My father told me that these four golden words and the Golden Rule itself, which manifests itself in every major philosophy in the world, are all the guidance needed for those of us who care about the future of the human race."

"Both my fathers told me the same thing," Jeff said, chuckling softly. "I suppose it's not too unbelievable that ideas follow family pathways as relentlessly as do genetic codes. We have been given hard tasks by all our fathers before us, have we not?"

Rolf laughed. "And mothers. Never forget the mothers. They are the solid foundations beneath our feet. Our fathers' ideals make for an interesting and productive life—if we can remain alive long enough to follow through! But the mothers are far more practical, especially in the 'keeping us alive' part!" His quick smile fading, Rolf sighed. "Let us rejoin the rest of the family and see what plans are being proposed now. I see Ewen is having a very serious powwow with Bernice."

"Can we adopt him, Grandfather?" Jeff grinned at Rolf.

"Who? Ewen?" Rolf laughed heartily. "Why not? Since I've met him, I've never had so much fun. He's the wizard, the Merlin, to our little coterie of knights. Our so-called Justice Seekers."

They were both chuckling companionably when they reached the Thomas Family Guard Station No. 1.

When they walked through the back wall of the station into the natural cavern itself, they saw the case lying on one of the large tables. It had not yet been opened.

"Who will do the honors?" Bernice asked. She was the Thomas guarding the treasure.

"Jeff Maratti," Ewen said decisively. "He deserves this moment."

No one questioned Ewen's statement.

CHAPTER 16

J eff looked around. Close beside him were Jeb, Randy, Ewen, Rolf—his most trusted compatriots. There was the genius trio of Bill, Ivan, and Jared. He saw Emily's beautiful dark-skinned sister, Bernice, so many of whose genes matched his own. Then there was his extended family, including Vince, whose dark features were also so tellingly like his. Behind them were ten or more men, all of whose faces—black, white, or anywhere in between—were as familiar to him as if he had never left home. This, he knew, was only a handful of the male contingent of the extended Thomas family, all of whom had been involved in secrecy from the time they were in the cradle—as had their parents before them. It was apparent that Isaac Preston had left his direct kin a difficult legacy.

"I don't have to tell you folks how important this moment is," Jeff said to these special people. "We have no idea what's in here, where it was obtained, or what Jon Junior was going to do with it. But if he was willing to put his life on the line to obtain it, it must be vital to our family. It kept many unwilling Searchers, including Jeb here," he waved his hand toward his friend, "on the trail for almost a century, trying to get it back."

He grinned. "Open it," Jeb growled in response.

As curious as the rest, Jeff chuckled and turned back to his duties. "Okay! Let's see what we have here." He opened the flap and looked inside.

"Anything?" someone said impatiently.

Jeff looked up. "I'm going to have to be really careful here. It's parchment paper, as I suspected. I don't know how well it's weathered through all this time. Rolf, will you help me, please?"

The older man was by his side in an instant, saying, "Hold a moment." He pulled two sets of thin rubber gloves from his pocket and handed one set to Jeff. Once their hands were covered, Rolf helped Jeff to work out from folds of aged leather a stack of drawings rendered on what indeed seemed to be very large sheets of parchment paper.

With gloved hands, he and Rolf worked at separating one parchment sheet from another. The drawings were then carefully spread out as flat as parchment could be after having been rolled and encased for over a hundred years! With the assistance of their mystified kin, they worked at arranging the sheets in like pairs across the quickly cleared tops of three now spotless tables. Unopened condiment bottles—quickly supplied by one of Bernice's younger sons—were used to anchor the pages flat to the tabletops. There were twelve pages, all covered with inked line drawings and carefully labeled.

"These seem to be house plans," Jeff said softly.

"What house is it?" someone asked. Silence. Jeff turned first to Ewen for guidance and then looked around at the other faces surrounding him. "Can anyone find an identifying mark? Anything?"

The only house plans Jeff had ever seen were the ones Moses had sketched out for the construction of Oak Hill Plantation. They had appeared quite similar to these but not close enough.

Ewen leaned across the table, examining them with a critical eye. Agitated, he let his gaze move upward to meet Jeff's.

"This is Randolph House," he growled under his breath. "Why the hell would The Compact have the plans of Randolph House?"

Indeed, now that Jeff looked more carefully, the renderings did seem familiar to those Moses had drawn up for him when he first proposed his building plans for a station on the Underground. A massive effort had then been undertaken and the plans brought to life.

Those plans, however, had clearly been identified as "Oak Hill Plantation. Oak Hill, Georgia" at the bottom of each page.

Not so here. Jeff noted a raw area at the bottom of one of the pages where it seemed that printed words had been carefully removed, perhaps with a sharp blade. "It's similar," he told Ewen, now pointing, "but not identical. Somebody has gone to great pains to eliminate the address. But I suspect this house is located somewhere in Maryland. That looks to me like an *M*. Don't you think so? Next to it is an *A*." He pointed again. "And there's another, on this page too." A short pause. "Or is it a *V*?"

Except for heavy breathing, the silence held.

"No pillars," Jeff said, then, after scrolling carefully through the pages. "It's not quite Randolph House. It's a Georgian façade, I think, created of brick." Again, he scrutinized the first massive page, the second, the third.

"Why would Junior have risked everything to take away these drawings?" Vince asked softly. "Where did he find them and why was he so was willing to risk his life to steal them?"

"The interior is quite similar to the Randolph House plans, hidden rooms and all," Jeff mused. "For those who don't know, Randolph House is the residence Mr. Jon Randolph III occupied before his recent death in Randolph City, Georgia. The original was built before the Civil War by an early relative who died in that war." He looked up into the concerned faces surrounding him. "What I think is that this house is the prototype for that one. For one thing, it's much older."

"But these blueprints were not the same ones used to construct Randolph House!" Jeff continued after a pause, "Your questions are quite to the point, Vince. Why, indeed, would Junior have taken the drawings? Let's take this problem one step at a time. First, architects are not shy about their work! Look for an architect's name inscribed on any of the pages. If there's no name, then someone removed it purposefully. We need a magnifying glass to see if we can find a lifted signature."

Bernice came forward, holding a small magnifier she had just found in her purse.

"Thanks." He examined the writing, suddenly spotting something he had not expected. A frisson of excitement came across him. He looked up at his friends, grinning. "It's a gazelle." He turned to another page and then another. "Every page has the same signature."

Randy's mouth dropped open. "Just like the symbol—Moses's mark!" he said excitedly. He didn't need Jeff's warning glance to silence him from explaining further. When Moses's priceless ancestor vase had been shattered by an assassin's bullet, Randy and Lorie had found a magnificent diamond cluster embedded within its remains, a seemingly secure hiding place exposed by the same bullet that had nearly killed Jeff. That vase and the precious contents it had contained were now permanently embedded in concrete beneath the monument to the late Major Jefferson Richard Preston.

"Moses?" Rolf said, staring at Jeff, eyebrows arched. "He was the architect who drew up these plans?"

Jeff asked softly. "Is it possible that these were the house plans that brought Moses to America in the first place? It must have been someone in The Compact who commissioned his work."

"They wouldn't still be so interested in locating this set of plans unless the house still exists and is in use," Ewen put in. "If we can find it, I bet we can breach the walls of the fortress itself! Maybe we'll find The Compact there!"

Suddenly understanding, Jeff said softly, "I know why Jon Randolph Jr. took this blueprint! He had to take it because another house, with which he was very familiar, was created with virtually the same plans! If The Compact is privy to all the secrets built into this house, the secrets of the first house lay wide open!"

Even the usually unflappable Rolf was becoming excited. "It's Randolph House you're talking about, isn't it? This is its prototype, isn't it? Is there a date on these plans?"

"You are going to have to brief us on this Randolph House you keep talking about," Vince put in. "But I have another question first. If The Compact document you told us about was supposed to be kept at this house, might it still be there? Wherever *there* is," he added briskly.

"Very likely." Ewen was getting more excited as he examined the documents. "Here are some dates inked on the first page, probably inscribed after the house was finished. '1820–1824.' That does it! This house was constructed a long time before Randolph House was even thought of." He looked up and grinned. "Not your usual house, that's for sure. Take a look. Lots of hidden passageways. Very much like Randolph House. Enough to be fearful of it, if for nothing else, the secrets it exposes!"

"Is there an address?" Randy asked. "Or a location." His cell phone was in his hand, ready to connect to the internet.

"All I can see is river," Jeff said.

Randy asked dryly, "Can we narrow that down a little?"

Jeff looked through the sheaf of papers. "No number. No town. Could be anything. Anywhere."

"Here's something on the page, nearby the house, I think," Ewen said. "An anonymous squiggle. I really can't tell. It looks like canal. Or channel?"

"Look in the Washington, DC area or Maryland," one of Emily's cousins added quickly, and Ewen concurred.

"So many houses along the canal road," he said after searching the computer database for a familiar Compact name and coming up empty. "If that's where it is, we'll probably have to search the whole area house by house to find it."

Bernice, who had been quiet up to that time, finally offered a suggestion. "We have *friends* in the real estate business. Let's do a little workup of the more noteworthy elements of this blueprint and get some eyes out on the road."

Ewen said, "My guys can scan the prints and merge them, so we'll have a sense of what we're looking for—in three dimensions."

The sun had disappeared. The symphony of the forest now rose and fell with the presence of night creatures and roosting birds. Most of the people in attendance had been on the road for some time—none had yet eaten dinner—as some were quietly reminding Bernice.

Chuckling, she produced baskets of food and the plates and utensils to serve it. Tables and chairs were once again set, and delicious soul-satisfying chili—hot from a portable stove—was quickly served out, along with home-made corn bread and a salad of greens.

"How do you do this so well every day?" Jeff asked her.

Bernice answered, "Been at it for a very long time, my friend. We excel at service, or so the Southern landed gentry believed! Then the Gilded Age imploded, and many things changed!"

It wasn't until after all the sweets and accompanying libations were satisfyingly consumed that Ewen had his "aha" moment. Jeff had heard of those moments but was unprepared for this one because it was decidedly not welcome!

He had already noticed Ewen sinking into uncharacteristic silences as the meal progressed—frowning a bit now and then, shaking his head, once even getting up and pacing about the gently lit courtyard. For a while, the tall man stood almost invisible in a darkened corner, away from the surround of pleasant conversation and occasional raucous laughter, only his wind-blown white hair a giveaway as to his presence. He walked back into the protected cave area where the large parchments were still laid out on the tables under subdued lights. He seemed to be examining them intensely, frowning as he did so.

Perhaps, Jeff thought, his friend was puzzling how to combine the large prints into one coherent computerized structure.

But it was something quite different. Jeff was standing beside Rolf, both getting better acquainted with Vince and Bernice when Ewen finally came to them, touched Jeff's arm, and pulled him out into the night. He seemed very disturbed, on the edge of speaking but not quite ready.

"You've been thinking," Jeff prodded.

Ewen ran a hand again through his hair. Jeff could still see in the dim light coming from the office building how troubled he appeared. "I think I've been there," he finally said.

"Where?"

"I've been in that house."

Jeff wasn't sure how to respond. "Well?" he finally said softly.

"I can't believe it, but I've been there. More than once."

"Do you remember the occasions?"

"Yes, I do." Ewen obviously was finding this very difficult. His voice was so soft now that Jeff could hardly hear him. And then, louder, almost as if he were confessing something unpleasant, he said, "Most recently, it was the occasion of a celebration." Again, a pause. A long pause. Then very softly again, he said. "One of my state's senators has recently decided to run for president. I was invited to a fund-raising party at his campaign manager's house."

"A senator?"

"It wasn't his house. The house belongs to his campaign manager, one of my business friends. I would never have thought...!"

Jeff could almost visualize the conflict roiling through Ewen's skill. "Shall we talk with Bernice and Vince?" he said softly.

After a very long moment, Ewen said in a slow, deep monotone as if he hadn't heard Jeff's words at all, "That's what they do, isn't it? They grab unsuspecting people and try to trap them into doing things they wouldn't otherwise think of doing. Then when they've shaded the edges of activities that don't have to be compromised under normal circumstances, you're in too deep to turn around..."

"Don't make any quick presumptions one way or the other," Jeff cautioned. "Let's lay it on Bernice's plate and see what she comes up with first before we make accusations we can't back down from—and before we have to go into the metaphysics of what's happening."

Ewen's shoulders slumped. He looked miserable. "Now
that I think about it, that house always seemed a little familiar to me. It does resemble Randolph House in many ways.
I've been in the clandestine service for a long time. Why did
I not put two and two together? Because it didn't suit me?"

"No reason to, Ewen. Many houses have similar floor
plans."

"Not that close." He seemed very depressed. When his
head came up again, there was anger written across his strong
features. "We've got to get rid of this Compact abomination!
It's ruining the lives of people who might otherwise be fine
and decent folks. It's friends of mine…being forced into taking action they would never take otherwise. Major…?" Tears
were forming at the corners of his eyes. Jeff had never seen
Ewen like this. Never expected to. It was wrenching…

"Now all I can think," Ewen's voice was near to breaking, "is…who can we trust?"

"That has always been the question, hasn't it?" Jeff
hoped Ewen would explain. Soon.

The sound of singing wafted from the inner courtyard
of the cave. Soft strands of guitar music mingled with the
pungent forest air. Melodies—soft, rhythmic, and plain-
tive—began to fill the darkness of evening. "Let's go back
in," Jeff finally said. "You've done yeoman duty for our cause.
You're tired. Let's relax for a time, my friend. Listen to the
sounds of the soul."

He took Ewen's arm and directed him, too, back into
the warmth of a family's heart. A spiritual was being sung,
deep voices rising in intricate harmony. The soft beat of a
drum merged into the melody, and the African roots of this
very American family began to surface. They were old songs.
Jeff had heard variations in other places other times. The
melodies were still as beautiful, he thought, but with harmo-

nies more complex and varied than what he had heard during his childhood.

At a pause, Jeff stepped out into the night and called Lorie. "We won't be home until tomorrow afternoon at best," he said to her as her voice came clearly to him from so far a distance. "It's too hazardous to drive these roads in the dark, but Bernice says there are sleeping bags and mattresses enough for all of us here."

"I miss you, sweetheart," he heard her say, "but you stay safe, hear? I'm eager to talk with you. I have so much to tell you of your father."

"And I have much to tell you of my sister's grandson," he said to her softly. "We found what he wanted us to have, Lorie, and now he is at rest. I could feel it deep inside. A great calm has settled across me."

Lorie was very quiet for a time.

"Love, what are you thinking?"

"That you are surrounded on all sides by your family right now…"

"So it seems," he said softly. "But all I want to do now is to hold you in my arms and not think about anything else." He had to admit, though, that he was still a little reluctant to read any of the words his father had put to paper. He was still puzzled and angered by the thought that Isaac Preston might have lured Saree, a tiny and defenseless child, into the very real danger she had faced. Dropping her down a well? How could any spirit, even benign, have done that?

And why would Isaac Preston sign his name to something as demonstrably evil as The Compact, unless he had been warped by those same people? Judging by what he had gathered from the early journals, his father had experienced firsthand the grief and injury brought by real world piracy. Had Isaac, as he matured, finally begun to accept as minimal the emotional damage foisted upon victims of theft, rape, and murder? How could any living soul ignore that kind of injury?

"I miss those arms, my darling," he heard her saying softly. "You be careful, hear?"

He was pensive when he hung up. She was the most remarkable person he had ever met. Her observations were generally so on-target that he had never had cause to complain or even disagree when he thought about them. He would ask her about his thoughts on Isaac when he returned to Virginia.

But as he turned back to the ongoing party, he realized he had something way more pressing on his hands right now.

Ewen Taylor was approaching him distractedly, hair flying about his face as if the man had been rubbing his hands through it, creating sparks. "I would never have thought Calhoun Talbot was Compact material. He's a responsible member of society. A top-notch Washington lawyer. Sometimes a lobbyist for various causes, generally big business now that I think of it. But nothing I had reason to question or complain about. He's already helped to reelect a very influential congressman, someone who is a little too conservative for my liking but who sometimes surprises everyone by doing the right thing. Right now, Cal is acting as campaign manager for Virginia Congressman Frank Selby, an up-and-coming politician who's about to throw his hat into ring and run for president. They wanted my help. And my cash.

"Jeff, it's clear I can't trust any of those men anymore." The expression on his face was more than grim. He looked drawn, a little ill.

"Don't come to any conclusions yet," Jeff said, trying to smooth the waters. "Let's do a little digging first and see what we come up with. By my reckoning, our spies are a good deal better than their spies." He smiled warmly at his friend, whose shoulders were still tight with anger.

As he watched, Ewen look around abruptly, as if suddenly remembering where he was. The entrepreneur stared for a long moment at the businesslike banks of computers against the far wall, the small flashing lights. His attention turned to the relaxed group of men chatting at the far back of the cave, occasionally bursting into harmonic variations on familiar themes and then stopping, laughing, and starting over. Ewen shook himself, stared full into Jeff's face. He took a deep breath. His shoulders finally relaxed but only, Jeff thought, because he was willing them to. A moment later, he said evenly to Jeff, "Well, for better or worse, we've got some names. It's time to devise new plans, isn't it? In the meantime, if we can't yet blow up The Compact, let's blow up some air mattresses."

CHAPTER 17

Monday, April 18, 2016

Lorie woke early, still a little uneasy at being in a new place, remembering why she didn't like sleeping alone anymore. Life felt no longer safe. For her, it had been a fitful night. Saree had not slept well either, but by morning, a gum problem had worked itself out with the simultaneous eruption of two new teeth. Lorie's little girl was now deep in dreamland. One more step away from babyhood, she mused, but how exciting it was to watch Sara Maria growing into childhood, learning so many things so rapidly. Bright little Saree could have the opportunity of a good life ahead—if The Compact would keep its big intrusive nose out of their family nest.

On that score, Lorie was buoyed by what Jeff had told her the last time he phoned. Speaking in coded language, he indicated they had found something quite valuable. And Ewen's involvement had put them many steps ahead already in their battle against the forces still arrayed against them.

He had also told her that it was too late to start the hazardous trip home—they would all be camping out in sleeping bags. He was looking forward to roughing it just to see if he still could, but he also told her he missed her sweet lips.

She didn't need to hear anything else.

Her job today, she decided, was to get back to her review of Isaac's journals.

The first date recorded inside the cover of her selected book was 1814, early June. It tracked from the previous book, which had ended with an accounting of Isaac's terrible illness. She turned to the first page.

> I have just turned eleven years old, at least I think I have. When I was very small, my mother and father always gave me a special cake on my birthday. It was during the time of the year when the roses had just started blooming. My mother always put a small rose on top of the cake, and my father gave me as many gold pieces as my age to put into my Chinese box. I have 15 gold pieces hidden there, which means I was five years old the last time he gave me a gift. Six more years have passed, and that makes eleven years. I still remember my parents, thanks to what Lak told me about writing down my memories. I can even see them in my mind. I have tried to draw pictures of them, but they don't look quite right. I expect some of my older memories are no longer with me.
>
> I wonder what they would think about me now. I am still the deaf-dumb boy to all the people I dislike. Will and I saw some deaf French people talking to each other with their fingers, and Will

asked their teacher to show us how to do it. Finger talking is not the same as writing words on paper. I think it is more like an idea language, so it does not matter what spoken language a person is using. Finger language is good to know also when we are working high up in the rigging. I am eager to get up there again, but Will won't let me until he is convinced I am completely well and have my balance back.

I have almost conquered the terrible plague that took so many people across the countryside. I do not know why I did not die. I must count myself among the fortunate and give back by way of thanks to many people. Will was by my side day and night to make sure I could breathe. He took the yellow phlegm out of my throat when there was too much of it and blew his breath into my mouth when I was having trouble. Sometimes he put a poultice on my chest and sat beside me while I slept. I was afraid he would become sick too. But he told me the same disease had overtaken him many years ago, and he survived and cannot be infected by it again.

Lak was here a lot of times in many disguises, which is very hard when you think of his size and his color. It makes me laugh to think about it—and I think that is why he did it. He is so smart. He brought soups and herb concoctions he thought would be good for me. His friends had many different ideas about what would help. They all sent gifts of food or medicine. Because of them, I know I soon will be the healthiest person alive. I am grateful to have so many good friends. I hope I can help them someday like they have helped me.

Will has been keeping me on shore while I was sick. I hope he will come home soon because I am all alone right now and I am very lonely.

"As am I," Lorie said softly to herself. "But my little girl is in the next room. Good friends, old and new, are drinking coffee and talking nonstop over at the big house. I could call in the babysitter and go over there to join them, but I won't do it because it will be so gratifying for my Jeff to learn that his father wasn't a big bad pirate at all. Just a scared gutsy little boy all alone in the world except for a fellow captive who loved him as his own son, as did good friends of many colors who were beguiled by the bright young orphan."

She spoke a little louder now. "Isaac, is this what you wanted your son to know, who his father really was?" Perhaps he wanted his surviving children to know who Will was too. Jeff's older brother had obviously been named for Will Deerfield.

There was no doubt Isaac wanted his only remaining son and his daughter Sara to understand their father. He had probably not been able to share these stories personally because of a fear of being overheard by someone of questionable trust. But in addition, what she was reading, written in Isaac's own hand, undoubtedly provided invaluable information about the people who comprised The Compact. Otherwise, why was it so important that Jeff had been summoned to find it?

She thought about it again. Had Isaac played any part in the near tragedy that had befallen their little daughter?

Personally, she still felt Saree's fall to be a simple, perhaps fortuitous accident.

On the other hand, Jeff never would have found that trunk if their daughter hadn't been chasing after a little fox, a small creature who just might be hosting a spark of life once named Isaac!

In all his journals, it was the humanity in the young boy's recalling of the tale that stunned her. His words simply glowed. A child that deeply moral under such adverse circumstances could not have changed much as he grew older. He could not have knowingly put a baby into grave danger.

Could it have been the imminent danger to Saree that had linked Isaac's spirit to that of the little orphaned fox? Perhaps it was simply a case of being at the right place at the right time.

Lorie turned back to her reading and was still immersed in the old book when she felt the thrum of tires turning onto the long driveway. Gathering her still sleepy child into her arms, she hurried to the main house to greet the adventurers. Five exhausted men were straggling from the big car, pulling out bags and boxes and trying to sort them into separate piles.

"Daddy," Saree squealed, a big smile lighting her face. She held out her arms. Jeff looked around and grinned at his daughter and then at Lorie. Striding toward them, he took Saree into a warm hug and covered her forehead and cheeks with kisses. He then brushed Lorie's cheek with his lips and breathed, "So much to tell you."

Rolf, who had just come back from depositing his camping gear onto the back porch of the big house, reached out eagerly for his great-granddaughter while Jeff returned to the SUV to continue the ongoing retrieval of gear and bags, coats, and unfamiliar-looking equipment, which seemed to be forbiddingly scientific. Everyone was laughing, almost giddy with success. As they should be, Lorie thought. She saw Emily hurrying over from their quarters, Todd bouncing in her arms. Jeb strode across the lawn toward his small family, arms wide open. "Em, your kinfolks is somethin' else, and there's no doubt about it! Now I know where Celly gets her spunk."

Emily laughed. "You met my sister, I take it."

"The bossy one? Sure did!" He hugged his wife and his little son tightly and then returned to the car. The unpacking continued, and excited voices filled the air, especially voices requesting an early meal.

Shortly thereafter, Lorie went on babysitting duty in the sunroom, leaving the kitchen chores to Chefs Alexi and Em. She and the children were joined shortly by Randy, whom Lorie was delighted to discover was quite a good chef himself. The excitement was palpable. The air vibrated with it. Lorie could hardly wait for the recap to begin.

CHAPTER 18

I t wasn't until all the worn-out youngsters were put into their respective beds that talk commenced. A circle of friends again assembled about the fireplace in the now darkened sunroom. As everyone seemed to feel she was the *de facto* chairman of their enterprise, they looked to Lorie, who waited only for everyone to be seated before formally opening the meeting. "I've been gleaning some knowledge of your adventures by just listening to you guys talk around me," she began, "but it would be nice if someone who was on-site could give those of us who held the distant fort a blow-by-blow account."

"Ewen is our hero," Randy said, chuckling appreciatively. "He actually got into the most god-awful sling contraption I've ever seen so he could be dropped over the edge of a mile-high cliff…"

"Not quite that high," Ewen demurred.

"Enough that you'd have been smashed into bits if they'd dropped you…"

"Which they didn't. And it was really an ingenious climbing apparatus…"

"Get on with it," Alexi said, beaming with pride. "We all know Ewen's a hero's hero!"

Ewen pressed the compliment aside with some embarrassment. "It was safe as anything I've ever done. But it was really exciting because I could actually see that old bi-wing plane and what was left of its propeller blades. One of those blades was reflecting sunlight up through a hole in the rock. Twice a year it did that!"

"The mysterious ghost lights," Emily said with a squeal of delight. "I've been hearing people talk about them. So the lights were real. Wow! A simple scientific explanation. Who would have believed it?"

"That's what it usually is," Rolf responded softly, as if reconfirming in his own mind the bedrock precepts of science he had always lived and worked by. "But this time, it may be putting people into grave danger. Bernice told us that a couple of naïve charlatans who believe all the Appalachian haunt stories are true—or more likely just want to make a quick buck—have published a definitive book about hauntings and ghost lights in the hill country. Unfortunately, the only ghost lights they are aware of seem to be ours. The relatives figure that over the next few days, they're in for a deluge of ghost hunters trampling the woods over the cave, looking for a way to get into it. And we can't say a blessed thing."

"But they wouldn't find anything, would they?" Guy asked, frowning. "You brought all the pertinent stuff back with you, didn't you?"

Lorie looked again to Ewen, who seemed to be obsessively running his long fingers through progressively spikier hair. He spoke in a solemn tone, turning the tenor of the conversation to one less of triumph than to that of caution. "We talked about this a lot on the way home. The problem is not that people might find something we don't want them to find. It's that if they try to enter the cave, they are likely to get hurt. They don't know what we just discovered—that the floor of that cave, as well as its ceiling, are quite unstable. Who knows why? Maybe it was the collision in 1918 that killed Junior Randolph. More than likely, it's the geology of the area, ancient sedimentary rock layers shifting across one another under pressure, or…" He paused, leaving alternate possibilities unspoken. After a brief shrug, he continued, "In any case, that whole section of the cliff could collapse around an unknowing treasure hunter, either burying him or sending him sliding off the edge." Again, he paused. "But because we don't want anyone to know we were probing around in there, we can't say anything!" Lorie could tell he was genuinely concerned.

"Can't someone put up warning signs?" Alexi said.

Policeman Randy spoke with disgust. "It's already well posted. But tell me, anybody, how many so-called treasure hunters pay attention to signs?" He barked out a hard laugh. "We put some pressure on Bernice, and she said they would keep a couple of the scarier-looking relatives on-site. Bushy beards. Big muscles. White and black faces both. They'll be toting rifles. That might warn people off and save us from logging a couple of unnecessary deaths caused by stupidity!"

"Thank goodness for family," Lorie said, chuckling. Jeff reached for her hand and gripped it rather more firmly than usual. She sensed that even though he was safely back on solid ground, he was still remembering the queasy gut hollowness he always felt when he stood at the edge of high places. "Let's stop talking about dropping off cliffs," she said with a smile. "It's time to show us what you've found."

"We've got the blueprints of a mansion much like Randolph House spread out on the big green table downstairs," Jeff said, squeezing her hand in gratitude. "We knew you'd all want to see the treasure. Hands off as much as possible, please, unless you want to pull those tight gloves over your fingers, latex I think you call them. The old parchment is fragile. We have a couple of magnifying glasses available if you'd like to get up close. Let us know what you think you're seeing in the drawings. And if any of you have any idea where the house might be located, please don't keep it a secret."

Thanks to living with its builder, Lorie knew enough by now about Randolph House's ins and outs to recognize the similarities. Leaning over the drawings, occasionally using one of the magnifying glasses, she scanned the areas she felt were essentially duplicated in the old house Jeff and Moses had constructed without modern equipment in a virgin forest in Georgia—with the willing assistance of many freed blacks and escaped slaves.

Aside from a modest third-floor storage attic—quite different from Randolph House's secret bedrooms and assorted passageways—Lorie felt that the biggest difference between the two houses lay in the quality and importance of an exit tunnel, one that took an abrupt turn to the north at the back corner. There appeared to be only a cursory basement plan. And the tunnel, which seemed to originate under raised back steps, appeared to terminate in a water source described as three parallel wavy lines. It was a feature of only minor note and ended as if the artist had simply lifted his pen, thinking to come back and fill in details later. Possibly it indicated a wastewater drainage ditch to be built or not as circumstances allowed. She glanced at Jeff. He shook his head, eyebrows raised, questions unanswered.

Alexi, who had been examining the blueprints with intense concentration, seemed to grow increasingly silent as many speculations ping-ponged around her. "I've been here." The words were spoken in a very soft voice, but suddenly all conversation in the room went quiet.

Lorie glanced up at the young woman. Alexi's face seemed suddenly drained, gaunt. Without warning, she slumped to the basement floor.

Her husband was the first to respond, crying out. He knelt and pulled her up against his shoulder. "Honey, what's the matter? Alexi, honey, what's wrong?"

"Lay her flat," Lorie instructed him briskly. As he lowered his wife's body, Lorie grabbed Alexi's ankles and pulled her legs upward, bending her knees and depositing her heels into her surprised husband's outstretched hands. "She's had a shock. We need to get blood back to her head." She felt for Alexi's pulse and found it beating strongly. A moment later, the young woman's eyes opened, and she realized she was surrounded by legs. She turned her head, looked up into Guy's face, and burst into deep heaving sobs, which left her unable to speak. Again, he pulled her into his arms, and this time, she clung to him, burying her face against his shoulder.

"What's wrong?" Ewen asked, also crouching next to his son and daughter-in-law.

"I don't know!" Guy said. "Alexi, darling, please tell us."

"Now they know where we live." Her muffled voice reflected deep distress. "Guy, I didn't dream she could be one of them."

"Who, Alexi?" Ewen asked. "Who have you been speaking with?"

"Patsy Talbot."

Lorie's heart sank. Jeff had told her of Ewen's speculation. This was the same name that had troubled Ewen.

"How did you meet this woman?" Ewen said, his voice urgent.

"A girl. She's one of my riding students. She's only thirteen, but she's been asking me so many questions about our lives—where did we come from? Why did we come here?

How did we select our horses? Everything about our backgrounds! I took her home from a lesson last week when her brother didn't show up to give her a ride, and she couldn't get him on her phone. Those plans! Guy, that's her house! Oh, Ewen…she invited me in. Even showed me one of the secret rooms because she thought it was so cool!"

The previously unflappable Alexi once more burst into tears. Her husband handed her a tissue and put his arms around her, soothing, kissing her face, trying to help bring her emotions under control. "I have just destroyed us," Lorie heard her whisper. "How can I even apologize when I have betrayed our family so completely? We will have to go into hiding, too, won't we?" Tearfully she turned to her father-in-law. "Ewen? I'm so sorry!"

Jeff had told Lorie about Ewen's recent reaction to the thought that he might have betrayed the Justice Seekers by trusting the wrong people. A queasy feeling began working its way through the pit of her stomach. Even if this thirteen-year old girl were totally innocent, never intending malice, might she inadvertently have taken information back to the enemy?

Ravenwing had only just arrived, so Patsy Talbot could not yet have seen him. Thank goodness for that!

But the big stallion still might give everything away. How could the girl avoid admiring him in the pastures if she remained one of Alexi's students? Surely Alexi would talk about Ravenwing—call him by name—cementing this family's relationship to Ewen. Lorie's own mind was now churning.

Would her family and Em's have to move again? All they had wanted was to settle into the rituals of ordinary life. Where would they go? Could they ever escape The Compact? Maybe she and Jeff could move in with her parents in Illinois.

Or maybe Em's family in West Virginia, if they could be found, would take them in for a while!

This time, it was Ewen who calmed the gathering. "Folks," he said in a tone of authority, getting everyone's attention, "trust me, our cover remains unbroken." He reached out to his daughter-in-law and took both her hands into his. "Alexi, darlin', The Compact knows nothing about these plans nor does it know we have them. Better yet, these people have no clue about your relationship to me unless they're a lot smarter than we know they are. But because of your compassion for a stranded student, my dear, we have gained an unexpected *entrée* into their rotten little world. We are now in a position to discover more about them than they will ever find out about us. Take it from an old spy master." He looked around. "It's time to pull together all our thoughts. We must lay out exactly what we're facing and then follow up quickly while we still have the advantage. Let's go back upstairs and start making some notes."

About thirty minutes later, everyone was settled comfortably in the sunroom, which was illuminated now only by a crackling fire in the central fireplace. In the shadowy darkness, Lorie, as moderator and chief note taker solely through the illumination of a penlight held by Jeff, encouraged the talk to resume.

Ewen spoke first, once more turning to his daughter-in-law. "I have always felt I was a master at reading devious behavior, Alexi. Hubris on my part, I fear, as your revelation has just opened my eyes to how easy it is to be taken in, even for someone as cagey as I supposed myself to be. Only with me it wasn't by a thirteen-year-old child who probably has no idea who her father really is but by the so-called respected business person himself, Calhoun Talbot. Until this time, I had always judged Cal to be completely trustworthy, and

I'm still having trouble thinking of him as a bad guy." Ewen looked around at the friends surrounding him. "But Alexi's experience has just confirmed what hit me so hard about the revelation that almost consumed me twenty-four hours ago." He reached out to his still shaken daughter-in-law and took a firm grip on her hands. "Alexi, do you remember the address of the house where you took your young student?"

"I've got it in my purse." So saying, she went into the kitchen to find it. When she returned, she said, "It's the anchor mansion in a new housing subdivision in Virginia. It's on a hill looking north across the Potomac River. That whole area was once a large estate. Talbot Estates!" Seemingly still trying to organize her thoughts, she scrabbled through her purse, pulled out a small address book, and opened it. "There it is." She held it up to show the fluid writing to Ewen.

"I've been there myself several times," he said grimly. "You're right, the house is relatively old, but it seemed to me that it had a distinctly *art nouveau* flavor to it—all those beautiful ornate stained-glass windows…Tiffany glassware everywhere. Beautiful. Verging on overkill, if you ask me!" He confirmed the address with a similar entry in his own address book and looked up at everyone. "They call it Talbot House, of course. Apparently, the Talbots came up short on cash a few years ago, so they quietly sold off large chunks of their estate lands to a developer. Georgian-style homes now cluster tastefully around the old house, which gives the sub-division its name and its *cachet*. Why didn't I put two and two together earlier? The Talbot mansion does looks similar to our blueprints.

"But it is *not*—repeat *not*—the house for which those blueprints were drawn. The official records say Talbot House was built in the late eighteen to early nineteen hundreds. I checked it out yesterday after a sudden conviction came over me that I was the one who had betrayed us all." He turned again to his daughter-in-law, this time with a gentle smile on his face. "You saw the date on those old parchments, Allie, the same as I did. There is almost a century's gap between the plans we just recovered and the date when the Talbot's house was constructed. Someone must have tried to construct a reproduction of the original dwelling. But they were unaware of all the secrets because Jon Randolph Jr. took the blueprints away a long time ago, never to be seen again…until now!

"Here's an instance to prove what I'm saying." He pointed. "The tunnel. Talbot's house is sitting on top of a hill. When I was there, I distinctly remember seeing a driveway heading down and around the house into a well-lit underground garage. Tunnel? A garage exiting a basement opening at the top of a hill? No water there except when it rains hard!"

Alexi looked up at him and nodded eagerly.

"There are other differences as well," Ewen went on. "Which means that we have not yet found the house that matches the blueprints."

Alexi's husband again wiped tears from her cheeks, gave her a kiss of support, and drew her into his arms. She huddled close against him, clinging to him. "I understand now why you wanted us to use my last name instead of yours, Ewen," Lorie heard her say softly. "And I'm glad you coached me so well in the answers I should not respond to when people ask questions that shouldn't be asked. Even if the questioner is a cute little thirteen-year-old redheaded girl. I was very careful, even with her."

"Redheaded girl?" Jeb Wallace's head came up abruptly. "Where was that house again?"

Alexi repeated the address.

He let out a huge sigh. "God Almighty! I know that house too well. I did lots of work there back when I was an apprentice Searcher. It looked fancy, but it had plumbin' problems all the time, leakin' roofs, windows that let cold air in—you name it, I fixed it. Or tried to." He turned to Jeff and said suddenly, "Remember, Jeff? I told you I once saw a picture of a pirate chief they called Redbeard, who might of won the Civil War single-handed if he hadn't been killed by Injuns first? And scalped! That's the house I saw it in!"

Emily Thomas cried out softly. "Oh my god—this Mr. Talbot—is he bald?"

Jeb turned to his wife. "Em, honey?"

"He has his head shaved every day to honor one of his ancestors. He told me that because he wanted me to rub it… very tenderly." She shuddered. "God knows why! He talked nice to me at first, but…" She turned her face away from Jeb and buried it in her hands. "He told me he was taking his revenge… I didn't know what he was talking about!"

Jeff's expression was one of shock and revulsion.

Victimization takes a deep toll, Lorie thought. Remembering the hell her friend had been dealt with at the hands of her Compact hostage takers, she went immediately to Emily, knelt, and embraced her. When she looked up, Guy and Alexi were standing aside, mystified. "Long story," Lorie said to them quietly. "Em was held hostage by The Compact for more than a year. Bad things happened."

Alexi sucked in her breath. "Oh my god! I can only…!"

"He's one of the pack I've already decided I'm goin' to smash to pulp one day," Jeb muttered under his breath. "But the DNA we got from him don't match."

"There's more to it than that," Jeff said softly.

"That one—he hurt me bad every time and liked doing it," Emily said before Jeff could explain. "But it wasn't him. I know exactly who it is now." Em closed her eyes and put her hands across them once again. "It was someone who had curly red hair." She said it very softly and then reached out to Jeb.

Lorie remained silent. Not everyone in the room was aware of the circumstances of Todd's conception. It was Em's tale to tell, if she chose.

"It seemed to be a special evening for them. He was tall then but still only a child," Emily continued softly. "So scared. I think he was convinced that they would kill him if he didn't do what they were forcing him to do. It was some kind of initiation. He whispered apologies to me over and over. He was crying when he told me he didn't want to do it...that he didn't feel inclined to have sex with women and I shouldn't take any blame on myself."

"Who was it?" Alexi whispered.

"Talbot's son, Brian."

Alexi's voice rose with disbelief and anger. "Patsy's brother? But he seems to be such a nice young man, so respectful and so... I thought he was gay!"

Emily smiled at her sadly. "All of the above, Alexi. Quite handsome. Sweet. And that beautiful head of hair! I never considered that anything might come of it because close as we got—which was sometimes uncomfortably close—as far as I was concerned, nothing happened between the two of us...although we put on a good show for them, taking our time about it under the silk sheet and moaning like we both really liked it. It was the first time they'd ever heard 'boo' out of me, and for weeks, they let me know how annoyed they were about it. I'm sure they knew I was mocking them...in the only way I could!"

"Oh, Em, how humiliating...for both of you."

"Not that time," Emily said, her mouth set tight. "Not that time! I made damn sure we both had our revenge. All those men watching, trying to embarrass and humiliate the boy because they all knew he was gay. And me, no matter what any of them did to me, well, this time was revenge! I whispered to him, told him to get angry and follow my lead. He caught on early enough to what I was up to, and we both ended up smiling and cooing and kissing, putting on a great show—and of course, I never did see him again."

"Oh my god," Alexi said again. She reached out to Emily and held her hands tightly. Tears were streaming across her cheeks. "How awful for you. How can you bear it?"

"I have good friends," Em said, responding generously to the young woman's concern. "And an absolutely wonderful husband." She smiled up at Jeb, who was respectfully standing to one side, trying not to react, although his face was a study of pent-up anger and agonized concern. Em smiled gently at him and turned to Alexi. "And our beautiful little boy," she said softly.

The younger woman recoiled, almost as if she had been struck.

"I think," Lorie said, feeling as if she had just been pulled through a knothole by her hair, "that we are going to adjourn. A night's sleep would do us all a lot of good."

CHAPTER 19

Tuesday morning, April 19, 2016

Jeff had to admit he felt much more able to cope with the potential dramas of a new day after his warm bath the night before, a satisfying cuddle with his shaken and more than willing wife, and a good night's sleep. Saree had seemed to sense the tension surrounding everyone the previous evening, and this morning, she was exceedingly well behaved, playing contentedly with her toys while the household remained quiet. She snuggled down for a while in her playpen with her blanket and pillow and then munched on some sweetened cereal Jeff gave her to try out her new teeth. He could tell how glad she was to have her daddy home. Once she was released from the playpen, she kept toddling to his knee so she could be held and hugged in short intimate bursts. Then she would crawl off his lap and go walking about the house once again, exploring everything within her range, especially Randy, who was well on the way to becoming her new favorite person.

Jeff let Lorie sleep as he prepared breakfast with Randy's help.

It wasn't long before she joined them, however. Her short hair was still bed-tousled, and she was wearing her old bathrobe, but as always, his heart gave an extra beat when he saw her. "How can a girl get any sleep when people are cracking jokes out in the kitchen?" There was a decided twinkle in her eyes. "What are you two guys laughing about now?"

"It's almost noon, darlin'." He grinned. "We've been getting our morning exercise, unlike you, who only have to chase babies around all day. Right now, it's all about food!"

"You goofballs!" With a giggle, she disappeared into the bathroom, leaving him wondering what *goofball* meant. When she returned, she was refreshed and beautiful, dressed in jeans and a warm plaid shirt and ready for anything. "What's next?" She pulled Saree's high chair to the table, strapped the baby into place, and seated herself. "Besides food."

"We're planning our next move," Jeff told her, reaching for the coffee pot. "Finding the house."

After giving notice with a quick rap at the back door, Jeb Wallace strode into the kitchen carrying huge rolls of maps. "The real deal," he crowed. "Geologic survey maps. Ever'thing's on here. I'm gonna look at canals because I think these guys was smugglers." Brunch behind them, Lorie quickly cleared the table. The assembled plotters spread out the maps and gathered around the table.

"C&O Canal," Randy mumbled softly, pointing. "The letters we found seemed to be abbreviations for something but not C&O. F—or is that a P? O for *ohwhatthehell!* A couple of those, but it doesn't make sense even if you unscrew your eyes backward a couple of turns and turn the paper upside down. Here's the Potomac River. It runs between the two states. We've got to keep the canal in mind. It's on the Maryland side of the Potomac. How old is the house? We need to start somewhere. Are those Ewen's maps? He told us he called one of his contacts."

Jeb nodded all the way through Randy's flow of words, concurring with everything. "All we have to do," he said, "is piece these together—they're made from aerial photos, so they show all the houses that are built alongside. We have to locate any houses that have generally the same footprint as the house on the old plans."

The explorers went to work, bending over the maps with magnifying glasses, checking maps with photographs of the same areas.

"There's got to be a better way," Jeff finally grumbled. "These house footprints are so small you can't even see them."

"How about using the satellite maps that real estate agents use?" Lorie suggested. "You can zoom in on whatever it is you want to see."

"Zoom in?" Jeb said. "What's that?" Randy looked up at her, frowning. Jeff simply waited. He knew it would be good. It always was.

"Haven't you guys ever looked to see what houses were selling?" Lorie said with a mock air of superiority.

"Why would we?" Randy said.

Lorie went silent but for only a moment. "Well, I guess if you never needed…okay." She grinned and shrugged. "But even if you don't need to, it's so much fun to drive the computer camera down the road and see what houses are there on either side."

Jeff stared at her as if she had just lost her mind, making her giggle. "Show us," he said.

She took a seat in front of her laptop computer and was soon displaying an astonishing program, which showed in great detail the area they had been exploring on printed maps. It looked as if the pictures had been taken from an airplane flying low over the property. "Satellites circling the earth," Lorie said rather smugly. "Use these photos in conjunction with computer scans of selected roads taken from ground level." She zoomed the camera lens downward toward the road, as a bird might do, turned the bird's eye toward a house, and focused in on specifics. "Buyers from Colorado can search for a house in Maryland or Virginia without even making the trip. All very up-to-date."

Jeff had to admit it: he was more than amazed.

"I've heard about this," Randy said excitedly. "Can you find the C&O Canal?"

She plugged "C&O" into the search engine and turned the computer over to Randy. "Have fun," she said, laughing, and went off to take care of Saree, who seemed to be a little annoyed because no one was paying attention to her anymore.

After a great deal of joint exploration of the roads from White's Ferry on the Maryland side of the river down to the District of Columbia, Randy looked up at Jeff, a little discouraged. "Unless there is a large house here that's totally hidden behind foliage, I don't think we've found anything that looks like the place in our old blueprints."

"Why," Jeff asked, "don't we look on the other side of the river?"

Fifteen more minutes were consumed in futile searches.

"Give us the dates again when that old house was built?" Jeb asked plaintively.

Randy checked. "The dates on the blueprints, 1820 to 1824, probably the construction dates. I bet we could find out something about this if we read more of those journals Isaac left."

"What would he have known about it?" Jeff asked.

Randy's eyes opened wide. "Are you kidding me? Why else would he have wanted you to have the journals?"

It was like a light turning on.

"Lorie," Jeb called out, and she stepped into the kitchen. "We're settin' up a readin' club here. Can you put a few of those journal/diaries out on this table? And a beer or two?"

"Or three," Randy put in.

Jeff saw his wife's face soften, and the big smile begin. She opened the refrigerator and handed out some bottles. "We've got milk, fruit juice, iced tea, beer, barrels of rum… what's your poison?"

To general laughter she left and came back a moment later carrying a dozen books. Although they didn't all look alike, they were all of a like size. The wraparound covers—in a variety of rich natural browns—were created of fine leather, some embossed with floral patterns, some plain. All seemed quite worn but were surprisingly intact. Many of the books were held shut with narrow bands of stiff leather inserted through loops affixed for that purpose. Several had narrow leather tie bands around them. She handed them to Jeff, who looked up into her now serious face and asked, "Could you and Randy give us a brief rundown on what Isaac has written in the books you've already read?"

"I'm ready to do just that," she replied briskly. "The old-est book." She held up a slight volume with a much-weath-ered cover. She opened the journal, turned to the first page, and read the words Jeff had now read multiple times, always with the same aching sorrow: "Marseille, France. April 2 in the year of one-thousand-eight-hundred and ten. My first name is Isaac. My last name is Preston. I think I am seven years old."

From the corner of his eye, Jeff saw that the door to the backyard was moving inward very slowly. He turned, mys-tified, and then heard the scratch of a paw on the floor and caught a glimpse of red fur, a white ruff. He held his hand downward to scratch Doggy's neck. How had the little fox escaped his kennel? What's more, how had he managed to get through the screen door without anyone noticing?

"Let him stay," Lorie said softly. "He won't cause any mischief." He looked into her eyes, knowing she was trying to tell him something important. Once again, without emotion, she read aloud the first words Isaac had written in the book, finishing with Moses's pronouncement about Isaac after he had saved the boy's life: "Little man, you are the boy they call deaf-dumb... When I first saw you, I knew you were a wily little fox and neither deaf nor dumb..."

Suddenly startled, Jeff stared into his wife's face. It was there, plain as could be, in her wide loving eyes—she somehow believed this little fox was the reincarnation of his father, this strange little creature who, perhaps, had not lured Saree into danger but, seeing what had happened, had plunged into the well shaft after her, distracting her so that she would not move from her perilous perch on an old trunk wedged fifteen feet below the surface of the earth with cold dark water rippling too close below—water that could easily have swallowed his baby if she had tried to rise to unsteady feet.

He realized he was holding his breath. He let it out slowly, his eyes still focused on Lorie, who, attention now concentrated on the book, continued in measured words to read of his father's first encounter with Prince Ukuhlakanipho, the wise man known to him all his life as Moses and to his father as Lak.

Entranced as they were with Lorie's soft voice reading a little boy's description of the man who was to be one of the major life guides of not only Isaac himself but also of his second son, neither Jeb nor Randy were aware of the emotions now engulfing Jeff.

He looked down into the big brown eyes gazing up at him. "Thank you," he said softly.

The little fox approached him, put his long nose and jaw into Jeff's extended hand, and let it rest there for a time. Then he trotted off toward the playpen and settled himself on the floor where he could stand guard over Saree, who was once again napping. Jeff looked up at Lorie and, through the lump in his throat and the tears that were forming in his eyes, gave her a big smile.

She smiled back, understanding the importance of what had just happened.

So often it seemed to Jeff that he and Lorie never needed words to communicate with each other. With no argument on her part, she had cleansed a tragically mistaken notion from the pathways of his mind. She had given his father back to him. He could now focus his full attention on the important journals he had wasted so much time avoiding.

"Since you've done all this background reading," he heard Randy say to Lorie, "can you give us a two-minute update before we begin our assignments?"

Nodding, she pulled out a small notebook and turned a couple of pages. "Here are some dates to remember—1801, the Pasha of Tripoli declares war on the United States."

Randy grumbled, "Tripoli? That's in Libya. How many wars or shadow wars have we fought in that part of the world in the past couple hundred years?"

"That first one," Lorie said with mock sternness, pointing her finger at Randy, "was called the First Barbary War because someone just knew there were to be more Barbary wars!"

With straight faces, both Randy and Jeb turned toward Lorie and folded their hands into their laps. "Yes, Teacher," Randy said. Jeb followed his lead. Jeff grinned.

Teacher-like, Lorie went on with a straight face, nodding briskly to her students. "Our friend and ally, Isaac

Preston, was born in 1803. That was the same year the USS *Philadelphia* was captured by the Pasha's formidable navy off the coast of Tripoli, the crew sold into slavery, and the captain humiliated.

"The United States decided that while it loved its ship, the *Philadelphia* had to be sacrificed so its big guns couldn't be turned against our own navy. So a group of American sailors, led by a young officer named Stephen Decatur, gave it a try. He was a tricky dude. First, he *borrowed*, you might say, a local boat. Now this is not unlike some of the enterprises we have pulled off, although it was on a lot larger scale. With a lot more blood." Lorie grinned as the men nodded their vigorous assent.

"With the assistance of some of Decatur's closest friends," she went on, "who just happened to be tucked away out of sight below decks, they floated their garden variety boat into the harbor, snugged up next to the *Philadelphia* like they were maybe having a little trouble managing their craft, and then, without warning, swarmed onto the ship. They attacked and killed its crew, set fires that burned the *Philadelphia* beyond any hope of repair, and, most remarkable of all, made their escape to great acclaim once they got back to the States. There are lots of towns called Decatur in the US because of this scoundrel." She looked up, grinning. "We've never had anybody name a town after us yet. We haven't killed anybody yet either!"

"Oh, snap!" Randy said. Jeb laughed. As usual, Jeff didn't quite understand the humor. He would ask Lorie once they were alone. It did not keep him from grinning.

"Hostilities with Tripoli ceased in 1805, at least temporarily." Her voice now took on a very solemn tone. This conversation was not meant to be a lighthearted dip into swash-buckling adventure. Jeff heard the creaking of chairs as listeners settled themselves to serious business.

"You've all heard about Isaac Preston by now, haven't you?" Lorie began. "Our baseline lies with Isaac, as he is the author of these tales. He was Jeff and Sara Preston's father and, not too coincidentally, one of Jon Randolph Third's grandfathers. Isaac Preston's parents, Gerard Preston and Elisa, his beautiful wife, lived in Georgia at the time we've been researching. Write that down, people. We've got a lot of names to give you now, but these will be the only names listed at the lower level of the family tree. Gerard and Elisa were partners, along with both sets of parents, in a cotton mill. The joint trading vessel in this enterprise was named the *Red Rose*." Lorie paused.

When her listeners urged her to continue, she went on: the young Prestons were Southerners born and bred, but they hated slavery and everything that went with it. It seemed to them that the growing and manufacture of cotton in Georgia was actually keeping the slave trade alive when every effort should have been made to eliminate a scourge the earth certainly did not require. When they discovered that no slaves were involved in the production of Egyptian cotton, an exceptional product, they shuttered the mill—to the horror of both sets of parents—and resolved to discover for themselves what the Egyptians knew that they didn't.

"In 1806, the *Red Rose* was finally able to sail out to the Mediterranean," Lorie went on. "Isaac's father felt that because of the derring-do of the US Navy in that part of the world and because that navy was now patrolling the area to keep shipping free from pirates, it would be safe to take his wife, Elisa, and their five-year-old, Isaac, along with him. It was to be a very great adventure for the three of them!

"Tragically, as we now know, he was very wrong. Unfortunately, the *Red Rose* expedition got trapped in the Mediterranean by the Embargo Act, something President Thomas Jefferson and his friends thought would keep the new country out of Europe's wars. Even if the Prestons wanted to go home, they couldn't! So they decided they'd just cruise around the Med for a while, doing what trading they could. Well, there may not have been Barbary pirates *per se* out there in the Med, but what was there was something just as evil, and it targeted the *Red Rose*.

Lorie looked up. "Poor little five-year-old Isaac's account of what happened when the *Red Rose* was boarded is very hard to read. His parents met horrible deaths right in front of him. The pirates took the ship, painted it black, changed its name to the *Black Rose*, and went on pirating.

"Isaac was kept safe by Sailing Master Will Deerfield, captive and, therefore, slave of the pirates, always closely watched but so valuable to them because of his years of experience that the pirates respected his wish to treat silent Isaac as his own son.

"In Marseilles, Isaac met Moses, aka Zulu Prince Ukuhlakanipho"—she did her best with the word—"and got invited to gala parties with interesting people from all over the world. Isaac also tells how Moses helped him to survive the African disease he caught when he was seven years old. Anyone who wants to read these early books can do it later. It's hard to read, folks, I'm warning you! Okay," she finished with a flourish. "Let's see where else this journey takes us. Who has the next book?"

Randy held it up, a thickish journal covered in a time-worn wrap: "Eighteen eleven and thereabouts. Eight to nine years old," he recounted. "Parties, parties, parties. Watercolor paintings of a variety of clothing worn by people from different parts of the African continent and even Asia, I do believe. Very ornate, some of these things. Some garb a little scant. Moses didn't discriminate as to whom he invited to his parties, except they all seemed to have lots of money. Interesting notes. Nothing pertinent to what we need right now, but it will be interesting to check this one out when we have time to go back.

He went on. "I also found bits of musical scales in this book with notes on them and composer's names. Isaac must have been a very smart kid. He was like a sponge, absorbing at firsthand stuff our current crop of kids never even think about. And he may well have met some people whose names we learn about in school or music class." He flipped a few pages. "There are also lots of sketches of types and configurations of sails, all labeled. Very nice pictures of ships, he could have been an artist. He was learning the differences between the classifications of sailing ships, as well as how to rig the sails to meet whatever winds were coming at them. A learning year, I would guess."

"But happiness and fun were rare commodities in his life," Jeff put in once Randy came to a halt. He held up the next book, a thick tome, well thumbed. "Nine years to eleven. As a young child, Isaac seems to have witnessed numerous pirate encounters flowing with blood and gore. Fortunately for him, the powers that be wouldn't let either Will Deerfield or silent Isaac participate in the raids. It was suspected they might try to take advantage of the situation if the people they were attacking started attacking back. Instead, they were part of the on-craft crew that had to continue to navigate and sail the *Black Rose* and afterward clear the decks of blood and whatever else was flopping around."

Everyone groaned.

"Isaac always helped with the wounded," Jeff continued after the uneasy laughter subsided. "It seems poor Isaac learned about anatomy and medicine the hard way, including how to stitch people up when it needed doing, which is something I *saw* him do often in later years. But it seems he also let several people die—those who had been unkind to him. He remarks that no one can offer complaints when the people responsible for that job delegate the unpleasant mending parts to a ten-year-old child."

"At least he was honest about it," Lorie said softly. "But I'm a little surprised he let anyone die on purpose. I wouldn't have thought he was that kind of child, even if some of the pirates had been hostile to him."

"Perhaps," Jeff replied softly, mindful that Lorie knew nothing yet about the bloody scalps, "he did not think of some of them as *people*."

Lorie was silent for a time. "There may be something to that," she finally conceded and turned back to her book.

CHAPTER 20

When a whistle issued from Jeb's lips half an hour later, Jeff looked up abruptly. Jeb's face was creased with a big grin. "I've got some good stuff here, folks. Jeff, you're gonna like the first part of this 1814 book. I reckon this is the one where the *Black Rose* gits blown out of the water."

Jeff grinned back. "Let's hear it."

"Isaac has just turned eleven years old."

Now Jeff put a bookmark into his own journal. He looked around him. All eyes were focused on Emily's husband.

"I'll just read plain out what he wrote," Jeb said solemnly:

> It was real dark when Will rolled me out of my hammock two nights ago. He said very softly, "Get dressed. Even though there is only a light wind, we have a Yankee warship coming up fast behind us. There is no doubt they outgun us and they can surely outrun us. I have already stashed my sea chest inside a dinghy and lowered it." Will then said to me, "I'll help you put yours over the side, and we'll tie it to the dinghy before we push

away." We carefully made our way to the deck. My sea chest was very heavy, and Will had to help me lift it, but I was so excited I was certain I could carry twice as much. We snugged a long rope around both sides and lowered it carefully into the water right beside our little boat. It made a splashing noise but no more than a big fish breaching. Because of the cunning way Lak had constructed it, it floated well, even with all the gold inside. Will secured a rope to the ship's rail, and we walked down it right onto the chest and from there climbed quietly into the dingy. I cut away as much of the rope as I could reach from the *Rose*, making sure my sea chest would not leave us. When we pulled away, it followed obediently behind like a big dog.

We dipped our oars quietly and were well away when the general alarm was sounded. Seeing the big American warship approaching, everyone on deck was running around like frightened chickens and did not notice us at all out on that dark water headed to shore.

It took most of the night, and sunlight was a danger to be feared, but between the two of us, we managed to make it all the way to the docks in Marseilles. I was very tired but so excited I ran to Lak's apartment and got his help with some of his friends to bring our chests to his rooms. We had heard the cannons while we were on the water. Now Lak told us that even from his apartment, he could hear the guns and see from the window a big fire out at the edge of the world. He told me he had been very worried about me, and he hugged me in a tight hug for a very long time. When I remembered the way I felt when my parents were killed, I knew what he was feeling, and I let him hug me as long as it took.

When the sun came up and the smoke in the sky finally cleared away, we knew the *Rose* was gone. I do not think I have ever been so happy—and Lak and his friends were as glad as we were that we had escaped.

"Then," Jeb went on excitedly, "Isaac talks about how they decide what to do next. Lak tells them to find out where the big warship that took out the *Black Rose* is docked. He says, 'Go to that boat. Tell them who you are and why you are here and ask them if you can go home with them.' They both liked that idea, so they hung around on and off at the dock for the next couple of days, waiting for the warship to come in with its prisoners and all…"

"Don't stop now," Lorie said eagerly. She was sitting at the table mesmerized, a forgotten coffee cup dangling from her fingers.

Jeff grinned at her. "Watch it," he warned softly. She quickly set the cup on the table and leaned forward, as drawn as he was to the adventures unfolding before them. His father had never talked about these things. He realized again how little he had known about Isaac Preston.

He wondered if his brother Will had ever heard any of this. A sharp pang of regret pierced him as he realized how much his siblings, especially Will, would have enjoyed sharing these tales of adventure as they had grown to maturity. An afterthought crept into his mind—would his father have used the word *adventure* to describe his experiences? Perhaps he had been silent about them because he did not want to recall anything about that part of his life.

"Now, Jeff," Jeb said very seriously, turning to him. His voice had taken on a different tone altogether. "This stuff is what makes your father—and I might add, his son—so different from the rest of those bastards they was hangin' around with—pardon the language, Miss Lorie," he said apologetically and then began to summarize, finally addressing Jeff directly. "In the end, he says it this way, 'It seemed to take a good while for the American ship to come into the dock. When it finally did, we put on clothes that made us look like gentlemen and hats we figured would hide our faces and went to see who had been caught and what was going to happen to them.'

"Here's what he says about that, 'We saw one fellow we knew follow another off the boat, all with their hands bound behind them and roped together so none could get away without dragging a half-dozen others with them. We saw more than twenty seamen led off, but we did not see the captain nor the quartermaster nor the first mate nor many of the regular crew.' What would you bet," Jeb said, looking up, "there'd been another dinghy or two on board, and the captain and the quartermaster, and a few of them other rascals escaped early with their own gold, not carin' whether the ship would burn or be taken captive, leavin' the left-behind crew members to swing in the breeze without 'em if they was captured?"

He turned back to the journal. "Okay, here's what Isaac says next about all those roped-up men, 'When I looked at who was coming down the gangplank, what I saw most of were the seamen who had been captured from other ships and kept alive because they were useful at their tasks. I finger-signed Will, asking him to tell the captain of the warship who the sailors were so they would not be mistaken for pirates and hanged on the spot, as it seemed to me that the people on the dock watching the action were angry enough at them to tear them limb from limb. I did not think that to be a fair assessment of those mostly innocent sailors who would not have lived two seconds more had they crossed one of their pirate captors. I was willing to give myself up if it would save any of those men.'"

"How much some of us are like our parents," Jeb said softly, looking up at Jeff. He shifted back to the written words:

> Will pointed up to a stern-faced man in fancy clothing who was standing at the bow of the ship, looking down on the proceedings. Will told me with his fingers not to talk with any person but that one. He said this was a man who would believe us. He went to one of the sailors, tugged on his sleeve, and spoke with him very softly.
>
> The sailor took both of us up the gangplank onto the main deck, put us into the captain's cabin, and locked the door behind us. When the captain came

in, it was the stern-faced man himself. The man looked very surprised. First, he held out his hand to Will, then both hands. Then he embraced my friend, and before I knew it, they were both crying like babies. It made me cry too. "I thought you were dead and gone," the captain said, and Will said he was too mean to die. I had to take exception to that, which I did in no uncertain terms. That was when Will finally introduced me to the captain, who was one of his closest cousins, and explained what had happened to my father's boat and told him a little about my longtime deception of the pirates.

I was getting a little impatient by now and I told the captain right out loud that not all of the men they had bound should be hung—they were captives just as we had been.

He told me it would all be straightened out and no innocent man would hang. In the end, holding Will and me as his sole source of who was innocent or guilty, he sorted the wheat from the chaff. I think he will be true to his word.

Jeb skimmed a few pages and then looked up at his waiting friends. "Here goes with some more of the good stuff, dated two days later, 'We were invited to come back to the ship to greet our seaman friends, all of them signed on as American sailors. To a man, they are excited about going back to America.'"

Smiles, cheers, and hearty clapping filled the room. Smiling, Jeb nodded.

"Is there more?" Jeff settled himself on the couch, relishing this moment. Lorie came to sit beside him.

A big smile lingering on his face, Jeb now turned several pages. "Here goes, 'Will and I have joined this crew by writing our names on the rolls, and the captain has promised he will take both of us home. I do not know if my grandparents are still alive, nor do I know if I would recognize them if I saw them. But if they are alive, they would want to know what happened to my parents and to the *Red Rose*, in which I think they also had a large stake.'" Jeb stopped. "This is as far as I've read."

Jeff heard a knock at the door and got up to meet his twenty-first-century grandfather. Rolf was dressed comfortably this morning in jeans and a wool plaid shirt. A delighted Saree pushed herself to her feet and held her little hands up to be held. As Rolf lifted her into his embrace, she put her arms around his neck, and the kiss she gave him on his cheek brought a big smile.

Jeff grinned. "What's going on over at the big house?"

"Bernice called." Rolf seated himself at the other end of the couch and pulled Saree into his lap. Smiling up at his face, she moved her little hands around, talking a mile a minute in words only she understood. When he answered as if he knew what she was saying, she gave him an adoring look and leaned back into his shoulder, gazing into his face.

Jeff knew that look. Complete contentment! Rolf wrapped his arms comfortably around her and turned back to Jeff. "The Family is still keeping track of the Searchers. No Hostiles seem to be headed in the right direction yet. This new Compact effort seems to be more a weeding out of the easy places. They zoom in with field glasses, and if nothing looks likely, they don't even bother to unpack their climbing gear. They're getting closer, but so far we're still in the clear."

"What have you heard about the ghost light book that Bernice was so afraid of?" Lorie asked. Rolf shook his head in exasperation.

"It's a given they've heard of it, hence this flurry of activity so close! Ghost lights are tantalizing in theory, but to our favor, it's pretty hard to pin something down when it appears only once or twice a year."

"Any aerial surveys of the cliffs yet?" Randy asked.

"Not our cliffs," Rolf answered. "But the Family suspects we will be lucky to escape a closer look this time. We're on standby for a quick summoning. What else have you found out from the Isaac books? Any solid leads? Suggestions as to where we look for our blueprint house?"

"Gut-wrenching tales," Randy replied solemnly, "but a little too early in Isaac's life for the answers we really need. All we can do is keep reading and hoping for some answers."

To which Jeff added, "Jeb's journal is from Isaac's eleventh year, 1814. It's quite an exciting tale."

"It's the part," Em's husband put in enthusiastically, "when Isaac and Will try to shuck the pirates off their case once and for all. I reckon this is the meat and potatoes part of the story."

"Jeb tells us we're only halfway through the meal," Jeff said, grinning at Lorie, who had seated herself beside him on the couch. "We're all slavering for the meat."

His friend flashed an answering grin. "I know it's comin', and it'll taste real good!"

Jeff handed a volume to his grandfather, who took it eagerly. "1817?" he said with a grin. "How old was Isaac in 1817?"

Lorie did a quick calculation. "Fourteen, most of that year."

He nodded, and with his great-granddaughter resting comfortably inside the circle of his arms, Rolf settled himself to his task. Silence once more fell across the room. A drowsy Saree finally fell asleep while diary readers immersed themselves once more into tales of a young boy's precarious life.

CHAPTER 21

—————

Jeb finally broke the silence with a sigh of disgust. "Well, we suspected one of us was gonna see it sometime. I'm almost sorry now that I had to be the one."

Jeff looked up abruptly.

"I haven't read it all yet," his friend said softly, "but for better or worse, I reckon this is the grit of what we have to know!" When Jeff nodded, Jeb commenced reading—in deference to the sleeping child a bit more softly than he had before:

> It is several months since I have written down anything in this book. But I owe it to myself, and especially to Will and to anyone else who might someday read this account, to relate the plain truth of the matter. Some very evil things have happened and are still happening. If people are not given the cold plain facts as seen by my own eyes, it will be far harder to change the outcome down the road. Once the document this pirate crew has devised is used as a weapon to press someone to do what they know is wrong,

many innocent people far into the future will be put in great and terrible peril through no fault of their own.

Stunned into silence by Isaac's pronouncement, Jeff first turned to Jeb and then to Lorie. Their faces said it all. Even as an eleven-year-old child, Jeff's father had been acutely aware of the lasting importance of The Compact.

"Well, here goes nothin'!" Jeb took a deep breath and began to read aloud.

Will and I finally were given to believe that we had been acting a bit too cocky. We had talked with Will's cousin in plain view a time or two—an error we should have foreseen.

When we were informed that the American ship was planning to head back to sea and that we were to travel with it, we determined to retrieve our sea chests from Moses's apartment. It seemed such a simple thing at that time. We chose the dark of evening to mount our personal expedition.

Even before we could leave the dockyards, however, we found our way blocked. On hand was the red-haired captain of the pirate ship and a goodly number of his crew members—all those who had contrived to manage their escape before the *Rose* was destroyed. It was clear someone had told them of our survival, as we had not made any big secret of it. They were lying in wait for us.

There were only two of us and at least a dozen of them. Hard as we struggled, our heads were quickly covered with bags, our hands were bound behind our backs, and we were hustled around many corners and finally down some stairs into a basement room lit only by a few candles. I was certain we were to be tortured and killed.

They treated us rough during the journey, but instead of beating us, as I supposed they might do, they sat us down and read to us a document they demanded we sign. Nor were they willing to take no for an answer.

They called it a Compact, the Blackheart Compact. The first part they insisted that we sign was short and, in many respects, the same rules we had lived under aboard the *Black Rose*. The admiral, the captain, and the other officers would be in complete control of our lives. We were told that, regardless of our doubts, we had to say out loud that we were binding ourselves to their rules of our own free will. We also had to agree that all our progeny—Will signed to me that this means "children"—would also be loyal to this Compact until the end of time. The penalty for not obeying would be extreme torture and then a slow painful death.

I had no doubt the captain expected
to be on hand well after his life on earth
was over to personally mete out that
punishment. I have seen for many years
how he enjoys the job of discipline. I will
never understand why some people like
to make others suffer.

Nor do I think that free will was
offered freely to any of the other men
who seem to have unhappily signed the
paper before we were asked to do so.

"'For those good folk reading this account sometime in
the future...'" Jeb abruptly stopped reading. He looked up
at Jeff and said, now in a whisper, "Did you feel it? It's like
Isaac's here... talkin' to us direct..."

"I think you're right," Jeff said quietly. A shiver had just
crept up his spine. He glanced at Lorie and knew without
words that she had also felt something. Her eyes were large.

"I felt it too," Rolf said softly. "We are getting close to
the answers we need, I think. Please continue, Jeb." Saree
stirred. Lorie quietly took the sleeping child into her arms
and moved her into the bedroom. She returned a moment
later, resuming her place beside Jeff.

Randy moved his chair a little closer as well.

Jeb took a deep breath. "Here we go," he said. "Isaac's
words again, my friends..."

Even though I deem these events to
be perhaps as terrible as the early loss of
my beloved parents—and I do not want
to think on that—if I do not explain in
detail what happened that day, there will

be no way to reverse the damage that is now being done to so many people, guilty or innocent, especially to those who have yet to be born and bear no blame for any of what happened in this time and place.

The captain explained to Will and myself that all his men had already signed a paper committing themselves to the organization and its commandments. We were the last to sign, they told us. They tried first to force me to put my name to their drivel. I pretended a lack of understanding, even though I clearly understood every terrible word. Still pretending to be what I was not, I did not speak but cried and fought when two bullies took my hand to slash it for blood.

In spite of also being heavily pressed, Will pulled me away from them, saying he would help me to understand. He gave me the finger signal to keep fighting and then he grabbed a knife and ran it along the side of my hand deep enough to make me cry out with pain. He did contrive to make me appear bloody, although there was in truth not enough blood to sign one name, much less two. He whispered, "Use my blood," and in the darkness, he offered his own right hand, which he had already slashed. I kept whooping it up, but in the end, they did not relent.

Jeb looked up, deeply distressed. His voice dropping almost to a whisper, he continued,

> Finally, I took the pen and signed "i s a k" with Will's blood—mixed with not a drop of my own. With no warning, the captain then raised his saber, and before I knew what was happening, he brought the blade down on Will's wrist, severing his right hand from his arm. It flopped at my feet. I almost fainted. He had known we were trying to trick him.

Jeff heard Lorie gasp and saw tears welling in her eyes. She moved closer, and he wrapped his arms about her.

Jeb was not yet done.

> The captain then said to Will, "You will no longer speak to this boy without my permission, and the way your life blood is gushing out, you will not live long enough henceforth that your signature is of any importance. You have let us know that you do not wish to sign our agreement, Mr. Deerfield! Be it known, then, you are now released from that requirement!"
>
> I screamed as Will sank down in deep shock. I flung myself on the floor beside him and pulled his head onto my lap. All I could see by the candlelight was his dimming eyes looking up at me from a very white face. Buttons snapped

off my shirt in my haste to remove it. I wrapped his wrist tightly within its confines, trying to stop his precious blood from flowing into the dirt floor.

The captain slapped my face hard and yanked at my hair to pull me off, but I clung to Will, holding onto his poor arm as tightly as I could to stop the steady flow of blood. I was screaming at the top of my lungs. Finally, the captain screamed back, saying that he could not put up with my racket—someone might hear and call the authorities. They quickly decided to leave me to come to my senses. Everyone went up the steps and out into the street. The candles were snuffed out one by one as men walked out.

When the door closed behind the last, it was as dark as I have ever known darkness to be. I heard the key being turned in the lock and knew we were securely confined. They thought Will would die in my arms, and that would serve as punishment for my resistance. They would kill me when they returned, of that I had no doubt. I was no longer of any use to them.

I searched the dark floor around me as best I could with my foot and finally touched Will's severed hand. I retrieved it and secured it tightly inside the shirt I was using to bind his wound. It was within touch of his wrist, which I had tied off as tightly as I could with a strip torn from my shirt.

A long time seemed to pass. It might have been minutes. It could have been hours. I had no way to tell, confused and angry and sorrowful as I was. The binding and the constant pressure of my joined hands on my friend's wound finally did its duty. Will regained consciousness for a short time, long enough to whisper my name. He was suffering terribly and very weak. I told him not to speak. I told him I would be with him as long as it took. I kept his head in my lap. Sometimes it was only by a single labored breath that I knew he was still alive.

When sometime later I heard a rattle at the door, I was very frightened. It cracked opened, and in the dim light from the street, I saw a shadowy figure press through. Saying nothing, he shut the door behind him. After a few attempts to light a flint, he contrived successfully to do so and put flame to a candle pulled from inside his shirt. It was a seaman from my father's crew who had also been forced into service on the *Rose*. His name is Jebediah Griffiths.

Jeb ceased his narration. His lips remained open, as if he wanted to say something more but was unsure how.

"These events did not happen just yesterday, my friend," Jeff reminded him softly. "Many years have passed since."

When Jeb Wallace spoke again, it was in a surprisingly broken voice. "Jebediah Griffiths. That's my given name, first and second, the whole of it! Ma named me for this man. He was one of her great-granddaddies. He died long before she came on the scene, but Ma said from what she heard about him, he was brave and resourceful and probably her favorite relative. I always thought my Compact connections," he continued softly, "came through my unknown father's side."

"Keep reading," Jeff suggested, intrigued and, Lorie could tell, quite moved. "Answers may yet be found."

Excitement could now be heard in Jeb's voice as the flow of words resumed.

> Jebediah had been my father's man first, one of the few spared by the pirates. He was an escaped prisoner from an English debtors' prison whose story of deprivation had touched my father's heart. But I had learned since that he was also a storyteller of great skill who could manipulate certain situations to his advantage. This was probably why he remained mostly unharmed while many others from my father's crew had been disposed of early on.

Jeb looked up at Jeff with a half smile on his lips and then eagerly turned back to the book.

> Jebediah had often worked with us quite expertly on the sails, showing that

he was also an accomplished sailor, and I realized then how he was so adept at finding ways to avoid entering the fray during battles by being far above them. This led me to believe he did not countenance piracy but felt he had no choice in the matter if he were to save himself in the long run. His arrival at this time was an unexpected blessing.

"Point me where to take you," he said to me, still not knowing that I could speak and likely doubting I could hear. But he knew I could read lips. "I know you are friendly with the big black African king who sometimes walks these docks. I presume you know where he lives?"

We did not know until Jeb Griffiths lifted his candle to see what he could use to help us that the pirate crew had saved their flag from the unlamented *Black Rose* and brought it with them to this place for their so-called loyalty ceremony. It was nailed to the wall. When I saw it, I got up in a rage and ripped it down. Griffiths quieted me with the idea that we could use it as a sling to transport Will to Moses's apartment, and this we did. Once it was stained with Will's blood, Griffiths said firmly, they should never get it back! I agreed with him in no uncertain terms, and he began to laugh, finally realizing I could both hear and

speak. He told me I was far more devious
than he, and that took a lot of skill.

Jeff looked hard at Jeb Wallace. Both grinned! "That's
why it was in the trunk!" They said it together!

"Damn!" The exclamation came from Randy, who had
risen to his feet. He sank back into his chair, tears rolling
from his eyes, and reached his hand out to Jeb, who took it
firmly in his for a very long minute.

Jeb turned back to the book with a great eagerness,
scanning for more pertinent information, summarizing.
"Isaac says that Moses sent for the best doctor he knew to
deal with Will's injury. Between them, they saved his life and
kept the hand!"

Lorie said meekly, "I hope it's not in that trunk!"

After a moment of silence, everyone laughed. For a
moment, the mood was lightened. "Is there more?" Jeff asked.

Having read ahead, Jeb now came up with a short syn-
opsis: "Moses's doctor tied off the artery and took flesh from
Will's severed hand to stitch over the raw bone, and at the
time Isaac was writin' this account, the wound seemed to be
healin' fairly well, though Isaac is angry as sin at the pirates.
He says he'll search 'em out and kill all of 'em once he grows
up! Once he simmers down a bit, he goes on to say that
Moses has promised to have a leather hand made for Will,
with all the bones in it intact, and he—Isaac—declares as a
solemn vow that he will care for Will for the rest of his life.
He also says at the end that he is writin' this day's account
from his hammock on the American warship, and they are
well away, under full sail, and headed west toward home. His
good friend Will, y'all will be happy to note, is recoverin'
as best he can from his ordeal in the captain's cabin in the
captain's own bed. And to top it all off, my relative, Jebediah

Griffiths, is sailing home with 'em. He might of signed The Compact, but it really was with a knife at his throat, and for now, he's joined up as a sailor on an American warship!"

Lorie sat up straight, grinning. "Spunky little Isaac!" she declared. "He and your Jeb captured the flag! Hooray for our side! Wait till Ewen hears about this!"

Quiet "hoorays" sounded around the room, with many arms lifted briskly into the air!

"The flag!" Rolf said excitedly. "Would there be any way to find it?"

Grinning broadly, Jeff said, "We have it, Grandpa! It was on top of everything else in the trunk! And the trunk is in about the safest place in the world—in Ewen's Georgia office. Under lock and key!" He felt a brush of fur against his ankle and looked down. The little fox was there looking up at him and then at Lorie, almost as if he were grinning. Lorie picked up the little animal, gave him a big hug, kissed the top of his head, and cradled him in her arms.

"He's purring, I think," she whispered. And then to herself, she said, "Do foxes purr?"

CHAPTER 22

Tuesday evening, April 19, 2016

D inner that night was again held at the big house. Lorie realized with relief that despite the unexpected dramas of the previous day, or perhaps because of them, Emily and Alexi had bonded. Together they had cooked up a storm of a meal.

Food to live for, Ewen Taylor declared, pulling melt-in-your-mouth pork off ribs the ladies had spent hours preparing and tucking it lovingly into his mouth. At least one of each person's favorite dishes was on the table that night, and Lorie was warmed by the tight camaraderie she could feel among these brave special people.

When dinner was done, the kitchen rendered spotless, and sleepy children put to bed with babysitters standing by, if needed, a meeting was again convened in the now darkened sunroom.

Alexi and Guy had been invited to this session, as Ewen had felt it was necessary to brief his son and daughter-in-law in regard to some of the more unusual conversations they were overhearing. They were both exceedingly curious, he had reported quietly back to Lorie, who had grinned and nodded, saying, "Perhaps it's time they enter the fold!"

Drinks were offered, and everyone gathered around the fireplace, a comforting bulwark against the cool breezes of evening. A hint of rain was hitting the now closed windows—a welcome spring downpour on the way, Lorie mused.

"How's the diary reading going?" Lorie heard Emily ask softly as she settled onto a couch next to her husband. Jeb reached for her hand.

"Rough generally." He recapped his previous narrative for the benefit of all. "But," he concluded, looking down at his wife, "here's the good thing, Em. I've found an ancestor I can be real proud of. I'm hopin' we hear more about him. For all his bad luck early on, he must finally have found a girl he could love and had a couple or two children because here I am!" He looked around, chuckling contentedly. "Here I am!" he said even more thoughtfully, looking down into Em's glowing face.

"It's no wonder Compact goons were after Isaac all those years," Ewen declared with a big grin. "Little brat! He kept them fooled from the start, managed somehow to avoid putting a legal signature on The Compact that everyone else had been compelled to sign, and then captured their flag! Flummoxed by a child! How humiliating! What I'm wondering is whether Will survived?"

"I expect we'll find out if we keep reading!" Rolf Maratti was also grinning. "But have you ever considered, my friends, what damage Isaac's descendants have wrought to a couple of versions of the Inner Circle these past few years? And this was even before we had Isaac's journals to tell us what kind of brigands we were battling. Guess we're chips off the old block!"

"We have Isaac's son as our leader!" Randy put in with a laugh. "The biggest gift of all!"

Everyone applauded, to Jeff's great embarrassment. "Maybe so," he said, "but there is no question mine are the superior troops! What good is a leader, I ask you, without brilliant troops!" From her cozy spot within the circle of Jeff's left arm, Lorie looked up warmly at her husband as he continued, "There's a new word I've learned that describes the way I have sometimes felt about my *modus operandi*."

"*Brilliant*?" Lorie offered.

"No." He looked down, seemingly thinking carefully. "It's more like *clueless*!"

Hoots of laughter rang out.

"No more excuses," Lorie said briskly. "We've got the blueprints. And now that we have the diaries, we're invincible!" Lorie turned her face up for a kiss. His lips were magic, and she snuggled closer.

"Let's recap what we've learned so far about The Compact," Ewen suggested, now rocking himself forward on his chair, reaching his hands toward the warmth of the fireplace. "We have some notion as to what that document actually demanded. I suppose there's a possibility that the full rendition is buried someplace in Isaac's journals and we just haven't found it yet. Keep looking, folks.

"In the meantime, I've transmitted Isaac's list of original signatories to headquarters, and we're already compiling information on their descendants and noting whether, by Isaac's assessment, they're bad guys or victims, like Jeb's great-gramps. Hands down, I'm confident we now know a whole lot more about The Compact people than they do about us."

"These little diaries are solid gold!" Rolf declared. "Jeff, you couldn't have found anything more useful."

"It wasn't me who found them," Jeff said with a chuckle. "It was our baby and a little fox!"

"So much for our great intellect," Ewen said dryly, "and banks and banks of intelligently programmed supercomputers."

For all the angst Saree's well adventure had brought to Lorie, she still had to laugh.

"There must be a compelling reason my grandfather gave up his life for these drawings," Rolf said thoughtfully. "He must have felt they were vital."

"I'm of the opinion it's their headquarters building," Jeb replied firmly.

"Why is no location noted?" Rolf asked. "Generally, blueprints have an address."

Alexi said a bit hesitantly, "Lorie and I have been searching real estate in the area we've pinpointed and not finding anything at all similar. But I think, well, maybe we need to be looking for it a bit differently..."

Lorie noted Jeff's sudden snap to attention. "Sometimes," he said very softly, "folks who've been standing a little farther away from a problem have clearer ideas than those who are too wrapped up in it. Please share, if you would, my friend."

Rolf Maratti added gently, "Alexi, please don't be shy."

"Well...it's kind of dumb maybe..."

Lorie sensed that the young woman felt she might be intruding into family matters that were none of her business. "Come on," she urged gently. "We're all too stuffed to bite!"

Alexi flashed a wry grin, which turned into rather embarrassed laughter. "Well, okay... It's just that, well, I was watching the kids tonight, and Jack was playing with his mashed potatoes and gravy... Oh, maybe it's too dumb." Again, she hesitated.

"Go ahead," Jeff prompted again, "I think you're onto something."

"Well, it seemed to me that he was looking at those potatoes as a kind of island in the middle of a gravy river, and he put a small cooked carrot castle on top of the potatoes and mashed it down…"

"Alexi, that's brilliant!" Rolf said. "As I recall, there are any number of islands in the Potomac."

Ewen responded enthusiastically, "Of course. Some are large enough to have multiple houses on them. I joined a friend a while back on a motorboat trip upstream from Great Falls to Harper's Ferry and noticed, much to my surprise, a working farm in the middle of the river. I also noticed there were vacation houses on some of the other islands. Alexi, my dear, you have just opened up to us a whole new dimension. Thank you!"

Randy, who had been quietly following the ping-pong of conversation, said abruptly, "Let's get that program back up and fly the satellite over the river. Good thinking, partner!"

A glow transformed Alexi's face, and Lorie smiled. Guy's beautiful wife had just become a *bona fide* contributing member of the team!

Ewen quickly found his laptop and placed it on a large work table. "Which map site did you use?" he asked Lorie as he pulled open the cover and settled himself comfortably. Following her suggestions, he entered the desired location—River Road north to northwest of the Maryland suburbs of Washington, DC.

"Okay," Ewen said. "River Road's a wipeout, you say, so let's move our view closer to the river and simply follow it upstream."

Above Great Falls, the Potomac meandered back and forth across a rocky bed, its shifting borders clearly discerned by a satellite locked into orbit far above the earth. The river divided and came together again around any number of islands, some rocky and relatively cleared, some heavily wooded.

"If any buildings are located here, they're awfully hard to see," Emily remarked.

"Look for outbuildings, man-made objects," Ewen told her. "Alexi, my dear, initially I would not have given your suggestion a first thought, much less a second. My immediate thought was, floods would make it impractical. But this island"—he pointed toward the screen—"looks like a piece of broken-off mountainside, probably high enough in places that floods never touch it. Moreover, it's surrounded by wide branches of relatively shallow water. Look here, folks—take a look at these little square dots placed on the island! Houses, as seen from space!" He zoomed the computer camera in on the island. "Can't get it close enough to see details," he said finally, "but even at this resolution, you can clearly tell that they're houses. No mansion here, however. Let's move on."

"Here's another wannabe island," Randy said, pointing, "where it looks like flooding debris over the years piled up and filled in the gap on the Maryland side." He had positioned himself where he could see the map quite clearly.

"You know what?" Lorie said with rising excitement, hanging over Ewen's shoulder. "That just might be it! Did you see it?" A sensation of certainty was building inside her. "Look there! Zoom in again, Ewen." She pointed, and he brought the image as close as he could without its breaking into indecipherable dots. "There's a straight line there"— Lorie pointed again—"obviously man-made, see it?" She glanced at her fellow computer explorers, all of whom were now bunched tightly around the monitor. "This first straight line here"—again she pointed—"looks like it might be the side of a structure, and there's a tiny little line, kind of like a footpath, jutting off from the side of the building and headed away from the riverbank and up into what I think might be hills. It seems to me that it's at the same odd angle as the dashed line I spotted on the blueprint in the study! See there! The last part of it, the part jutting off, points directly north according to the compass lines on the screen. Away from the river? Up into the hills? Strange!"

"Damn," Lorie heard Ewen say sharply. "Let's get the blueprint and check that out."

"On it!" was Jeff's quick reply. He left the room and came back in less than five minutes. "Sorry for the delay," he said softly. "I had to put the gloves on—not so easy! Here, let me spread it out on the table, and we can all take a look."

Ewen plugged his laptop into one of his printers, and Lorie made a quick color copy of the scan. Ewen handed it to Rolf, their resident expert on geology. "Exactly the same," he said, trying with little success to hold his excitement in check. "The bent end is oriented to the north. And look here," he added almost breathlessly, placing his finger again on the computer printout. Two other man-made objects could be seen, one on the Riverside that seemed of sufficient size to be a small boathouse, another apparently twice its size on the other side of an obvious driveway, the second structure halfway hidden by trees.

"If that's a garage or a carport," Rolf said softly, "there must be a dry land access area."

"I'll make a print with the same dimensions as our survey map." Ewen fiddled with the computer, produced a bird's-eye view of the area, and sent an image to a different printer. "Let's correlate this area with the geologic survey map Ewen has laid out over there. All the current roads are located on that map, with no treetops to get in the way."

Guy said, chuckling, "If any roads are there, I bet they're all posted 'No Trespassing.'"

"I have some devices," his father said slyly, "that might provide us with a little more intimate information without anyone being the wiser."

"Bring in the drones!" Lorie said with relish. "Serves 'em right, doesn't it? They're the ones who started it!"

Shortly, exhaustion by now outweighing exhilaration, the party broke up. "Get a good night's sleep," Ewen said quietly as he walked out the door and pulled it carefully shut behind him. "We've got lots to do tomorrow."

CHAPTER 23

Wednesday morning, April 20, 2016, 11:00 a.m.

Lorie rose late, finally feeling more or less rested. She found a note from Jeff saying that he had gone over to the big house with Saree. Take her time, he had written, he would let her know immediately if anything vital was occurring!

She was pleased and not surprised. She had been up several times during the night to tend to their teething child, and her thoughtful husband had given her the chance this morning to get some unbroken rest. He was always mindful of such things, and once again, she thanked her lucky stars that she had found him.

Found? That wasn't really the right word for it, was it? He had been sent into this new world for a purpose, and she just happened to be on-site when he arrived. Luck? Coincidence?

None at all! If there was any issue she was unclear about, it was not this one. She had been handpicked. She'd never quite figured out by whom. Sara? Isaac? Maybe Isaac's good friend Lak, aka Moses?

Her side of the family perhaps? Just before Jeff, in Confederate gray, had been killed by a Yankee trooper understandably mistaking him for a Reb, he had left his bereaved sister Sara in the hands of Lorie's own multi-great-grandfather Marshall Manning, one of his West Point friends. Marshall, a recent widower, took Sara out of harm's way, over time grew to love the grieving young widow and later married her, combining their family fortunes for all time.

Marshall and Sara's marriage had been an extraordinarily good one according to every account. They died within a week of one another, both in their nineties. Lorie had read an old obituary for Marshall, which went on for many paragraphs, not only about Marshall but also his accomplished wife and their three brilliant sons plus reminders of the many successful grandchildren and great-grandchildren they had to show for their devotion to each other and their joined families. Not hype, as it was a local paper. It was a heartfelt account by someone who had known them both, and it was lovely to read.

She was digressing. Her worries were still with her. How many of their own small band, waging a shadow war against a much larger army, would survive the conflict if the two sides actually came to blows? Once Jeff completed the tasks he was sent here to do, would her precious husband be allowed to remain? His child, perhaps—or *children*, if they dared to have more—might encourage fate to smile upon him!

She tried to ignore the roiling burn rising in her stomach. There had been too many near misses already in this guerilla conflict between the too-elusive Compact association and the high-powered mop-up squad to which she now belonged. So far, thank goodness, the decisive hits had always landed on the other side. Many descendants of the original Compact pirates had been taken out of play in the last two years.

But careful planning could go only so far. They had been very lucky to date, but too many retrieved bullets were tucked away in drawers as reminders of what could happen if they were not always at the top of their game! Could that kind of luck last?

The death of any one of these brave souls working so hard around her, she now realized, would be hell for her to handle.

She gave a deep sigh. Failure was simply not an option.

Girded with what resolve she could pull together, she strode through the beginnings of a rainy morning across the lawn to the big house and found, not surprisingly, an extra contingent of busy, very familiar people set up in the sunroom. Bill, Ivan, and Jared had arrived with computers, printers, and all the wires and other connective devices they seemed to require. "Hi, guys," she said. "Fancy meeting the Three Musketeers here! Don't you ever sleep?"

Since she had last seen him, Bill, the super-intense genius, had shaved off his ragged mustache and chin whiskers. No one would have known even a week ago what a good-looking young man he really was, although he certainly didn't seem to care that much. This morning, his attention was riveted to a large computer monitor. "This is one of the grandest houses I've ever seen," she heard him say to no one in particular, awe softening a voice he seldom used.

She paused to watch. His drone seemed to be exploring at very close range the interior of a large magnificently furnished home, seemingly unoccupied—at least for the moment. The rooms were dark outside the broad beam of a drone-equipped spotlight. From what Lorie could discern, while the building was similar to Randolph House, it was far more ornate and furnished in a completely different style!

She stopped to stare. "Headquarters!" she whispered, awed. "We did find it!"

"We did!" Bill echoed back with smug satisfaction. "We are good!"

Sitting at another computer, Jared was occupied with a different kind of image. He seemed to be wandering through sections of damp wooded areas, swooping here and there across rain-glistened treetops, dropping down occasionally, apparently noting access to various places of interest along and away from the Potomac river. Now and then, he reached toward the large map lying on the desk in front of him and made marks with different colored pens. Lorie could not even guess what he was doing, nor did she ask. In response to her cheery greeting, he raised his hand in acknowledgment, his attention still glued to the monitor in front of him.

"Greetings, Lorie! Welcome to Drone Central." The bald parts of Ivan's head gleamed in the overhead lights as did his broad smile. "The answer to your interesting question about sleep is—during the odd breaks! It's sufficient for now because this is more exciting than anything I've ever done before. Bar none!

"Great breakfast spread in the dining room, girl! Grab a cuppa and a sweet something and come back to see what we've found!"

"In a minute," she said, grinning despite all. "I've got to check on my kin first."

Surprise came from seeing her computer-averse husband sitting in front of one of the machines, actually using the keyboard, monitoring, manipulating and pulling out of various printers a series of sharp-colored images.

As she walked through the computer enclave, impressed by all the paper streaming out around her, Alexi, standing by as traffic cop, greeted her with a huge satisfied smile.

"Babysitting service in the kids' room," she said from her position of gravest importance. "Saree is happy as a clam playing with the boys. They think she's the cutest thing they've ever seen. And they adore that little fox, who doesn't seem to mind being schlepped like a rag doll from place to place and stroked like a kitty by lots of small hands! He never bites, does he? We've got both babysitters working overtime today. Lots of goodies for the small fry to munch on and enough new books and toys to keep them distracted. Grown-up plans are being compiled elsewhere."

Emily Wallace came next through the doorway, carrying her little redheaded son. She headed automatically toward the kids' room. "Get some real breakfast, Lorie. We're going gung ho now that we've found the hive or whatever they call a place where wasps go to sharpen their stingers, if you don't mind me mixing a metaphor or two!"

She disappeared into the next room for a moment and came back quickly. "All's well. Saree is queen of the hill. Todd was thrilled to see her—he adores her!" Then she continued as if no interruption had taken place, "It doesn't seem like anyone's in residence at the river residence right now, according to the trio, except maybe a couple of outside guards who both seem a little bored with a tendency toward nappish thoughts because the raindrops are mesmerizing them. It probably wouldn't even occur to them that a sneak recon is being carried out right under their noses, inside the building they are being paid to guard, to put it more exactly!

"Ewen told me his guys figured out how to avoid the interior cameras and turn off all The Compact alarms. They substituted their own green 'all clear' lights so no one suspects our little drones are swishing about inside the house, spying on everything. Getting very interesting pictures too.

That house is obviously Control Central. What we're worrying about is why no one is there."

Lorie grinned. Ewen's guys had come through again! She replied airily, "They're probably all wandering out in the woods looking for Junior's airplane." It was when she turned at last toward the kitchen and caught a brief glimpse against the window of the golden glow she associated with Sara that she realized how very close they were to something of great import. Much as she admired Jeff's sister, Sara's presence was always jarring to Lorie, it being an indication that something big was just about to happen.

"Hello, Sara," Lorie said softly and noted a momentary answering pulse. "Don't you worry! We'll handle it," she said and then added to herself, "If we can figure out what *it* is!"

Trying now to tamp down a rising anxiety, she sweetened a large cup of hot tea, picked up a doughnut, and came directly back to the sunroom where she found Jeff staring intently at a monitor displaying the same interior Bill had been looking at earlier. She noticed his hand moving, the curser keeping time, small movements, as if he were searching for something specific. "Your sister's here," she said quietly as she moved up beside him.

He turned to her, nodded, and gave her a warm smile. "I know. She's been looking over my shoulder!" He pointed across the room. "She liked these." The ancient blueprints— as the team was still calling Moses's meticulously detailed etchings of the mansion, which it seemed was now being intimately explored by two drones—were spread across several worktables, each parchment now covered by window glass specifically cut to fit each individual page. From his spot in front of the computer monitor, he turned toward her again. "I'm spying out all the pictures hanging on the walls, Lorie. All the past admirals, captains, quartermasters, mates, other important personages. Many names, some very familiar in this century, many dates. On top of that, we are gathering confidential information, handwritten texts of history long hidden, recorded in great detail and now snapped up into our computers in the twinkling of an eye. It was nice of The Compact people to do all this work for us, wasn't it?"

Chuckling, he added, "As you can tell, very early this morning the genius trio inserted a couple of small spy drones into that overflow drain you remarked about that goes down toward the river or...," he paused and then added, "provides a short place of rest for people who have just been transported quietly across the river, headed toward mountaintops from which they can search out and follow the north star! We found this star symbol embedded in many of the sections of what was pawned off on these Compact people as drainpipes." He looked up at Lorie, his eyes crinkling with humor. "What do you think?"

"It is very specific, isn't it?" she answered thoughtfully. "I'd say you were on to something Moses's clueless clients completely missed!"

He looked up at Lorie and again grinned. "Try this one, Rolf told me 'the leach field for the septic system is located on the downward side of the yard'—not a word of which I understood, but you might. There is also a water well located somewhere safely away from waste products. Bill waited to see what might happen when one of the guards used a bathroom. Apparently, no waste or water appeared to be draining from what we were initially calling an overflow pipe. So while there are drains tied into the house plumbing, this is not one of them. There! Did I sound like I knew what I was saying?"

She couldn't help but laugh.

"Knowing that," Jeff continued undaunted, "he sent Chuck through that strange little drainpipe." He turned toward her, his blue eyes crinkling with suppressed laughter. "I can't believe they've named these little winged things like they're people!

"Unfortunately, Chuck was stopped at the outer basement wall by a large louvered cover fixed across a hole cut through the wall but completely hidden by years and years' worth of fast-growing vines. But nothing stops Bill. He took charge of one of Chuck's narrow sharp arms, moved it through one of the louvers, and suddenly all the screws were loose, the cover was carefully lowered to the floor, and Chuck—or shall we say, Chuck's eyes—were on watch inside a largish hidey hole.

"Lorie, it was a resting place for escaping slaves! Lanterns were stored there with intact fuel cans. We don't know if the cans were still full or empty because Chuck didn't care one way or another. He showed us an assortment of warm clothing, canned food, hand weapons, hand-drawn maps—everything that might be needed in the hills!" He looked up at Lorie and broke into laughter. "Right under their noses! Someone on our side was working for them right under their noses! And they never tumbled! Not to this day!

"The drone I'm watching now—they're calling this one Guppy—is the main spy with the best camera. It followed Chuck into the interior of the house, and both are taking pictures. Bill is controlling Chuck. Ivan was on Guppy's controls.

"From the outside, the pathway that leads to the hillside is invisible. It's covered by high grass. We saw it only because our geniuses are using a different form of light, which finds impacted dirt and assumes that a road or a pathway used to be there. The owners probably never knew about it.

"There's a heavy vine-smothered grate disguising the outside opening. It's a grate, apparently meant to keep out small animals and creeping vines. Easily removed from the inside, as our drones did it first time 'round! We tried it from the outside too. Those blasted vines made it a lot harder to get inside, but they were replaced so precisely they appear to be untouched!" He chuckled. "We urged our little winged friends to go in and come out a couple of times just to make sure we could do it right. It's the only unguarded entryway to the house, and even though we now know we can enter the house bodily, we'd rather not. Chuck and Guppy are our men, so to speak, but we have to be able to retrieve them at the drop of a hat!"

Jeff took a deep breath and went on. "The house isn't occupied at the moment. Two gunmen are sitting outside, completely unaware we're inside! Many bedrooms in the house, none in use. No clothes in the closets. Bedding and cleaning products are on the shelves. Someone suggests that the house might serve as an upscale venue for formal meetings or planning sessions. Staples in the cupboards are in large bags and boxes—the kind of supplies useful for catering companies, I am told. One of the upstairs rooms is clearly an office with a large desk, phones, typing machines of some kind, copying machines, things I can't describe and have no idea what they are—the works, as someone phrased it! In another of the upstairs rooms, there are several rows of file cabinets. That may be where their correspondence and working papers are kept."

Lorie whispered, "It really is Control Central, isn't it? Compact Headquarters!"

He nodded, grinning broadly. "Our drones are quite facile at *picking* locks, but the interior basement door wasn't even locked." He grinned. "Why should it be? The property itself is posted every six feet with skull and crossbones warning signs. It's surrounded by rolled barbed wire and businesslike guard dogs. There are two human guards on duty right now, trying to look like they know what they're doing. This morning, when our drones came, however, the dogs were sound asleep. Didn't wake up either!

"So Bill taught our drones how to turn off the inside intruder alarms before they began their reconnaissance and also told them how to warn us if anyone wants to run a check on the alarm system. In that case, we turn all alarms back on and our adversaries can check away as much as they like! Our presence remains a secret. Lorie, that man is uncommonly brilliant! He thinks of everything!"

Lorie nodded. No surprise there.

"Chuck and Guppy have entered room after room, taking pictures for us and sending them back." His voice grew even more excited. "Honey, we've gone practically everywhere in the house. It's virtually a duplicate of Oak Hill, although it's not quite as large. The other exception is the attic. Except for several rows of file cabinets filled with historical documents, it's as empty as the basement. We will want to take a look inside all the cabinets eventually, but that can wait. The locked room, the only one we haven't entered yet, is the one we always called the drawing room at Oak Hill. We suspect that The Compact document is there because, as our geniuses put it, that room is alarmed to the teeth!"

He lapsed into silence for a moment and finally said, "I keep thinking how my father would have loved to be part of all this! Do you suppose anyone would mind if Doggy joins us for a while?" He grinned a little sheepishly. "If he's really...well, I know you think... Anyway, we're going to be needing as much help as we can get during the next couple of days, and he might appreciate being part of this productive confusion. Might even join in, bark or whine or something."

"Doggy is in with the kids," she finally said, trying to hold back a giggle, "being dragged around like a rag doll, doing a lot more babysitting than he ever signed up for! He'd probably welcome a break! I'll get him."

Not easily done, Lorie discovered when she heard the wails of distress coming from Doggy's adoring crowd as she retrieved the poor animal. "I just need to take him for a little while," she said soothingly as she wrapped him in her arms. "Uncle Jeff needs to ask him a few things."

"Doggies don't talk," Tony said firmly.

"My Doggy talks," Saree said with equal firmness to Tony, who harrumphed and stalked off. She turned her big blue eyes to her mother and nodded. "My Doggy talks," she said again with a big smile as she waved goodbye to her friend. *Well, that's very interesting!* Lorie said to herself as she hurried back to Jeff with a relieved Doggy safely huddled close in her arms." Jeff grinned when she told him.

"Not very likely!" he said. But when he looked down at their small new pet and that pet looked up at him with what seemed ever-so-much like a relieved smile, he frowned. "Really?"

CHAPTER 24

Early Wednesday afternoon, April 20, 2016

"**W**e've got an even dozen of Isaac's books left," Lorie said to all the folk gathered around the dining room table at the big house. They had suspended everything they had been working on in favor of a simple but tasty buffet lunch. Now the table was cleared, and the children had been put down for naps—or not, depending on the determined child! In any case, Lorie noted with relief, the little ones were being tended and were doing well and causing no problems, realizing that *very serious things* were going on with the "big people" in the house. Randy brought in a stack of leather-covered books. Lorie reached for them and set them on the table in front of her.

"These are the rest of the journals written in English," she said, taking the 1814 volume into her own possession. "Ewen's translators are having a field day with the Zulu books. Jeff and I have gone through those he wrote when he was a child, and you folks who are late to the game will be glad to learn that Isaac has said his final goodbye to the *Black Rose*! Maybe we'll hear more about our new player in these remaining volumes. You've already heard of him. Jeb's kin. Isaac calls him Griffiths."

"These accounts are vital to what we're doing here," Jeff said, taking a seat beside her. "If you find anything of relevance in what you are reading, please speak up. Any takers?"

All hands rose, including those of the computer geniuses, not only relieved to be getting a break from their duties but also eager to be considered full members of the crew.

"Here we go," Lorie said enthusiastically, sorting the books into chronological order and handing them out the same way. "Here's one for you, Jeb, 1815. Next year for Em, 1816. Here's a real pretty one for Rolf, 1817." She looked around. "Ewen?"

"Right here," Ewen said enthusiastically, holding out his hand. "1818?"

"Yep. Jared? You game for 1819?"

"Gung ho!" the mountain climbing genius said, catching the small leather-bound volume she tossed to him.

"Know all about it? 1819?" Bill said to him with a grin.

"Not a damn thing!" Jared shot back, laughing. "But I'm sure as hell willing to learn!"

Books went quickly to the other two wizards, who were just as eager to participate: Ivan first with the 1820 book and Bill the following year. Lorie's stack was diminishing rapidly.

She looked at Randy, who had been momentarily absent and now came in with a sandwich in one hand and a beer in the other. "Randy? We're up to 1822."

Munching away, he put down his beer, grabbed the book, and found a place to sit, nodding between bites.

The 1823 book went to Alexi. Her husband, Guy, eagerly claimed the next.

"And the final one, 1825, for Jeff," Lorie said, putting it into his hand. "That's the last book written in English. After that, it's Zulu talk all the way. Ewen is letting his computers scan those. We've already read some of the earlier books, so

I can catch you up if needed. Here in my hand I've got one written by Isaac when he was eleven. The year was 1814. All right, people, one, two, three—go!"

For some time, the room remained quiet. All that Lorie could hear was the faint whispering of page against page and human breath coming forth in muttered ejaculations as people read of things they had never experienced, didn't much like what they were seeing, or were hopefully impressed.

"Anyone ready to make a report yet?" Lorie asked half an hour later. Her book was a rather more hopeful volume relating the specifics of Isaac's rescue by the American Navy in 1814, and his and Will Deerfield's repatriation and transport back to an America neither of them remembered nor at that point felt any part of. "Chronological order then," she said after getting no enthusiastic response. "Guess I'm up first. You don't need to read Isaac's actual words if you don't want to, people. Just give us an idea of the territory."

She began reading, paraphrasing the written words: "In 1814, Jeb Griffiths was encouraged to join Isaac and Will Deerfield on the American warship, and Isaac noted that Griffiths fast proved himself to be an exceptionally valued addition to the crew." She grinned at Jeb when she read that part.

"Once they reached home shores," she continued, "and discovered that both sets of Will's grandparents were still alive, Jeb Griffiths was hand-selected by Will to accompany Isaac back to his family's home in Georgia."

She moved on, laying out the story in bits and pieces, picking up what she felt were the most important points: it was Will's great sorrow that he could not physically do what he felt was his duty to the boy. But Captain Phineas Spaulding had, in modern-day terms, "grounded" him. Will needed to take time to recover from the loss of his hand, both physically and mentally, and Captain Spaulding knew just the place to go—a Maryland navy hospital with specialists attending. Will was not a happy patient, but his seafaring cousin insisted he would not let Will go anywhere until he had seen all the surgeons he needed to see—the best in the world—and had consulted with whomever might be able to secure a good prosthesis for Will and teach the "stubborn old man" how to use it.

Isaac offered some of his pirate gold to Will's cousin, but the man just smiled at the small boy and told him he had it covered, thank you very much. Isaac wondered why the big man didn't want the little boy's money, which was just as good as anyone's.

Laughing, Lorie informed her audience that Captain Spaulding had no idea how much gold Isaac had stored in that very heavy trunk! Nor did they know to this day, she added with a wry grin, because nobody had yet been willing to open it far enough to do a count.

She went on: the captain was very accommodating to Isaac and his new escort. He helped them to obtain a carriage and a coachman to make the journey to Georgia and smoothed their way with all the necessary documentation, letters to friends they could call upon, addresses of inns willing to accommodate friends of Captain Spaulding for less than their posted rates, and all the maps they needed to find the places they needed to find. He also issued a blanket invitation for them to return and rejoin the crew of the warship if they wished to, informing them he was highly impressed with both.

Isaac was a little nervous about the entire process of entering such a large country. Having lived all the life he remembered clearly either on the sea or in a small French apartment in a very big city near the ocean, he had never been confronted with such a vast expanse of unbroken woodlands as this country seemed to contain, and had real qualms about venturing beyond the confines of the cities or towns.

Lorie read the next section aloud:

> "Are there bears?" I asked Will when I went to the hospital to say goodbye. It was hard for me to stop crying and I was embarrassed about it.
>
> "They are as afraid of you as you are of them," Will Deerfield had said to him, smiling through the many hugs. "Same as with the people you meet, Isaac. But at least the bear is honest about his likes and dislikes. Be very wary, my dear boy. Watch what's going on around you all the time. Remember, the pirates, they are everywhere. You don't see them unless you keep your eyes open. Don't tell people too much, don't let anyone fool you. You are a smart young man, my silent Isaac, and I have every expectation you will get along just fine."
>
> "What if I don't like my grandparents?" Isaac had asked.
>
> "Take this journey one day at a time," Will replied, in Isaac's estimation, more seriously than he had ever been in all their time together. "But don't you forget me, Isaac!"

Isaac had broken down at that point, and tears also came to Lorie's eyes as she read his exact words: "'I started to cry like a baby, hating it but having no control over it. Having lost my parents when I was a little child, I have considered Will as both my father and my mother. I can scarcely bear the thought of being separated now from the only family I have known. If you find something for us, Isaac—maybe a farm where peaches can be raised,'" Lorie read Will's words now with a tremor in her voice, "'see what we can do about purchasing it. As soon as I get out of this damn hospital, I'll join you. You'll not be rid of me so soon!'

"Finally understanding that Will truly intended to join him as soon as he was able, Isaac Preston went bravely out into a big new world, Jeb Griffiths at his side."

Lorie looked up, grinning. "Not bad," she said. "A new life in a new world with a new trusted friend."

Jeb Wallace glowed, realizing that Griffiths was still in the picture. "I'm convinced we was bound to meet sometime, Jeff," he said. With a big smile, Jeff reached out for Jeb's hand. "There's lots in the book I'm reading," Jeb went on warmly, "about the friendship between them."

"Was the bond of friendship broken for a time?" Jeff asked. "It seems pretty solid in this book I'm reading too, but he's saying here that Griffiths has just returned. There are a goodly number of years unaccounted for, I believe."

"The bond was never broken," Jeb replied with a grin. "Just put on hold. And here's the reason..." He turned back to his volume of Isaac's history and paraphrased the words: "In 1815, Griffiths got an official letter from Captain Phineas Spaulding, wondering if he—Griffiths—would join the crew of Spaulding's ship, as he needed an experienced sailor, currently unemployed, to teach raw recruits, and he couldn't think of anyone better! At the same time, Isaac got a letter of his own from the captain, this one with an apology: Captain Spaulding regretted not being able to ask for Isaac's help as he had done for Griffiths. But he wanted to explain. At the age of twelve, Isaac was far younger than any of the men he would be teaching. Isaac understood. Regretfully.

"But he was having a ton of trouble livin' with his father's parents," Jeb went on. "Secretly he was lookin' forward to buildin' a house for himself and Will. Griffiths took Spaulding up on the offer to go back to sea, as he had discovered that he wasn't that much of a farmer. What I suspect," Jeb looked up at Jeff, "is that Griffiths and Isaac simply lost contact during that time—no internet back then, folks. But I'm bettin' it was a good solid friendship, and likely one day we'll find a letter or two that went between them."

Emily added, "This Jeb Griffiths may have been an accomplished storyteller who liked to add a few exaggerations when he was spinning sea tales, but I like him almost as much as I like my Jeb! His heart was pure! The DNA link is strong in this one, my love!" She leaned over and kissed her husband.

"What about the 1816 book?" Rolf asked Em, who was next in line.

"Not much action," Em replied, "except in Isaac's bright little thirteen-year-old noggin'. Because he had not yet attained his full height, poor Isaac was treated as a child by both sets of grandparents. They couldn't get their heads around the fact that he'd been plunged into the school of very hard knocks when he was only five. He didn't need all the *crap*—excuse the expression, folks," Em looked up with a smile as everyone laughed and continued, "that his grandparents were trying to foist off on him. Slavery was the big thing"—now Em became serious—"especially their excuses for it. He found the treatment of black people appalling, the whippings, the constant humiliation, the maiming of those who tried to leave. He hated it! He lived with his father's folks for a while, and when he couldn't stand it any more than they could, he switched to the other.

"The root of the trouble was the same in both houses. Isaac took issue both with slavery and being told what to do as if he were a child. Except aboard a ship, he was pretty much used to doing what he wanted. More than that, he longed to get personally acquainted with the African populations at both plantation homes. He was conversant in a number of African languages, he was familiar with many of the complex African cultures, and he knew where most black and brown people originated on the African continent by the way they talked and looked. For his grandparents, those kinds of conversations were forbidden. He couldn't understand why.

"From the cradle, he knew how his parents felt about slavery, and from personal observation, whatever stigma was attached by many of the members of the white race to skin color or facial characteristics was simply a nonstarter with him. What he hadn't known and quickly picked up on," Em finally concluded, "was that his grandparents' acceptance of the Southern norm and the way they treated their own slaves had been the driving force behind his parents' determination to search for cotton products produced without the use of slave labor. Everyone was uncomfortable when young Isaac made his father's oft-declared hatred of slavery crystal clear to his grandparents or when he recalled syllable by syllable the last six words he had heard from his mother's lips as she leaped from the ship into the sea—words, he says, that were burned into his very being—'I will never be a slave!'

"Then," Em said with a huge grin, "he was approached by a group trying to help slaves escape to the north. From that moment, he had a calling."

Surprised, Jeff turned to Lorie. "I never knew Father set his goal that early on!" he said softly. "I thought the Freedom Road was Mother's idea!"

Three heads popped up. "Oops!" Lorie said softly. The genius trio had not yet been let in on Jeff's secret. They were the realists, even more so than Ewen: engineers, scientists, mathematicians. They would surely consider Jeff delusional—would it make a difference to their willingness to help?"

"Your multi-great-grandfather, Jeff," Rolf said quickly, holding up his book dated 1817, "learned about the Freedom Road less than a year after his return to Georgia, and at the end of his first year, he was completely involved." He paused, "But I must digress for a moment to let you folks in on a secret known only to my close kin. During the Second World War, my own mother was a guide for fugitives trying to escape Italy into Switzerland."

Those words accomplished their goal. Every face turned to Rolf, and with a relieved sigh, Lorie resumed her note-taking. Rolf, as the old saying goes, had them wrapped around his little finger now—attention riveted!

"My mother's *clients*," Rolf continued, "were spies from the Western Alliance or downed American airmen—sometimes the same thing—who needed to get across the Italian border into noncombatant Switzerland. Jon Randolph Third was one of the airmen she rescued." Rolf seldom told his own story, and he chuckled at the surprise it aroused. "And I am the ultimate result of that meeting. Such a coincidence it is that this parallel book is the one I have drawn."

Rolf returned to his nineteenth-century report with an awed audience, his faint European accent simply reinforcing the Old World roots of his great-great-grandfather Isaac—not because Isaac had been born in Europe but because he had out of necessity grown up there.

But the story Rolf relayed was of Isaac's entry into a world of intrigue once he returned to his homeland, the world of the Freedom Road.

Lorie had to admit she felt privileged to hear once more a few of the secrets Rolf seldom revealed, relating it this time in relationship to his own ancestor's experience.

Rolf continued: Isaac learned much in conversations with the slaves on his paternal grandfather's plantation, in many cases in their own languages. He had to be careful that his grandparents didn't catch on to what he was doing, or he would without question have been sent away to school. That was the last thing he wanted.

After he shifted caregivers because his father's parents decided they just couldn't deal with their *willful* grandson, his maternal grandparents also began to notice that many times he was not around when they wanted him. Since none of their own slaves had disappeared, they never related his absences to their neighbors' missing slaves, but there was a reason for that. Isaac knew when to be where he needed to be. Nothing was left to chance.

Still, his maternal grandparents felt he needed formal schooling. They preferred, however, that it be done at home. They had taken great pride in their only child. They still mourned her, and now, by God's grace, a part of her had been given back to them: her handsome but very undisciplined child. They vowed they would do their best to raise him as she would have done. He knew all this and he sympathized with them because he still remembered, as did they, her beautiful blue eyes and the warmth of her loving arms.

Most of the children in their part of the country were being taught by tutors, so he was furnished a tutor. For his grandparents' sake, he tried his best.

Isaac already spoke colloquial French, Italian and Spanish fluently, some German, and classical English— Shakespeare was his favorite. He also knew mostly American slang and profanities that were in use aboard the *Black Rose*. He didn't tell his grandparents or his tutor, but he knew enough to get along in dozens more languages than they were aware of, and although he hadn't realized right away that languages all had formal structures behind them, he could speak or write enough to get by at least in the most prevalent of those languages.

The language tutor arrived, but when that worthy realized that Isaac's knowledge and skill in the tongues his grandparents thought he should know was of greater depth and facility than that of his own, he resigned.

Isaac's knowledge of mathematics, hard won by his daily handling of lengths of ropes that had to be exact, as well as working nightly with the navigator to make sure the ship was on a correct course, far exceeded the simple practicality of any tutor's lessons, as the subsequent tutor discovered. That tutor also discovered that Isaac knew a great deal about astronomy!

Intrigued, that brave soul persisted when it came to geography and history. But old sailors' reminiscences of journeys around the Equator or the Horn of Africa, about battles fought in unexplored places, personal yarns containing much of the seafaring history of countries bounding the Mediterranean, and, in Isaac's case, cautious forays up the coast of France and across to the British Isles a time or two to take on supplies not easily purchased from suspicious vendors elsewhere had helped give Isaac a decent sense of European geography as well as history. Isaac's tutor threw up his hands when he realized how much Isaac knew about Europe.

"But not America," Rolf concluded. "Isaac's knowledge of American history had fallen into a dark hole. So the intrepid tutor changed his approach and bore down on the history of the United States. He proceeded to teach the young man what he had missed during the years he had been abroad. Isaac was fascinated. He asked for books and got them. He asked for maps and got them. The tutor was pleased at the progress his young charge was making. What he didn't know was that Isaac had a driving agenda of his own.

"What he learned," Rolf concluded as he put the book down, "was that while he found the motives of the Founders of his home country laudable—political freedom for every citizen—that simply did not go far enough. Slavery had mostly been abolished in the Northern States, but where he lived, slaves were not considered citizens nor, in some cases, humans! That was unacceptable!"

No one spoke for a moment. After a short period of introspection, conversation, and questioning, Lorie announced that it was time for Ewen's report. The date on the front of his volume was 1818.

"Isaac is growing up," Ewen began. "He turned fourteen in early spring, and he's quickly gaining height and weight, much to his delight. He's also pleased to discover that as his beard begins to erupt, he's being mistaken for a grownup. During the time of this book, he is still being tutored at his maternal grandparents' home. Because he's doing so well in his studies, his mother's parents are now willing to give him more leeway about taking jaunts about the countryside on their riding horses or in one of the carriages. During one of those field trips, he finds what he thinks is a suitable piece of property for himself and Will."

Ewen looked up and around the table. "Folks, the property he's talking about is Riverside Plantation. It's on the

Chattahoochee River, he says. There's a space on a bluff, high enough above the river that if he builds something there, it won't get flooded. He writes about peach trees and he begins to ask questions about how to care for them."

Ewen skipped to another page and continued, "Will Deerfield is still living at his cousin's home in Annapolis, being taken care of during the captain's many absences by Captain Spaulding's efficient and well-meaning wife. But Will has gone into a deep depression, Isaac says. Isaac had received a letter to that effect from the captain, and our boy thinks he knows the cure. He's determined to travel to Annapolis to pick up Will and bring him back to Georgia."

"The rest of the book contains sketch after detailed sketch of the plantation house he proposes to build, the flower gardens he will put around it, the peach orchard he will create, and the kitchen gardens he will grow to support the two of them and whatever helpers they might need—free men and women, he says, who will get decent wages. He talks about having sheep and pigs and a few cows for milking and beautiful horses to pull the carriages."

"He manages through intermediaries to buy the property at a good price—in pirate gold, of course—unbeknownst to either set of grandparents. Very shortly, with the help of a few of his friends, including at least two of his paternal grandfather's house slaves whom he has bought through an intermediary and freed and to whom he is now paying a living wage…" Ewen looked up, grinning into the eruption of laughter. He lifted his thumb in agreement and continued, "The house starts to take shape. After several months work, when he feels it's ready for occupancy, he finalizes his plans to travel to Annapolis and bring Will back."

Guy interrupted, "This is a fourteen-year-old boy?"

"Fourteen going on forty." Ewen chuckled. "The lovely thing is, he succeeds! The rest of the book is about his trip to Annapolis in the fall of the year in his maternal grandparents' best carriage. It's quite a large carriage, actually, pulled by two horses. He has rationalized the use of it by telling his maternal grandparents he will have to bring all Will's possessions back with him!

"They are very worried, since he has told them he must take this journey by himself. He says to them very rationally that he has faced down pirates and thinks he knows fairly well how to take care of himself, thank you very much! With reluctance, they finally agree. He's never really given them any trouble. When he leaves, however, he takes two escaping slaves with him concealed in the space usually allocated for luggage.

"Not his grandparents' property, however. He thought that might be pushing it too far!" This again brought about a roomful of laughter.

"Finally," Ewen went on, "he describes his tearful reunion with Will Deerfield, and then he recounts the interesting and occasionally hazardous trip they make back to the plantation house. He thinks Will looks terrible when he first sees him, gaunt and all pulled into himself. But as they begin to travel south—in the relative comfort of his grandparents' best—the older man's spirits begin to revive. He's laughing and joking again and telling old sea tales he has told many times before, and by the time they arrive at Riverside in early fall, this Will is way more like the *old* Will that Isaac remembers from his *pirate* years."

There was clapping and hollering in the room, and all the children, including Saree, poked their heads around the corner to see what was going on.

Jeff swept his daughter up into his arms. "Little one," he said, "your grandfather has proved to be one of the finest and most intrepid people I have ever known."

Grinning happily, she hugged her daddy and then reached out for Rolf, who took her into his own arms with a big laugh and gave her the best hug of her life!

"Hold up!" Lorie said finally, to quiet everyone down. "It's not quite dinnertime yet, the cook tells me," she grinned at Alexi, "but there are some pretty good-looking snacks on the table over there. And do I see some wine?"

CHAPTER 25

A fter a short break, Jared was eagerly on tap to share what he had discovered. Lorie had noticed how avidly the young man was reading his book, pages turned forward and then back, the book itself shifted sideways many times, then another long dip into solid reading.

"1819," he said excitedly. "And I have found out more about escape routes in this book," he said with an expression of reverence Lorie had been hard-pressed to explain until now, "than I've ever known. Do you know how early the effort began to free slaves and how extensive the escape routes were? The Appalachian Trail—an Indian cross-country pathway, of course—but according to this book, it was also an important escape route to freedom from where our own personal heroes were located. Harriet Tubman's name is associated with it, she called herself Moses, you know. And now Isaac and his friends are doing it too! With the assistance of their own Moses."

He continued, "I've been on that trail many times. It's rough when you don't have hiking boots and proper gear. Even if a person knows one area really well, they'd still need guides farther along—someone who knows where travelers can get food and water and a bed to sleep in—and the names of reliable ferry-boat men at river crossings, people who put their lives on the line to get fugitives to safe havens. Without all these brave unnamed folks, fugitives might have got lost or been drowned or starved to death. There were wild animals out there too—bears, panthers, who knows what? Escapees could easily have become victims when you think of how wild the country was back then!"

"Many probably perished," Jeff said softly, "for lack of local guides."

The mountain climber nodded. "There were other routes to the North, though, aside from our trail," Jared went on thoughtfully. "In this book, Isaac describes guides pretending to be businessmen who suddenly have a pressing need to bring black apprentices or secretaries with them when they travel to the north on business. Proper identification papers were always required! Making *papers* was an occasional occupation for sympathetic artists back then. A hazardous profession, but believe it or not, this little book indicates that our Isaac was very good at it!

"I also found lists here of the locations of houses—coded, of course—where fugitives could be hidden in attics or crawl spaces during the day, then sent out during the night with fresh guides to get them to the next safe house, another place to get some food or to sleep.

"It was virtually—no, not virtually—*physically* impossible to make it to the north alone, and I'm blown away by the number of people involved in this effort, both black and white, who never spoke of it after the war. It wasn't because they were ashamed of it! I know for a fact that some were privately quite proud of their efforts. But fear of slave-owner associations like the KKK forced them to keep their mouths shut. Even after emancipation, lives and livelihoods would have been in danger if people had spoken aloud what they had been doing not only during the war but for many hazardous years before and after!

"Isaac has put coded trail maps into this book showing where some of the hiding places are located. He's also got code names of guides and other useful stuff, if it could be translated. I'd like a copy of this book, if you don't mind, folks, to add to my research. I know I don't look it," the young mountain climber then added, "but I have black roots, along with my white. My great-great-great-grandmother was a mostly black slave who was spirited out of the South by a young man who loved her enough to take her North and marry her. Legitimately! And have six children with her. He defied his family to do it, and I'm proud as hell of him! He saw to it they all went to college, by the way, and that they got good jobs afterward!"

Again, the readers erupted in clapping and shouts, and again, the children came to see what was happening, as did Doggy.

"It's okay," Lorie said to her daughter, seeing the worry on Saree's face. "Big people sometimes get excited because of good things!"

Saree looked up into her mother's eyes and grinned in what now seemed complete understanding. "Football?" she said.

"Something like that," Lorie said with a laugh. She leaned down to give a big hug to her dear little daughter.

Ivan, the married genius, was up next. "In 1820," he said, "when spring finally comes, Isaac decides to made a break with his grandparents—to their great relief, I expect—and moves into the brand-new Riverside house with his good friend, Will Deerfield. They begin to put in peach trees, many varieties, to see what might work best. They plant some cotton but consider the effort a little too time-intensive. So they get some sheep. That seems to work really well. The sheep are thriving, but they realize they have a lot more to learn about sheep. So they hire a sheep man and a couple of Indian ladies who have spent lots of time weaving beautiful woolens.

"Since he can't fully participate, Will Deerfield is finding it hard to deal with his life. One day, while he and Isaac are watching the weavers, however, Isaac comes up with a way for Will to handle some of the weaving himself. They rig a device which makes it relatively easy for Will to work left-handed, with the assistance of a hook strapped to the leather hand his sea captain cousin has purchased for him. Sometimes he has the help of one of the Indian ladies, who is pleased with his innovations. She's pretty, she's patient, and Isaac notes that she smiles at Will a lot. Isaac wonders if love is in bloom, at least on Will's side, but he doesn't want to ask.

"There are many sketches in here of machines Isaac is trying to come up with so Will can work with the leather hand. Will is trying different ways to utilize it—he wants to make colorful rugs, Isaac says. Or wall hangings. At the end of the book, Isaac has left some watercolor pictures of a number of the small rugs Will made during that first year. It looks as if Will's doing a damned good job of it. At that point, they both seem very pleased about his progress.

"Will is also pleased when his sea captain cousin and the cousin's sympathetic wife come to visit at Christmastime. They are quite enthusiastic about the plantation, about the canned peaches produced from their first crop, about all the woolen artwork and the extensive gardens. They are so pleased they ask Isaac if they can buy in. Isaac bristles. He assumes they feel he's getting in too deep and is on the path to failure. His pride gets too much in the way, and he turns them down—quite politely, however. That's when Captain Phineas Spaulding drops the bombshell!"

There was an extensive sigh at the use of that word. But Ivan was quick to explain: "No, no! That's not what I mean! Captain Spaulding tells Isaac that he has submitted Isaac Preston's name for an appointment to the United States Military Academy, and with a big smile, he informs Isaac that he has been accepted. Isaac is dumbstruck. He had never even considered that as an option!"

After a round of complete silence, the room again erupted with shouts and cheers. No children appeared this time. Only Doggy came to see what the fuss was all about. He stood beside Lorie, giving her his funny little grin. She picked him up, hugged him for a time, and handed him to Jeff, who also gave a round of hugs and ear scratches.

"Good for you, Isaac!" Lorie whispered when she took him back, and Doggy reciprocated by licking her ear.

Bill was up next, the red-haired super-genius. "1821. West Point, cover to cover," he said. "Early in the year, Isaac is still working with Will, trying to get everything pulled together so things will go well during his absence. One of the things I think we've learned about Isaac is that he understands people sufficiently that when he picks someone to do something, he pretty much makes the right choice first time around."

"I'll agree with that," Jeff said softly, and Bill looked up for a moment with a small smile and quickly turned back to the book.

"He tries to persuade Captain and Mrs. Spaulding to stay with Will at the plantation at least during the first year of his absence, and they have graciously agreed," Bill went on. "The drill at West Point, once he gets there, sounds like double what I went through at boot camp! But he's been through the mill many times, our Isaac! He takes it all in stride and actually seems to enjoy it. He is still amazed—yes, amazed—that he's one of the selected few. After what he's been through, he's riding high.

"I'd consider him a modest kid for the most part, and he's not much of a talker, as we realize from his early years, but he makes lots of friends, and we'll just see as we go along whether or not most of them stay friends with him throughout their careers. The way he talks, he's the kind of person who'd be a really good candidate for our little group of conspirators."

Bill looked around the room, grinned, and added, "Nothing more of note—it's a working diary, it seems. He's probably using the pages more as a study guide than anything else. Chances are, his letters to Will and Captain Spaulding tell more of his life at West Point than this book does."

"If we could find them," Lorie said softly. "So much seems to have been lost in that big fire at the plantation house during the Civil War, that horrible night when Sara's whole remaining family died! Randy, how about your book?"

"Ditto on the study guide description," Randy concurred. "Some pretty specific stuff in this 1822 book, including mathematics I didn't know existed back in those days. They were learning to be engineers, weren't they?"

"In order to be a general," Jeff put in, "you have to think the way engineers do. There are many moving parts to a battle campaign. A general has to have at least an idea of where everything is at every moment and what it's supposed to be doing there."

"Well," Randy put in, "he's not a general yet, and he's lost track of what's been happening at home, and I think he's more than a little concerned about what's going on back there. Apparently, he got a letter from Will saying that strangers have been moving in around them. Apparently, Will has had nightmares about The Compact catching up with him one day, and now he's afraid his hiding place has been discovered. He feels the Spauldings might be in danger too.

"The Spauldings don't appear to be particularly worried, but they have summoned a few extra friends of theirs to join them, friends with black faces. These guys are pretending to be house servants but are in fact military aides, armed guards! Six of them! That's reassuring to Will. He doesn't want his cousins to be caught in the line of fire.

"But Isaac is now more concerned about Will than about the Spauldings. He wonders about coming home. Will won't let Isaac even think of quitting." Chuckling, Randy continued, "In addition, the Spauldings throw some weight around, and a few relatively trashy people move out when other people a little higher up on the social scale offer top dollar for their property. Then somehow all that property gets deeded over to Will, so the plantation grows by leaps and bounds during Isaac's absence, thanks to the Spauldings.

"Aside from that, most of the book is about life at West Point. Isaac's a tough kid, and he not only takes it, he eats it up!"

Lorie looked up at Randy. "That's it?"

"Can't be," Randy said. "Who comes next?"

Lorie turned to Alexi. "How about it?" she said.

"I really like this guy," Alexi responded, holding up her book. "He's so old-fashioned about his approach to girls."

"This is 1822 we're talking about!" Randy pointed out with a big laugh. "He *is* old-fashioned!"

"Well," she shot back with spirit, "it's refreshing to read it in a young man's own words! And," she added emphatically, "it's nice to see him admiring people for their attributes rather than simply their looks!"

"For instance?" Emily asked, a smile playing about her lips.

"It's still Christmas break when he's writing this. He's talking about a party he went to in Boston at the home of one of his West Point friends, a guy named Andrew Lewis. A lot of girls were there, including Andrew's sister, Margaret. According to this book, she's very pretty and also smart as a whip and knowledgeable about all the current politics, literature, and music.

"Later he escorts her to a dance at the home of another West Point friend, and they have a terrific time. It's his first time dancing, and she has a terrible time teaching him. She does it slowly with lots of laughter, and he says here he's finally getting the idea. He's very interested in her and says he'd like to meet her again."

"My mother's name was Rachel," Jeff said softly to Lorie.

"I know," she whispered. "When did they get married?"

"In 1832. Ten years to go."

"When was your mother born?"

"In 1812. Okay, I get your point." He grinned at her and squeezed her hand. "He deserves a little fun," he whispered.

"But this is the interesting part," Alexi went on, oblivious to the footnotes being discussed privately. "He says he really likes Margaret, but when he picks her up at Andrew's home on their second date and he's introduced to her younger sister, Rachel, he's 'blown away.'" Alexi looked up, grinning. "He didn't say it that way, actually, but the way he talks about her, it's obvious."

She turned back to the book and began to read aloud. "'Rachel has hair like gossamer and a smile like an angel and the most beautiful blue eyes I've ever seen. The only problem is, Rachel is only ten years old!'" Alexi laughed. "He writes later, 'When this young lady grows up, I am going to find her again and ask her to marry me. All my children must have eyes as beautiful as hers. And she is the model of decorum, which I think is rare for a child that young.'"

Lorie laughed along with Alexi and squeezed Jeff's hand. "She's got him!" she whispered.

Alexi continued, "Most of the rest of the book is about classes and drilling and learning how to be an officer. I don't see anything else of great significance here, although some of you who know more about what you're looking for than I do might want to skim through it. I was very impressed by this young man, however. He's articulate and interested in just about everything."

Guy agreed with his wife. "Nothing of great interest here during 1824 but classes, classes, classes, marching, marching, marching, and drilling, drilling, drilling. Some dances and other social events now and then. Nothing of immediate interest that I can see. He's beginning to write letters, he says, to his young lady friend in Boston." Guy looked up and around and grinned. "She has blue eyes and she is interested in kittens, so he paints kitten pictures to send to her and pictures of cadets in uniform." He turned back to the small book. "Isaac also reports he's heard from Georgia several times, sometimes from Will Deerfield, sometimes from his grandparents, and all seems to be going well. Peaches are growing like crazy, they're being picked and processed, lots of wool products are being produced and sold. The neighborhood is stable again, the larder is full, and all is golden with Will and with the cousins.

"When December rolls around, Isaac gets to come home for a couple of weeks. Will is doing exceedingly well, although he's coughing more than Isaac thinks is good for him, and he won't take any patent medicines for it. The Spauldings are also doing well. Both sets of grandparents are thriving—although the hated slavery continues—with occasional local escapes, much to his grandparents' mystification and chagrin." Guy concluded his book with a laugh. "He is reassured on all fronts. And then the book ends."

Jeff picked up his volume. "1825. Last one in English," he declared. "Momentous year—graduation! Diploma granted! Hats thrown in the air! He's not the top graduate in the class—he's been a little too feisty sometimes to claim that position, and some of his classwork has been a bit slack—but he's got the most exciting assignment he can possibly imagine for a newly graduated officer. For the next two years, he will be on detached duty. The staff at West Point has picked up on the fact that he's a linguist and excellent at disguises!

"They want him to do undercover work for them, specifically in the western part of the country. His assignment is to learn as many of the native Indian dialects as he can so he can help the army negotiate with the tribes. Sounds a bit hazardous to me, but obviously he survived!

"The last half of this book is written in Zulu, and I do not speak nor read Zulu with any great facility. So this will go to our good friend Ewen's translators so we can discover what happened to Isaac during the remainder of this year!"

"Time to fix dinner then," Alexi said, rising finally to her feet. "And, Jeff, I must thank you for one of the most riveting ventures I have ever taken into history. It was blah-blah-blah to me when I took it in school. This young man has certainly made it come alive!"

"You are most welcome," Jeff said, grinning at her. Smiling, she disappeared into the kitchen, Emily and Jeb right behind her. Guy and his father also excused themselves, saying they thought the proposed menu seemed a bit too spare in view of all the menfolk being fed this time around, plus all the little ones involved, and the ladies might need help pulling it all together.

CHAPTER 26

Wednesday evening, April 20, 2016

When Lorie got up to join the women, Jeff held out his hand. "Please stay," he said softly. "I'm still reeling from all that I've heard about my father. I need you to help me put my thoughts into perspective. You are my anchor in this world, Mrs. Preston-Maratti-Randolph…and my shield." He took her hands into his. His expressive eyes were filling with tears. She, who relied so much upon his strength during these often dark times, had not quite realized how vulnerable he still was. She sank back onto the couch beside him.

"See!" Lorie heard Jared say quietly to his compatriots. Since the books had been put away, they had been huddled together in a corner of the room, talking under their breaths. "It happens all the time when he thinks no outsiders are listening. He just did it again!" He looked up, saw Jeff returning the look, and frowned. "We're smarter than we look, sir! And our ears are as well tuned as our brains! Isaac really was your father, wasn't he, Major Preston?"

Lorie sucked in her breath, but her husband simply gave her hand a quick squeeze and turned to face the genius trio. "Can you actually believe something that unbelievable, Jared?" he asked.

"We do unbelievable stuff every day," the mountain climber responded. "It works because it's fact-based. If one knows what the facts are and how different pieces of hardware and software relate to each other and if a person has a creative flair, one can do remarkable things."

"We're all into science fiction too," Bill, the redhead, explained, "because, who knows, one day some of those screwy ideas thrown out by science-savvy writers might actually turn out to be feasible! It has actually happened! But this...?"

Jeff grinned disarmingly. "If you were to do a background check on my DNA, fellows, you would be reassured that I am Rolf's grandson, Jeff Maratti. Rolf is a grandfather to be treasured. His son, Carl, is my father, a terrific guy with a loving heart. Just to clarify, we call ourselves Maratti rather than Randolph to protect the family from The Compact."

Lorie saw the glance he gave his present-day grandfather, who was at this moment sitting at the other end of the same couch, sharing a secret with a giggling Saree. She knew Jeff would not say more to these newcomers unless Rolf was comfortable about divulging their inexplicable double bond.

Rolf gave Saree a quick parting hug, watched her totter fearlessly away, curls bouncing atop her head, and leaned back, grinning at the genius trio. "Why don't you just lay it out, Jeff?" he said with a nod. "After all they've done for us, these fellows deserve to be let in on our little family conundrum. Perhaps they can someday explain it."

"I can try," Jeff said, the question in his tone relaying the possibility that there might be no explanation available—not to scientists, at any rate.

The young men who comprised what Lorie called the genius trio pulled their chairs closer, clustering around Jeff almost as a single unbroken entity. Lorie moved even closer to Rolf, away from the tight huddle at the other end.

Jeff was quiet for a time. Lorie thought he was searching for a reasonable explanation that might make sense to these bright young men because, frankly speaking, none of it had ever made sense to her. It was just what it was!

Finally, he began, "My brain, the flesh and blood brain of Jeff Maratti, was seriously damaged in combat in Afghanistan several years ago. Those injuries and those memories were almost unbearable for the Jeff Maratti I was then, every day drawing me away from sanity and closer to the raw edge of madness."

"We understand that," Ivan added softly. "We've wondered if it's a factor…not that you've shown any sign of dementia…way far from it, actually! It's just that sometimes…"

There was another moment of silent contemplation from Jeff, respectfully waiting on the other side.

"Gentlemen," he said finally, "I will give you a very short explanation of the situation as I understand it. I was kidnapped by members of The Compact two years ago, taken forcibly from an army rehab center where I was undergoing treatment for wounds I had sustained overseas. I was held for ransom. Treated roughly. During that time, perhaps to compensate for the fear and pain I was experiencing, I became another person—someone I admired greatly.

"He was someone whose journals I had devoured eagerly when, as a child, I was visiting my great-grandfather. The books were stacked in the corner of a secret room I had just come across. As I read them, I grew to admire the writer and wanted to be just like him. He had been a soldier, a good soldier, loathe to kill or maim but with an honorable goal in his sights, an end to slavery once and for all. His own memories were clean of the torture I later endured while I was being held captive by our current enemies. Many of the memories I bear now, for better or worse, seem to be those of that distant relative, Jefferson Richard Preston."

Lorie saw three faces looking at her Jeff with doubt in their expressions, wondering how he could claim as fact such bare-faced fiction. What surprised her was their willingness to believe anything more than what he said. Even she still wondered where the truth actually lay.

Bill spoke first in an awed kind of voice. "If you really have those memories, Jeff, then there are a few things I'm dying to ask you. Do you mind?"

Medical stuff, Lorie supposed, these men were scientists above all, searching for real-world explanations: what kind of brain, for instance, could experience the slings and arrows of active battle yet manage to avoid the traumatic brain damage that had crippled so many veterans over the years? It took no more than two seconds into Bill's question for Lorie to realize that was not where this conversation was heading!

"From what I've heard about it," Bill continued eagerly, "Isaac was tight with the architect who built the house we've just located. I couldn't understand at first why a black architect would sign a building contract with this Compact organization. But now I think I'm beginning to get the bigger picture! I was just going at it from the wrong end.

"The Compact people needed an architect, a really good one if they wanted to have secret rooms and so forth. But it had to be someone who was *expendable*, didn't it? How devious they were to seek out a black architect who was an expert on hidden features. He could be ambushed afterward, and no one would look very hard for the murderer!

"But this black architect was slipping one over on 'em all that time, wasn't he—this Moses fellow? Constructing escape routes we're finding every time we turn around, secret tunnels, concealed doorways. The Compact people sure weren't trying to help slaves escape to the north, we know that! But somebody was doing it out of this house big-time!"

"Escape routes?" Jeff asked, looking a bit blank. He wasn't pretending a thing right now. Lorie drew in a long breath.

Rolf looked at her and grinned. She relaxed, took a deep breath, recalibrated her thinking. Quietly Rolf raised his thumb. Grinning at him, she returned the motion.

"That crooked drainpipe," Bill now persisted, "is certainly large enough to accommodate several escaping slaves for a night or two in complete safety because no water can get into it, much less out! Unless it's Noah's flood on the Potomac, which never happens! But people can get out of that place quite easily once they're let into the pipe because all the screws for the drain covers are on the inside of the pipe, not the outside, and little screwdrivers for those screws are attached on the inside, one to each of the grates. I bet nobody who lived there ever knew that. We found out because our drones saw them from the inside."

"And that odd bend in the line," he added, talking across Ivan, who was increasingly eager to break in, "it points directly north toward one of the primary underground routes I've been mapping. Underground trails are a hobby of mine. A passion, really! One of my ancestors escaped along this route!"

Ivan began speaking in an excited voice the second Jared's voice ceased. "We know the architect of the house was a Zulu prince named Ukuhlakanipho." Lorie realized with shock that the tall man's rendition of the name was spot-on perfect. "It's a Zulu word that translates more as 'wisdom' than anything else. I knew we were onto something when we found his symbols on these etchings. He was an accomplished artist, you see, besides being a noted architect.

"My wife and I saw some of his fabulous paintings when we were in South Africa on our honeymoon two years ago. I was so taken by them I've been putting out feelers to purchase more. I have a pretty good collection already, and I suspect there are lots more to be found. It was apparent he'd been in the Deep South of this country, as several of his paintings were of Africans working on cotton plantations. Nobody was ever able to explain to me how an African prince came to be painting views of slavery from a Southern plantation! But they told me," he went on, much more deliberately now, "in fact, it was rumored—even there in that little art shop in Johannesburg, South Africa—that he had been a guide on the Underground Railroad in America. No one in the shop knew what had happened to him, as there is no record of his ever having returned to South Africa. Was he in Georgia pre-Civil War? Was he actually working the Underground?"

Now his voice went low, solemn. "I didn't really want to bring it up, Jeff, but another of my South African etchings is of a young white man who looks exactly like you, sitting just the way you sit, looking off into the distance the way you often do. It's signed by someone calling himself Moses. The identifying mark on Moses's etching—I call it his *brand*—is exactly like the symbol the person you call Ukuhlakanipho puts on his paintings. A little gazelle. Three or four swift small marks, and there it is. When I remembered that, everything came together for me! I've been trying to tell these guys that we're working with the real Major Preston. They've never believed me!"

"Until now!" Jared said.

"Likewise!" red-haired Bill echoed. "And I've also got quite a few questions to ask you myself."

Lorie saw Randy step quietly into the room. He had been helping in the kitchen. A dishtowel was dangling from his fingers. He stood silent by the door, watching, listening.

Into the waiting silence, Jeff said softly, "Moses helped us set up several of the routes that were used on the Georgia section of the Freedom Road."

It was as if a soundless bomb had just exploded. Three sets of eyes opened wide. Mouths dropped open. Their wish had just been granted!

CHAPTER 27

L orie saw Rolf lean forward, watching his grandson, listening carefully.

Jeff continued, "He had the assistance of many sympathetic whites, freed Africans trying to make do on little or nothing, and especially Native Americans who were furious that their Indian brothers and sisters had been *cleared* from the eastern woodlands that had been their home for centuries, and forced to walk hundreds of miles to the treeless expanses of the west—in chains."

"The Trail of Tears, they called it," Bill said softly, nodding, "because so many died on the way to Oklahoma and points west. That whole episode was a travesty and a crime to humanity! But what happened to him, this man called Moses? He seems to have met the same fate. Did you ever meet him, Major Preston?"

"In what I now call my first life," Jeff began carefully, glancing across at Rolf, who gave him a solemn nod, "I knew him as a friend and mentor, as had my father, Isaac."

The three young men looked at each other and nodded in unison.

"Moses was a very big man in many ways," Jeff went on. "A kind and loving soul with the heart of a teacher and the most talented artist and architect I have ever been privileged to meet. What happened to Moses when he walked into that carefully planned and executed ambush should happen to no one in what we call a civilized world!"

A long, somewhat uncomfortable silence followed.

"Would you be willing to tell us exactly what happened to him?" Ivan asked in a soft voice.

"I don't like to think on it," Jeff answered in a voice of equal softness, "but the life he led," he cleared his voice when it suddenly broke and swallowed hard, "and his courageous heart and those of his two brave Zulu warriors deserve to be honored by those who see Moses for what he was, someone even I didn't know until now—a brilliant artist, architect and teacher, a consummate warrior, and, above all, a gentleman of distinction who could function with excellence in any society he wished to join."

Ewen had returned to the quiet sunroom. He also was now watching intently.

When Jeff finally spoke, his words reflected a degree of distancing that Lorie had never before heard in his voice. He had tried to put certain memories behind him, locked them away. These people were asking him to unseal the lock, and he feared the pain it would cause him!

She reached out what she hoped was a reassuring hand. Grasping it tightly, as if it were a lifeline, he cleared his throat and again began to speak: "Because of her pregnancy, my young sister Sara returned to our father's house, Riverside, when her husband was dragooned by Confederate recruiters. When she received what she thought was a message from Jonny Randolph saying that he was at Fox Haven, that he'd been wounded and needed her, she was almost frantic to see him, find out why it had taken him so long to contact her, and so forth. She needed to reassure herself of all these things, even though she was very close to her time of delivery.

"Jonny Randolph was a tall, handsome, generous, and principled young man who revered the Constitution and the Union. Even though he was a Southerner born and bred, he was a staunch advocate for Abraham Lincoln and his policies. He hated the institution of slavery. But as frequently happened in the Confederacy, young men in small communities were many times forced—under threat of immediate death—to serve as foot soldiers in an army of secessionists, defending an illegal government they did not support. He knew that if he said no to armed recruiters, he would be shot, and if he deserted after they dragged him away, he would be shot. His only recourse was to march away wearing a gray coat and carrying a rifle on his shoulder with the hope that in actual battle the bullets might miss.

"Sara did not know nor did any of us that Jonny had been killed several months earlier in the Wilderness of Virginia, one of the many young Confederate foot soldiers who lay unclaimed, their bodies moldering and yet unlamented because their families did not know they had already met their fates. On this day, when my father arose from his sickbed and found that Sara and Moses and two of Moses's best men were gone, he immediately sent for me.

"Sergeant Ben Ross and I were preparing for an undercover mission to the Atlanta area to gather information for General Sherman. Confederate grays were tucked inside our saddle blankets. I always left a coded message regarding my current assignment at a signpost checked frequently by my father's aides. My father's caregiver, Rastus, managed to catch us before we reached the Chattahoochee. When he told us Sara had left for Fox Haven, we immediately turned north, fearing the worst.

"The farm was a good day's ride, and Sara and her party had left midmorning. We traveled at top speed to catch up, arriving after sundown. Too late. After a round of needless torture to the three black men, indicating that these marauders were not soldiers of any legitimate army, savage murder had been done. Three naked, bleeding bodies were hanging from a tree, and fire had consumed most of the farm. We buried them together next to that same tree, which has since grown to a mighty size. Its roots cradle what is left of their precious flesh and bones. To me, Fox Haven Farm will always remain a sacred site.

"The battle those brave Zulu warriors waged against a much larger force gave Sara time to reach a place of safety. Ben and I found her in the dark of night, huddled inside one of the hiding places we had created along that trail. She was too grieved even to speak, and her labor was well underway, several weeks ahead of time."

"We discovered an old wagon in some bushes behind the still burning barn, probably the only thing on the farm that hadn't been stolen or destroyed. We hitched our riding horses to it and were taking Sara back to Riverside when, by great good chance, just as morning broke, we encountered Captain Marshall Manning on the trail. He was a West Pointer of my era and a good friend."

"Lorie's relative," Emily said softly. "One of her grandfathers." She had just come quietly into the room, and she sank into a chair beside the fireplace so she could hear more clearly. A moment later, her husband joined her and remained to listen in respectful silence.

Jeff halted for a moment. When he turned to Lorie, she could see his eyes brimming with tears. He wiped at his face with the tissue she held out to him. He cleared his throat and paused for a deep breath. "Captain Manning," he finally said, "had been searching out locals with medical experience, sympathetic Southerners not tied to secession, people willing to assist army physicians at the field hospitals. He had come with a small contingent of troops, for safety's sake. When we told him we were carrying orders from General Sherman, he said he would care for Sara. He and his troops, along with one of his mountain volunteers, a young healer named Elijah Benning, assumed command of the wagon bearing Sara and immediately turned their mounts toward Riverside.

"We cautioned them to be on guard, suspecting Riverside might also have been targeted. Captain Manning sent one of his aides at top speed to request that a relief column be sent to Riverside, and he and young Benning proceeded to take Sara away from Fox Haven Farm.

"The Yankees loaned us two of their own mounts to replace ours, which were still hitched to the wagon. They said they would leave our horses at Riverside in return for the wagon, which seemed a better bargain for us than for them given the condition of our horses at that point."

After a momentary smile at the memory, he went on. "We changed into Confederate gray on the spot and resumed our original assignment. But we were forever dodging Yankee troops that day, wondering why there were so many so far from the field of battle. We thought we were doing well, nevertheless, and that we could get to the river with enough time to cross once the sun went down again. Instead, we were both shot, ironically enough, by Yankee troops.

"I have learned since my return," Jeff continued softly, "that Captain Manning generously took upon himself all the unfinished business Ben and I had been compelled to leave behind. He saw to Ben Ross's family, making sure Ben's wife received the government pension Ben had ably earned. And he cared more than capably for my young sister and her new child. Within two years' time, they fell deeply in love, were married and living in Illinois, far to the north. Marshall was a good father not only to his own first child—whose mother had died upon her son's birth—but to Sara's first son, and to the child he and Sara shared through their own love."

"It wasn't until I read Sara's journals that I discovered her son was born the same night our father was murdered within view of the still smoking ruins of Riverside Plantation, her childhood home. She called the baby Jon Randolph Jr. for her husband, whom she now knew, to be gone forever.

"That child," Jeff said quietly but with significant emphasis, "born on a field of murder and arson, grew to be the brave pilot whose remains we have just put to rest."

Three breaths exhaled as one.

Lorie saw Randy move closer to the now mesmerized group of computer gurus. "Time for a break," Randy said quietly. "Come eat."

Once again, friends gathered around the long table in the kitchen. After a period of thoughtful solemnity, small talk finally returned. Children were fed. Delicious foods were passed around. With nourishment at hand, life gently restored itself. Lorie looked out the window and saw through the pale twilight rain still falling quietly on silent peaceful meadows. Nature, she thought sadly, grieving for all the fallen young men.

CHAPTER 28

—

After dinner, as fathers and others of their sex cleaned up the kitchen, mothers moved to the task of putting their children to bed. As she kissed her sleepy daughter and handed her over to one of the resident babysitters, Lorie could still feel the melancholy now surrounding the entire company of friends.

Shortly thereafter, the men reconvened in the darkened sunroom. Lorie joined them, moving into a snug place beside Jeff on the couch. A very long period of meditative silence lay over the company as they watched flames flare and dance.

Jared, the mountain climber, could finally wait no longer. He said softly to Jeff, "What happened to you that night, Major Preston? If you don't mind my asking, sir."

"I died," Jeff replied matter-of-factly, "as did one of the kindest, bravest, most loyal gentlemen I've ever met—Master Sergeant Ben Ross of the United States Army, my second-in-command. We had been leading a resistance group brought together to protect our small community of Unionists from Georgia Secessionists. That town is now known as Randolph City." He motioned toward Randy, the last kitchen holdout, who had just entered the room with a fragrant cup of coffee in his hand. "Ben was this man's grandfather four or five notches back. Every bit as entertaining to be with as this one, and just about the smartest soldier I have ever had the pleasure of working with."

Randy grinned at Jeff. "Wow," he said. "Why didn't you tell me all this before?"

Lorie smiled to herself as she watched the genius trio take a new admiring look at Randy.

"Ben's death still haunts me, my friend." Lorie strained to hear Jeff's voice; she knew that reviving these memories was very difficult for him, but he was grateful for the work the trio was doing, and he would not deny them their answers. "Ben and I had been asked by General Sherman to assist him as he and General Grant devised their grand plan to split the Confederacy. Our assignment from General Sherman was to infiltrate Confederate lines and gather as much information on their tactics and numbers as we could. He was eager to move on to Atlanta and needed to know the lay of the land.

"A preliminary change of tactics had been made at Kennesaw Mountain, unknown to us. General Sherman would have had no way to find us at that point. Taking a battlefield advantage during the fighting, the general had ordered Yankee troops to move to the east, scouting the best way to get across the Chattahoochee.

"After turning Sara over to Captain Manning that dark night, Ben and I lay low for a time, tired to the bone. On horseback, we worked our way slowly back toward the river, hiding several times during that day to get a little sleep. It wasn't nearly enough. When darkness came again, we made our move—right into a Yankee bivouac. One of their pickets saw our gray coats before we saw his blue. Ben took the first bullet and died instantly.

"I put his body where it would be found and properly identified. I don't remember much about what happened after that, except being suddenly propelled off my mount by another well-placed shot." The stillness in the room lasted too long for Jeff's comfort.

"You were spies, weren't you?" Jared asked softly.

Jeff responded, now in a more normal tone of voice. "Like my father, I was a graduate of the Military Academy. Also like him, I remained on detached duty once my required enlistment was put behind me. It depended entirely on the status of my father's health whether I was away or at home, but when I went out, my missions took me far afield. In answer to your question, yes, I suppose I've always been a spy from early childhood, working on the Underground Railroad." He added softly, "I have worked for freedom for my fellow human beings my entire life. Fighting other Southerners was difficult but necessary because they were so wrong-headed. However, the hardest battle my family has ever been engaged in is this one."

"We want to help," Bill said. "Can you brief us on what's needed right now?"

Gratified by their eager response, he nodded. "As you know, we've just discovered from reading my father's diaries that The Compact was a document forced upon the crew members of the *Black Rose*, a pirate ship sailing the Mediterranean, shortly after that vessel was sunk by a US Navy warship. We are certain that many of the crew members signed with swords at their throats, and we know from folks still caught in its snare that its *rules* or *commandments* or whatever The Compact called them then are even today followed to the letter by its leaders as if they are Gospel. A person's personal commitment to decency is never taken into account.

"The most pernicious part of The Compact, though, is that a person's signature binds not only the signer but his entire family forever! How can such a peremptory, imperious demand be legal? They say it's a valid contract. Surely it's not! Still, we've found that people have been murdered for even thinking of trying to challenge it!

"Compact officers were men of limited natural skill and no conscience. They gave no thought whatsoever to their abandoned crewmembers trapped on a rudderless ship in foreign waters. What angers me the most is that still they demanded that these men, having been rescued by others, commit their souls and their families to the Blackhearts, as they were then calling themselves, by signing a document to that effect in their own blood!

"When the officers of the ship returned to the country of their birth, most were drawn to the Southern states. Slavery equaled big money, so that's where they wanted to be. Once they had drawn their spider webs around various areas where communication with each other was possible, they closed the trap on those who had been compelled to sign their document. It's clear to me, however, that folks enslaved by a dead relative's signature on a document that can't possibly be held legal in any court of law are simply slaves. No more, no less."

Jeb spoke quietly. "Damn right!"

"Despite current laws against such a savage practice," Jeff went on with a nod, "The Compact's demands remain unchallenged and unchanged. No way to challenge, no recourse available. I know that Jeb will agree with me that the harm they are doing to innocent hardworking people is not only criminal but unforgivable. We are here to stop them!"

Questions now bombarded him from every direction. Jeff held up a hand. "Believe me, friends, we are learning many things together. But first, let's get everyone's thoughts straight about the mansion we have just located. At the time the Blackheart mansion was being built, long before the Civil War, only the top officers of The Compact were aware of its

hiding places and secret rooms. Those features were specifically requested by a group called the Inner Circle.

"Moses had been specifically sought after as the architect for this job because he was the leading expert in his field.
He had traveled extensively and had long studied castles, pal-
aces, and stately mansions that contained such rooms. And
he was a noted fabricator of the hardware, which creates the
magic. Years after he designed The Compact's headquarters,
he was the architect who helped me to build what is now
known as Randolph House."

"Why was it so important to have secret passageways
and rooms?" Ivan asked.

Jeff's answer was terse. "The house we have found is
obviously not a home to be lived in. It's a destination created
solely in which to conduct Compact business. It is also most
perniciously a place to ferret out spies and traitors. Remember,
only the people comprising the Inner Circle knew about the
rooms. If from behind the walls any person is overheard speaking of revolution or disloyalty, he is immediately dispatched.

"This was also unfortunately the fate that befell all the
builders and craftsmen who worked on the house. Apparently,
Moses was warned about this wholesale slaughter by someone who admired the architect more than he feared the officers. As soon as they realized what was happening, Moses was
whisked out of sight by loyal friends.

"An unexpected change of plans occurred when my
father intervened, and eventually Moses came to Riverside
Plantation, except for his size looking very unlike the royal
architect Compact members had come to know. I doubt that
even the Fox Haven killers were aware of his true identity.
They simply knew him as a big uppity black slave.

"When Jon Randolph Jr. stole those plans away years
later, I suspect one of his goals was to open The Compact's

secrets to the public. That, of course, was more frightening to the Inner Circle than anything they could imagine. I realize now that they have spent many dollars and many more man hours searching for those plans than John Junior could ever have imagined.

"They are never going to give up this search until they discover what happened to that plane. If it were destroyed by fire, so be it. But if the plane still exists somewhere in these hills, the Inner Circle is fixated on retrieving what Jon Randolph Jr. took away from them."

"In regard to the unexplained drainpipe, however," Jeff added with a laugh that now hinted at humor, "I think you are correct there, gentlemen. Moses must have stumbled on their plans and was taking his small revenge by leaving an Underground station inside their Confederate clubhouse. We will probably never know if the drainpipe was used as a resting place along the Freedom Road, but wouldn't that be ironic? What's more ironic, it should be very easy for us to enter the house using that pipe once we get past the barbed wire, the guards, and the dogs!" He grinned and a chuckle traveled around the room. A nervous sound, Jeff reckoned. But they had faced worse! In this case, they would be met with a virtual handshake.

"When was this house built?" Ivan asked finally.

Ewen answered, "Between 1820 and 1824." He had just reentered the room to see if anyone wanted another drink or something containing calories, either sweet or salty. "An update, folks, now that we know where it's located, we have asked the people in charge if we might be read in on whatever legal information about it is on file. We have just received the first answer to our request. The house is deeded to a group actually called the Blackheart Compact."

Rolf laughed. "At least we're not going to be breaking in on strangers!" He looked up at Ewen. "Do you have a good red?"

"Several," Ewen answered, pointing toward bottles clustered on the sideboard in the sunroom. "Pick your poison and I'll pour!"

"Something the color of blood!"

"Right on!" Ewen hurried to serve drinks all around. "Now let's hear the rest of the story."

Jeff took a sip of wine and continued, "Until I was restored to life, I knew no more of this bloody history than you did. Sometimes I wish I had never asked. I have also come to realize from reviewing the records that had Ben and I got back to Sherman with the information he required, Atlanta would not have been burned. More's the pity! But of more importance now, what I also realize with the greatest of disgust is that the Blackheart savages have yet to be called to account." His voice raised a notch, anger spilling over. "The extent of my current mission is quite clear—dismantle the organization itself, bring justice where it is long overdue, and destroy that damned document!"

"Oh," Randy said wryly, "is that all?" He winked at Lorie, who gave him a thumbs-up signal—all would be well…she hoped!

CHAPTER 29

Early morning, Thursday, April 21, 2016

Lorie woke. Her eyes opened abruptly. An oppressive darkness still enveloped the farm. What had awakened her? Not Jeff. He was lying beside her, his strong face relaxed in peaceful sleep. She heard nothing coming from Saree's room, no whimper, no partial cry.

Then she knew what it was. Silence! No longer was the spring rain pattering down on the horse farm. A feeling of dread enveloped her. Just then, the phone rang!

It was someone named Vince, asking for Jeff.

He pushed himself to his elbow and grabbed the cell phone she held out to him. "Damn!" he said a moment later. "When do you think they'll be in your area?" He waited for a few minutes. "Thanks for the warning, Vince. We'll gather our gear and be on the road before noon latest. Expect us by early evening. Are you sure that's enough time for you folks?" A pause. "We'll do what we can. Call in the park police if you need to, but frankly, I'd rather have an army division." He laughed and added, "Knowing your crew, you may be right, bro!"

"Em's brother," he said to Lorie, handing the phone back. "Searchers from The Compact have found their valley and are setting up tents. It's a good bet they'll spot the cave sometime tomorrow, if they're at all competent. We want to have everything and everybody in place in case they do."

She could not disguise her fears. Had her own wake-up call been a warning? Should she tell Jeff?

He pulled her into his arms and held her close to his chest, brushing her face and hair with tender kisses. "Honey, we're only going to be watching them, monitoring from a distance. There is nothing they can find there but a broken airplane, a sad desiccated corpse, and a lot of skinny flat rocks that shift across each other like they're greased. We will not let them hurt themselves if we can help it, but if they really want to be stupid, we may have to stand by and watch them destroy themselves!" His laugh was hard. "This may well be the end of The Compact, my love. Or if not the end, the beginning of the end!"

"I hope so," she said. "I have a really uneasy feeling this time, Jeff. Way more than I've felt before. Please be double careful...for me and Saree!"

"I know how sound your instincts are, my love," he said quietly. "I will be especially careful, I promise! To the nth degree!"

"Love me," she said to him. It was dark outside the window. There was still time before he had to rise. "Right now, Jeff. I need you right now."

He bent over and kissed her lips softly. His hands moved tenderly up her arms. When they reached her shoulders, he gently lifted the straps of her gown, and in moments, it was gone. He laid her back on the bed and began the kisses only he could give. Lips, eyes, neck, shoulders...she closed her eyes and gave herself over to feelings she had never experienced with anyone but her beloved husband. Surely this was not the last time she would lie with him!

"Do not be afraid, my love," he said softly. "I am stronger than you quite realize."

The next half hour was exquisite. It was something to remember in case he never came back... No, she should not be thinking that way! *Enjoy the moment*, she thought fiercely. *Treasure the moment you are in. Don't think back! Don't think forward! Savor this moment, this moment alone! Revel in it! Give everything you have to give!* Again, she lifted her lips to those of her beloved husband and, sometime later, fell asleep inside his warm encompassing arms.

When the phone rang again, she hesitated before answering. Another sharp ring. She reached for the phone and realized she was alone in the bed.

She grabbed for the phone! "Come give me a kiss before we leave." It was Jeff.

"You're still here? Oh, thank God! Why didn't you wake me!"

"You needed the sleep, love. We're outside in the drive. Ready to go. I want to hold you again before we leave."

"I'll be right there." She took five minutes to beautify and then pulled on slacks and a shirt, covering all with her red sweater. Slipping bare feet into moccasins, she tiptoed into Saree's room, carefully wrapped and lifted her still sleeping child, and made her way out of the house and across the yard to the big barn, where in the early light of dawn she saw a group of men standing beside two dark vans.

Four were dressed for the mountains: Jeff, of course, in black climbing gear; Ewen in clothing reflective of Swiss climbers; Randy also clad in jeans and climbing boots—as always, ready for anything; and Jeb! She was surprised, shocked actually, that he was taking that chance! If anyone of the Searchers recognized him there in the hills, he would be shot on the spot! She saw Emily standing in the doorway, holding her sweet titian-haired Todd. Both were fully dressed. Em's expression was of dread, tears rolling across her cheeks.

Ewen's son was still bringing gear out of the barn, dividing it equally into the luggage space behind the seats of each of the two vans. He was also dressed in climbing gear. Guy was going too? She then saw the young genius, Jared, coming from the bunkhouse, carrying his own mountaineering gear. How many did that make? Six!

Who was left? Were they leaving the women behind? Alone?

Not quite! Bill came out the door of the bunkhouse, followed by Ivan. "Keep in constant contact," Ivan called out. "We're manning computers, radios, and cells 24-7, and you'd better let us know exactly what's happening when it happens, folks, so we can get help to you immediately if it's necessary! Do you all have your headsets? Drones packed?"

Nods all around.

"Does everything work A-okay?"

Again, nods.

Rolf strode out of the house just then. He saw Lorie with her sleepy, tousle-haired child and came, smiling, to relieve her of Saree. "Hello, Mama, and good morning to my little darling," he said, taking his great-grandchild into his arms. "Do you want to give a big kiss to your daddy? He's going to be away for a day or so." He smiled at Lorie, but it was not a reassuring smile—only one of commiseration. He moved toward Jeff.

So Rolf was to stay at the horse farm with them and a communications team of the highest skill. She took great comfort from that.

Then she saw the other men, at least six. A second jeep also arrived. Another. And then another! They were at the fence line, talking with Ewen and Guy. She saw rifles. The men parted, some going one direction along the property line, some the other.

The women and children were not being ignored. They were being placed in safekeeping during what might escalate into a bloodbath if today's outcome did not go the way it should. Suddenly, there was a lump inside her where her stomach had once rested.

She glanced toward the house again. Alexi was standing in the doorway beside Em, wiping at her eyes with a wadded-up tissue. Lorie hurried toward the two women. "Guy's going?" she asked.

"He's a better climber than his father ever was," Alexi said in a broken voice. "He would never forgive himself if anything happened to Grandpa Ewen. I told him it was okay for him to go. Oh, Lorie, how can you stand it?" Lorie put her arms around the young woman and held her for a time until the sobs ceased.

"It's time to end this war," she said to Alexi, stroking her back. "These are the only people who can do it. I've seen how they work. They are brilliant. I'm not going to say everything is going to be automatically okay, Alex, but this is something that has to be done. None of these men has ever shirked a duty he felt was right, and we can't stand in their way!"

"I know," Alexi said. She mopped at her eyes. Resolutely, the ladies moved toward their husbands for what could be their last embrace.

Each husband, Lorie knew, offered words of reassurance. But Lorie had just heard once again the story of how her beloved husband had met his fate the first time! It could happen again just as quickly, as soundlessly, not at the hands of allies to his cause but at the hands of enemies so heartless it was impossible to think of them as rational beings.

She snuggled into Jeff's arms, held her cheek against his chest, and heard his beating heart. "If you have to go out on those ropes, love," she whispered, "please remember how much I love you and need you! Come back to us, you hear?"

"I will always come back to you, Lorie," he said softly. "I promise! But you're in charge of the home guard now, love. You and Rolf. And by the way, those extra troops are Rolf's security guards. After what happened in Randolph City, he's not taking any chances with Ewen's family, his family, or mine!"

"I wish you didn't have to do this," Lorie said, "but I know it's part of your mission. Keep closely in touch! And get back here as soon as you can!"

He pulled himself up straight, clicked his heels, and saluted. "Yes, ma'am!" he said.

She couldn't help it, and a laugh bubbled up in her throat. He swept her into his arms again to give her another loving kiss, and then touching her cheek most tenderly with the tips of his fingers, he turned and walked away toward the van.

"Goodbye," she whispered behind him.

He heard her, turned, and blew her another kiss.

As the men boarded their respective vehicles and rolled almost soundlessly away, headed toward the endless chain of mountains that so prominently dominated the western horizon, Lorie felt a heaviness in her heart. It was a mindless fear—she hoped! Each of those men knew his business. If there were any group of people who could defeat The Compact, they would be the ones. But there were so few of them. So very few...

CHAPTER 30

Midmorning, Thursday, April 21, 2016

As the vans disappeared from the long driveway, she walked slowly back toward the ladies, three of them: Emily, Alexi, and herself.

Rolf was again holding Saree, who was rubbing at her eyes, still wondering why she was outside saying bye-bye to her daddy, who had just got into the car without her. Grandfather gave his granddaughter a big hug. "Let's get some breakfast, little one," he said and turned toward the house.

"Let's get fed!" Alexi said. "After we eat something, we can either worry ourselves sick or do something useful like cleaning the house or washing clothes or ironing."

All three ladies laughed. "Ironing!" Em said, snorting at the thought. "I'm way past that! I'd rather talk!"

"Sounds good to me," Lorie said, realizing that the first option, house cleaning, was exactly where her mind had first taken her.

Good grief! Worry was threatening to overwhelm her good sense!

"Coffee!" she said, chuckling wryly as she reached for the pot. "I wish I could read Zulu so I could go back to the books."

"Doesn't the Defense Department or the CIA have those books?" Alexi asked.

"I think it's a nameless someone else," she replied. "And I don't usually worry about Jeff very much because he's very capable, but this time… Oh, forget it!" She shook her head, resolved to stand strong. "There are six big brave men going over there to help out the Family, and according to Jeff, they've got dozens of people on-site or on call!"

Rolf had by now taken complete charge of Saree. She was sitting sweetly in the baby chair, smiling, laughing, and talking up a storm with Grandpa, who was making little pictures on her tray with small flakes of sugared cereal. Whenever she ate a piece, he replaced it with another flake and another variation on a theme. The giggles were continuous.

"I keep hearing about the Family. What is it, exactly?" Alexi asked, wrapping her hands around a half-filled cup of hot coffee. The kitchen table had already been cleared off, and the dishwasher was swishing away the remains of a substantial breakfast consumed by warrior husbands headed out to battle—if it came to that! Again, Lorie felt her heart turn over!

"Jeff's father, Isaac Preston, had a child by another woman," she answered softly and she started to giggle, thinking about the way Jeff had told her about it, "before he married Rachel. Rachel was Jeff's mother.

"The first child's name was Rosette. Her mother was a young woman named Celé. Last name unknown. Long story there, ladies!"

"Tell us!" Alexi said with excitement in her voice.

"Rachel died along with all but two of her children as a result of germ warfare perpetrated by The Compact. Her only survivors were Jeff and Sara.

"It's the kin of Isaac's first child whom Jeff calls the Family." Lorie reached for one of the few sweet rolls remaining on the plate, refilled her cup with more fresh brew, and seated herself across from Emily. "After that horrible night during the Civil War when everyone but Sara was killed, those people were the only family that poor girl had left."

From a corner of her eye, she spotted a small reddish-brown animal prying open the screen door. Doggy caught her glance and remained poised in place for a moment until Lorie dropped her hand down, holding a small piece of buttered toast. Quickly he scurried across the floor, accepted the toast, and placed himself directly on her feet.

"You're worried, aren't you?" Em said to her softly—a statement, not a question.

"Dreadfully!"

Em again asked, "Because Jeff doesn't like high places?"

"He's terrified of them!" Lorie sighed and put her cup down. "But he'll do whatever it takes. I've seen him. He's the bravest man I've ever met."

"Lorie, I'm not sure exactly what your husband does." This time, it was Alexi asking. It was a question without a question mark, not demanding an answer if one was not offered.

"He's a spy," Lorie said lightly. "It's his family business."

The young woman laughed. "You're teasing me, aren't you?"

"No," Lorie answered, attempts at humor fading. "Unfortunately, his whole purpose in this life is to rid the world of the Blackheart Compact."

Alexi looked hard at Lorie and then she looked at Emily; neither was smiling. "You're not kidding about all this, are you? What I've been told—privately—is that he's a reincarnated soul who has come to rid the world of a pack of bad guys. I thought people were just letting him think that until he finally figures out who he really is after being knocked around somewhere in a combat zone."

"I wish," Lorie said softly.

The young woman turned to Emily. "Do you believe this nonsense too?"

"I have no reason to doubt it, Alex. He knows far too much. He's also trying to bring both halves of Isaac Preston's family together. Rolf's side"—she indicated the elegant older man, who smilingly put up his hand in assent—"and my family's side. I'm part of the Family."

"You two are related?" Alexi said softly. "But, Em, you're…you're partly black, at least, and Rolf's as white as, well, as white as I obviously am."

Now Rolf spoke up, his Italian accent quite distinct this morning. "And both Em and I have Isaac Preston's blood running in our veins. Good blood it is, my dear."

Alexi looked at Rolf. Then she looked back at Em. "So…?" The obvious question was left hanging in the air for a while before Lorie snickered.

"You know what?" she said. "I have no idea how the connection came about! Jeff's never been able to bring himself to tell me. I think it's kind of embarrassing to him. He's told me a skeleton story of their relationship in so many words and left all the good stuff out. Em, do you know why there's a whole second family belonging to Isaac?"

"My family," Emily said, a little gleam coming into her eyes. "Oh, indeed, I do. I know all about it! It's one of the stories we ladies like to relate when there's no one else to gossip about."

"Do you mind...?" Lorie said, eyebrows lifted. "Don't chuckle like that, lady, if you're not going to let us hear the good bits! All I've heard was that Jeff's mother, Rachel, was very angry at Isaac when she first came to Riverside Plantation after her huge society wedding and a long romantic honeymoon and found a little brown baby being wet-nursed by someone not her mother. That was when she first met Rosette and was told that the baby's mother, Celé last name unknown, had been sold by the plantation manager to their next-door neighbor. Word came down that the neighbor was now abusing Celé dreadfully in the most horrible of ways, and Rachel went just as ballistic as Isaac did at the news!"

Em knew all about The Compact's horrible ways. She nodded and said, "And?"

Lorie continued, "Jeff also told me that his mom had deep connections with the Underground—different connections than Isaac's because she was associated with a New England Abolitionist group—so she was able on her own to spirit the beautiful but abused Celé, lately of New Orleans, away from Isaac's neighbor's plantation to a place in West Virginia where Rachel's friends had turned up some of Celé's blood relatives. I have also been told that Celé's true love, Jamie Cormier, was there with them and that Celé and Jamie got married, and that was that!

"But poor Celé wasn't able to take Rosette with her because then everyone would realize that Isaac's new bride had connections with the railroad!

Again, Em said, "And?"

"Okay, okay! When Rachel discovered a few years later that Rosette was her children's half sister, she almost left Isaac—not from jealousy but because she was furious that he hadn't trusted her enough to tell her about the relationship. Even worse in her eyes, he had never quite treated Rosette the same way he treated his other children. Rachel forced Isaac to take Rosette to live with her mother so Rosette and Celé could get to know each other and have a little peace of mind. She also wanted Celé to see how lovely her child was and how talented, especially because Celé had discovered she was unable to have any more children after her time with the odious neighbor!

"Life settled back into place for a short time, I was told, until everyone at Riverside died of that dreadful African flu. Apparently, that trip to relocate Rosette with Celé did indeed arouse some attention, and as a result, an assassination attempt was made against the family via an early type of germ warfare. Everyone died but Isaac and Moses, both of whom were immune to the disease, and a few of the household help who also happened to be immune. Jeff and Sara were spared only because neither of them were home when the lethal germ was brought in."

"Okay," Em said. "Just so we don't have to think about people dying of African diseases, I'll tell you folk all about Celé's long journey but only because—not your fault, Lorie—Jeff didn't know everything, and you've got some of it partially wrong."

Rolf gave another little gift to Saree, something to keep her productively occupied for a while. He moved his chair closer to the table. "Can I listen in?" he asked.

"Sure," Em said, her eyes once more full of mischief. "Just don't blush and put your handkerchief to your lips, saying, 'Lawdy, Lawdy, how you do gossip!'"

Ancient tragedy was put aside for the moment, and even Lorie had to laugh out loud.

Emily dropped her voice, causing everyone to momentarily bend toward her. "It all started when Isaac was on a mission to New Orleans. He never told anyone what the mission was, but if he was being graded, he probably got an *F* for this one because he blew it big-time!"

"Don't keep us waiting," Lorie growled.

Em laughed. "Okay, here's the dirt—when Isaac got to New Orleans, Mardi Gras was in full swing, and about the only place he could find a room was in an establishment just outside the French Quarter, in a pool room/bar that had a few private rooms upstairs for letting out to travelers." She gave a sly glance around the room to assure that everyone knew what she meant.

After a few subtle whistles and "oh-ohs" around the room, accompanied by a soft chuckle from Rolf, Em continued, "Well, after Isaac had looked around the Quarter for a while and had gotten something to eat, he went back to this place, which, as you can imagine, was pretty noisy. But the reason here wasn't Mardi Gras. It was an auction that was being held in the pool room. Several beautiful quadroon women were up for bid. Isaac looked them over and decided they looked plenty tough enough to take care of themselves, and he didn't need to draw attention.

"It's always been clear to us that Isaac was pretty disgusted by the whole idea of slavery, but he was in enemy territory, so he couldn't draw attention to himself. However, he suddenly noticed in this string of women who were up for sale a beautiful little tanned girl with big dark eyes and long straight black hair. She was wearing a full-skirted gown that had a deep neckline cut to show off her smooth shoulders and full bosom. She couldn't have been more than fourteen or fifteen, he figured, and he said she seemed so scared his heart flipped over.

"He didn't know what to do. He thought about ignoring the whole thing and decided he'd just go to bed. But as he walked up those stairs, his eyes kept straying back to the girl. She was watching him, and the hopeless expression on her face seemed to say to him, 'Please save me from this!'"

"Good grief!" Lorie said under her breath.

Alexi was sitting motionless, her mouth open.

"Well, what could he do? He'd seen dozens, if not hundreds, of women raped on that pirate ship, and he couldn't help but sense her fear. There were a few more women ahead of her in the group, with bidding going on hot and heavy, and Isaac figured it might take some time to sell them all. So he went back to his room, packed his travel gear, opened the window to the fire escape, scooted outside, and relocated his horse to a spot just under the window. Couldn't have taken more than five, six minutes.

"Then he climbed the stairs back up to his room, came out his door—leaving it open a crack—walked casually down the big staircase into the bar, strolled big as you please into the pool room, and struck up a conversation with the owner, complimenting him on the new pool table and the spectacular bar. In the meantime, he was trying to find out what he could about the auction.

"Well, it wasn't the auction that the owner was obsessed with. These were just extra no-'count quadroon slaves belonging to his recently deceased partner, and he had the dubious honor of having to liquidate his partner's half of the estate. What it boiled down to was that most of the cash would go to his ex-partner's wife. But he didn't mind lining his pockets at the same time by taking a portion off the top of the profits, so he was jazzing up the goods.

"What he really wanted to show off was his new pool table, and what's better than to have the auction in the pool room with the women on display right there in the middle of the table, standing—or lounging—on real Oriental rugs that were also for sale.

"Needless to say, Isaac was a little nervous about what he was going to do, and he was awfully tired after riding all day. But by now, he was madder'n hell. So he bought a drink at the bar to give himself a shot of courage. Now he'd only had one drink or two in his life. He found out that it made him kind of woozy. But he judged it might also give him the gumption to do a thing he'd never do otherwise! Or so he told our family elders when he finally met them to explain his side of the story!"

Emily chuckled and paused for a long sip of hot coffee. Her eyes were still twinkling.

"Come on," Alexi scolded. "You've dragged us this far. Let's take it the rest of the way!"

"Funny you should say that," said Emily, giggling first and then bursting into quickly suppressed laughter. "Well, most of the women," she finally continued, "had been auctioned off by the time he got back, and everyone was now waiting for the beautiful little girl to be put up on that table, to find out just what was under that big skirt. She was boosted up and she just stood there quaking in her new high-heeled shoes, especially bought to show off her perfect legs. Men kept lifting the hem of her skirt to catch glimpses of her legs. She was mortified because she was only wearing a silk shift under that big skirt, not even stockings!

"She was getting red in the face and ready to cry when Isaac finally called out, 'I'm gonna bid on that little girl, but I gotta see what I'm gettin' first. Gimme a few minutes, will ya.' He jumped up on the table, wrapped the skirt of her big new dress around her body, and flung her over his shoulder. He pulled a gold doubloon out of his shirt pocket and flipped it to the bar owner, who was standing there like he'd been turned into marble. 'I'll bring her back if I don't like her,' Isaac said. He jumped down from the table, girl still over his shoulder, and headed into the hallway and up the stairs."

Lorie's mouth dropped open.

Em went on, "That—he told our elders—was the first and only time he had ever done such a thing, and he really didn't know why he was doing it, except he was determined to get her out of there before any of those fat, drooling old pirates put their hands on her. He had planned to do whatever it took to keep her away from them, and he thought that might do it!"

Lorie finally couldn't stand it. She started giggling.

Alexi, thinking about it, was red-faced now with suppressed laughter. Then it just burst out of her.

Rolf's belly laugh rolled on and on. "Good old Isaac! Where there's a will…!"

"Anyway," Emily continued, now in a firm tone, trying hard to keep herself from giggling, "here's the way it went down, so to speak! Everyone was so stunned they acted just like you guys just did—mouths open, no words, nothing!

"The owner finally yelled up the staircase at Isaac, 'That's not the way an auction works, mister.' He was kind of sputtering. 'She's worth twice as much as that!' To which Isaac opened the upstairs door and called back, 'Damaged goods, sir!' He shut the door behind him and propped a chair and a chest against it."

Lorie burst into laughter that wouldn't stop. Rolf's face was red, as he was laughing so hard. Alexi had hiccups. Tears were running across Emily's cheeks. Saree simply looked on, mystified, but grinning at all the crazy people around her.

"What happened next?" Lorie finally sputtered.

"Well, it was touch and go after that," Em continued when she could find her voice again. "He gave Celé his spare clothes to pull on real quick, including his own thick socks for her bare feet because they heard a lot of people coming up the stairs, and he knew they'd have to run real fast if anybody could ever get that door open!

"Now if you remember, his sturdy little horse was saddled and ready to go at the base of the fire ladder. The minute they got down, they were in the saddle and out of there! Isaac said he and Celé never looked back until they were so far away from New Orleans they couldn't see nor hear it. They camped out somewhere that first night in the brush wrapped together in saddle blankets for warmth, hoping no rattlesnakes or other vermin would find them! That's what became a problem, in retrospect."

Lorie chuckled. "Sounds like a different serpent attacked."

"Right! The one in the story of Adam and Eve!" Em was laughing. "He was real tired and more than a little drunk probably high on adrenalin, and she was not only really grateful to him but entranced by his physical beauty and his willingness to put himself on the line for her. It was something neither one of them could keep from doing, but I'm told it only happened once! Well, as I'm also told, once is all it takes!

"They discussed all the possibilities the next morning. That's when he told her he couldn't marry her because he was promised to another. And she told him, 'I'm promised to another too. Can you take me to him? His name is Jamie Cormier.' He couldn't promise her anything, he told her, until they got to some safe place so they could read maps and find out exactly where they were, and then they'd sort out what each of them needed to do."

"So," Emily concluded, "that's what Isaac told the elders of her family when he finally met them. That's after he was coerced by his new wife, Rachel, into reuniting Rosette with her true mother. Celé never disputed the relationship. She always said that Isaac looked just like the most handsome Greek god she'd ever seen, grabbing her up like that, claiming his prize. She was truly entranced by him." Em shrugged her shoulders with a "sometimes it happens" expression and said cheerfully, "Well, if he hadn't done the deed, I wouldn't be here," and once more burst into laughter.

"Oops!" Lorie said. The laughter didn't stop, nor did the stories.

CHAPTER 31

On the road
Thursday, April 21, 2016

"A re we there yet?" Randy asked, making his voice sound whiny like a child. Jeff laughed. Jeb, who was driving, also gave a big laugh—exactly as Randy had intended, Jeff figured, something to break the solemn silence.

"Only halfway, mister," Jeb said, grinning, "and you know it! We'll stop for lunch at this little town comin' up. I called someone on our contact list to ask if anybody knew a place to eat where we wouldn't be noticed as strangers, so to speak, and that last call I took was someone associated with the FBI over in DC. He said the people who run the only restaurant on this road just happen to be theirs. They've been in place for a few weeks now, keepin' an eye on the tourist trade. They're the ones who alerted Em's family about Searchers in the area." He added, "Maybe this'll give us a chance to look over those new maps Bernice sent before we head up to the hills. I betcha we find a change in the routing!"

Jeb was right. As soon as they pulled out the new instructions, they realized that Bernice had given them quite a different route this time. Her new directions did not bounce them across the steep mountain roads Jeff still recalled with a queasy stomach, nor did it make sharp turns onto narrow roads that seemed to trace by mere yards the summit of steep precipices.

Instead, once they were briefed by agents eager for updates, fed well, and sent on their way, Jeff realized they were following well-maintained Forest Service roadways until they reached a paved road defined quite sternly as "private." Jeb turned onto the private road, remarking that he felt right privileged to be included in the "private" category this time 'round!

The roadway rose comfortably upward through deep woodlands on roads expertly sliced out of the face of successive hillsides. It bridged sparkling waterfalls, passed through gold and green mountain meadows, and finally intersected with another easily navigable blacktopped road, which wound even more gently upward to a ridge top road blessed with views of surpassing beauty at both sides.

Jeff was as gratified as he was surprised.

Again, to his surprise, along their new route, they encountered a small town modestly proclaiming itself to be Nowhere City. It consisted of several square blocks of houses Jeff clearly recognized as having been designed in the exuberant mid-nineteenth century—two-story, four-square-styled homes surrounded by spacious yards. The town also boasted of a downtown area consisting of stores displaying not only contemporary clothing but equally modern household goods on display behind big glass windows. There were trees in this small town, sidewalks, mowed lawns, and tended flower beds.

No people.

"Go six miles past Nowhere," the new directions had said, and Jeb made some soft comment about how oddly unsettling the feel of an empty town was.

Six miles past Nowhere City, judging by the odometer, they were...well, somewhere! To Jeff's right, the woodlands were still thick and uncompromising. But as the van made a gentle turn to the left around the next hillside, he saw ahead quite the most handsome log cabin he had ever set eyes on, its high gable roof covered by overlapping cedar shakes. Blooming flower beds were artistically scattered across its sloping front acreage.

Still following Bernice's new directions, Jeb turned the van from the main road onto a driveway that wound its way upward toward the grand home. It now became apparent that the timber mansion was part of a much larger operation. A number of outbuildings could be seen in the forest beyond, the most apparent being two rows of smaller independent log homes built in generally the same style as the main residence but on a more human scale.

Jeff spotted a structure that could possibly be a bunk-house, as well as other undefined buildings, all constructed of logs that must have been cut from the surrounding forest many years before, as there was no sign of new timbering activity.

The main residence was sequestered from the rest by a split-rail fence, which seemed to quite adequately provide the large house with an independence of its own. Following the written directions being barked out by Randy, Jeb turned the van up the long driveway of the home and continued following arrowed signs into a large parking lot.

Bernice Richards herself met them at the big front door. "Welcome to the Richards Family Command Center! Watch out, KJ!" she said as a very young person on a scooter circled her legs. She shooed him (or her) away and, with determination, led the six newcomers through a sun-drenched Great Room. It was a huge space filled with comfortable couches, armchairs, magazine-covered tables, filled bookcases, multiple display cases—too much to take in all at once—and finally through a swinging door that opened into a long hallway.

Jeff couldn't help but smile. This must be the *cabin* Jon Randolph's first son, Junior, had come to in his spare moments so many years ago when he visited with his *other* family! These were the people who shared flying adventures with him, tried desperately to help him when he needed it the most, and now honored his memory.

Jeff hoped Sara had visited here as well. He had by now read with pleasure many of the letters that had been passed between his only surviving siblings. He had seen stories written by Rosette about Sara's parents—his parents—and their other siblings. Those letters could well have warmed and comforted his youngest sister, as the thought of it did just now for him.

Bernice turned to the right and led her guests along the hallway cut through with several unremarkable doors. Where was she taking them? She paused in front of a door, which seemed not unlike any of the others, pulled a key from her pocket, unlocked the door, and ushered her five surprised visitors into a generous-sized, quite handsome study lined with bookshelves and crammed with office equipment. The room was dominated by a long table and multiple chairs. Bernice shut the door firmly behind her and relocked the door.

"Whew," she said with a mock wipe to her brow, leaning her back against the door. "There are eight of them here already and more on the way. Grandkids! Gotta love 'em! But until they're older, there are parts of this house which are simply off-limits! Those kids zero in on the computers, get on the internet, and run through reams of paper…well, you probably know the whole story yourselves!"

Ewen, who had already started to chuckle, gave a hearty laugh. "I totally understand!" He winked at his son, who was also laughing. All ice, if there ever had been any, was broken!

Bernice went on. "Three of my four boys are already on-site and their families are with them, all determined to protect Grandma! The last is on his way without the benefit of small fry. Lots of manpower here already. More coming! Male cousins and uncles are either patrolling this acreage or are posted somewhere on the road, no male in this family over eighteen and living within one hundred miles has opted out. Nowhere City will be a thriving community tonight."

Jeff blinked—Nowhere City was a real town? Well, it sure sounded like it, especially when the Family came to visit!

"The string of cabins out back are filling up too," Bernice went on. "This used to be a pretty swanky summer estate for some very wealthy people. We've upgraded and converted everything that isn't related to our family business into guest quarters. Lots of fun in the summer." She looked directly at Jeff then. "Wish this visit were going to be fun and games, guys, but I'm afraid our *cave* has finally been spotted!"

"The Searchers!" Jeb said. "We knew they was close. Have they set up a base camp yet?"

"They have." Bernice shook her head. "A whole passel of shave-tail kids, most of them no more than seventeen... eighteen. They've got a couple or three older babysitters who probably don't want to be here any more than their charges. But we've also noticed there's an older guy with a rifle and a holstered gun monitoring the whole thing.

"They're all down there at the base of the cliff with their camping and climbing gear. They set up their whole tent village already, and they've been searching every ridge with high-powered binoculars and telescopes. I saw how excited they got when they finally spotted our shifty little cave. They haven't started climbing yet. Possibly the 'No Trespassing,' 'Trespassers Will Be Prosecuted,' 'Warning—Danger of Rockslides' signs are stopping them...temporarily! I presume they're waiting for someone more senior to come onto the scene and start yelling and telling them not to pay attention to the signs."

Suddenly, she turned to Jeb and looked at him long and hard. "You know about Searchers, do you? Former Searcher yourself?"

He nodded. He seemed quite uncomfortable, Jeff thought.

"Then you must be Jebediah!" Bernice held out her arms. "Welcome, brother-in-law! Finally, we meet! Like it or not, you're gonna have to face up to your wife's whole family all at once! Don't worry. They won't eat you!" She put her hands on Jeb's shoulders, went up on tiptoe and reached her face up to give him a big kiss on the cheek. "Em has told me so much about you!" She released him with a broad smile on her face. "I'm really glad to have you here, Jebediah Wallace, fighting the good fight with us. And such a handsome man at that! I think Em did real good for herself, and you can tell her that for me. Just don't you go and get yourself hurt, or Em will have my head!"

Jeff grinned at his friend, who was still standing mute as if in shock. It was obvious Jeb had not expected a welcome of any kind, much less one so effusive! "Uh, thanks!" he mumbled, but Bernice had already turned to her next visitor. Jeff saw a tear rolling across Jeb's cheek, followed by a second. Greatly pleased, Jeff turned his face quickly away so as not to embarrass his friend.

"Chief Randy Ross, the policeman." Bernice turned to him. "Another indispensable asset! Thanks so much for joining us!" She took his hand in a warm grasp and then focused on Ewen. "Nice to see you again too, Mr. Taylor. Welcome to the Family Command Center! We want to begin liaison work with you so both our Command Centers speak the same language!"

"Call me Ewen," he said with a big grin, reaching out for her hand.

Beaming, she turned next to Guy. Her eyes widened. "I bet this one is related to you, Ewen. Your eyes are very much the same, you know. Determination, along with all that intellect!"

"And you'd bet right," he replied proudly. "Guy is my youngest and the best climber in my family. If someone needs to be rescued, we'll certainly give it our best try."

"Well, I appreciate your both being here. In regard to rescue work, keep in mind that we have foolproof ways of anchoring people onto this hilltop for rescue purposes. I'll show you our equipment before anyone does any climbing. We've had to figure out ways around gravity over the years because that cliff seems to look so inviting. But don't let it fool you! It doesn't want anyone near it! Unfortunately, before we figured that out, we experienced more than one fatality. We try the best we can to protect the general public, but sometimes it takes a little more cooperation than aggressive climbers are willing to accept!"

Now she turned to Jared. "I've met this young man before too. Only I was led to believe then that he was nothing more—nor less—than a genius at computers. You're a climber too, young man?"

"Jared Bryant, ma'am," he said, reaching for her hand. "I climb anything anytime. And yes, I would have been tempted. But I'm an inveterate sign reader, and I pay attention to what I read!" He continued with a big grin, "I've been told you have some ancient safety devices and climbing equipment, I'd appreciate taking a look at them, if it's possible."

Bernice grinned. "You're most welcome to inspect the old pulley and sling and the harness. It was constructed by an old sailor, name of Deerfield, who really knew what he was doing! In regard to the safe-climber devices, it's simply a matter of fastening the highest-quality metal chains to posts screwed deeply into solid bedrock, and we know exactly where that bedrock lies. We secure our climbing ropes to those Deerfield chains before we go out, which is infrequent, just to let you know. None of us likes to tackle the high spaces. Gives you a kind of queasy feeling in the stomach!"

Jared grinned. "If I had that problem, I wouldn't be a climber."

"You can have it! So tell me this, climber, how do we keep those kids from doing it and sliding off the cliff, taking half of it with them?"

Jeb grinned. "We was just talkin' about this. When they wake up in the mornin', all their climbin' gear is gone! Think they'll be pushed to climb up those cliffs then?"

"That would make it impossible, of course! But those poor kids...," she said sadly. "When the guys with guns finally find the road to the top, they'll just try to make the kids climb down. That floor shifts when a person steps on it! Besides which, the roof of the cave is almost ready to crumble. We don't go out there at all! What scares me is that kids apparently can't 'just say no.' My heart bleeds for their parents! We've got to find a good way to stop them!"

"I was in that category myself," Jeb said softly. "And you are right about the casualties. Several boys in my group never made it home to their lovin' mamas. Some of 'em was good friends of mine." He paused for a moment, swallowed hard, wiped at tearing eyes with a folded handkerchief, and finally said very softly, "You know what makes me want to fight back? I want to see my mama again. She's probably written me off as one of the lost ones. I went by once where we used to live. No one was there.

"I don't even know how to start lookin' for her, or if I should, but I'd sure like her to meet my Emily. And Celly. And our little Todd. Thing is, we don't even know where to start lookin'. If my mama is still alive, I'm sure The Compact honchos know exactly where she is, and they're checkin' on her every now and then to see if I get in touch. It really ain't fair, is it?"

"But," Jeff finally put in, "we've done some serious work on this problem, Bernice, and we're pretty sure we know where those Compact documents are, including address lists. We're going to grab everything, including The Compact itself, the minute an opportunity presents itself!"

"The Compact? The actual...?" Bernice's eyes grew wide. "It's real? You know where it is?"

"Got it pegged!" Jeb said rather sharply. He took a deep breath and added, "Only trick is gettin' to it. There's an electric fence and guard dogs."

"If we need to," Jeff put in, "we have ways to deal with the dogs and the guards...and the fence. Our problem was that we couldn't think of an outside diversion so compelling that few or no living souls would be lingering inside the mansion where it's kept. If we had that kind of diversion, then we'd simply enter the place, get The Compact, and bring it home."

Bernice's eyebrows rose. "What kind of diversion do you need?"

Now Jeff grinned. "I believe we've just discovered it. Look around you, friends! Look at all these people congregating up here because of what's happening at the base of the cliff. Our diversion is happening, even as we speak!"

Bernice's eyes lit. A big laugh erupted from deep inside her. "Forget the maps I was trying to find for you. Let's head for the kitchen! Coffee and munchies for all. And we can talk about what's on your planning boards right now and what you might need down the line."

Jeff grinned. This Bernice was quite different from the bossy lady they had met at the restaurant. This was the genuine Bernice—sharply intelligent, decisive, and focused. It was going to be a pleasure working with her, especially if the going got rough!

And then she said just the thing to peg his assessment of her. On her way back to the long kitchen table, holding a full pot of coffee in her hand and surrounded by a whole bunch of very tired men, she said, "You know what, guys, stealing their equipment is the best idea I've heard yet. Too simple to even consider guarding against, especially their first night out. Coffee or tea, if you want it, folks, and I'll show you right now to your rooms. Get as much rest as you can, sleep, if possible! And then let's firm up your splendid plan."

"Sleep?" Jeff said.

Bernice raised her eyebrows. "If you're gonna beat 'em, you've gotta get some sleep. We'll get you up well before the cock crows! Our guys can easily take out the guards in the dark, a little pinprick of something blown through a tube. The kids who are out there? First night out? They'll be so exhausted no one will even know you were there. One o'clock wake up? Two?"

It took Jeff a couple of seconds to comprehend Bernice's plan. When he did, he let out a hoot of laughter. "Ma'am, you are a hell of a general! Make it two o'clock. More sleep is better. Wish you'd been around during the Civil War. Guys," he said to his crew, "get some sleep. We'll be gone and back well before sunup. It's a good bet they'll be deep in dreamland the whole time we're there!"

CHAPTER 32

In the mountains of West Virginia
Shortly before dawn, Friday, April 22, 2016

"**H**ow'd it go?" a tired-eyed Bernice asked as Jeff and his crew dragged themselves onto the back patio of the log house and stood bedraggled and mute in front of the wide-open back door. The bundles they were carrying looked like Santa Claus's bags filled with Christmas gifts consisting mostly, if not entirely, of climbing apparatus. They had just returned from what some might consider hazardous duty.

Bernice pointed toward a patio door, which opened into a large dark cavern, a nearly empty storage area, as lawn chairs and tables had been pulled onto the patio to be repurposed elsewhere. The bags were deposited noisily into a massive heap inside. The key to the padlock, which ultimately secured the door, was dropped directly into Bernice's apron pocket.

The kitchen reminded Jeff of the one in which he had often dined at Ewen's bunkhouse complex in Georgia. One of the gleaming tables inside the brightly lit room was already set for breakfast. It looked capacious enough to seat fourteen grown men easily, perhaps eighteen to twenty folks of various ages if no one minded rubbing elbows.

On this early morning, however, the table was set for only six plus Bernice. Despite the few hours of sleep, his men were very tired, operating by now, Jeff thought, only on determination and adrenalin.

"Smooth as silk," Ewen said, grinning. But he looked old this morning, Jeff thought with alarm, older than he had appeared before! The entrepreneur slumped into his chair and brought an overfilled coffee cup carefully to his lips. "They won't know what hit 'em till they open their sleepy little eyes!" He sipped gingerly at the contents and then puffed at the steaming brew a couple of times before taking another sip. "Good stuff, Bernice! I needed that."

Jeff watched with concern as Ewen downed half a cup in one gulp. Then the older man looked up, smiling like a cat that's just caught the canary. "Well, Bernice, you saw what we found down there in the camp. Everything gone in an instant. Our story is that it was spirited away by mountain sprites, and we're not admitting to anything else."

"How did you do it?" Chuckles rumbled in Bernice's throat.

A bit of sunshine peeked over the summit of an eastern mountain just then, throwing golden rays through the clear cool air and the kitchen windows, just as a couple of Bernice's daughters-in-law and several teenaged granddaughters came through the swinging kitchen doors. They gave friendly waves and greetings to Grandma and her friends and went immediately to work at the stoves and counters, mixing, baking, frying, toasting, gossiping among themselves. Simple breakfasts were being provided, served up cafeteria-style with goodwill, camaraderie, and a sense of everything in perfect order.

"Our silent little drones snapped up the big loose stuff piece by piece," Ewen said in response to Bernice's question.

He grabbed an offered plate and started filling it. "And each piece flew quietly away."

Now Guy grinned at his father. "My dad likes to do this kind of 'behind the scenes' mysterious stuff." The young man's plate was as full as his father's. He reseated himself at the table and began to fork food ravenously into his mouth.

The rest of the men followed in like fashion. Jared laughed as he sat down. "We've got a bunch of work drones that are marvels at retrieving hard-to-reach equipment. But these so-called Searchers made it real easy for us to get the big things. The kids aren't careful with their gear at all. Easy to see they're total novices. *Safety* is just a word to them, not a concept!"

Jeff saw the wry grin on Jeb's face. He'd been one of those Searchers, and he knew how little those young men really cared about their tools, even tools that might save their lives in a pinch. "Whatever was layin' around was snatched up first," Jeb said.

"Then we took aerial pictures of the campsite with night cameras," Randy put in to expand on what the others were saying, "and located what else we needed to look into. I was in Special Forces for a time. So was Jared, we've been comparing notes on who had the worst deployments. Jeff's better than all of us combined, though. He was an Airborne Ranger, so he's sneaky. Like a snake!" Emphasizing the *S* sound, he looked around, met Jeff's tired grin, and chuckled.

"We slithered into their site..." Jared's face beamed in the glow of the rising sun as he continued the *S* emphasis, "and found them snoring. It was horrendous!" Everyone laughed, relieved to be able to blow off a little steam. "We went through bags and backpacks, and I don't believe we missed a thing. Even if they want to climb this morning, there are no ropes, carabineers, harnesses, slings, belay gloves, brakes... We even took their helmets and climbing shoes."

Bernice's chuckles also morphed into a big laugh. "Slippery spies slyly succeed!" Her smile faded quickly, though, as she looked around and then out the back window. Frowning, she said quietly, "They'll still want to get up top, I expect. If they're smart, all they have to do is look at a map. They'll find the county road. Probably the last resort for these guys," she added, "because they've always seemed pretty dense. 'Go with the *hard* first because if it's *easy*, there must be something wrong with the planning.'" She looked at Jeff with a wry expression on her face. "We'll have them up top soon, which is just as dangerous as climbing the closer you get to the edge."

She looked around the kitchen and saw her grown male kin beginning to assemble, fiercely ready to defend their way of life. She turned toward them and said in a firm voice, "I want you guys to all be on Deerfield harnesses the whole time you're out there on the cliffs. There are plenty to go around."

Jeff glanced at Randy, at Jeb, at Ewen… "Deerfield harnesses?" he mouthed. His eyebrows raised significantly. "Will Deerfield?" he said casually to Bernice, making it a question.

"Best engineer in the business!" she answered. "He came here early, when Isaac got here. Isaac came and went when he needed to. Will was a good friend of Isaac's—his mentor, I believe—but he stayed on here. He was a sailor, but he was mesmerized by the magnificence of the mountains! Better than the ocean, he said to our early kin." Again, addressing her young relatives, she said, "You know where the harnesses are, we've practiced this scenario many times. Make double sure your ropes are secure before you cross the red line. Okay? Don't forget, you guys who haven't been here for a while, edges on the other side of that line have been known to break off right under people's feet! It's been a couple of weeks since we measured and marked the edge line, so be extra careful.

"Next directive—when it seems possible to do it without being seen, once this operation starts, we want you to grab any of the young men who seem to be standing back a bit. Have you grabbed any already?" She grinned at the nods. "A few, I see. Quiet, are they?" Again, grim nods. She looked around again. A multitude of young men had just arrived and were beginning to assemble their climbing gear.

"All our hostages will be stored temporarily in the tunnel," she said firmly. "Tie and gag anyone who objects. Don't choke anyone! Just make sure they can't yell. Also," she added, "keep eyes open to rescue Compact personnel if the ground breaks under them. We're not vindictive. We're just looking for justice. Keep that in mind, people! If all else fails, we'll call the big burly cousins"—she gave a nod to a couple of older men now entering the kitchen—"to step out of the brush, give the evil eye, and scare everyone to bejesus!"

"Stopped us!" Jeb said with a big grin at Randy, who winked. "Damned intimidating!" Jeb continued. "But we weren't carrying handguns, and these guys might be."

Bernice pulled a phone from her pocket and punched in a number. "Everyone okay out there?" she said to someone far away. "Yes, they're back in great shape, with lots of toys." She paused again and looked backward for a moment. "They say the adult intruders might be carrying." Again, she listened. "If you think it's necessary…okay, I'll put out the call to hoist the red flags. They're all out of mothballs and ready to go. Thanks, guys." She turned back to her guests.

"First report from the cousins," she said, a chuckle in her voice. "Pandemonium down in the valley. Everybody running around like headless chickens. They'll sort it out eventually and maybe send for backups. But we've got more jeeps headed this way ourselves. We'll see who's better at this kind of skirmish."

Jeff thought breakfast had never tasted so good. But he really needed some sleep. He looked up at Bernice.

"Go," she mouthed soundlessly. Aloud, she said, "Get some rest, brother!"

CHAPTER 33

Friday, April 22, 2016

Jeff woke with a start about noon to find the atmosphere at the log cabin charged—something important was happening! He sat up abruptly.

"Compact hierarchy gathering below the cliff," Randy called out as he paused by Jeff's open doorway, headed for the kitchen. "Bernice's spies in the valley below have passed the word that an awful lot of the head honchos are on-site. You were right, it seems they all want to be in on the action. Guns bristling, bro!" His laughter seemed a bit caustic. "On the bright side, their posh mansion down on the Potomac is probably as deserted as it ever will be, and Ewen's troops can move forward with their plans—the sooner, the better, Bernice says! She also wants you to know that help is on its way to man the barricades up here."

Jeff immediately called Lorie to give her a status report. It was a short conversation. She was terribly worried, she told him.

Her continuing concern troubled him. She was not generally a worrier, but she had a kind of sixth sense about over-the-top disasters waiting to happen. He knew enough by now to realize that if she asked him to pay attention, he should most certainly pay attention!

Thanks to Rolf and his allies, Jeff was certain the women and children residing at Ewen's horse farm were in the best of hands. And because he knew and trusted every man who had come with him, he had no qualms on that score. Their selfless teamwork last night was smooth as any expedition he had commanded.

Nor was he particularly concerned about his own well-being, if he could be assured he would not be located near the edge of the high cliffs! He didn't want his compatriots to know how fast his heart got to beating just thinking about it! Was that what Lorie was sensing? His raw terror at high places! The bugaboo that had plagued him all his life!

He had promised Lorie he would be especially careful if he were called upon to do any climbing or rappelling. Ropes would be inspected, knots double-checked, and buckles set and jerked to make sure they had firmly caught. If he had to go out on those ropes, there was nothing he wouldn't inspect firsthand before he used it. There were plenty of experienced climbers in their party. Hopefully he wouldn't have to do any of it. But just in case...

"First time in this century," Bernice told him tersely when he finally entered into the kitchen, "that we've considered raising the red danger flag on the mountaintop. Had to pull the old flag out of mothballs when we got the alert from our watchers on the road below!"

"What happens now?"

"Family members close enough to see it will pass the warning to other family members. Red flags will go up from family to family. Every able-bodied male within two hour's drive will join us, armed!"

"Are they all trained?"

"This is the one threat nobody's ever taken lightly. Yes, they are all armed and well trained! Many service veterans are included in this batch of volunteers."

Jeff paused to sip at a cup of hot coffee. He ran scenario after scenario through his head. Bernice felt the Family was sufficiently prepared to meet the enemy's forces, but they didn't know The Compact! It had deep roots, unlimited funds!

What did the Family have?

Determination! And some of the smartest people Jeff had ever met. He smiled and then nodded to himself. The Compact would be in for a big surprise!

All of his gear-gathering compatriots were using their rest time to best advantage. Despite the pump of exhilaration that comes with success, everyone except Randy was still reveling in sound sleep. *Welcome sleep*, Jeff thought! But he couldn't quite go back there himself, no more than Randy could. Not yet.

As the day wore along, that red flag flying above the mountaintop proved to be very effective. Male members of the Family were arriving by the minute—all reliable men, Bernice told him proudly. They lived close by, and she knew them all.

Jeff noted with satisfaction as they arrived at the compound that their complexions were of many hues, from black to brown, from freckled through golden. Firearms and ammunition boxes were beginning to accumulate in the big common room, and amazingly enough, everyone seemed to be on friendly terms with everyone else, as if everyone knew each other, which they probably did!

Grandchildren who had been vacationing with Gramma Bernice had been rounded up and were on their way with mothers and sisters back to their own homes, protesting loudly. It was apparent to Jeff that his newfound relative was unbending when it came to protecting her family. The young cooks had been scheduled to leave the site earlier, but they insisted on keeping to their tasks, still producing luscious smelling casseroles, desserts, and salads—surely enough to feed the army still assembling.

Jeff suspected that the empty Nowhere City houses he and his men had seen on their way up to the big cabin were by now fully occupied! That would be a sight to see.

Randy popped into the kitchen to inform everyone within range that several Family members were posting "No Trespassing" signs at the base of the driveway that rose upward to the big house, and IDs were being checked by their guards before any vehicle was allowed to proceed farther. Emergency protocol plans developed long since had finally met the criteria this situation demanded.

The two- to three-mile barrier of deep woodlands extending beyond Family property to the cliffs had always been and still remained under the jurisdiction of the US Forest Service. That included not only the deep forests between the cabin and the jagged cliff but the cliffs themselves, which dropped abruptly several hundred feet into the narrow valley below. Knowing Family members to be responsible guardians of the forest, Forest Service personnel had always granted them free access to that area. Encroachment by armed Compact members upon National Forest property, Bernice had told him, was now being viewed as a hostile act!

If government personnel were threatened, Randy added, members of the Family would put out a call to action— Bernice's designation—and Family would instantly come to the rangers' defense. They had done so before in isolated instances and were prepared to do so again.

As Jeff looked around, it seemed to him that there was enough firepower already accumulated at Family headquarters to take on a small country! If Compact members defied the "Private Drive" sign on the roadway up the hill, there would be no recourse but self-defense. Everyone who arrived was acutely aware of it. Rifles were being stacked in the hallways, munitions boxes located within easy reach.

Jeff was almost stunned by the fact that most of the people he saw entering the house were related to him. Spouses excepted, these were genetically his father's people only because of a "slight miscalculation" with a young woman named Celé, someone Isaac had met before his marriage.

Jeff was proud of his father for acknowledging the small human product of that miscalculation and protecting and caring for Rosette and her mother as long as he had. He saw Rosette's face again in his memories: four years his older, pretty, funny, smart half sister, who had so many years before become one of his best friends. Now he remembered how very much he had missed her when, at his mother's insistence, she had been taken away to live with her mother. "Celé is Rosette's real mother," his mother had told him confidentially. "And she needs to know her mother's family as well as her father's."

As he looked around at the people coming into the big log house, he realized that without a doubt it was either Rosette's face or his father's that he saw in a sudden glance, a quick smile, even in the smallest of gestures!

Jeff had always known his father as a good, decent family man. This gathering confirmed his assessment. It was obvious to him that Isaac had given these people not only of himself but also of a large portion of his accumulated treasure. Bernice had recently told him that every member of the Family had received the benefits of a superior education, thanks to a perpetual and very well-placed endowment fund that Isaac had set up for their benefit!

Early members of the Family obviously knew about Will Deerfield, and just as surely those relatives were aware of, if not acquainted with, Jon Randolph's son, Jon Junior, who had died at the cliff a century ago. It was the almost simultaneous deaths of Sara and Rosette, Jeff had been told, that had unfortunately severed the close ties.

However, letters written to Sara and carefully stored in cousin Sue Bailey's attic were lovingly remembered just when they were needed—letters written by Rosette to her half sister when they were both mothers of their own.

Once again, the family and friends of Isaac Preston were working together! Let's see now, Jeff said to himself, who fared the best—the silent people who lied, cheated, and hurt or the quiet people who trusted, helped, and loved!

CHAPTER 34

I t was a time for waiting—the hardest part of any operation, Jeff thought. Seated in a virtually empty kitchen, nursing along another cup of coffee, he picked up the cell phone he had finally learned to use and punched in coded messages to the members of his active team still on duty in Virginia.

"Continue surveillance on the river house. In addition, please dispatch an observer to monitor activity around the mountain house and the cliffs beyond. Many intruders approaching the site. BR is preparing to defend."

"On it," came the answer at once.

Thinking to dissipate his increasing nervousness, he decided to tour the house. Despite what he supposed was an early attempt to appear rustic, he could tell it had always been a very fine home. A good number of the rooms contained museum-worthy furniture and fine art. He recognized some of the artists' names scribbled at the lower corners of exquisite paintings, people recognized as great artists even in this new world. His family had never lived in this fashion, even though they could have afforded it, he thought. There must be an explanation. He would ask Bernice next time he saw her.

Treading cautiously along one hallway on what were certainly priceless Oriental rugs, he turned a corner and was brought to a halt by a large double door, closed. He tried the door. It opened readily into a very large room cut through by many tall windows, allowing it to fill to the brim with golden sunshine.

The whole house reoriented itself for Jeff when he saw the embalmed forest creatures displayed in glass cases on shelves located throughout the room. This was the Great Room that Bernice had hurried them through when he and his troops had arrived to join forces with the Family.

Gaining confidence now in his bearings, he strode toward the front door and turned around to take a second look. An antlered stag's head was mounted above a huge stone fireplace built into one of the corners of the room. On a shelf created for the purpose, a long-deceased beaver, small stick inserted in its mouth, was raising its head from an artfully crafted ceramic pond. Jeff's first impression was of distaste! He had never understood the taking of animals for display.

He was joined moments later by a young man almost as tall as he was but one he had not yet met, a good-look-ing fellow with a deep suntanned complexion and black hair of much the same consistency as that tightly curled across the well-formed head of the dashing actor, Vince Thomas. "You're Jeff, they tell me," the young man said. "I'm Gus Richards. Gus for Augustus. But mind, if you call me that, I'll deck you!" Grinning to show he was only partly jesting, he held out his hand in welcome. "I've been sent to be your personal guide."

Jeff chuckled as he grasped the outstretched hand. "Hello, Gus! To whom do you belong?"

"I'm Bernice's. The middle son of her three. The lone bachelor. Her favorite, of course! How could it be otherwise?" His dark twinkling eyes mirrored his mother's. Jeff could see Bernice's expressions in Gus's face, but surprisingly enough, he also discerned a reflection of his own father and very distinctly that of his older brother, Will. "And now you've met the three of us."

Jeff's heart swelled with admiration for this splendid young man, but the tears that sprang to his eyes, the lump that came into his throat, surprised him. If Will had not been felled along with his mother and the younger children when a fatal fever was brought deliberately into their home, if his own younger brothers and sisters had been allowed to grow and thrive, it could so easily have been one of their grandchildren standing before him.

And then he remembered—this young man was a direct descendant of his own father. The relationship was that close! The warmth of feeling for Gus that came across him was profound! "And what do you do in your spare time?" he said, hoping that sharp jab of emotion had not been apparent. "Are you the intrepid hunter of these…"—Jeff pointed to the taxidermy on display—"woodland creatures?"

"Good god, no! You should have started your tour at the swimming pool in that big white building out beyond. This is the original retreat—actually the raw beginnings of this complex. We've kept it the way it was in the old days to remind us that we not only built it from the forest up, we still own it today!"

Jeff's eyebrows shot up.

Gus chuckled. And when he finally realized that he was speaking with someone who actually wanted to learn the history of the house, he continued, "It was to be a safe haven and vacation playground for all the relatives in the late 1800s, you see. We weren't exactly welcome in most of the cushy places one went for vacations back then. I guess no one thought a black person in this part of the country deserved a little downtime. Nowhere City sprang up to house the expanding lists of our blood relatives who also liked mountain vacations—and real freedom instead of something just passing for it.

"But to keep the larder full enough to feed all those visitors, our intrepid ancestors decided to lease the big house out now and then to admiring summer people who came to the high forests in carriages or on horseback when it was too hot for them down below, in the sweltering flatlands that ended at the seashore." He laughed. "No one realized the people on the permanent staff of this grand place were also the people who greedily gathered up the rents when they were due, subdivided the funds, and slipped them into private accounts, which continued to draw good interest even during several depressions, because we was jest a little bit smarter and we never took nothin' for granted!"

Jeff's laughter rang out again. "Hooray for your side!"

"I expect you've pegged the fact that it was billed as a hunting lodge." Dropping into a patois very familiar to Jeff, Gus drawled, "The first folk who come, they was a'feared of them furry little things sneakin' around in the woods, so they took it upon theyselves to kill ever'thing that moved—weasels, skunks, foxes—shooting at 'em all till they was all vanquished. Then they put 'em on display under glass so they could brag how good they could shoot!"

"We Blackies was always here," he continued, a twinkle in his eye, "just as small as those creatures in their eyes, but we escaped the bullets 'cause we jest faded into the background like all good blackies should! We do so like to chuckle!"

Jeff couldn't help it, and he started laughing and couldn't stop!

Gus followed with generous laughter of his own. "So when push come to shove," he continued, "it was those poor little defenseless critters that ended up dead under glass, but we sneaky Blackies stayed healthy 'cause we really liked renting out our house each summer for increasingly larger sums of money! We made out like bandits, actually!"

Again, laughter! Worries regarding the continuation of animal homicide disappeared. "Have the smaller furrier game come back the way the rich whites did?" Jeff ventured.

"A goodly number of bears. A bit bigger than chipmunks, actually. But we encourage lots of those greedy little snack animals to stay around for the bears to feed on instead of us! Eat or be eaten—that's the motto outside these windows! Our advice is, stay inside with the darkies. You may not see 'em around much, but they's a lot more friendly!"

Jeff recognized the quirky sense of humor, as it so achingly reminded him of Rosette, whose speech had so easily transformed into one or another of the many dialects she heard around her every day at Riverside Plantation. Her children and grandchildren were the lucky ones in his family. They had survived!

Quite suddenly, Gus stopped talking. Jeff, who had been admiring the beautifully hand-carved wooden picture frames surrounding small painted faces that seemed very familiar to him, suddenly saw one of himself. He chuckled and then glanced up at Gus, who was staring at him now, silent, his eyes wide.

"Is it just this light?" Gus asked softly and then answered his own question. "No. That is you, isn't it?" He paused. "Is that possible?" His voice had dropped almost to a whisper.

Jeff straightened up, surprised. "What do you think?"

After a long moment of affirmative silence, Gus looked directly into Jeff's eyes for a long moment. Much to Jeff's surprise, he then gave a sharp salute and said in a subdued voice, "Welcome to our home, Colonel Preston. It seems you have been expected."

Jeff was silenced. Colonel? Colonel Preston? Expected? By whom?

"I...I have something to give to you," Gus went on, almost in a whisper. "It was sent here by your sister just before she moved north to safety during the Civil War. She asked that it be passed along to you if you were found alive. I believe you will want to see it before any confrontation with our enemies begins, with the people she called members of The Compact!"

"Colonel Preston?" Jeff paused, uncertain now how to proceed. This young man, whom he had not met until only a few moments ago at a house where he himself had never lived, was addressing him at his correct rank in the Union Army of the mid-1860s! The promotion papers must have been in his records when his sister was notified of his death. Yes, he *would* want to see what Gus had found!

"Explain," Jeff said quietly, "if you please!"

"I was looking..." Gus's dark face had blanched to near white. Discreetly, he moved a step backward. He became even more animated. "I was searching the attic here one day, recently I had suddenly become very curious about the origins of the house and was trying to find out all I could about it, how it came to be built, who the architect was, the names of the craftsmen who did the carving—all that. And in a back corner of the attic, I came across some really ancient stuff that had been sent here by...well, I'm now assuming it was Sara Randolph Preston Manning way back in the old days. Her note said, 'Do not destroy. Keep with Family artifacts.'"

He swallowed a time or two and then added, trying, Jeff supposed, to moderate what now appeared to be growing excitement, "It's in the closet in my room. If you promise me you won't disappear, I'll go get it and be right back because there is a sealed letter there with your name on it, and I want to see what that letter says as much as you do, Colonel Preston!"

He was back in less than five minutes with a small leather-covered box, which Jeff recognized with shock as the "message box" he and Sara had shared if they had important messages to pass on to each other. It had always been left tucked away in a squirrel hole in the branch of an ancient hollow tree at Riverside Plantation, a tree that no longer existed.

Stunned, he looked up at Gus, who said in a somewhat strained but excited voice, "I didn't think it would hurt for me to read it, as all these people died so many years ago… but for some reason, I have always felt that would be a breach of trust." He handed Jeff a formal envelope, yellow with age. The return address in the left corner said "Riverside Plantation, Roswell, Georgia."

"Thank you, Gus," Jeff said very softly. Silent now, he opened the flap and pulled out a folded piece of fine parchment, the kind of paper upon which his father had always penned important business letters. With some trepidation, he unfolded the letter.

My dearest son,

I have received word that Compact raiders are on their way to Riverside. I did not tell Sara. Instead, I sent her quickly off to Fox Haven Farm with Moses and two of his best Zulu warriors to care for her. She did not want to leave me, so I told her I had heard rumors that Jonny might be there waiting for her. I did not want to pass on to her the truly dire news I have received of the carnage remaining after the battle in the Wilderness of Virginia. I strongly suspect Jonny was one of the many conscripts killed there, along with all the other fellows who were marched away to fight for a cause that defies their deepest beliefs. Even more heartbreaking, Jonny's body will probably never be identified.

I feel such an intimate thing as birthing a child should be experienced in a mother's own home with her family around her rather than at a place of death and destruction. Unfortunately, that is what this home we have loved so dearly for so long will become in a few hours. My dear son, I am dying of a cancer that is growing in my lungs. I can scarcely breathe now, my mind is not as sharp, and my doctor has told me I have very little time left. I have sent the staff to the mountain home I once told you of in the Virginia mountain country. They will be well taken care of there by your eldest sister, Rosette, who knows most of them already. Moses can take you there or give you a map and the appropriate passwords.

I do not intend to let the people of The Compact conquer Riverside. Only two of my men are staying with me. I told my fellows not to martyr themselves, but two have volunteered to stay with me to the end. They know the escape routes as well as you and I do, and I hope they use them.

I will not be taken alive, Jeff. I will give as good as I get and then fall on my own sword. I am dying, anyway. I think you have suspected as much.

I have had a good life for the most part, with many loves, many sorrows, and only a few regrets. I have not told Sara, but I have only weeks left to me. It is a cancer growing in my lung, next to my heart. I would like to see you again before the end, but I think under the circumstances, that is not possible. I have already said my final goodbyes to your dear sister Sara—even if she was not aware of it—and to my best friend Moses and to this life we have built and lived together. The fellows of The Compact will not take this house, Jeff. It will long since have become my funeral pyre.

I have only one request, my dear son. I have left a map for you. Follow it and you will find your old friend, Celé, and her beloved husband. You will also find your dear sister, Rosette, who is as spunky as ever. I have told them they must keep their origins hidden to avoid the pirates' scourge, but they will take you and your sister to their hearts at a moment's notice. Celé and Rosette remember you with the greatest of love.

My profoundest love to you, my son. You and your sisters are my legacy to the world. When I think of the three of you, I realize I have left far more than gold to my fellow men.

Your loving father,
Isaac Preston

Jeff could not look up from the parchment. Tears were rolling from his eyes. He felt a motion against his side, and took the handkerchief the young man was handing him.

"Thank you, Gus," he said softly. "I am profoundly grateful to you for caring for my father's letter. It means the world to me. Some day I will tell you about it, in its full context—but not right now. I have a lot of thinking to do."

"I understand," Gus said in a very soft voice.

And Jeff was sure he did.

CHAPTER 35

I t was a much-subdued Gus who concluded his duty as tour guide and brought a still solemn Jeff back to the kitchen. Both were ready to sit down with a glass of something more bracing than tea when his mother abruptly entered the room. Gus looked up. "What's happening?"

"Nothing yet, but…," Bernice seemed nervous, "their jeep people are yelling at their SUV people, and the SUV people are yelling at each other and at everyone else. Our hidden mics are picking up a lot of words polite people don't say in public. The youngsters are cowering at the end of a barrage of obscenity, being roundly blamed for not setting out a watchman. They claim they did set out a watchman, but he disappeared." A grin flashed across her face. She relaxed. "Must be the guy our fellows grabbed. His name is Thad Simeon. We've got him in custody, and he's telling us all he knows, with relish, and asking for sanctuary, which, of course, we'll grant him!"

"Thad Simeon?" Jeff's overworked sense of wonder flooded into a huge burst of joy. "By god, I'll have to tell Jeb. Keep that young man safe, will you? It was Thad's father who warned us to leave Georgia. He started this whole rescue mission. We and all those boys owe him! But I have another question," he added with a sudden sense of urgency, "in terms of the Searchers. Do any of them have red hair?"

"Well," Bernice answered tentatively, "just let me find that out!" She pulled a phone from her pocket and dialed. The answer was brief. She turned back to Jeff. "Funny you should ask. I'm told there are no redheads among the Searchers. But…there are two who came in the bigwigs' SUV, with the bald guy who's loud and mean!"

"Any further descriptions?"

"The bald one is an older gent—the top guy, they think! A voice like steel, unprintable words aimed at those poor kids whose equipment went missing. Blaming them! The redhead, a middle-aged gent, apparently Baldy's second-in-command. Diplomatic but cold, whatever that means, maybe because he said something about 'sacrificing yourself for the sake of The Compact.' As if anyone would want to!

"The third, though, the one on the direct end of that suicide directive, he's no more than a kid. Same general age as the Searchers, eighteen maybe, no more than twenty tops. Must all be part of the same family. He's been told he'll be the first man to enter the cave in the mountainside. Apparently, he's to search for the treasure, and if he can't bring it out himself, they'll send in someone more *worthy*, or words to that effect! He's the canary in the coal mine, the sacrificial lamb, and it's obvious he's terrified!"

Big problem! Jeff shook his head. He took out his phone and dialed Jeb Wallace. "We've got to talk. Can you meet us in the kitchen?"

Jeb was there within minutes, eyebrows raised.

"The Family got your friend Davy's son. Thad Simeon is safely in our custody."

"Thank the Good Guys once again!" Jeb said with intense feeling.

Jeff's smile faded as he followed up the good news with the bad. "But little Todd's *daddy* is out there too," Jeff said softly, "with his father and another member of the hierarchy, being told he has to be the first to go into the cave to see if there's anything worth sending one of the big heroes out to bring back, meaning if a sacrifice has to be made, it going to be the gay kid!"

Jeb's face went white. He sat down suddenly on the nearest bench. When he looked up, Jeff could see distress written in every expression. "What can we do?"

"Hopefully we'll figure something out once we're on-site," Jeff said.

Bernice Richards understandably was as puzzled as her son. She looked first at Jeff, then at Emily's husband, and then back at Jeff. She motioned with her shoulders, something more than a shrug. "Anything we should know about?"

"Family matters," Jeb Wallace mumbled.

"We're Family," Bernice declared, going to him and putting a hand on his.

Tears were beginning to spill across his cheeks. He looked up at her. "Well, Family, this is one big problem we've got to fix real quick because I'm not gonna let that boy get hurt. I won't let it be said down the line sometime…" He choked up and stopped speaking.

Bernice glanced at Jeff. She looked at her son and motioned sideways with her head. "Private discussion, gents," she said softly. "Come back in ten."

Jeff and Gus moved outside to the garden to finish their beers. "Gus, that boy is Em's baby daddy," Jeff said softly to Gus, who did need to know. "He didn't want that personal encounter any more than Em did, forced rape on both their parts. If Emily hasn't spoken with your mother about it— which is a hard thing for Em to do, facts be known—Jeb can fill you in. This is top priority! For Em's sake and little Todd, too, we must keep that boy safe!"

Bernice beckoned to them a few moments later. They returned to the kitchen just as Bernice was saying, "We can try to grab him…" her tone as she spoke with Jeb was pure compassion, "like we did your friend's son. Shall we call a strategy meeting?"

Jeff interrupted, "Let's keep this inside your own personal family group, Bernice. It's quite sensitive for Emily and Jeb."

Bernice turned to Gus. "Get Vince on the phone, would you? He's above the cave with our jeep. It'll only take a few minutes for him to get here. Let's run this by him."

Gus grabbed a phone from his pocket and made the call.

Jeb was pacing and Jeff was sitting silent when a smiling Vince came through the door. He asked everyone to join him in the small private office he utilized for keeping track of his theatrical schedule. Bernice's expression was an interesting study of outrage and concern, but for the moment, she did not speak. She closed the office door tightly behind them.

"Greetings, both of you," Vince said, shaking hands cordially with Jeff and then with Jeb. "You've done us a terrific service eliminating all the climbing equipment at one fell swoop! Brilliant! Beats anything I've ever done on screen! What can I do for you in exchange?"

"First," Jeff said as they seated themselves at a small table, "give us an update."

Vince laughed sharply. "It would be funny if it were a movie, but it's not! They're dithering down at the base in loud angry voices. It's clear there's a headbutting match between the two older guys. I've spotted maps out, though, and I think the loudest voices are for coming up the county road. The steep one."

"Is your private road shown on the maps?"

"Geologic survey maps, yes. I haven't seen one of those spread out over the hoods of their SUVs yet, but our guys are out on the road protecting Nowhere City, just in case. FYI," Vince went on, "the thinking at the base of the cliff seems to be this—if they can find a way to get above the cliff, they can fasten ropes to trees and simply drop down to see what's in the cave and snag it if something is there.

"It has not yet occurred to them that if the cliff face is as dangerous as the posted signs indicate, the top of the cave might be as well. We are acutely aware of the danger because we have unfortunately lost people up there! However, much as I dislike all of them, I don't want their deaths on my conscience! Especially those boys who are here under duress."

"What do you suggest, then?" Jeff asked. "Stopping them at the guard shack?"

"That armed guard approach was just for you folks. Movie stuff! We've never done that kind of overacting in real life. Do you have any suggestions?"

Emily's husband looked up at Vince. His private conversation with Bernice had been helpful, the edge of his emotion finally blunted. "You guys scared the bejesus out of us, comin' out of the shack like that! But if you do the same thing to them, they'll probably shoot first, ask questions later! We never would of. But our heads are screwed on different from theirs."

Jeff, who had been ruminating on the problem, finally spoke out. "Unfortunately, Vince, we've got a different problem to solve first. That red-haired young man must be snatched away before any ropes start dropping or lead starts flying."

Vince looked hard at Jeff, then at Bernice, and then at Jeb, whose eyes were focused tightly on Vince's face. "Dare I ask why?" Vince said softly.

Jeb's words came as a growl. "He's Brian Talbot, Todd's real daddy!"

Vince took a step backward, genuine shock apparent in his expression. "That youngster is baby Todd's gene donor? How did that happen?"

Jeb said grimly, "Forced rape. A punishment for his bein' gay, a humiliation! Emily feels for him because of what happened, and we both decided to keep the baby! That boy was hounded to do what he did with a lot of old guys gathered around watchin' and hootin' and hollerin'. He needs to be got away from 'em—not killed because of 'em!"

"That's...despicable!" Vince's tanned forehead and cheeks had turned a noticeable red. "Oh my god! That poor kid! I understand what you're saying. I understand! We'll do what we can do, Jeb! Oh my god, what Em's had to go through! And you! And the boy! I can't even imagine...the understanding you've shown!" He strode toward Jeb and took him into a tight embrace.

Jeb didn't seem to know how to respond. His hands flailed a bit before they finally touched flesh and stuck. There were tears welling in his eyes when Vince released him.

Vince stepped back then and wiped at his eyes too. "Up till now, this has been kind of a daily ritual, fighting these people. It's been our legacy, you might say, an isolating kind of duty we've had to face because...well, I wasn't real sure what the because was. It seemed like such a lame reason to have to lock ourselves away from the world—because of a document someone might or might not have signed under threat of death! Race was never part of this equation, was it? We've often wondered.

"Now you're confirming the document story with that much power over people…? My god!" He took a deep breath and continued, "Okay! Now it's personal! I don't think I've ever felt so much hate…anger…rage! It just boiled up in me…" He turned away, tears streaming down his cheeks again. "Poor Emily, my poor sweetheart of a sister! The humiliation she must have endured! They didn't even know she was a blood relative of Mr. Jon Randolph III! She was just a *throwaway*! Oh my god! No wonder you went into hiding. How brave she's been…and you too, Jeb! What can we do to help?"

"For the record, Vince," Jeff answered quietly, "and this is only because you've had no occasion yet to experience the full depth of The Compact problem—Em's *relationship* to the Blackheart Compact in this case was unknown to them! The connection came through Jeb. One of his ancestors, a seaman named Jebediah Griffiths, signed the original Blackheart Compact under extreme duress! It didn't matter that Griffiths fought to keep from signing. In the end, it was either that or his life! He chose life! So Jeb is bound to The Compact the same way we are.

"Jeb met Emily while he was a Searcher. You might say that was pure bad luck on Em's part, except for the fact that Jeb is one of the best people I've ever had the good fortune to meet, and he and Em love each other. Moreover, he's helping us to destroy The Compact by telling us what he knows about how their side of it works!" Jeff nodded at Jeb, who now appeared more determined than angry. "As far as The Compact goes, your family's relationship to ours seems always to have been kept a secret. We didn't even know about you until we discovered Rosette's letters to Sara, which are now concealed in a very safe place. You folks could walk away at any time with no one the wiser as to your genetic relationship to Mr. Jon Randolph III."

Jeff's voice now resonated with a seriousness he had never used before. "But here's the bigger picture, folks, something you may not completely be aware of—Compact people are everywhere! They're embedded in many professions, governmental bodies, police departments, corporations, you name it. You won't know if you're working with someone who's connected, unless they want you to know! And by then, you're on the hook to them!

"This organization has been building on itself for a long time, like an upside-down pyramid. Most of its participants are reluctant and fearful and quite willing to abandon their membership in the club if they ever could. If we can take out those people down there at the base of this cliff, the current governing hierarchy—the Inner Circle, they call themselves—and destroy their origination documents, including the original Compact, we can begin to unravel the whole organization. It's going to be a massive job, but we're determined to get it started!"

Vince looked hard at Jeff. "I'm in! Just tell me what to do?" He looked up at his sister and then at his nephew. They both nodded.

"We're pretty sure we know where The Compact document is," Jeff answered with a grin that seemed to surprise them, "and we're after it!"

Vince frowned. "The document? The actual Blackheart Compact, you mean it still exists?"

"Remember the blueprints we found here in the plane?" Jeff answered. "I trust you've been updated by Bernice, those blueprints were Moses's plans for The Compact headquarters building. We've found that headquarters building, and once we get in, we'll know all its secrets!"

Vince's eyes went wide. "Compact headquarters? Where is it?"

"It's on a nice little acreage of mountain rock and woodland butted up on an island in the Potomac River upstream of Washington, DC. Because we've studied the defensive devices surrounding the headquarters, which are grim and include armed guards, we're convinced that's where the origination documents are being kept, including the actual Compact. The only barriers left to grabbing the documents right this minute are a couple of watchdogs inside the barbed-wire fence and possibly a couple of armed guards. Would you like an updated report from our off-site spies? They are working on this even as we speak!"

"Hell, yes!" Vince growled.

Jeb looked up at Jeff, grinning broadly. "You gave them the GO, didn't you?"

As he pulled his cell phone into his hand, Jeff grinned back. "If all the hierarchy is here at the base of our cliff, including a couple of truckloads of armed guards, who's left to mind the shop? Let's see if our guys have had any luck." He punched in Bill's number. "How about it?"

At the answer, Jeff whooped! His fist went into the air. While he was still online, he gave a running summary of Bill's excited narrative to his eager compatriots: "Not *just* The Compact document? A microchip too? From the same sealed display case? Pages and pages of names and addresses! It's in your computer, and you're actually looking at them? And the display case has been resealed with a little smoke bomb, so it appears that the contents simply burst into flame! God, you're good! Bill! Ivan! Great job!" He looked up, grinning. "Chuck got one. Guppy got the other!" he said, looking up and around the room. "We've got them!"

"How?" Gus asked. "What? Who?" He seemed genuinely bewildered, and with good reason, Jeff thought! Gus would get his answers, though, in a few minutes, along with Vince and Bernice.

The Compact would never know what the hell had happened!

A great big grin lit Bernice's beautiful face. She hugged her son tightly. "They've got geniuses working on their side too, Augustus."

"And drones with names?" Vince still appeared stunned.

Jeff explained, "Guppy and Chuck are very small but powerful. They can wait quietly in high shadows hidden from guards and dogs. Having access to those blueprints we found in the cave allowed Guppy and Chuck to quietly swoop from empty drainpipes into secret passageways created by a very clever architect named Moses, thus giving them entry to any room in that house.

"Jon Randolph Jr.'s untimely death forced us to take a generational break—death does that sometimes. But with the aid of those blueprints he rescued for us and with two smart drones helping behind the lines, success is finally within our grasp. Our guys back at the ranch have snatched away The Compact organization's most important possessions, the seminal documents and the address lists of all Compact members. Guppy and Chuck flew silently through secret passageways filled with spider webs, indicating, of course, that no human had been there in many years. They scooted unseen into a locked and alarmed room, took the ancient documents, including The Compact itself, from a closed case, which is once again closed and locked, and brought 'em home! With no one the wiser!" He grinned. "Now we have to prepare for the next task, snatching away the slave labor!"

"Some of us are way sneakier than others, that's for sure!" Bernice said triumphantly. "But now that all of Isaac Preston's kin are aware of each other and are working together, we cannot fail!" With a hearty laugh, she added, "Rule number one, don't ever underestimate Family!"

Vince threw his arms around Jeff and then hugged his brother-in-law once again. Tears of joy in the accomplishment of the daring coup were streaming from many eyes.

*****

The first chance Jeff got, he called Lorie. Stretched out in a comfortable bed with his head propped on a pillow and a blanket wrapped around him, he was tired as he ever had been—and that was really, really tired!

"Are you okay?" she asked with a bit of tremor in her voice.

"I'm going to fall asleep the minute I hang up, but on the whole, we're all doing well. What I need to know is your assessment of the acquisition that was sent to you by airmail?"

"Oh, Jeff," she answered, her voice tremulous, "oh my god, I can't believe I have actually seen that…that abomination! None of us can! Isaac's signature is just the way he described it! I burst into tears when I saw it there on the first page, that poor little boy! It's not just a legend. It's real! Then I remembered what happened next!" She was silent for a time. Before Jeff could think of anything to say that might prove comforting, she exploded. "It has a dark feel to it, Jeff! What you feel first is the slashing of the blade because of all that blood soaked into the parchment! And then you remember the purposes for which its words have been used! I've never been affected like this before—by anything! This may be a historical document, but it needs to disappear! Permanently!

"The guys had Chuck drop The Compact document itself into a black plastic trash bag. And then every handwritten page of the member lists followed. Then they shoved the bag into the vault in Ewen's room. Alexi knows the combination, and she was certain Ewen would agree it can't be stored anywhere else except inside that closely guarded room. The computer chip, which we assume contains address lists, is in the bag with it. It was handled by Guppy, who put it into the computer all by his little electronic self so we could examine it and pulled it out, too, after we'd recorded the data. We didn't touch either object, Jeff. We didn't even want to. Later, perhaps, after we do some Navaho purification chants or something! Guppy then did a little exotic dance of sorts before he settled down, and his power went off. I think he was scrubbing his electronic hands. Not sure!" She laughed a bit nervously. "He may have had a mental breakdown!"

"Thank you, my love," Jeff answered, chuckling with quiet exhilaration. "We'll decide what we're going to do with those things when we get back. Now here's my update on what's happening—The Compact people wasted most of their evening in a screaming match among themselves, but plans are finally starting to jell. They're searching all kinds of maps for a way to get to the top of the ridge early tomorrow morning, and we've heard talk about rappelling into the cave from above. They have no idea how dangerous that is!

"We're expecting the log house to get some company tomorrow, but they will find it padlocked and alarmed with stern notifications attached to the doors that trespassers will be confronted by Pinkerton guards who will feel free to use deadly force or something to that effect! Many of us will be out in the forest in interesting places where we can see but not be seen. And we've got Forest Service personnel and Park Rangers on call if we can't handle these guys ourselves. Also,

I've volunteered to help pluck kids back from the brink if the ground above the cave gives way."

Lorie gasped. "How?"

He chuckled a bit nervously. "I'll be using a tried-and-true rescue device that's rigged up near the edge for that purpose. Apparently, a rescue apparatus was built near the edge back in the day, and it still works. I'll have a crew to help me, which is especially reassuring."

"Rescue apparatus?" Lorie repeated anxiously.

"They call it a Deerfield device. It's built in a dense part of the forest close by the drop-off, concealed inside a shack that was built to keep it from being tampered with. They tell me it was put together by an old sailor who knew all about pulleys and ratchets and wheels and chains and everything seaworthy. The base of the device is anchored into the solid part of this mountain, but it's as close to the edge as possible. They say that it works so well that if a rescuer is hanging onto a person who's hurt, it doesn't take more than one person on the rope above to bring both up, although more hands make it easier. And don't worry, Lorie love, there's been no chances taken here! The ropes are changed out every year. I'll be using the same climbing gear I used last year when we reclaimed Moses's diamond masterpiece, and I was hanging ten stories over the streets of Washington, DC! Once I'm hooked onto the crane attached to this device, the crew can swing me wherever I need to go off the face of the cliff and lift me back when I tell them to."

"Your father's 'Will' built it for them?" Lorie asked quietly.

"Of course, it was Will Deerfield," Jeff said quietly. "My father regularly got letters from him, and I met him several times while I was growing up. He was brilliant. And isn't that an unexpected twist?"

"My world has just brightened a lot," Lorie answered, sounding more secure. She added, "How is Ewen doing? Do you still think he's at risk?"

Jeff answered this time with confidence, "I've already asked him to lead a rescue party into the forest to snatch the young men away from their Compact guards with a quiet promise that we will get them home to their parents as soon as we can, free of all Compact commitments. He snatched up that assignment. In any case, he won't be doing any active climbing for a while! Does that calm your fears, love?"

Again, Lorie was quiet. "The queasy stomach feels a bit better now that I've heard you're going to be assisted by a crew. Please be especially careful. I'm beginning to take my stomach problems very seriously!"

"I am too," he replied bluntly. "I think someone or something with a broader perspective on this situation than we have is working the math on our chances of prevailing over our foes and perhaps giving us early warnings… Your queasy stomach, perhaps? This is a hazardous operation at best! So thank you, love. We'll be as prepared as we can for unexpected ambushes. Get some sleep now. I'll call you in the morning. Kiss the baby for me, please!"

Lorie chuckled. "I will do that, Daddy. We both love you, you know!"

"I know," he said quietly. "And I love you both right back. Forever!" With another kiss, he hung up and was asleep moments later.

CHAPTER 36

Before dawn, Saturday, April 23, 2016

H e was awakened by Vince holding a small flashlight and shaking him gently. "They are on the move. They wisely rejected the steep road because it's too hazardous in the dark. They ignored our 'Private' signs, of course. Six SUVs and several jeeps are already approaching Nowhere City. All the lights are off in town, so maybe they'll ignore it. They'd better, or they're in big trouble!"

"I'm up," Jeff said, following his words with action. He pulled on his clothes: jeans, a dark shirt, climbing boots, and a jacket against the lingering chill. He picked up the climbing gear he had brought with him and slung it over his shoulder.

Breakfast was a cold one in a kitchen lit only by pocket flashlights. Bernice didn't want lights on or aromas lingering. A wise precaution, he thought. If the intruders did not see nor smell indicators of human presence, they would likely ignore the secluded log cabin at the top of the hill and simply follow the gravel county road toward the edge of the cliff, roughly two and a half miles ahead as the newly installed arrow sign to the "Scenic View Parking Lot" indicated.

Jeff was aware that many of the darkened dwellings in Nowhere City, as well as the hallways inside the lodge itself, were bristling with men carrying loaded rifles and that they were itching to use them. At Bernice's request, the Park Service had furnished a contingent of law enforcement people to oversee and possibly intervene if an actual confrontation seemed likely. State Police had been notified as well. Several radio-equipped personnel from each service were already on-site, and every one of them was carrying at least one weapon.

If Compact members were aware that this particular part of the mountain on this particular day was an arsenal itching to explode, would they continue their quest? A toss-up, Jeff figured. At this point, they had to be sensing that a showdown of some kind was looming. Otherwise, they would not have brought so many men with them.

Soft conversations were going on throughout the kitchen. Jeff saw Bernice circling, refilling coffee cups with brew heated in the microwave, offering breakfast rolls and/or salt jerky made only as Bernice could create either food for body and soul!

Ewen found Jeff in the solemn crowd. "My brother Bob is here," he said quietly. "He's brought in some other folks from the FBI. Since the forest belongs to the US government, the Forest Service has jurisdiction, but a lot of collaboration is going on right now."

"A couple of SUVs came past the house an hour or so ago filled with armed men," Jeff told him. "Theirs! We've matched them with more troops. Forest Service rangers and sheriff's deputies have been mobilized. Ours came in a convoy early this morning, after theirs got here. On the other hand, maybe The Compact doesn't know they're being watched, but they're itchy. They've never seemed too intelligent," Jeff added, hoping that was still the case.

Bernice came by, still refreshing coffee cups. "I've been told that all of the young Searchers are on top already," she said quietly. "They were brought up before dark, but they spotted the warning signs and won't venture near the edge—none of them! A minor upheaval, I understand! A strike, of sorts! Hopefully they're still huddling in their tents."

Ewen replied, "Everyone knows our primary task is rescue. After we've confused and scattered the adults, it'll probably be easy to grab the young men, several at a time or separately. Slow and steady until we get them all!"

"We are the masters of stealth!" Jeff chuckled. Bernice grinned and moved on with her coffee pot.

Ewen looked hard at Jeff and held up crossed fingers. "You concentrate on that red-haired kid. We'll take care of the others!"

"Thanks, Ewen," Jeff said warmly. He stepped quietly through the back door into predawn on the porch of the big log cabin and took a deep breath of cool air. He would always associate that pungent incense of pine with the moment of incredulity that had begun when he realized he had reemerged into life from the darkness of death. He had a sudden warm remembrance of the wind-swept grasses that had caressed his face like soft fingers, wakening him as he lay at the bottom of the ravine and then the cacophony of forest sounds nearly overwhelming him as life and awareness flowed back into his body.

He heard the sounds clearly once again. Against the silence of the woods, he discerned the occasional sharp bursting of a pine cone, twitters of nesting birds, soft whispers of the wind that brushed his forehead, cleansing and clearing his mind. He was alive, and now he knew why. He had been summoned back not only to help his own extended family but to release the unending band of young men dragooned into doing The Compact's dirty work, an unwarranted servitude on their part, based on fear not just for themselves but for all the people they loved.

He was also keenly aware of the presence of a great number of determined, well-armed, unnaturally silent men now on the alert in cleverly camouflaged "blinds" surrounding this mountaintop Command Center. These surprisingly innovative descendants of his father Isaac and the beautiful Celé were intent on guarding their legacy—their way of life—indeed, their very existence!

Strangely enough, until now they had not been fully aware of the scourge called The Compact. If without prior warning these proud people had been confronted by the heavily armed Compact killers who were now invading their mountaintop focused on finding a lost treasure, his sister Rosette's family might never have had a fighting chance at survival.

In general, the Family had what it took to defend itself. But the hostile firepower now arrayed on this mountaintop was far more deadly than the Family could ever have anticipated. No wonder he had been summoned! It seemed that he and his small but unusually well-armed crew had arrived just in the nick of time!

He felt a hand on his arm. He turned to see Gus. "Sorry," the young man whispered. "Mom told me she's heard that things are already popping and that I should escort you to the cliff by our short route. I doubt anyone has shown you this one till now."

"Short route?"

"Our tunnel!" He grinned. "I see you've got your gear on. Good."

Jeff grinned back as he once again adjusted and tightened straps intended to suspend him far above the earth. Tunnel? Why was he not surprised? This was his family after all!

What surprised him was where the entrance was located: in an unused outhouse! The old wooden building located at the rear of a kitchen garden far beyond the main house offered a serviceable three-seater that had very long ago been abandoned. Its *aromatic* contents, his guide told him, had judiciously—after a certain amount of purification—been used as fertilizer for the beautiful flower gardens spread across the front acreage. When Gus pulled the wooden seat covers up, his small flashlight pinpointed handles cleverly concealed in packed earth at each side of the structure. "You reach down through the holes and pull up both sides simultaneously. It takes two people to do this, as they have to be pulled at exactly the same time. We're just going to lock this privy from the inside because we don't want the seat put back into place before we crawl out!"

Jeff had to laugh!

They lifted. With a dirt-filled box dangling beneath it, the seat came out smoothly and was stored in an out-of-the-way place. Gus again retrieved his flashlight and pointed the beam downward, illuminating a ladder descending into a deep dark hole!

"How in hell did you do this?" Jeff was incredulous.

"Dynamite," Gus laughed. "Some of our family members worked for the railroad back in the day, blasting holes through mountains so train tracks could be laid. They borrowed a few extra sticks, calculated, drilled, and then backed off and let her rip! Several times! Just so! Very precise! They were trained engineers. They knew exactly where they were going and how to get there. It's a really neat tunnel over to the cliff." He now became serious. "What Mom wants us to do is grab and hide those poor fellows who were dragged out here for no business of their own. We'll keep them in seclusion until we can smuggle them back to their families. Doesn't that sound kind of like what the underground railroad did?"

"What do you know about the Underground?" Jeff looked at the young man with new appreciation.

"Everything! Chapter and verse! Come on, let's go. Put your light on." Gus retrieved an elastic strap from his pocket and pulled it across his forehead. Jeff, remembering he also had a light strap in his equipment, followed suit. A moment later, two powerful lights blinked on.

"Next," Gus said, handing Jeff a coil of rope, "clip this to your carabineer. You'll probably have to use it." He then looked at Jeff, a querulous half-smile on his lips. After a long moment of silence, he said very softly, "You're scared, aren't you?" He glanced toward the hole and nodded, indicating Jeff should go down first.

Jeff looked up at the young man, momentarily uncertain what to say. "Yes," he said truthfully. "Aren't you?"

"Not of the hole. I honestly don't know about the rest," Gus said. "Should I be?"

Jeff answered, "Be cautious, Gus. We're not dealing with ordinary people here. Their actions define them differently. We've discovered that some of them are pure evil. These young people we are hoping to take back to their parents, they are only pawns in what The Compact hierarchy considers its primary goal above all else—acquiring power. Their parents have been told in no uncertain terms, 'If you ever want your child back, do exactly what we tell you to do. Never question! Never fail!'"

"Oh my god! That *is* evil!"

"I want us to blow as big a hole in The Compact today as you folks did to this mountain to finally break all their hostages free. I will do my best, Gus, but if I fail, can I count on you to continue my mission?"

Gus was silent now…stunned, it seemed. Then he swallowed a time or two and said softly in a deep querulous voice, "You'll probably have to clarify for me what that exact mission is, Major Preston."

Something pivotal could well happen in these next few hours. I'm not certain what, except to warn you that the outcome is not a settled business! Our presence, Gus, is the deciding factor. Stay alert! Call in help if and when it's necessary. My body is all too mortal. I hope I will survive, but that depends entirely on how the cards are dealt and how well they are played. We are on the brink of a significant battle. Are you afraid?"

"I wasn't before!" Gus breathed. "Now I am—damn it!"

"Stay afraid. It will keep you sharp!"

Gus nodded briskly and began the descent. Jeff followed, counting the steps as they moved downward. At forty-eight, his very human knees were beginning to buckle, and he felt a burn in the back of his legs. "How much farther?" he asked, trying to keep the words from sounding like a complaint.

The answer reverberated eerily from below him. "Only ten more steps, Major. Then we move into the tunnel. We're headed to the exit just above the cave. Follow me closely."

Gus stepped off the ladder and reached out a hand. Jeff grabbed it and pulled himself finally onto a solid floor! An opening in the rock surrounding them revealed itself in the glow of Gus's headlight. Suddenly, lights came on. "Electric eyes make life a lot easier," Gus said.

The tunnel lights, Jeff discovered, were activated by movement. When travelers left one portion of the cave and turned a corner, fresh lights appeared and the previous lights went out. "We have to walk half a mile rather than two and a half," Gus told him. "The dirt auto road is quite slow, it bends and turns many times around the cliffs. We go straight through the mountain. Anytime we see cars headed toward the cliff, we make a beeline and we issue stern warnings to the drivers as they arrive at the parking lot. There are always jerks who don't want to listen. If they survive, they tell us how sorry they were to have ignored us. The few who tumbled down…well, we'll never know how they felt, but the one I saw fall…" Gus's voice faltered.

"It must have been difficult," Jeff said quietly.

"I was just a kid! I was scared of the slightest hillside for months after that. Mom was really worried about me, it took a long time to get past it. I'm functional again, but it's made me way more wary when I'm up here. The first thing I do is put on a harness and clip a rope to one of the Deerfield anchors. No running around out on this cliff!"

"I've been afraid of heights all my life," Jeff told him quietly, adjusting his own gear once again.

Gus's grin was spontaneous. "I thought Yankee Major Preston wasn't afraid of anything!"

Jeff chuckled softly. "I never thought the Yankees would be my downfall, but it was two of their bullets that knocked me off a cliff and broke my head open. How's that for irony?"

Gus came to a halt, the grin gone. "Forgive me if I don't laugh." His voice was quite solemn. "It's hard enough for me to think of you as a living person, but to hear from you about the way you died…I'm sorry, Major, but please tell me you won't repeat that scenario on my watch!"

"Gus," he said quietly, "I have a loving wife and the cutest little two-year-old daughter you ever saw. I'm not intending to die anytime soon!"

"Thank goodness for that!" Gus's voice was still a bit shaky. "All you have to do is call out if you're in trouble, you can count on me!"

"Thank you, Gus. I appreciate that!"

The young man paused for a long moment, again looking hard at Jeff. Finally, he turned back to his guide duties, and it was the "joker in the pack" who quietly led Major Preston to the camouflaged exit on the mountaintop.

CHAPTER 37

Saturday, April 23, still early morning

They came out through a small metal door cleverly set into a crevasse in one of the granite walls that comprised the enduring, rather than eroding, section of the mountainside. Once closed, there was no sign that an entryway existed. Jeff hoped he would be able to remember where that door was and how to open it if he needed to! Almost as if he'd read Jeff's mind, Gus whispered, "This is the whitest cliff in the area. Look for the crooked little pine tree sticking out sideways about four feet above the trail. It's a fake that hides the operating lever. This pathway takes us to the observation post we set up on the only ridge that overlooks the cave. It seems we've been anticipating this crisis for a long time!"

"Lead on!"

A short distance from the Family's concealed exit, a bright red line had been spray-painted across the path and a message in the same medium: HALT!

No mistaking that message!

Gus pointed upward, and quickly they mounted the rugged staircase that had been cut from a slope on the side of the mountain and supplied with a taut rope railing. Now from a vantage point slightly above and to one side of the final resting place of Sara's brave son, they could get a broad view of what was happening below. Two middle-aged men in climbing gear had cut wide open the wire security fence above the cave and were preparing to pass into the danger zone, perhaps thinking themselves more privileged than ordinary mortals! Also on-site were at least a dozen slender young men wearing brightly colored jackets, jeans, and climbing boots. Searchers. Unlike their masters, they were standing far back from the edge as a pack unwilling to venture past the Family's wood and wire fence with its long-posted skull and crossbones. Not one was wearing climbing gear, all of which remained secure in the big cabin's storage shed.

A tall young man—this one unfortunately rigged with climbing equipment—was also standing near the danger zone but apart from the others. Gus handed Jeff the binoculars, and he trained them on the lone climber. *More than a boy*, Jeff thought. *Twenty, maybe. Not much more.* Curls of russet hair were plastered to the sides of his face by the sweat of recent exertions. In the pale light of early morning, Jeff watched him reach to push the damp hair away from his temples. His face was open, with regular features, a slightly tilted nose, and well-placed eyes. A good-looking fellow on the whole, grown tall but not quite yet a man.

At this moment, the sullen resentment typical of late adolescence seemed to be battling with what dignity he might have exerted were he in any other situation than a father-son conflict. Little Todd's biological father, Brian Talbot.

The older men and a couple of burly fellows who appeared to be guards blatantly strode past the warning signs and across the upper lip of the cave, zeroing in on the chain-link fence installed by the Family to stop the ever-present know-it-alls who ignore posted signs. Jeff wondered, did these folks think warnings were a joke and the fence simply a symbol of disclaimer of responsibility in case someone tried to sue? The intruders were standing in a place where unstable ground had several times dropped unwary walkers into dangerous territory—in one case, at least, headlong down the side of the cliff. Being inveterate liars themselves, was it possible they could not recognize truth when it was displayed for all to see? The bald man turned to his son and gestured for him to come forward.

Jeff spotted a dark-skinned member of the Family striding resolutely through the forest toward the cliff. He heard the arrested breath behind him and Gus's soft voice. "My brother, Jerome. Oh my god, what's he doing?"

Jerome broke out through the cover of trees. "Hold up, you fellows," he said sharply. "It's too dangerous to go out there! You're already on shaky ground!"

The man turned to him. "It's our business, nigger! None of yours!"

"It's everybody's business when a person commits suicide!" Jerome snapped back. "And it's the law's business when someone commits murder! If you cut that fence, mister, I'll call the law on you!"

"Boy howdy!" Gus said softly. "He's really asking for trouble!"

Talbot beckoned to three of the young Searchers who had been hanging back. "Take care of this!" he said harshly.

The young men looked first at Talbot and then at each other. A moment later, they moved hesitantly toward Jerome, who beckoned, whirled, and headed back into the forest at a quick trot. The Searchers started after him slowly and then accelerated their efforts. Moments later, a few more Searchers disappeared from sight, apparently willing to chance their own escapes.

From Jeff's higher vantage point, however, it was possible to track the chase. Jerome led his pursuers through thick scrub, moving farther away from the cliff with each step. He then took an abrupt turn back into the forest. All the pursuing Searchers followed, only to be confronted by Jerome's companions, those who had remained concealed in the nearby brush. "My other brothers," Gus whispered, grinning, "and a few cousins."

There was a short scuffle, the Searchers quickly acknowledging the fact that they had been fairly apprehended. Their hands shot into the air. After a short discussion, hands went down and everyone disappeared.

"The other tunnel entryway is over there," Gus said with laughter in his voice.

Jeff grinned. This Family knew what it was doing!

As that small drama was transpiring, Brian's father again motioned for his son to come forward. Their companion remained silent. Once more, Brian refused. Talbot beckoned to the remaining Searchers, the five that were left, and, seeing no movement, gave the same "come forward" signal to a group of armed men standing behind them. The gunmen moved forward, herding the remaining young men before them. "These fellows will help you out, Brian!" Talbot said coldly.

His words cut through the trees like a death sentence.

"No!" Brian said abruptly. "Not because of me!" He stood silent for a long minute. "I'll go alone, Father," he said stoutly. "This is my birthright. My death. Not theirs!"

Jeff let out a deep sigh. With those defiant words, the boy had taken a huge step toward adulthood—if perhaps his last to life!

Another soft "Oh, crap" came from Gus, and Jeff decided it was time to act. "He'll need help. How do we get down there?"

"Secure your climbing rope," Gus told him, pointing toward a metal ring embedded a few feet away in gray stone. It was done in a second. Gus then handed him a stout red rope with a businesslike red metal clip affixed firmly to its end. "It strikes me that you might be the one who was meant to use this, Major. Clip it to your belt for now. As you go down, play out both ropes behind you." Jeff looked up sharply. The rope with the red clip seemed to be coming from a distant point higher up on the mountainside.

"It's attached to our Deerfield winch," Gus continued, nodding at him. "Don't worry. We keep it well serviced, so I know it won't tangle or freeze up. We've used it many times for rescue work. It's very old, but it's a trooper, kind of like the old geezer who threw in his lot with us when the Family first came here to build the big log house."

"Will Deerfield, I reckon!" He'd heard about this winch from the old geezer himself a very long time ago.

Gus gave him a startled glance. "Did you," he said in a tentative tone, "ever meet him?"

"I knew him well," Jeff said softly, now drawing upon very old memories. "I was around eight, I think, the first time I met him. Maybe ten the next time. He'd been a sailor. He was a very good friend of my father, and he had a curious leather hand. He was a cheerful person who liked to talk, especially about sailing ships. As far as I was concerned, he knew absolutely everything, and I worshipped him! I never met his children, but he talked about them all the time. And about his beautiful wife, a Cherokee woman, I believe! He said she'd brought him back to life!"

Well, I think we're going to beat the hell out of these people, Major! I don't know how you got here, but it's just sinking in how disastrous this invasion could have been without your early warnings!" Gus stayed close beside him as they moved cautiously toward the edge of the cliff. "Time to put your headgear on now! If you have qualms, I'll talk you through it."

"I've done this before," Jeff answered, "but I'll admit, heights make me dizzy!"

"You're safely harnessed, Major. None of these ropes has ever failed. We use them for lifting injured people off the face of the cliff. We've done it plenty enough times to know what works! Got your radio activated?"

Jeff flicked the switch and realized he was now hearing Gus's voice through his earpiece. "Yes," he said softly into the mic.

The quiet words came through clearly. "Stay out of sight for now. Too many guns out there! We'll wait just behind the fence."

"Understood," Jeff answered softly.

CHAPTER 38

I t took only a few moments to descend. Jeff could now see why Gus had selected this position. Flat on their stomachs, located somewhat higher than the cave, they were able to remain concealed while retaining an informed view of the intruders' progress.

All three of The Compact invaders' ropes had since been attached to the trunk of a sturdy pine tree growing a few yards back from the rim. Young Brian, his father, and their companion began the descent directly into the cave just below them. Their dependence on that tree, Jeff said to himself, was ill-advised! But no warning would have stopped them in their willful arrogance.

Jeff caught a slim glimpse of the old airplane, twisted and partially upended like a discarded child's toy, one blade of its propeller forced firmly into a jagged fissure at the rear of the cave. Once wide wings drooped sadly to the cave's floor; the skeletal remains of Jon Randolph Jr. still rested peacefully inside the ripped-open cabin. Thanks to Ewen's careful extraction of the portfolio, there was no indication anything had been touched since the day Junior's airplane had smashed into the cliff.

The second climber's excited voice said, "Look there, a skeleton still in the wreck. Must be Randolph. I can't believe he's still here!"

"If he's here, so is the package!" Talbot said. "Brian! A chance to redeem yourself! Get over there and bring it out."

The young man had just touched down onto the floor of the cave. He paused, his hands still clinging to the rope. "I don't see anything…" Suddenly, his rope went slack. As falling loops curled into a heap around his boots, he tripped and lost his balance, coming down hard on his backside. Feet extended forward, he began to slide toward the opening. Quickly dropping onto his back, he threw his arms upward. One hand touched a strut of the old plane, and he grasped at it, reached out the other hand, and held fast with both. His motion toward the lip of the cave stopped as suddenly as it had begun. The airplane remained solidly in place.

"What's going on?" his father exclaimed.

A frantic voice floated down from above. "Hi, down there. Watch out! The tree just upended! Better move outta the way quick. It's all coming down on you!"

"Pull it backward," Talbot yelled. "Get together, all of you. Pull it backward!"

Too late! The vine-heavy area just above the cave entrance began to sag. Men standing at the edge above backed away quickly. Some escaped. Several tumbled downward as rock, soil, shiny pine needles, and vine debris disintegrated beneath booted feet. A panicked voice said, "Watch out. Get back, fellows! Behind the fence! Run! Run!"

With a soft rushing sound, a large portion of the cave cover crumbled, bringing the tree with it, thick branches now concealing most of the airplane's nose section. Broken parts of the pine bounded downward unimpeded for many long moments to the foot of the cliff, spraying needles, ripped-off branches, and soil. To his relief, Jeff saw no bodies tumbling behind it.

Another voice said, "Hey, you guys, you out there in the woods, we need a little help here. Can you throw us some ropes?"

Jeff heard a voice coming from the distance. The Family was already on-site. "How many ropes?"

"Five or six, maybe more. We've got some guys down there on the ledge with the captain and the quartermaster, and a few of us might need some help too."

At least three of the gunmen who had been on the edge of the cliff could be seen trying to pick their way out of the debris inside the cave. They, at least, had survived! It was apparent that some had not—the broken bodies of at least two others could be seen crumpled at the back of the cave, held temporarily in place by fractured rock.

"Stay put," the rescuers called back. "Don't move a muscle. We'll be right there!"

"How long?" The voice sounded desperate.

"Hang on! We're getting our gear together!"

As dust began to settle, Jeff searched the area for further signs of life. He saw Brian still clinging to one of the struts of the airplane, trying to pull himself up. "I'll get you, Father," he was gasping. But it was difficult, if not impossible, for him to gain traction on loose debris, which had been widely broadcast and now covered the entire base of an already insecure area.

Jeff finally spotted the third man—the quartermaster?—crouching in a back corner, trying to find a handhold of any kind. He had managed to disengage his rope from the remainder of the fallen tree, which continued to move slowly outward with a tilt toward what would inevitably be its final destination.

The same could not be said for the elder Talbot. He was lying flat at the mouth of the cave, his head at a strange angle, eerily similar to that of the body in the airplane. Talbot's body was being held in place only by the aircraft's back wheel and one large branch that had broken off and now rested across him like a giant hand, its thumb caught by a portion of the right front landing gear.

"Don't bother about me," the quartermaster called out to Brian. "Get your father. I think he's hurt!"

"He's dead," Jeff said softly to Gus. "If young Talbot tries to retrieve the body, they'll both go down the side of the cliff!" Jeff stepped forward to the edge of the mountain, holding tightly to his ropes. "I'll get the young man. Take your pick of the others."

"Right, Major," Gus said. He came to stand beside Jeff. "Let's go get 'em!"

Silently they went over the edge, swinging gently until they were even with what remained of the roof of the cave. Once in place, Gus started a gentle swing out across the valley and on rebound played his gear expertly, landing on what remained of the shelf. He released more rope, bounded across to the man behind the plane, and reached out a hand. The quartermaster grabbed it eagerly and was finally able to work himself to his feet. Gus clipped his bindings to the man's gear and spoke into his helmet mic. "Two coming up. Stand by!"

Someone above answered, "Tell us when you're ready."

"We're linked for the lift," Gus said a moment later. "Pull away." As Jeff watched, both men were gently lifted into the air and a moment later disappeared from sight.

Now it was Jeff's turn. He lowered himself to the ledge, touched down gingerly, and slowly worked his way toward Brian.

The young man had other ideas. "We're bringing Father up with us," he said. Now flat on his stomach, he was inching himself across the cave toward his fallen parent.

"I'm sorry," Jeff said, "but we can't take him, Brian."

"We can't leave him here!"

"I'll come back for his body after I help you out."

"I need to do this!" Brian said. "If I don't, he'll say I failed him!" He put his arms about his father, lifted him to a sitting position, and hung on tight. "Come on, Captain. Let's go!" The bald head of the older man drooped sideways at an odd angle. There was no life in the wide-open eyes, no pulse in his neck.

"Brian," Jeff said firmly, "your father is dead! Let him go!"

The young man looked up at Jeff, shock reflected in his face. "He can't be dead! He's the captain!"

"I'm not going to argue with you," Jeff said evenly, trying to be reasonable. "He is dead. You are not. We're going up!"

"I can't leave him!" Brian cried out, terror apparent in his voice. "He's the captain! He has powers the rest of us do not! He'll punish me if I leave him here!" The young man was clearly more frightened of his parent than of the situation in which he now found himself and was speaking no sense at all.

Jeff maneuvered himself into a better position and touched down next to Brian. "I understand you are upset and in shock," he said as calmly as he could manage, "but your father is incapable of punishing you—or anyone else. It's time to let him go, Brian!" He reached out to the young man from behind, clipped Brian's climbing gear to his own, and put his arms about young Talbot's waist. Still, Brian refused to drop Cal Talbot's body, and no amount of tugging from above was effective. "What's going on down there?" A voice came down. Vince.

"Give us a moment!" Jeff called out. "He's trying to bring his father up too."

Again, he heard Vince's voice. "We can't do it by hand, Jeff. Too much weight. Do you have the winch rope?"

"I've fastened both ropes. Brian is not yet secured."

"Just give us a moment."

During that long "moment," Jeff again tried to convince the young man to drop his hold on his father's body. Nothing seemed to penetrate Brian's sensibilities!

"We're attached to the winch and standing ready," Vince called down.

"Stand up," Jeff said sharply to Brian. The sternness of an adult's voice finally got through to the young man, and he clambered to his feet. Still, he refused to release his grip on his father's climbing gear. "He's gone, Brian," Jeff said again. He seldom lost his temper, but right now, it was being pushed to its limit. He took a deep breath and began again. "You've done all you were required to do, sir. Let's get you up and away from here. You need time and space to grieve your loss!"

Brian burst into tears. "I can't do that," he said, sobbing so wildly it was difficult to make out his words. "I was born to my duties," he cried out brokenly. "If my father is dead, by the Blackheart power of hierarchy, which is Blackheart law, my uncle becomes captain, and I take over the quartermaster duties from my uncle. They're convinced I'm not capable of dealing with anything, much less a crisis. I've got to make sure I do this right!"

Finally getting hold of a bit of the logic of Brian's confused dilemma, Jeff called up to Vince. "Give me a minute or two, will you? We've got a couple of things to work out." Once more, he focused on the young man. "Let him go, Brian. Time is wasting!"

"I can't let him go! He's the captain! I have to save the captain or die trying."

Another portion of the cliff tumbled downward with a low but ominous roar, leaving another gaping crack in the floor. Jeff could see further partings of the floor of the cave working their way along multiple fault lines—another beginning to form directly under the portion of the cliff where he and a determined young man were engaged in a monumental battle of wills. Jeff struggled to keep a firm grip on Brian.

Vince called down. "We've got you attached to the winch, but it can't handle three people, Jeff. Four hundred pounds tops. An added body is too much weight even if we help out. Tell him that as soon as you're both up, we'll send someone down to get his father's body."

"Someone from The Compact?" Brian said in a loud voice.

Vince heard the request, and this time, his voice was sharp. "One of our people! All of yours, young man, are being questioned by the authorities!"

Brian fell silent.

"Do you mean to go down with the cliff?" Jeff finally said, now exasperated as he had ever been! In view of the problematic land on which the young man's feet now rested, this was a crisis only moments from happening!

"Why not?" Brian said wildly. "Why not? I don't have anything to gain by going back up. My mother's gone, I don't know where she is! I'm a blot on the family name and on The Compact itself. My father is always telling me how much I've betrayed him and the whole organization by…by claiming to be queer! I'll never have a family member to hand the position down to, anyway, no matter what my father says. Only one person really means anything to me! My little sister! She's the only person who's ever liked me… I've got to tell her what happened…but I'm not sure I can tell her I let our father drop down the cliff! I'm worthless, just like he always said!"

"Patsy?" Jeff said softly.

For the first time, Brian looked up into Jeff's face. "Good God! You people know about her too? You'll take her away from me," he went on, his voice rising, "and then no matter what I do, I'll be all alone! Let me fall into the abyss. Just let go of me! I don't want to have to suffer anymore."

"Pull yourself together, dammit!" Jeff said forcefully and then fell silent. Anger would not help this situation. The boy was already hysterical. There was no need to add to his pressure!

He thought a moment. A quick little spark of light showed the answer in a new way. "You are not without family," Jeff said softly directly into his ear. "There is your son to consider."

Brian lapsed into utter silence. "What...what son?" he finally sputtered. "I'm not married. I'm gay!"

"His name is Todd. He's a beautiful child. His mother loves him more than words can tell. And her husband, Jeb, his foster father, dotes on him."

"You mean...there was the one time...I was so embarrassed...she was a pretty lady and so kind!" Silent tears began to slip across his cheeks. "She had my child?" His voice softened. "I have helped to create a child? She didn't reject him... the way I've always been rejected! A baby? With my genes!"

Jeff heaved a giant sigh. "How could anyone reject Todd...or you, Brian. You are a person of great warmth no matter what your father or anyone else tries to tell you. You helped Emily through a terrible ordeal! She speaks of you with genuine gratitude."

Brian looked hard at Jeff. "I'd like to see her again, if it doesn't embarrass her, to let her know how much I valued her help. And...I'd like to see...I'd like to see the baby too." There was a long contemplative pause, and then he said, "I'd really like to meet the child I helped create. Would she let me see him?"

Jeff was silent, thinking. What came next would be crucial to many people. "Emily Wallace is one of the world's great ladies," he said quietly. "Her family is all around you. All of these good people…people with black faces, brown faces, white faces…all trying very hard to rescue you, they are her family. They are my family too! They will most certainly take you in, Brian. They all love Todd. If you let them, they will love you as they truly love him."

Brian looked hard at Jeff, silent. Tears continued to stream from his eyes. "What is the price?" he said quietly, his voice near to breaking. "There is always a price!"

"Release your father's body, and we will ascend to a safe place on this mountain—surrounded by many friends."

No further words spoken, Brian quietly unbuckled his father's gear from his own. He let the older man's body slip to the ground and, as the earth shook, took two giant steps backward, now pushing Jeff almost frantically behind him. Almost simultaneously, the area surrounding the cave entry split off, and Calhoun Talbot's body jerked downward into the roaring, raging maelstrom of a major landslide, almost as if having been grabbed by a giant hand.

As the dust began to settle, Brian Talbot, now standing precariously on the edge of nothingness, turned to look into Jeff's eyes. "Please ask them to bring us up," he said in an unusually reasonable tone of voice. "I need to see my son…and to thank his beautiful mother for giving me the first chance I've ever had to be a worthy person of my own."

"Ready to be lifted," Jeff called out.

They were quickly drawn to safety as everything, except the broken airplane and its long dead pilot, continued to plunge wholesale to the forest floor.

It would be hours before the cloud of dirt and debris settled into place. Jeff doubted that Talbot's body or any of the others would ever be found. The remains of Sara's brave son, Jon Randolph Jr., and most of his broken airplane had been captured by the mountain and were now sealed securely for the ages, high above the valley floor.

CHAPTER 39

Saturday, April 23, 2016, noon

After answering reasonably well the many questions posed by law enforcement officials on-site, the boy—Jeff corrected himself once again—the young man walked back to stand silent atop the cliff close behind the barriers the Family had long ago erected to prevent the disaster that had finally happened. He was gazing downward past the raw scar at the edge of the cliff to the still restless pile of dirt and forest debris far below when Jeff came up silently behind him and put a hand on his shoulder. Jeff felt the startled reaction and recognized anguish, as well as puzzlement in the young man's tear-blurred eyes.

"What have I done?" Brian's voice was barely audible.

"Saved yourself to start a new life! There is no shame in that!"

"He was my father."

Jeff let that observation pass with tight-lipped silence. No man of his acquaintance had ever treated one of his own sons the way that arrogant bastard had treated Brian! Calhoun Talbot had not deserved even a jot of loyalty from a son whose inborn humanity must surely have come from his mother's side of the family. If any child needed to be ripped away from his paternal heritage, this was the one!

"Where is your mother?" Jeff asked.

"I don't know. We haven't heard from her in over a year. I've been looking everywhere I can think of, and Patsy and I think she might be dead. Our father hit Mother pretty hard that night, with our uncle egging him on. He's her older brother, so she was used to being hit. But the last time we saw her was when Patsy and I left her at the hospital after we finally got her out of the house. Both of her eyes were black, and she was bleeding pretty hard from her forehead when she kissed us and told us goodbye." A tear trickled across his cheek and then another. "When we went to see her the next day, she wasn't there, and no one would tell us a thing!"

"We have resources," Jeff said softly. "Do you mind if we help you search?"

Brian looked up at Jeff, surprised, and wiped at his face.

"You would do that for me?"

"Of course. If you wish us to."

"At least," Brian said softly, "I would know whether or not he killed her. If he did…then I don't care where he lies tonight!"

Again, Jeff's heart turned over. "And where is your sister right now?" he asked.

"Patsy? She's at a friend's house. Someone my father doesn't know about. When I was told where we were going, I dropped her off there so she wouldn't have to come with us. I didn't know what might happen to her if she were left all alone with these rough guys! Her mother's gone already, and now her father—for better or worse!"

"We have a safe place for her," Jeff said softly. "She will be well cared for."

"The same place where Todd is?"

"No, not yet, but she will be safe."

His face lit. "I would be so grateful! I think she would be too!"

"Come with me, Brian," Jeff said softly. "You've already been questioned, so there is no reason for you to remain here. We will isolate you from those of your father's associates who may wish to do you harm."

Brian Talbot said in a low voice, "By virtue of The Compact document, I'm officially the new quartermaster. You are correct. They will not welcome me with open arms!"

"Can you reject the position?" Jeff asked. He physically turned the young man around and, with a firm grip on his arm, started moving him upward toward the concealed doorway into the mountainside.

"Nobody defies the dictates of The Compact! My uncle won't be happy, though, even though he's the captain now. He'd been looking forward to leaving the quartermaster position for years and moving up to become captain. He wasn't stupid enough to actually kill his brother-in-law when both of them were so well known in Washington. But he didn't mean me to survive this little expedition! I knew I was expected to die! They had already picked a quartermaster. It wasn't me."

"Surely they didn't tell you this!"

"My uncle made no secret of it."

Jeff paused in stride and turned to face the young man.

"And still you came with them?"

"I had no choice!"

"You have a lot to learn, Brian," Jeff grumbled as he led the way into the tunnel. Gus had been waiting for them quite patiently. He greeted Brian with a handshake. No smile. Without a word, he turned toward the dark tunnel that would eventually lead the way back to Family headquarters.

"Where are we going?" Brian Talbot whispered nervously.

"To a place of safety," Jeff replied.

Thirty silent minutes later, when they finally reached the tall ladder, Gus said very sternly to Brian, "You must trust us now! I'm going to put a blindfold across your eyes. Then I'm going to climb up first. You climb next. There are a lot of steps. Jeff will be right behind you to assist you if you need help. Follow me until I tell you to stop. You will have to lift yourself out of a hole into a small building. We will keep you blindfolded until we get well away from the entrance. Please pay attention to these rules, or we cannot guarantee your safety."

"I'll do it right," Brian said in a penitent voice. "I'm damned lucky to be alive right now, and I won't mess up."

He was surprisingly strong and did not stumble along the way. It was as if he were drawing upon a resource of will he had never had reason to access before.

Gus insisted on Brian's being continually blindfolded until he reached the back steps of the big log house, where a previously alerted Bernice was waiting for them.

"Many people want to chat with you, Jeff," she told him once quick introductions were made. "Don't worry about this young man. We'll make sure he gets something good to eat...and maybe a little rest as well. I suspect he's got a long ordeal ahead of him."

"Thanks, sis," Jeff said softly. "He's going to need a lot of looking after. And thank you for Gus. He is a son to treasure!"

Bernice beamed. "He may be the joker, but he always comes through." Her voice turned solemn. "You'd better get on out to the front of the house. Lots of stuff going on out there. Authorities everywhere you look! No reporters yet. Everybody wants to talk with you and Ewen first."

Jeff laughed. "I expect it's going to be a very long day. And why," he said somewhat under his breath, "do they not want to talk with you? You're the ringleader of this whole shebang!"

"Because I'm jest a fat ol' black lady who cooks," she said with a chuckle, "and who don't know nothin'. I'm leavin' all the talkin' up to you good-looking white guys who can dang well alibi us out of anythin' we done that wasn't quite kosher!"

Jeff roared with laughter. What a family he had! He had never felt so proud!

As he headed toward the front door, Ewen caught up with him. "Well done!" the entrepreneur said softly. "We came out of this with kudos up the kazoo, if you know what I mean! We're finding out that some of these guys are so tied to organized crime and other generalized criminal activities that once they head into the legal system, they will never again see the light of day! With Guppy's and Chuck's help, we've got all the corroborating evidence that we need to put them away, which is going to be a little hard to explain, actually!" He stopped to think about it. Then he started laughing too. "This is going to make lawyers rich and keep judges working hard for years! I think we've actually broken up The Compact, Jeff! The whole network! We've dismantled its whole ruling class!"

"To say nothing of having that genuine bloodstained document itself in our possession," Jeff added, grimacing a bit.

Ewen whistled softly. "They don't even know that yet. Let's not confess too quickly. Strictly speaking, we stole it! Keep an eye out, Jeff, when you go outside. A great number of people are assembled there, ours and theirs, and if we don't recognize them, we don't really know which is which. The major difference is that the real law enforcement agencies are looking for law breakers and snapping them up one by one.

Their people, on the other hand, are just itching to snap us in two!" He grinned at Jeff. "Unfortunately, it seems one of The Compact's head honchos is a congressman. He hasn't been tagged as a bad guy yet, and he's really been throwing his weight around."

"Which one?" Jeff asked.

"Cal Talbot's brother-in-law, Franklin Selby. One of the members of Congress from Virginia. The same man whose campaign I'd been asked to help finance. He says he knows nothing about an organization called The Compact. He was just helping his brother-in-law with a group of teenagers."

Jeff's eyebrows rose. "He's the quartermaster—the money man—now on track to become captain. Brian Talbot gave me the whole relationship. Brian was in the loop before they found out he was gay. He was aware that this assignment was destined to be his last one!"

Ewen gasped. "They were going to kill him and say it was an accident? Good God! *Depravity* is too kind a word. So Selby, Congressman from Virginia, was The Compact's money man! And now that his brother-in-law is dead, he's the new captain! Damn! There'll be hell to pay in Congress when they find out. He'll deny everything, of course."

"How could he deny anything?" Jeff barked. "He was caught red-handed! He was one of the people in the cave."

Ewen exploded at that. "He has already explained that he thought it was simply an exciting treasure hunt cooked up by his brother-in-law for their church youth group and he was giving a helping hand! What a hypocrite! Worse yet, he's claiming they did nothing wrong except to trespass on government land, and he's a member of Congress! So why are they holding him, he asks? Very indignant about it. He lost his brother-in-law, and his nephew is now mentally crippled by watching his father die in such a terrible way... Don't believe a thing his nephew says…such a sad thing! People should be crying for his loss. Not crying foul!"

"Oh my god," Jeff said with even more exasperation, "how could anyone believe that garbage?"

"The FBI knows everything, of course. They've been in this with us from the beginning, and they were on the scene, watching all this go down literally! The State Police and the Forest Service have known Bernice and her family forever, so they have a good handle on the truth. I don't think any of the law enforcement people will question our explanations. But lawyers and press people are beginning to arrive. Lots of money and publicity involved here. Very high-profile stuff. People in high places. Members of Congress! We'll be butting heads with sharks."

"We must keep Talbot's son in hiding and away from his uncle," Jeff said. "If my instincts are right about the boy, he might be open to revealing all the secrets of The Compact. He's been on the inside. He knows everything!"

"I think," Ewen said, now with deep compassion, "Brian Talbot needs to be placed into witness protection immediately. His uncle is furious at him for not bringing his father's body back to be properly buried."

"His uncle is the very face of evil," Jeff growled. "Talbot's body is buried just where it needs to be!"

"In hell, I hope!" Ewen concurred.

"Makes one want to believe, doesn't it?" Jeff said softly.

CHAPTER 40

Saturday, April 23, 2016, midafternoon

With those thoughts racing through his head—and Ewen flanking him—Jeff stepped outside onto the broad porch of the elegant log cabin. They were instantly surrounded on the lawn below by lawmen of many jurisdictions, and a few reporters who had been listening to police reports had somehow managed to find their way to Nowhere City and, following police vehicles, to Family headquarters.

Ewen gave the assembled onlookers a condensed version of what had just happened at the cliffs and then said in a calm and authoritative voice, "I'm sure you have questions. One at a time, please." Being a high-profile entrepreneur, he was used to this kind of thing.

Jeff took a deep breath, uncertain as to what might come next. He remembered Lorie's premonitions with nagging unease.

"How did you get involved in this, Mr. Taylor?" "Did you know the Congressman and his friends were coming here?" "What were they trying to find?" "Why didn't you call in the law when you knew what was happening?" The same general questions came from many lips almost simultaneously. The few media people in attendance who seemed to make a practice of listening in on police calls also seemed to recognize Ewen immediately.

Nor did it take law enforcement personnel long to recognize Ewen. Big-time entrepreneur. Aircraft manufacturer. Inventor of cunningly innovative devices for display and advertising purposes. Government contractor for who-knew-what military agency! The list went on and on and on. Never any record of improprieties. Known as a straight arrow…

"The FBI was the first to notify us the looters were on the move," Ewen replied, his voice calm and his words precise. "Initially, our presence here was motivated by an urgent request for assistance from the owners of this property, the Thomas family. They have been guardians of the cave in the cliff for well over a century. One of their close relatives was interred in that cliff, Jon Randolph Jr. His body remains there." A buzz of comments and questions swept through the small audience. Jeff's presence was noted: "Who is your friend?"

Ewen glanced toward Jeff and held out his hand. "Jeff Maratti. He's related both to the Randolph family and to the Thomas family. When he was informed that people who had no business here were planning to invade the Thomas holdings with the intention of either climbing up to the cave from the base of the cliff or climbing down from the top, he asked if my organization could offer some assistance—first in protecting the gravesite, but of more importance, he knew the area was unstable and climbers would be in serious danger.

"I am a longtime friend of Jeff's. He asked me about suitable equipment for use in rescue work if that was necessary, and I was more than willing to help. We have had a number of related problems with these same people over the past few years. This time, however, our involvement was primarily rescue, which we accomplished as well as we could under extremely hazardous conditions.

"As you can tell while you are traveling through the Thomas property, warning signs are posted everywhere. But because of the indifference—or more to the point, disdain—that these people have for legitimate safety concerns and the rights of property owners, along with their attempt to whitewash their depredation, even calling it a treasure search, the very worst outcome has been realized! Half the cliff has crumbled into rubble, desecrating the century-old gravesite of an honored member of the family and killing several of the men who came with them to serve as foot soldiers.

"We understand now that this gravesite was, in fact, the actual target of a search these same people have been conducting for over a century. We are not entirely clear as to what they are looking for, as no one is willing to tell us!" His voice rose in genuine indignation. "Perhaps if you ask them, they will attempt to offer some kind of coherent answer. It better be a good one! Lives have been lost. The number of people buried under that rock pile at the base of the cliff is still in question. Perhaps one or two of the survivors will be able to sort out those names to your satisfaction and that of the victims' next of kin.

"None of the young men commandeered to perform the grunt work here were hurt, by the way, as we spirited them out of harm's way as rapidly as we could. We have as many questions as you do for the people who planned this so-called treasure hunt. But I will tell you this right now, these young people are innocent of any wrongdoing. It was never their intention to put their lives into grave danger while trespassing in hazardous conditions on private land and in National Forest property. The very idea that this was a treasure hunt with a church group is totally repugnant! And untrue!

"In fact, armed guards had been hired to keep them in servitude and to fight off the Thomas family if there were any attempt at defense of their private property! You might want to ask the hired mercenaries—at least those who survived—some very pointed questions! And you might have even sharper questions for the people who hired them in the first place."

As Ewen addressed the law enforcement personnel, his attention riveted. Seeing his friend's reaction and then taking a quick look himself across the front yard, Jeff smiled. The slow but heavy hand of justice was about to descend on the very person who was charging up the hill toward the lawmen.

"If you want to find out why they encroached on private property to destroy a part of the National Forest," Ewen said to the still hushed group, "there's your man! Ask him." He pointed, and everyone turned at once, and their adversary was suddenly surrounded by uniformed officers. "His name is Franklin Selby. The first victim of the cave was Calhoun Talbot, his brother-in-law. And if you haven't yet recognized him, Mr. Selby is currently one of Virginia's representatives to the United States Congress. Even now he is preparing to run for a second term. He was in the cave when it began to crumble, and ironically, he was rescued by one of the young Thomas family members on whom he should be pouring down grateful thanks for saving his skin. Ask him, if you will, what he and his group of mercenaries were doing here!"

Selby suddenly realized who was speaking, what was happening. He turned on his heel, only to be blocked again by two large officers. Swiveling quickly back toward the house, he broke abruptly away from the lawmen and resumed his swift forward stride. "That's the man who's the cause of all this trouble!" he shouted, approaching the front porch in such an authoritative manner that everyone instinctively moved aside. For the same reason, he was not halted as he gained the steps to the porch. Jeff had only a moment's warning. Not quite enough!

Rather than the traditional open-handed slap denoting a challenge, this was a close-fisted blow meant to fell an opponent! Regaining his balance quickly, Jeff came to full attention, letting his arms fall to his sides. He tried to pretend the unprovoked assault had not rocked his senses.

"Sir?" he said, an automatic response. He knew well the reason for the attack and the consequences. His words were firm and distinct. "Am I to suppose you have challenged me to a duel?"

Selby stopped, surprised, finally realizing he had just given lawmen reason to arrest him on the spot. The idea of a duel seemed made in heaven!

"I have," Selby roared. Trying to gain some time, Jeff supposed—turn events to his benefit. "Name your weapon! Pistol or sword?"

The small crowd remained riveted in place, stunned into silence, as if time were standing still for this unexpected but deadly scenario to play itself out.

"Neither," Jeff said very calmly. His temple was smarting, but his brain was still fully functional. "There is only one weapon suitable for this duel."

"And that is…?"

"The cutlass!"

Selby stepped back, shocked.

"Surely you can obtain one, Mr. Congressman Selby," Jeff said evenly, letting his voice rise so as to be clearly heard across the full expanse of the lawn, "if you do not still retain the cutlass your ancestor used when, in another time and place, he was quartermaster of the pirate ship *Black Rose*—ranging under full sail on the Mediterranean Ocean until the American Navy bombarded and sank her in 1814."

self and possibly a tainted antique weapon. "Blunted blades.
Three certified judges. Our seconds will determine the time
and place."

"No," Jeff said in an authoritative voice, which boomed
out across the area where everyone was now standing open-
mouthed in astonishment. "You have challenged me suppos-
ing I would not be aware that, even with blunted blades, such
an event might well be illegal in this country. Having thus
retained what you thought was the upper hand, you would
not call attention to its illegality but call me a coward if I
declined.

"However, I am willing to accept your illegal challenge,
sir, despite its being frowned on, and because I now have
the upper hand, I will be the one to determine not only the
weapon but the time and place! One week from tonight.
Midnight. Saturday, April thirtieth, on the National Mall in
Washington, DC. Once we have received permission, we will
join blunted blades on the plaza area, which lies before the
great monument to our late President Abraham Lincoln...
and the best performance wins the dual. Be there with your
second, and I will meet you in fair and open duel, judges in
attendance!"

He looked around at the lawmen, wondering what their
responses would be. Seeing nothing but stunned puzzlement,
he then focused his attention on the much depleted, scraggly
band of Selby's paid ruffians who had finally found one another,
no doubt wondering what their fate would be at this juncture,
likely concluding that they were never going to get any of the
pay promised to them for hazardous duty and that they would

more likely be spending some time behind bars! They, too, were now standing mute, motionless, their eyes wide.

Jeff nodded toward his Family members, whose equally stunned expressions reflected utter disbelief at the scenario they were witnessing.

With a calm smile, he turned and, without looking back, he calmly strode across the porch to the door and reentered the Thomas family's log home.

Bernice met him without a word and shepherded him into the kitchen. "Let's get an ice compress on that cheek," she said, "before he knows how wounded you are…and how prone you are, I hope devoutly, to making jokes when you are smacked silly by a gloved fist."

"Thank you," he said gratefully. "I am reeling! But I am not joking, and he knows it!"

Gus was beside him the moment Jeff sank down on a kitchen stool, still feeling quite a little disconnected. What had he just done? "I've never been so proud in my life!" Gus said to him with awe in his voice.

Vince came through the door. "My god, I hope you really know how to use a cutlass. Those things are wicked, Jeff. You could get killed, even if the blade is blunted! I'm presuming you know how to use it, or you wouldn't have suggested it, but I'll ask one of my best trainers to work with you if you need a little brushing up."

"Thanks," Jeff answered, still wondering somewhat blankly what had come over him but knowing somehow deep in his heart that this resolution would prove to be decisive one way or another. "That might be a good idea. It's been a few years." Several lifetimes! "I'll probably need some updating, current rules and the like, if there are any! And a little practice so I don't get scalped by a blunted blade! What's going on out there now?"

"The rest of the press has finally arrived," Bernice said. "They all see it as a sporting event, not a duel to the death! Selby's intention, I'm sure, as he surely means to make it lethal! Ewen says it's time for you to go home, but I think you'd better hide until we can smuggle you out. Don't worry! We handle this kind of stuff real well!" Grinning, she gave him a big hug and then guided him to his room so he could contemplate in isolation what he was now facing.

Ewen woke him three hours later. His head was still throbbing. "My pilot is here with the helicopter. It's on the landing pad over by the cliff," Ewen said. "We wanted to get you back to the farm right away, but we had to wait for the crowd to disburse first. Reporters are hanging around, but no more questions for you, my friend! Ready to make a run for it?"

"A helicopter is the best idea I've heard yet!" He desperately needed to get back to Lorie to update her on what had happened and to get her advice—on everything! His acceptance of the duel had been as much a surprise to him as it had been to everyone else. He had heard the words coming from his own mouth. He was fairly certain he had not spoken them. He certainly had not planned to speak them, although he thought, with a strong measure of internal reassurance, he was perfectly capable of meeting and defeating anyone's blade!

"I believe my father has finally made his presence known," he said softly to Ewen.

Alarm apparent in his face, Ewen responded, "Can he help you fight a duel?"

"I can do that myself!" Jeff said softly. "I've had plenty of experience fending off my older brother's cutlass. I was a whole lot better at it than he was. And he was better than Father, who hated it but learned well how to use it to keep himself from being killed. You know who our tutor was, at least during the rare and delightful times he visited Riverside?" He gave a wan smile. Perhaps this *was* the best way after all! Sweet revenge!

"I daresay it was the same one-handed pirate retiree who helped to build this house."

"Ewen, you know my extended family pretty well by now."

"Down to and including all the ghosts, friend! A one-armed swordsman in later life?"

"One of the most accomplished swordsmen I've ever met, right- or left-handed. It's one of the reasons the pirate crew kept him on the sails. If Will had been on deck with either a saber or a cutlass, it might have been one of them upended into the ocean at the end of a skirmish, and no one left to know if the fatal blow was from foe or *friend!*"

*****

Jeff stepped out of the aircraft several hours later and into Lorie's arms. "Let's get you into bed, my love," she said softly. "You do look exhausted! Ewen tells me you took a hard blow to your head without warning. You need time to heal."

"Ever the nurse, my good wife," he said warmly. "Do you know how much I love you? If not, let me tell you in no uncertain terms...I could think of no one else on the ride back. Of how very much I love you and our little Sara Maria. I thought much of the strange life we have been living, trying to stay out of the hands of pirates—in the twenty-first century, for god's sake!"

"Ewen called me to let me know what happened, Jeff." Her voice was nearly cracking. "I've always been aware that the ultimate responsibility would fall to you. It's why you were brought back. You are the only one who's capable of repairing all that's broken. But we will help you, all of us together!"

She began by directing his steps across the yard toward the little ranch house. His head was still spinning. If not for Lorie's assistance, he might well have slumped to the ground.

"You'll get past this with a few hours' sleep," she said. "He couldn't possibly have hit you hard enough to destroy your brain, not by the way you're talking, love. What's even more pertinent, you have a very hard head!"

"It's my father I have to watch out for now!" he said with a short laugh. "Perhaps he got a little ahead of himself on this one!"

"The duel?"

"You heard!"

"From Randy. I have to admit, I'm terrified! How could it be legal? Why did no one put a quick stop to it? Surely someone who was there would know what the laws are. Regardless, the two of us are confident you can beat anyone, so forgive me for pampering you mercilessly this next week until the whole scenario has played itself out!"

Jeff spoke again. "For a while, it seemed our time had finally arrived. We could defeat them at last and begin a new life, free of fear! And now this! Is this why I was sent here? It seems I cannot avoid a face-to-face confrontation! What if I lose, Lorie? He won't *blunt* the blade, of that I'm convinced! I'm going to be facing steel!"

Lorie stopped in her tracks and gave him "that look"— one she had given him a few times before—of sheer incredulity. "You have got to be kidding me!" she said and let it go at that.

Jeff chuckled at last and let her put him to bed but only after he had given his delighted little daughter a warm coming-home hug and a big kiss. Things felt so much better now—he knew he could get some real sleep. Again, he laughed, privately this time. Lorie's *look* had brought back all the confidence he needed!

As he was drifting off, he felt a creature slip into bed with him under the covers and then under his hand. The little fox. His smile came back, even though he wanted to be cross. He scratched Doggy's neck several times before falling into a deep healing sleep.

CHAPTER 41

Saturday, April 23, 2016, twilight

When Lorie heard the hum of car tires on the driveway, she hurried to the window and followed the sharp glow of lights headed toward the big house. The remaining warriors had finally arrived home, in time for a late dinner that would have to wait just a bit longer but only because the conquering heroes needed to drag their equipment into the barn and do what they could to clean up properly for a meal at the big house.

Lorie hurried into the bedroom and touched Jeff gently to wake him. "They're back," she said softly. "You told me to let you know. Would you rather sleep?"

He turned slowly to face her. His cheek was still quite bruised where he had been punched and swollen despite the ice pack, but all in all, she told him, it didn't look as bad now. He would survive, as would his precious brain. She smiled. Hard heads had their uses!

"I'll get up," he said. "My thoughts are relatively coherent, and I'm eager to catch up on the aftermath of our 'great climbing adventure.'"

"How did you fare on the ropes?" she asked softly. "I hear you hung out over the abyss for many minutes talking to Brian Talbot and in the end saved the boy's life."

She saw surprise sweep across him. A broad laugh burst out until he winced. "I never once thought about my fear of heights! There was too much else going on!"

Lorie gave him a big grin. "Hooray! At least the day wasn't a total waste! I do want to warn you, though—Brian's here and he's coming to dinner!"

"Good! I told Ewen that Brian was welcome to take my place in the car if he wished. I'm pleased he did."

"Did Jeb tell Emily the young man was coming?" Had it been her, Lorie thought, she would have been more than grateful for the warning and locked herself away!

"He sure did! Reluctantly, to be sure, but Emily was her usual gracious self. Once Jeb explained how Brian lost his father, she immediately agreed to meet with him. Brian is a little wary of Jeb, needless to say, but he's eager to apologize again to Em and to meet Todd. That was something Jeb agreed to outright, good fellow that he is! He and I both want Brian to understand how a proper family functions. Poor youngster! He's got a lot to process right now. I hope he's strong enough."

"According to Emily," Lorie said softly, "he seems to be quite a bright young man. Hopefully he's stronger than even he realizes."

"I saw some evidence," Jeff told her, "that he will be capable of moving forward once he is able to process dispassionately all that has happened to him today. He had already taken many responsibilities upon his own shoulders despite his awareness of what he would surely face in that cave. He expected he would be the one to die, not his father! I'm hoping he will come through this ordeal on the correct side of the coin. Perhaps we can help make it easier for him!"

When the dinner bell rang, they walked as a family to the big house, she and Jeff, carrying their small excited child.

When they were greeted by Great-Grandpa Rolf, Lorie could see that she was not the only one for which a certain quality of life had changed. She had never been sure it would happen, and today she was convinced it was inevitable. Rolf was grinning in a more spontaneous way—more open, far less formal.

*****

Discussion at the dinner table was clamorous—everyone was buoyed!

"The FBI raided Compact headquarters now that they know where it is!" Ewen made the announcement after receiving a call from one of his contacts in Washington. A great cheer rose from those assembled. "They were surrounding that big old river house at just about the same time we were watching the cave disappear. Everything that seemed to be of value at the headquarters and more was taken back to their offices to sort through. My friends, The Compact is busted!"

Brian Talbot, who had been sitting quietly as far out of the way of conversation as he could manage at a huge dinner table, showed immediate signs of intellectual shock! As she watched the variety of ways in which her friends surrounding the young man pretended not to notice his discomfiture, Lorie turned at the sound of a soft cry and saw Emily approaching Brian with her just-wakened baby in her arms.

Brian's attention was wholly diverted from that moment on.

Lorie thought as she watched the introductions play out that, if for nothing else, the introduction of father to son was more than successful. She had a strong feeling that the relationship just begun would continue, even if the genetic relationship of Todd to Brian was never mentioned in the child's presence.

Rolf had news from alternate sources. He glanced briefly at Brian, now holding the baby in his arms, his expression one of pure rapture, and got a clearing nod from Jeff.

"The membership lists Guppy and Chuck got hold of for us are invaluable," he said quietly to Jeff. "Besides the people who participated in the mountain raid, the Feds have quickly identified scores of key players in the government who are associated with this organization. I think a number of people who were previously pooh-poohing are going to be shocked—likely horrified—by the familiar names that are showing up! I was!

"Charges have already been drawn up and subpoenas served," he continued. "All this happened quickly, so no one was prewarned and able to go into hiding or think up excuses! The proper authorities will shortly have all the incriminating evidence they require to put people under lock and key, some for a very long time. I think this will be the first night in years that I'm going to sleep soundly!"

A tremendous burden had just been lifted. Lorie could scarcely process the lightness affecting her own spirits. Those who would first be notified that they were free of The Compact's dangling blade were the descendants of the Blackheart's impressed crew, trapped front and center in The Compact's headlights throughout most of two centuries.

With the confiscation of that ancient list, as well as the related ancestral charts and the computer targeting program that had played havoc with so many people's lives, The Compact's lights would be forever darkened. There were hundreds, if not thousands, of innocent citizens who would once again be able to live their lives free of obligations imposed upon them by a force too genuinely sinister to be ignored, too widespread to hide from.

"First thing I'm gonna do," Lorie heard Jeb say to his wife, "is check that list myself to see if my ma's name and address is on it. And if it is, Em, you and me and the kids are gonna take a trip to find her and get reacquainted."

Lorie was still concerned. Was there any chance a new organization might spring up among the "true believers" of Compact rule? She asked Ewen what he thought.

"There's always a chance," Ewen said thoughtfully. "There are always grasping people who benefit from imposed corruption because they can so easily acquire wealth at the expense of others. Some people never consider that sharing what most of us think of as the common good is a good thing for everyone."

There was more to be said about it, but Lorie knew that was not what would generally be spoken of tonight. This was a celebration!

If there were a dark side to the evening, it was the upcoming duel looming over everything!

Lorie was also working her head around another problem. The surprisingly warm welcome Brian Talbot had met at the mountain home had resulted in an emotional meltdown on his part when he realized he was in fact being offered friendship and comfort by people he had always been told were "the enemy."

The challenge now facing him was wholly related to questions about the upcoming armed conflict. Of all the people present, only Lorie's unflappable Jeff was relatively comfortable with the idea of facing a slashing cutlass!

But Brian was aghast! "No!" he said urgently. "My uncle's too good with a sword!"

"Aren't there laws against dueling in Washington, DC?" Emily asked anxiously, taking a crowing Todd back into her own care as Brian's attention turned abruptly to the upcoming conflict. "I believe," Ewen answered Em's and Brian's questions softly, "all rules have been suspended for this showdown. Even the park police were unnaturally quiet when that possibility was presented to them. All they offered was that business on the National Mall would be restricted to certain select visitors on that particular night. The story they're presenting is that a big-screen movie scenario is being shot at the Lincoln Memorial."

"Curious," Lorie said. "Someone is putting pressure somewhere."

"Now that's a scary thought!" Emily said. "Who do we know who's in the movie business? Our side? Or their side?"

"Vince?" Lorie suggested. "Vince doesn't have that much clout in Hollywood! Does he?"

Brian Talbot remained very quiet. Lorie wondered about it—wondered, in fact, how the young man actually felt. He'd not said a direct word about his father's death. Perhaps he was still in shock. Anyone would be. Anger would surface, she thought, battling with the customary grief associated with losing a parent. The sacrifice he had been asked to make that morning would have upended anyone! He needed time to process what was happening to him.

Nevertheless, life goes on, and at the conclusion of the soul-satisfying meal, the Justice Seekers once again gathered around the fireplace in the darkened sunroom. A comfortable chair was added for Brian, who had, except for his introduction to the baby, for the most part maintained his silence throughout the meal. He now seemed to be awed and a bit puzzled not only by the company he was keeping but by the lighthearted tone of the conversations ping-ponging around the circle of friends. His special focus eventually turned to the youngsters, and especially back to Todd.

"He's a beautiful little boy, isn't he?" he said softly to Lorie, who was now beginning to reach conclusions that were more positive than negative but not yet settled.

"Todd's a darling," she agreed. "A very healthy, well-adjusted little boy."

"I'm going to have to get out into public life more often," Brian went on, speaking softly just to her, mumbling almost, "to see what 'real life' is like. I always knew there was something that felt comfortable…like you…we…are here tonight…but I figured I'd always be on the outside of that group looking in, never on the inside looking out!" He hesitated and finally said, "Have you been able to find my sister? She would love Todd."

Lorie turned to Guy's wife. "Any word on Patsy Talbot yet?"

Alexi turned to her husband and said quietly, "Have you located our missing child?"

Lorie saw Guy frown. He excused himself and left the room. After a brief absence, he came back grinning. "We've found your sister with her grandmother, Brian…and your mother."

The young man's mouth fell open. "I have a grandmother?" His face transformed from one of worry, shame, and fear to one of utter incredulity. "I have a grandmother," he repeated in a louder tone. "And my mother and Patsy are with her! Are you people wizards?" Lorie could almost see the young man's shoulders lift as so many of his burdens dropped away, and now she began to understand why he had not been as forthcoming as she had hoped earlier!

"We have contacts," Ewen said with a big grin. He reached for Brian's hand, which was gratefully offered.

"Those of us sitting here, Brian, joined forces several years ago," Ewen explained, "as individuals to work against The Compact hierarchy. Our resulting organization is strong and very effective. We need for you to lie low for a time, if you will. Your mother and your sister are already in the witness protection program...your grandmother has been there for many years! When things settle down, you can join them if you so desire. All we ask is that you continue to be as up front and truthful with us as possible!"

He broke in, "Mr. Taylor, if there is anything at all I can do to help you, I will. The organization related to that bloody old paper needs to be wiped off the face of the earth." He took a deep breath and continued speaking very rapidly, in what seemed to Lorie almost a frantic attempt to gain their acceptance. "I can hardly believe this has happened to me! First, you people appear. Second, I'm given my life back. Literally! My life! Someone thought I was important enough to save." A tear rolled down one cheek, glistening in the soft candlelight. More tears appeared. He glanced at Jeff almost worshipfully and then added in a soft, heartfelt tone, "And I've met a beautiful little boy who I'm told could be related to me." He was being deliberately discreet, Lorie realized, not knowing how many people were aware of the circumstances of the relationship. A very positive sign in Lorie's estimation! "And now you tell me my mom and my sister are still alive and well and that I have relatives I didn't know about! A grandmother! You are wizards!"

Jeff put a calming hand on Brian's shoulder. "We are just ordinary people," he said quietly. Lorie grinned at her husband and, with eyebrows lifted, gave a brief shake of her head. He winked at her. "What sets us apart," he continued firmly, turning back to the young man, "is our desire to help people who are struggling to find their way out of problems not of their making."

"That's me," the young man said softly, thoughtfully. "I've wanted out ever since I discovered the world doesn't work the way my *family* lives it. Now that you've let me experience a bit of that *alternate* world, I'd like so much to help others break free."

CHAPTER 42

Later that evening

"I think…," Lorie mused later that evening while only their small group of genetically related couples, including Randy, of course, was gathered again at the little guesthouse. She had just returned from the big house after seeing Brian settled comfortably in private quarters in the bunkhouse. "I think," she repeated thoughtfully to those people so very dear to her, "we may have gained a very important recruit."

Rolf nodded. "Agreed. I like him, and I'm inclined to believe him. This may be a turning point. We must wait for enough time to pass to see how genuine he is! It's easy to be blindsided, but my instincts are showing him settling on our side."

Laughing and joking now, the few defenders remaining at the modest guesthouse drank a little more wine, cracked a few more bad jokes, and were almost prepared to call it a day when Lorie said softly, "One more story, folks. Pertinent! It's from a separate journal that Isaac kept, a small one, which shows exactly what kind of man he was. Not criticizing, mind you! Just saying, keep this tale in mind when you go up against these people! Any of you, but especially Jeff!"

Seeing everyone settle comfortably back into their chairs, Lorie picked up the journal. "Got to set the stage," she said in a deep mysterious voice and proceeded to paraphrase the pertinent part. "Moses, aka Lak, was, in real life as we all know by now, a noted European architect named Ukuhlakanipho, a member of one of the Zulu royal families. He'd been selected from a group of other pricy architects to build a meeting house for what he thought was a legitimate *fraternity* type of organization that wanted a very special kind of structure. It was to be kind of like a Masonic temple or whatever. If anyone had mentioned the word *Blackheart*, Moses would have known in an instant who they were. But they were very careful not to drop any hint of their bloody history.

"So Moses drew up plans—mind you, folks, it's those very same drawings we have spread out across all the tables at Guy's house!" Eyebrows raised significantly! "And then he remained on-site for a while, since it was a rather complicated structure, and they had asked him, pretty please, if he would stay an extra day or so to make sure everything worked exactly right.

"He agreed to do that gladly. Everything was right on schedule, if not ahead of schedule. The building was complete as far as he was concerned. He was pleased with it, they seemed pleased with it. Everyone had shaken hands. What's more, he had actually been paid! In gold coins! He was at his hotel packing his gear and getting ready to leave when someone very close to the top people appeared at his door, asked to come in, and then quietly warned him—to his great shock—that his life was in danger.

"He had had no prior sense of treachery, since everyone he'd met had been cordial and businesslike. But if this contact, a highly placed black slave in his primary employer's household, was willing to put his life on the line to warn Moses that he'd better hightail it out of the country, then it was high time to high-tail! This brave soul told him quietly that many of the workers who had done special jobs on this project were dying off or had gone missing. Any questions so far?" Lorie asked with a sly smile.

"Keep going!" Emily said eagerly.

"Well, Moses checked the next day with a few trusted sources and discovered that what the informer had told him was chillingly correct. At least ten people had either been 'accidentally' killed or had mysteriously disappeared within the past week. All ten were people who had done work specifically on the hidden passageways or the mechanisms that opened secret doorways.

"Moses wasted no time checking out! He quickly gathered up his bags and baggage and contracted a carriage to take him to Baltimore, where he could get passage on a sea-going vessel headed to Southern Africa. It seemed that simply resuming a normal workaday life was probably out of the question, at least for a while. But he still did have a home to go to, after all, with parents who had finally decided they were very proud of their successful son, even if his sex life was a little confused." As an aside, Lorie added, "He was gay, in case any of you hadn't come to that conclusion already!"

She continued, "Isaac, in the meantime, had just come back from a tough but successful mission in Indian territory, only to have an urgent message waiting for him at Riverside that his bosses in DC wanted him to come in person to give a detailed report of his last mission so they could get more money from some of the political skinflints they had to deal with every time they turned around.

"He set out the next day. It took a few days to get from Georgia to Maryland, and when he finally reached the thriving little village of Georgetown, night was coming on. He'd come as direct as he could on a strong horse, and his bosses didn't expect him for another couple of days, so he thought he might just take a day off to sleep.

"He was extra tired and really hungry when he spotted a lively bar and grill establishment close by the warehouse area. Something was cooking that smelled delicious, so he tied up his horse and walked in. There weren't many restaurants back in those days, but there were a lot of out-of-town travelers who needed to eat, and because of the C&O Canal, which ran through Georgetown and up to Harper's Ferry, there were a lot of watermen too. This place was big, noisy, and crowded.

"He was lucky enough to get a table by himself off in a dark corner, and while he was eating, he couldn't help but notice two big burly watermen a couple of tables over. He'd seen them before—in a different context—and he knew they were not watermen but snakes. Silent Isaac had been a lip-reader forever, of course. He pulled his hat brim down so they wouldn't notice him and listened in by watching their lips if he couldn't actually hear their words. Pieced together, it seemed they were talking about someone they'd just been paid to eliminate, a big black dude who was on his way to Baltimore to catch a sailing vessel to Southern Africa. They were to be paid with the gold the big dude had on him.

"As they went on, Isaac wasn't too shocked to realize that they were hired assassins because he'd been told that a couple of times, but he was stunned to discover who they were after. 'He's a big nigger,' one of them said as if he didn't care who heard. Isaac didn't have to read lips to hear that. 'He don't speak English like real people do,' the other guy went on, a little more softly. 'He talks like a swell-headed Brit.'"

"Brit?" Randy said.

"He'd studied engineering at Cambridge," Lorie explained. "And I think architecture came in there somewhere, too, unless he took it up in Marseilles later. Got his British accent somewhere in that period."

"Anyway," she continued, "Isaac's antennas shot up, since he was pretty confident there weren't a lot of big black dudes in this country who spoke the King's English. He hadn't been aware that his friend Lak was here, though, and he was a little miffed because he thought he should have been told. But he was pretty certain that's who the two men were talking about. So when they left, he followed. He figured this was a lot more important than his new task for the government, which was not an emergency...yet.

"These bad dudes were also traveling by horseback. So Isaac retrieved his faithful pony, who by this time had been given oats and water and was standing by, raring to go. Pretty soon the bad guys left the tavern, got on their own mounts, and headed east but not toward the big town of Washington, DC. As Isaac had feared, they took a northeastern turn and headed cross-country directly toward Baltimore.

"It doesn't seem like very far from DC to Baltimore now, forty to fifty miles tops, but back then it was a couple days' ride, maybe a little more, depending on how much you wanted to push your mode of transportation and how many meals and drinks you wanted to indulge in. These guys weren't in any hurry. They just plodded along for a while. They finally found a place to camp and were soon sacked out for the night. Isaac figured from the lack of urgency that the boat wasn't leaving those Baltimore docks anytime soon, and maybe he'd have a chance to get there first, find his friend, and snatch him out of harm's way. He hadn't seen Lak since he'd left France many years before, although they had corresponded pretty regularly. He was excited about renewing their friendship.

"He wondered again why his friend hadn't told him about this particular project. Generally, Lak was pretty forthcoming about his schedule. He figured Lak must have had his own good reasons. Probably the secrecy imposed by his employers," Lorie speculated and continued, "Tired as he was, Isaac took off on his own. In a day and a half, he was at the Baltimore docks inquiring as to which boat might be heading for Southern Africa and when it was sailing. When a couple of dock workers pointed it out to him, he took up a lookout point. Didn't see Lak, though. Could these Baltimore dock workers have got it wrong?

"He hadn't seen the Georgetown guys yet either. That's what really worried him. Having no idea where Lak might be staying, he hid his horse in a nearby derelict shed and made a nesting place inside a big stack of wooden boxes waiting to be filled. He hunkered down. Waiting. Watching. Getting a little sleep. Not much.

"The next night, all that waiting paid off. He saw some activity around the boat and asked a couple of the crewmen when boarding would begin. They said, 'Tomorrow afternoon, but an important person is coming on tonight, early boarding, private.' Well, Isaac thought that was a little strange! If important people were coming on and if the boarding was supposed to be secret, those crewmen certainly shouldn't have told him about it! They were either dumb or indifferent. In that case, if anyone else asked, they'd probably spill the beans to them, too, especially if they were offered a little cash.

"So he got his horse saddled and packed and moved up as close as he could to the boat, still keeping out of sight as much as he could. Pretty soon a couple of fancy carriages arrived, and a big person wearing African robes got out of the first. The people from the second carriage lifted out lots of luggage. It was all carefully transported onto the ship by a whole raft of people. Then a uniformed official from the ship came down to the docks and welcomed this really important guy onto the ship.

"They walked up the gangplank together. Everything seemed perfectly on the square as far as Isaac was concerned. Even at that distance, he could tell it was Lak. He knew him, he says, by the way he walked and the generous way he moved his hands. Isaac's first thought was that he would swim out to the ship when everyone left, climb up one of the ropes—as he had done countless times—find Lak, and have a reunion in private. And then he would go back to DC for his meeting. He saw no sign of the assassins. He was beginning to feel way more reassured.

"Then he saw them, the two murderers, talking to a couple of the same guys who had just helped take Lak's luggage up to his quarters. The dockworkers pointed upward and walked away, and the other two guys moved toward the ship. It looked to Isaac like a major emergency. What could he do?"

Lorie felt something on her feet and suddenly realized that Doggy had parked himself there. She grinned, quietly handed him a piece of her cookie, and stroked his head.

"Okay, okay!" Em said.

Even Rolf had hunched toward her. "What happened next?"

She grinned. "He killed them. End of story!"

Mouths dropped open.

"Well," Lorie said in what she thought was a reasonable tone, "he knew their target was Lak. So he killed them first. Problem solved and favor paid back. Lak had done the same thing for him on the docks at Marseilles the day they first met."

"How?" Rolf asked quietly. "How did he kill them?"

"Knives. He had two—and excellent aim—and since he had already crept up pretty close, two targets within easy range. Two knives, two hits! Silent!" She used her hands to illustrate.

Another moment of shocked silence.

"What if it was not the people he thought it was?" Randy's question.

"Do you think Isaac would make that kind of mistake?" Lorie answered with a big grin. "He checked in later that day, though, with the authorities and was reassured that these were the guys he had suspected they were. Really bad boys! No strangers to law enforcement! Paid killers! Isaac would have been given a medal if he hadn't wanted the whole affair kept under wraps. The authorities gave him his knives back and said, 'Well done!'

"Isaac visited with Lak, told him what had happened, renewed his friendship, and, a day before the boat was scheduled to leave, persuaded him to come to Georgia as a newly acquired *slave*. Who would ever believe a Zulu prince would be working as a house slave on a no-count peach plantation in Central Georgia where the owner was away more than he was at home? Lak couldn't have had a better disguise.

"A long-freed black American businessman living in Baltimore was suddenly offered an opportunity to take a boat trip to Southern Africa to search for his family, courtesy of one of his countrymen. Almost contemporaneously, a big black slave moved onto Riverside Plantation to help with the growing peach and wool businesses. According to the account, each of the men felt it was the most productive journey he had ever made."

Cheers arose, quickly squelched in deference to the sleeping baby in the next room, although a number of arms pumped through the air in an expression of "Well done, Isaac!"

Doggy jumped up onto Lorie's lap and licked her chin, to general laughter. She gave him a big hug, kissed him on his nose, and handed him to her husband!

"You know the term 'no quarter'?" she said firmly. Everyone nodded. "Keep those words in mind!" she said softly.

CHAPTER 43

The following week…

Vince's fencing tutor, a splendid athlete named Grigori Rasikoff, arrived at the Virginia horse farm from California the day after the takedown at the cliff. Jeff was impressed. Grigori was sleek and wiry with smooth pliable muscles. He was almost as tall as Jeff, at least ten years older, and very serious about his duties. He spoke English with the faint remains of an accent and told Jeff that even though his parents had immigrated from Russia years before, he had spent the last part of his teen and university years in St. Louis, Missouri. He was now a permanent resident of Los Angeles, California, either doing stunt work himself or teaching others how to pretend to be doing something they would never attempt in real life.

Before Grigori's arrival at the Virginia horse farm, Rolf Maratti, more security conscious than ever, searched The Compact's confiscated lists for "Rasikoff" or similar names. After several hours of determined study on Rolf's part, the fencing tutor was cleared of any hint of Compact involvement.

Jeff liked him the moment they met and saw immediately that Grigori Rasikoff was intrigued, excited, in fact, by the challenge of a real duel. No faking it, as in the movies or on the stage! He was determined to prepare his client not only to defend his honor but, despite the proposed safety devices attached to the blades, to save his life in case someone cheated! Grigori was welcomed with greetings and friendship.

The hard work began almost at once. First, their opponent's representatives were met with in a neutral place—in this case a small restaurant at Dulles Airport—and the rules put into place. The weapons were to be blunted, with judges allowed to examine them before the duel commenced. Points would be given on technique and on hits to the body. The winner would be awarded ranking based on technique and hits made within a specified period of time. All decisions were final, and everyone signed binding agreements.

Then the specific training began. In light of the nature of the duel and its location—on the plaza at the base of the second set of steps, fifty-eight in number, leading upward to the statue of Abraham Lincoln in Washington, DC—it was a given that steps would be involved. Up, down, backward, forward—Grigori zeroed in on training the proper leg and foot muscles to respond to every possible cue. Combined with this were whole body responses to a number of complicated dueling techniques he felt Jeff might encounter, along with a tutorial on a few illegal moves he might need to fend off, given his opponent's basic nature.

Videos had been made of dueling events won by Franklin Selby. The events involved rapiers, not sabers, certainly not cutlasses. Selby had posted videos of his wins to family members. Fortunately, one of those members to whom he felt the need to brag had been his nephew, Brian Talbot. And Brian was more than willing to make copies of those videos for Jeff and Grigori.

Every sneaky deviation of Selby's form from standard fencing procedures was noted, and countermoves were created. Brian's eager helpfulness was very much appreciated, and thanks were forthcoming—a reaction that did not go unnoticed by the young man himself. Jeff grinned as he thought of it. Brian's response to a simple "thanks" was almost that of a small puppy responding to his master's "good boy" for proper behavior. He had eagerly made himself available if anyone needed help in the barn or the kitchen—or in the nursery, working with the youngsters—blossoming in response to unfamiliar but friendly relationships, which normal people consider normal in a normal world. Still, he had not talked with anyone about his father's death in the cave, and until he did, no one felt completely comfortable talking openly in front of him about the upcoming challenge.

Midweek

"More videos," Vince called out a couple of days after the tutoring had begun. He was standing outside the wire fence, Jeff, Guy, and Ewen had strung together so Jeff and Grigori could practice swordsmanship without inadvertently harming either farm animals or hands. "He just posted them," Vince went on, "probably trying to show you how good he is with a blade to intimidate you. Franklin Selby is a grandstander who thinks he's an Olympic wonder. He's a novice compared to you, Jeff. You'll have to be careful not to kill him. You're perfectly capable of it."

"I'll not slice him," Jeff answered solemnly. "How can I, with a blunted blade. However, I somehow doubt he shares the same ethics."

"I will prepare you for the unexpected," Grigori said with a grin. "I am delighted by how much you already know…and by how much you have learned in these last few days. Do you have a plan in mind already given the venue you selected?"

"I do," Jeff responded.

Grigori grinned. "I bet it has something to do with steps!"

He returned the smile. "Let's try these particular techniques again…"

The training went on with even more whole-body muscle strengthening and then specifically arms and legs. Jeff, who until a few days ago had felt he was quite strong enough, could feel himself still gaining in strength and agility. His capacity for deep breathing had increased, his attention grown more sensitive to minute changes in the approach angle of his trainer's blunted blade, and he was growing in flexibility at avoiding even a touch.

"You are formidable," Grigori said to him on Friday in a serious tone. "I would not like to face you in battle with a sharpened blade. You would have my head off in two seconds."

Jeff laughed. "I have few enough friends. Cutting off heads seems a bit counterproductive!"

"Keep in mind," Grigori said even more solemnly, "that this man truly wants you dead. Do not smile, young Mr. Maratti! It is not a joking matter! You've seen with what disdain he cheats! You must be prepared for anything. Okay, let us do it one more time!"

Saturday, April 30
The day of the duel

The last day of April arrived. Lorie rose from bed feeling a bit sick to her stomach. It was strange how often the day and the hour of the duel had eluded her. Was it because she had thought someone would think better of it and the whole thing would have been called off? The idea in and of itself was simply too improbable! People didn't fight duels in this day and age! They had not even tried to search the law books, but chances were good it was illegal, if there actually were any contemporary laws about something so unlikely!

"Midnight, tonight!" Jeff dropped his voice, making the words sound like a horror movie soundtrack. He grinned. She didn't feel like grinning back. Her stomach was tied in knots. So much bad stuff could happen tonight! She didn't want to think of it, but every moment her mind wasn't busy with something else, it reverted back to the duel, hanging over her head like a…like a cutlass!

Jeff, on the other hand, seemed buoyed! Excited! Looking forward to the challenge! Or at least looking forward to putting it behind him and moving on!

Lorie heard Jeff, Rolf, and Randy discussing strategies. They were standing on the patio, clustered around a laptop computer spread out on the picnic table, reading again all the information they could about the Lincoln memorial. How many stairs rose above the plaza area to the memorial itself? Fifty-eight! A fair number! Would Jeff have to climb the stairs? There was no reason to—the plaza in itself was quite large enough for a duel.

"Keep him moving," Randy said firmly. "Keep Selby away from you, man! He'll try to wound you where you're most vulnerable."

"I've got tough plastic shields to wear under my clothing in the heart and the groin areas," Lorie heard him answer, "and I'm going to be wearing what they tell me is impact-resistant clothing, if that's at all possible." She saw him frown almost imperceptibly. "The basic plan is to keep from getting hit! Even if the blades are blunted, they can still hurt!"

"He'll probably cover himself everywhere with hardened plastic," Randy said. "Like armor!"

"I hope so!" Jeff grinned. "It's hard enough to maneuver freely while you're trying to keep from being wacked like a rug hanging on a clothesline. Adding pounds to your body only makes it less supple. He'll tire quicker."

Lorie joined the men at the picnic table. Cups were already in place, and she had supplied the gathering with a variety of cookies. This time, she brought out a fresh pot of coffee and pulled up a chair to join them.

Randy asked in a quiet voice, "I'm still wondering why Selby challenged you in the first place. What was his motivation? The Compact organization is more or less a dead issue now, isn't it, now that we have all its stuff?"

Jeff thought about it and finally answered, "I don't think they ever considered what the loss of those documents would mean. Perhaps he expects to get everything back if he beats me. But…is it possible that he might not yet know that we have it?"

"Doesn't matter," Randy said, a grim expression on his freckled face. "What matters is who wins!"

Jeff laughed. "You question the outcome?"

In the most serious of tones, Randy said, "I know you won't maim Selby or try to kill him, Jeff, but I don't know about him! I've never seen a fencing match in my life. Something out of a movie, maybe, but that's only an imitation of life. Are there rules? If there are, will he follow them?"

"I have my own rules… I will not try to harm him!" Jeff said quietly. "But I have to be ready for anything with these people. They were pirates—still are, I expect. They obeyed no rules but those of their leaders! I have been focusing on defense—this is what will protect me, my friend!"

"The other thing is," Randy grumbled, "what do you win—if you win?"

Jeff smiled. "The end of The Compact!"

"Maybe! Maybe not! Have you ever considered the possibility that he might win, Jeff? Even if he doesn't kill you, a blunted blade could cause a concussion! Or worse!"

Jeff said slowly, "He would be arrested and jailed. Even if I could be proved to be a willing participant in this exhibition—which I decidedly am not—my death would be considered murder. Selby would be tried and likely sentenced to life imprisonment. Either way this goes, he loses!"

For Lorie, that was not really an answer! She didn't think it was an answer for Randy either as he walked away, shaking his head.

Neither Lorie nor Rolf really wanted to watch the men practicing. It was too unnerving! So unnerving, in fact, that Rolf had not even told his extended family in New Jersey what was about to happen. Jeff's twenty-first-century parents still knew nothing of it. Lorie hoped she wouldn't ever have to call them with any kind of bad news at the end of the day. One more worry on top of everything else! But at least Jeff Maratti's parents wouldn't be on-site to watch it happen!

*****

Early in the afternoon, a large helicopter skimmed low across the beautiful Virginia horse farm. A moment later, Guy Taylor burst from the big house and ran toward the guesthouse where Lorie and Rolf, with large cups of hot mint tea, were still trying to keep their nerves knit together while

Jeff continued to cross cutlass blows with Grigori in the big barn—their last formal practice, they claimed.

"We've got company!" Guy called out excitedly. "Our friends from West Virginia came to be on hand for the duel!"

Jeff appeared in the doorway of the barn, cutlass still in hand. "Great!" he called back. "Who all is here?"

"Vince! Bernice is with him! They wanted to stand by Emily and Jeb. I just gave them permission to land. Let's go out to the landing field to meet them! They've got some other people with them!"

The "people" who were with Vince and Bernice were introduced as Elihu Douglas, the pilot, and his wife, Constance. "Hi, folks," Vince called out as he stepped down from the helicopter. "I've brought my movie producer—our pilot—and his second-in-command, Connie. She's the real boss. We've also got a couple of fellows who know how to run cameras, et cetera."

Introductions were made, and then Vince dropped the surprise. "We're ready for you on the National Mall. We've already got the lights in place, Jeff. Even lighting all around. No shadows. We've made sure no extra people will be on the site by setting up barricades and a good deal of canvas so no stray tourists nor Compact members will be able to interfere. Ewen's there already, supervising the preparations. The Park Service was relieved that they wouldn't have to do the hard work themselves.

"No distractions tonight, my friends! This is the real thing! Connie and Hugh are in charge of the filming. Everything will be covered from a variety of positions, and we have a few world-renowned judges who will be there watching the proceedings so we will know instantly if Frank Selby tries to cheat. The only other visitors will be law enforcement personnel."

"So that's how we got permission to use the mall!" Lorie said softly. Grinning broadly, she turned to Sheriff Randy Ross and found him grinning back.

"It pays to have friends in high places, doesn't it?" he said softly.

"Rich friends!" she mouthed to him, and he nodded vigorously!

"Is Gus here?" Lorie asked.

Vince nodded. "But he won't be with us on the mall," he added. "He's babysitting Brian Talbot while we take care of business. That poor young man—Brian, not Gus—is beside himself with guilt and fear. He seems to be blaming himself for everything coming down the Pike."

"There's a lot more riding on this contest than we ever figured, isn't there?" Lorie said softly, once again terrified that her world might come crashing down.

"Our whole world, Lorie," Vince said quietly, echoing her fears. And then again, he said, "Our whole world! One we didn't even know was in jeopardy until you came to tell us!"

Lorie nodded, unable to respond without bursting into tears.

*****

Too soon, several of the ranch cars were turned out onto the driveway to transport interested parties to the capital city. Lorie knew that Grigori Rasikoff wanted to be on-site early to make sure everything was done right. Fortunately, he had enough credibility to call foul if it were necessary! He and Vince Thomas were sharing one of the cars. Jeb, Emily, and Bernice opted to join them. Jeff, Lorie, and Rolf came in a second car, Randy at the wheel.

Guy and Alexi did not want to attend, although they wanted to be informed instantly of the outcome, of course, as did the entire staff of the horse farm. All of the children, including Saree and Todd, would be cared for by Guy and Alexi, as well as their own trusted caretakers!

Their two-car caravan reached Washington, DC, at six in the evening. After parking close by the mall in an underground garage spot privately reserved for them, the small group found what passed for a fast-food restaurant in the Capitol City, and everyone, Lorie noted, ordered whatever came most easily to mind: a hamburger here, a hot dog there, fish sandwiches for sharing, many cups of coffee, a serving or two of ice cream.

Lorie didn't taste a thing, and if anyone was to ask her later what she had eaten, she couldn't have told them. She, Em, and Bernice teamed up and, speaking infrequently, trailed toward the mall behind their masculine counterparts, pushing mightily to keep up the pace. The men were bunched tightly together, chattering away in the arcane language of the world of sports. Grigori and Jeff led the pack. Jeff's cutlass, safely shoved into its scabbard, was concealed in a large canvas bag, which he had strapped to his back. Rolf, Jeb, and Randy followed, everyone carrying electronics equipment of some kind.

The weather was perfect. It had been a fine spring day altogether—when Lorie thought about it, not too hot, a slight breeze, blue sky above, flowers everywhere, just about perfect. Lorie looked at her watch: seven o'clock. And still a bright sky. Five hours to go. Why had they got here so early?

Many people were curious as to what was happening at the Memorial. It had been effectively blocked off to visitors for the evening, tall canvas barriers in place around the wide steps rising upward to the massive but beautifully rendered sculpture of a seated Abraham Lincoln.

"Movie stuff going on in a couple of hours," the mall guards were telling people. "Come see the monument tomorrow when these California people are done with their filming." Smiles were forthcoming, people vowing to return the next day, but—Lorie surmised—many would return tonight to watch the live action. Canvas barriers would deter no one in a park with no fences to keep people away! What unknown movie star would be filming at the Lincoln Memorial on a soft spring evening in April? Come find out! She shook her head, grinning briefly!

And then she wondered how many Compact people would be waiting there as well, ready to take revenge if their leader lost! Her smile disappeared!

Why were the hours taking so long?

The sun disappeared at its own graceful pace, the sky eventually grew dark, and the park donned a soft veil of twilight—as dark as it could make itself in the middle of an urban area illuminated by many streetlights.

Jeff, Grigori, Jeb, Vince, and Randy all had disappeared behind the barriers surrounding the monument. Lorie, Bernice, and Em, accompanied now only by Rolf functioning effectively as their protector and defender, decided to take up their portion of the time by strolling around the Reflecting Pool, looking avidly at everything and studiously avoiding speaking.

Part of the time they rested on park benches, watching tourists, listening to the sounds of many voices speaking many diverse tongues as people wandered by, curious as to what might possibly be happening at the western end of the mall on a warm weekend night in April.

As Lorie had surmised, many people were now beginning to stroll casually across the wide green lawn toward the Memorial. Sensing that something interesting was about to happen, some were fully equipped with picnic baskets. Others were carrying blankets so they could rest on the grass and indulge in food and fantasy. All seemed determined to stick around.

Ewen came abruptly across the four tourists, who by now were bored despite their unease and were sitting on a bench, gossiping about everything and nothing.

He looked around at his friends and then noted the slowly gathering crowd. He began to laugh. "Why not?" he said. "It'll serve The Compact right if we take some of the canvas down so everyone can watch them get skunked! These people will be witnesses to history, even if they don't know it!"

Rolf, who had been acting quite distant, looked up at Ewen. "You are that certain my grandson will win?"

"One hundred percent!" the entrepreneur answered. "One hundred percent, my friend! Blunted blades may smart and bruise, but they don't kill. And the dance, the beauty, the grace of this sport—the way Jeff moves—will be a joy for all to see! The destruction of The Compact tonight will be total!"

Lorie understood what he was saying, but she also knew that The Compact people cheated just because they could, and she also knew that sometimes things simply go wrong, even if there is no reason for it!

Time moved far too slowly. She understood that many things were going on behind the scenes—street clothing was being removed, tight dueling garb donned, protective devices put into place, zippers zipped, buttons buttoned. Boots were being pulled on. Belts with scabbards to hold the weapons were being strapped around waists. Gloves to protect vulnerable fingers were pulled across capable hands. Jeff had a large entourage tending to his needs.

Frank Selby's team remained hidden. The only people Lorie had seen flitting momentarily from Selby's side of the monument were a couple of relatively old men and a young man with a sheathed cutlass hanging from his belt, perhaps Selby's tutor or coach. The young man looked supremely confident. Lorie was shaken by that look, left fearful.

CHAPTER 44

I t was 11:30 p.m. when Rolf began to elbow his party's way through the crowd, allowing Lorie and sisters Emily and Bernice to move closer to the steps. They seated themselves on benches located at the edge of the Reflecting Pool, which lay at the base of the steps. Eighty-seven steps in all, Lorie recalled. She knew the number well by now. She shut her eyes.

Many other people were there, shadows in the darkness, talking softly, wondering with good cause what was happening at such an important location. At midnight! All that could be seen of the base of the Lincoln monument itself was canvas discreetly draped in such a way as to isolate and shield what was behind. Outside this zone, reflections from an uncommon number of bright lights danced across many nooks and crannies.

Suddenly, one of the canvasses suspended above the steps dropped downward gracefully with a somewhat muted *thump*. With the assistance of a large number of strong young men, it was flattened out across those steps and then rolled into what became in quick order a tight, relatively substantial barricade blocking all physical access to the steps above it. The plaza area where the duel would play itself out could be clearly seen, as well as the remaining steps leading upward to the massive sculpture. Fifty-eight of them. The number floated through her brain. Would they all be included in this duel?

From the generosity of light flooding the scene, it was apparent that someone somewhere would be filming the action. As of this moment, however, no one could be seen on the plaza nor the steps. Not yet.

Lorie felt her heart pounding in her stomach. This dark area where she was now seated in the heart of Washington, DC, was the last place she had ever wanted to be.

And yet she had to be here! It was her duty to be here!

Be strong, she told herself. *Be strong for Jeff. For Saree. For all the nameless, faceless people—many of whom might even be out there on the mall watching this drama unfold, praying silently that Jeff was there to free them from Compact slavery.*

Somewhere in the night, a bell began to toll. One peal. Another peal. Another. Resolutely the tolls continued, counting slowly down to midnight.

As the sound of the last bell faded away, Lorie's attention locked abruptly on the figure striding confidently from the left side of the patio toward the center. He was tall and slender. His thick blond hair glistened in the bright lights. Powerful in appearance, he was dressed entirely in tight white clothing that emphasized the musculature of his chest and arms, the toned muscles of his abdomen, the sinews in his legs. He was wearing calf-high white leather boots fitted to his legs, supple enough to shift with every motion of his foot—raw power walking. He carried the cutlass in his hand—larger than Lorie had thought it to be, curved steel, in this version blunted but still capable of serious injury. Its blade glistened in the light directed downward onto the patio. Lorie had brought opera glasses, and now she raised them to get a better look at her remarkable husband. Lorie had never seen her Jeff like this—she scarcely recognized him—but in tandem with the raw fear she felt for his well-being, she was possessed by a fierce swell of pride.

"Mr. Selby!" His deep authoritative voice could be heard quite clearly across the soft murmur of voices echoing through the audience gathered below, which instantly ceased! "You have challenged me to a duel. It is midnight. Are you now prepared to lift your cutlass against mine?"

Selby, almost as tall as Jeff, appeared a few seconds later, striding from his sheltered dressing area onto the patio with an almost overwhelming sense of bored disdain. He seemed to radiate power. His clothing was black, padded, making the wearer look more bulky than he actually was. His cutlass was still sheathed, his hand barely touching its hilt. He was accompanied by the young man Lorie had seen earlier. "Mr. Maratti," he said. "Let us get this business settled right away so we can get on with our lives, whatever is left of them."

Suddenly, he drew his cutlass and lunged at Jeff, weapon raised above his head. It came down with a *clang* onto Jeff's instantly raised blade and bounced upward. Selby almost lost his grip. He had not expected his opponent to be as devious as himself. The young man who had been tending to him skittered quickly out of the way and disappeared.

"*En gardé*," Jeff said with a bit of irony in his clearly audible voice, still standing motionless at the spot he had initially claimed. "Thank you for the warning, sir! I now understand your tactics."

He moved backward, acutely focused, awaiting the next blow. When it didn't come, he stood tall, strode nonchalantly behind Selby, nudged him with the side of his blade, and said, "Well?"

Selby flattened his weapon, held it out, and whirled around. Jeff ducked, and his adversary nearly fell over.

Quickly recovering, he chopped angrily at Jeff, who once again eluded the blade.

"Stand still, damn you!" Selby roared.

"I don't believe there is any rule to that effect." Jeff laughed, skipping nimbly away from subsequent thrusts. A roar arose from the crowd!

No matter how hard Selby tried, he could not land a blow. Lorie began to unwind, fascinated by the subtle swordsmanship her husband was exhibiting. He continued the elusive game now playing itself out, seemingly touching Selby gently with his blade anytime he wished.

"He's good," Rolf said softly behind her. "Strong! I've never seen such smooth movements with such a heavy blade!"

Jeff was using the tactics she had overheard him discussing with Rolf and with his coach. He was crowding Selby across the patio, toward the steps that rose behind him. The back of Selby's leg touched the edge of the first step. Frustrated, at last realizing he had no other option, Selby bent his knee, raised his other foot to the step behind him, and moved upward. Another step blocked his way, then another. Encouraged by the point of Jeff's cutlass against his chest, he continued to move upward—away from that increasingly frightening blade!

At one point, Selby let his weapon drop momentarily to his side. It was then Lorie spotted, through the small opera glass still gripped in her hand, the last thing she had ever wanted to see. Engraved on the side of his blade, clearly exposed now by the brilliant floodlights Vince's photographers had brought to the event, was an ugly black skull and crossbones surrounded by a crudely carved heart. Even more ominous was the glitter that defined the cutting edge of the blade—not blunted as promised and earlier judged! Selby's weapon had been switched at the last moment undoubtedly by that troublesome young aide who had skittered to one side as the match began. This, in fact, had to be the exact weapon that had eviscerated Isaac Preston's father, allowing the Blackhearts to take possession of the *Red Rose*! The shock almost unbalanced her.

Selby broke away momentarily and, with no warning, swung again at Jeff with full force. Jeff ducked as the blade swished across his head with little room to spare. The audience, silent a moment before, began to clap, whistle, and shout. "Get him, Jeff," someone called from below. Randy?

Now everyone knew his name!

"Go, Jeff!" someone else called out. The cry was taken up across the audience.

Jeff forced Selby up the next step. Backward. Again, Selby raised his heavy cutlass, stumbled a bit, and lost his grip! The steel weapon hit the ground with a *clang* seconds before he did.

Jeff helped him up and handed the quickly caught cutlass back to him. "Yours, I believe."

Words met with a steely "humpf." It was not until he heard his own voice that Selby realized every syllable was being amplified. With a start, he grabbed his weapon possessively and backed off, still leaving the dreaded symbol exposed!

Jeff could not miss seeing it now nor the gleaming edge of the blade. The ultimate betrayal!

With a sudden vigor she recognized as carefully contained anger, he forced his opponent up to the next step!

Fifty-eight steps! With no remorse, Jeff was now compelling Selby to move backward and upward, holding the very same weapon that two centuries before had killed Isaac Preston's father, Jeff's grandfather, allowing that good man's young wife no other option but suicide and thereby leaving their five-year-old son an orphan!

Lorie noted the older man shifting his heavy weapon back and forth as its weight began to wear at his arm muscles. Hard as he might try, however, there was no target he could reach, nor had he anything to hide behind. Just one broad empty step after another. Backward, upward, upward—using leg muscles he had probably never once considered the need to tone.

Someone in the audience noticed and began to count. "Eleven," he called out. "Twelve."

The crowd swiftly took up the chant. Lorie did, too, silently but fervently. Clearly Selby was rattled by the sound of voices favoring his opponent! He tried to move to one side to find a way back down to the plaza—to the easier playing field.

Jeff was always blocking his way. No matter which direction Selby turned, Jeff's quick blade was there. Even blunted, its effectiveness was devastating! Selby had only one route available to him.

By the mid-thirties, Selby was clearly losing any ability he might have had to escape. He could scarcely stumble up to the next step, Jeff's blunted steel ranging within inches of his all-too-vulnerable neck or his temple!

Jeff persisted. Selby moved—always upward—one uncertain step at a time. Sometimes trying to swing his blade. Often stumbling. Now and then putting his free hand down to the cement step to keep from stumbling.

"Forty," the chant from below went on. "Forty-one. Forty-two."

Jeff clearly had the advantage—had had it from the beginning, Lorie now realized! "Are you ready to declare defeat?" Lorie heard him ask.

"No, dammit!" the man shouted, striking out again. Jeff ducked as the blade approached him, rose, made a graceful turn, and returned to the forefront, his blunted blade still extended, blocking Selby's quite efficiently.

"You will continue to climb upward then," Jeff said resolutely. "We will visit Mr. Lincoln together, you and I!" The words may have been soft, but they were heard plainly by the silent crowd below.

A great swell of sound arose then, a rhythmic chant: "Go! Go! Go!"

Jeff placed the curve of his cutlass under Selby's chin and boosted it upward. "Mr. Selby, please stand. Mr. Lincoln awaits your presence."

Selby stood up, turned toward the steps, and, as he took a step upward, suddenly reversed his course, swinging his blade wildly.

Jeff dodged lightly away, obviously expecting the move! His cutlass caught Selby's blade mid-swing, lifted it directly from the man's hand, and released it as he turned away from the steps. It hit the steps below and continued clattering downward, too far away this time for Selby to reclaim. A great roar arose from what had now become a great crowd of partisan watchers.

Jeff turned back to his adversary, prodding him in the chest with the more virtuous blade. Selby began again, reluctantly, to climb to the top and then forward now, the curve of Jeff's weapon located lightly at the middle of his back ready not to thrust but poised to give a painful whack.

Again, the audience burst into wild applause. Jeff did not pause to acknowledge his win. That would happen, Lorie felt, after he and Selby had reached the top of the great staircase and were fully situated in front of the massive memorial to one of America's greatest leaders!

"He would not have asked you to bow before him," Jeff said firmly once they had arrived, his words clearly heard through the crisp night air, "nor will I! But Mr. Lincoln was without any doubt the better man, Mr. Congressman, although he had to die to accomplish his goals. I will not let you die. You must pay for the choices you have made in your life!"

At that moment, Lorie, her mouth open and jaw dropped, realized that the confrontation she had so feared was behind them! Her husband—her tender lover, her fierce protector, the father of her precious child, and her very best friend—was not dead nor wounded!

It was clear to everyone that Jefferson Richard Preston Maratti was the decisive victor, even if they did not know any one of his names!

He turned toward the people milling about below. An instant hush came across the crowd. "Mr. Selby," Jeff said, his amplified voice now booming out across the mall, "is a lawfully elected congressman from Virginia. Concurrently, he is a lifetime member of an organization associated with piracy and other murderous practices to which he and his family for the past two hundred years have pledged their complete loyalty. It is called the Blackheart Compact."

"His ancestors are among the founding members of the Blackhearts," he went on, now speaking into breathless silence, "a criminal organization dating to the eighteenth century during which time pirates roamed the oceans, praying upon innocent ships engaged in legitimate trade. Mr. Selby is the contemporary leader of this organization, as it has remained active and is still thriving in this century and in this country. His obligations to the Blackheart Compact, its founding document, have always superseded his obligations to the Constitution of the United States of America, and I have been the first signer of a petition asking him to give up his elected position because of this clear conflict of interest. If anyone wants to join me in signing the petition, there are people moving among you quite willing to accept signatures."

Lorie watched as onlookers paused, sought out petition holders, and took the time to sign. She was impressed as she had ever been, immersed in rapture at the unreality of the entire event, which had suddenly become very real!

Bernice came to her out of the dark, gave Lorie a huge hug, and then impulsively embraced her younger sister, Emily, followed by anyone else who seemed to need warm arms. She was laughing, crying, hugging all the sympathizers she found nearby! "I don't believe it!" she kept saying. "Freedom at last! After all these years!"

Suddenly, someone at the base of the monument cried out a warning. Lorie turned and looked up. Selby, who had been standing transfixed like a cornered beast beside Jeff, had made a sudden lunge toward her husband.

Jeff stepped back abruptly, countered the move with a few quick moves of his own, and was now holding Selby's arm high. He shook the captured arm, lifted it higher, and shook it again forcefully. A dagger slid to the ground from inside Selby's upraised sleeve. The clatter it made falling to the platform could be clearly heard across the mall. Silence suddenly encompassed the entire area.

Lorie saw Randy running toward Jeff from behind the monument, calling out.

"I'm fine!" Jeff's words did not waver. "Just a scratch." Blood had begun to well copiously from his cheek, course across his chin, and drip downward, spreading across the previously pristine whiteness of his shirt.

Two park policemen were quickly on the scene. Selby's arms were wrenched behind his back, cuffs snapped into place. The two officials whisked him behind the massive statue of Lincoln, the place from which Randy had been prepared to offer assistance if it were required. All four men disappeared.

Lorie could no longer see her husband, but before worry had a chance to take hold, he appeared once again. Some of the blood had been mopped away, and a faint bandage was now apparent on his cheek. "Mr. Selby has conceded the match," he called out and bowed again at the wild response. Before the clamor had ended, he turned to leave.

Another thunderous round of applause again stopped him. Jeff turned back to his supporters—to even more applause. He swept the blade of the cutlass slowly to the floor in front of him, paused as steel met cement, and firmly returned the blade to its scabbard. Making a graceful turn, he disappeared behind marble walls.

It took some time for the applause to finally subside. It wasn't until then that the bright lights previously directed at the monument went out. Only the customary park lighting remained, along with the continuing excited clamor of the huge crowd, now dissipating, albeit reluctantly, with many eagerly seeking out the petitions that were still being passed around.

CHAPTER 45

L orie rose from her seat. Rolf said numbly, "Now what do we do?"

"I was going to ask you that exact question," Lorie answered. Sisters Emily and Bernice stood silent beside her, both as stunned as she. "This is not something we even talked about. Let's see if we can find Randy."

Excited spectators were moving away rapidly, disappearing into the darkness, chattering excitedly among themselves, wondering who that person was who had so soundly defeated a crazy homicidal congressman! Was he an actor from a TV show or a movie? Had this been a real duel or something cooked up as PR for a new show?

But Lorie could also tell from the conversation around her it was apparent that many people had recognized the congressman from Virginia. Many of these workers lived in his congressional district in Virginia!

"That cutlass Selby was using," she said quietly to her companions, several of whom had missed that part of the byplay, "was switched for one that had never been blunted. It was the same one we read about in Isaac Preston's first journal, the blade that killed his father! It would have been sharp enough to cut Jeff in two." Before she could elaborate, they were approached by two uniformed park policemen.

438

"We're here to escort you folks to a temporary emergency room," one said politely. "A vehicle is available if you wish."

"Thanks!" Rolf Maratti replied, acknowledged spokesman now for his small party. "Better than walking." But it was with some concern in his voice that he asked, "Where are we going?"

"It's an office building," was all they would say, and since his group didn't seem to have much, if any, option, they agreed to the transportation.

In the long black limousine that pulled to the curb alongside, they were driven several blocks to a tall glass building in the very heart of the district. They were escorted through a huge modern lobby encased inside luminous walls. Lorie spotted a banking institution within those walls, several boutique stores, a small coffee shop—all now closed— and a long row of elevators, one of which Lorie's party was encouraged to enter. They were subsequently let off at what seemed to be the top floor by a young police officer who then led them past a darkened receptionist's area and into a large well-appointed office, obviously the workspace of one of the top executives of the firm.

Jeff was there, looking very tired, sitting as still as he could in the office secretary's swivel chair. A middle-aged man answering to the title of "Doctor" was replacing facial tissues and transparent tape with a seriously workmanlike bandage, and it appeared to Lorie as if more than a few stitches had been taken. "They're not too deep," the doctor said in a comforting voice. "It will hurt for a while, but you are very lucky, Mr. Maratti! You will not die from this wound, as you might well have if your reaction had been less brisk!"

"However, regrettably, I'm afraid you will always bear the scar in some form or other. But look on the bright side!"

he added with a bright humorous smile. "You'll have a lot to tell your grandchildren if they point and ask, 'Where did you get that one, Gramps?' You can always wow them by saying you got it in a midnight duel with a pirate on the steps of the Lincoln Memorial in Washington, DC. The bizarre thing is," he laughed out loud and then shook his head in a "now I've seen everything" kind of way, "you won't be kidding! It's a good thing you're quicker than he was! He really was 'trying for the jugular'! Not cool for an 'exhibition match'!"

The doctor turned, saw his visitors, and smiled. "Hi, Family! He outsmarted the bad guy and survived! We're all relieved! It was 'touch and go' there for a moment! Representative Selby was stark raving mad when the park police wrestled him down and finally managed to dislodge the rest of his concealed weapons! He will spend the rest of his days behind bars in a cell, maybe padded! He keeps saying the match was stolen!"

"He was convinced he could kill my husband in front of hundreds of people and walk away free?" Lorie was still shaken by the very thought of it.

"Premeditated murder!" the doctor said very seriously, looking up at her. "Even in front of all those witnesses! Nor did he expect to pay for it! Crazy as a hoot owl!"

"They probably had some bizarre excuse cooked up to cover slipped blade syndrome," Ewen said. He had just walked into the room, escorted, as they had been, by park police. "Hi, Doc. Thanks for coming. We feared there might be some blood let tonight! Jeff, how do you feel?"

"I'm not really sure!" he said quietly.

"It was a great show!" Ewen went on, as excited as he'd ever been. "We've got it all taped and filmed, including every damn word he said to his seconds—all incriminating, including his express intention to kill you, Jeff! Grigori and Vince are so excited between the two of them that they can scarcely put two coherent words together. Last I saw of them, they were jumping up and down, slapping hands, knocking each other's shoulders, being quite ridiculous about it. They think you're terrific, my friend, as do we all!"

"Much depended on my winning," Jeff said softly.

"You are by far the superior athlete, no question about it, and, it goes without saying, a transparently principled man! Now you and Lorie"—his eyes turned toward her—"and your little daughter can finally take a long vacation and get some much-needed rest, go up to the mountains with your newly found family, and just do nothing for a while!"

"I don't think so," Jeff said, a stunned expression creasing his bandaged face.

"Why not?" Ewen asked, genuinely surprised.

"It was something Selby said just before they put him into the police car. A large number of other people came to me out of the darkness, and all of them told me the same thing…mostly with congratulations and wishes for a better future! They all seemed so happy about it I think it might be fact!"

"What was it?" Lorie asked.

It seemed an awfully long time before the answer came. She remained patient—reluctantly! What she really wanted to do was yell, but she would not do that to a wounded husband!

He took a deep breath and sighed! "By Compact Rules, the person who defeats the captain in saber battle, with witnesses to attest that it was a fair fight, becomes the new captain!"

Lorie gasped. "Becomes…?" But of course! Somehow he—or the spirit of the person who had compelled Jeff to call Selby out—had known exactly what had to be done to destroy The Compact!

Isaac Preston himself? Will Deerfield? A conspiracy of spirits, perhaps!

Jeff dropped his head into his hands. The quiet in the room seemed to take an inordinately long time to get past. No one wanted to speak—at least until Jeff did!

Finally, he looked up, grim-faced. "I'm too tired to talk about it. Can we just go home? We can talk about it tomorrow."

"What are we thinking?" Ewen roared. "Let's get this show on the road! Drivers?"

"On it!" Bernice trumpeted and headed out to the lobby where open elevators awaited them. Her car keys were in her hand. Once they retrieved their cars, police officers escorted their small party through town—both to ease their way through the heavy traffic they seemed to be encountering on their way to the bridge over the Potomac River; primarily, they realized, for their protection. It took some time, but at last they found themselves on the correct highway, headed back to the secluded horse farm in Virginia.

Gripping her husband's hand as if it were a lifeline, Lorie breathed a vast sigh of relief! She thought she would never let it go!

CHAPTER 46

May 1, 2016
Back at the Virginia Horse Farm

N o one got up early the next morning, but when Lorie finally managed to lift her eyelids just before eleven o'clock and realized that Jeff was not there beside her, she fairly leaped out of bed. "Are you okay?" she asked when she found him in their small bathroom, carefully lifting the bandage that had been spread across his right cheek. He was trying to examine, with some difficulty, the stitches holding together the jagged edges of a fearful bloody slash. "Does it hurt?" she asked.

He turned to her and, after letting her do her medical/ wifely thing—replacing the bandage in its entirety—drew her into his arms. "Yes, I am very okay," he said to her first question. With even more good humor in his voice, he added in regard to the second question, "And yes, it hurts like the dickens! Also, I think Randy is up. I heard him talking with Saree, telling her that the genius trio has just arrived. He just hollered out that we've been invited to go to the big house for a late breakfast, I think he called it brunch. That okay with you?"

Nodding, she turned her face upward for a kiss and clung to him for a long time afterward. "I was terrified I would lose you last night!" she whispered. "I've always known that you were called here to do a great and dangerous thing, my dear love. But that *thing* was so terrifying I couldn't possibly have imagined it!"

"And yet," he responded with great warmth, totally embracing her, letting his chin rest lightly atop her head, "without a single whine or whimper, you were willing to let me follow my destiny, take my chances, and ultimately have my moment of glory! You are a remarkable wife and companion." He pulled back and looked squarely into her eyes. "I mean to tell you this over and over again as we travel the rest of our lives together, battling whatever forces of evil we may yet encounter, you are and always will be my very best friend! If I don't say it once a day, then reprimand me for becoming senile!" Seeing her big grin and after another moment of silent reflection, he put his arms tightly about her again and added, "So I must tell you a little guilty secret, my love. There were more souls at that encounter early this morning than Selby and myself." Again, he paused, seemingly trying to find the right words. "I was well prepared, of course," he finally said, "beforehand! But just the same, I could feel them with me, cheering me on!"

A huge burden she had not realized she was still carrying instantly lifted from Lorie's shoulders. "Telling you exactly what Selby was planning?"

"Good grief, wife!" he remonstrated with a big laugh and a broad wink. "That would be cheating!"

Now wearing a triumphant grin, she said, "Let's gather up Randy and that small chatterbox he's having a serious conversation with and head for the big house! I bet we'll have champagne for breakfast!"

"Knowing Ewen, you may be right!"

Indeed, she was. Big bottles of high-quality champagne were located in a number of places around the big gathering room that opened onto the outdoor patio, although only one cork had yet been pulled and that bottle had scarcely been touched! That plus all the rest, Lorie opined, would be relocated to the discard pile before the end of the day!

Of more significance, many members of the Thomas family of West Virginia—fully aware by now that their connection to the Randolph family of Virginia would from this day on be publicly confirmed by Jeff's astonishing similarity in appearance to Vince Thomas, black movie hero *par excellence*—were happily enjoying a sumptuous outdoor breakfast with new and welcome relatives and friends!

Randy walked the still chattering Saree into the playroom where many children had congregated, and finally, a few minutes later, still grinning but nearly exhausted by small-fry chaos, he emerged onto the patio and headed for the food table. "Jeb's stuck there for a while," he said to Lorie, "teaching Brian Selby how to be a really great big brother to their sweet little Todd. Brian's taking to it like a duck to water! That's one massive problem well solved!"

Lorie grinned at Randy and gave him a thumbs-up.

"Come on, you laggards back there in the house," Bernice called out from her workstation at the outdoor grill. "Come join in the conversation and eats!" When she spotted Jeff, she called out, "The conquering hero emerges! Speech! Speech!"

A great cheer went up, led by fencing coaches Grigori and Vince, who threw their arms high into the air. Jeff grinned and made a grand bow to Grigori, similar to the one he had made very early that morning in a very different place, and then said to Vince and Bernice, "You folks are now free to claim your full heritage without worry about any kind of retribution from the Blackheart Compact organization!" With a victorious smile, he stood tall again and said loudly to all around him, "The Compact organization is out of business once and for all! As its new captain, I have just declared it so—you are my witnesses—thereby putting myself out of a really cushy job!"

Again, a cheer arose, even more raucous, with a few cat-calls included!

"And I have a feeling that it will be the multitudes who were gathered below the monument last night," Jeff went on with a bit more moderation, his eyes still twinkling, "who will spread our message far and wide. They will pass along the truth about Congressman Selby, facts they saw up close and in person. Selby's supporters will no longer be able to claim the high ground when the sun shines brightly, as it now will, on his many misdeeds! The Compact organization will crumble under its own weight as the *Blackheart* sinks once and for all into the depths from which it arose!"

Again, cheers arose from assembled relatives and friends! Many wineglasses were raised into the fresh country air—Lorie's included!

"But don't ask for a repeat performance from me any-time soon," Jeff said decisively, turning his smile into a fake frown. "It hurts like hell!"

To calls of "Awww, poor baby" and similar jocular dis-paragements, Jeff ran the gauntlet of all his friends and rela-tives lined up at the grill, shaking hands and clasping shoul-ders. He selected two platters to offer to Bernice, who filled them with special attention. He finally made his way back to Lorie, handed her one of the overflowing plates, and carefully seated himself.

Rolf Maratti was seated at Lorie's other side, glowing with obvious pride. "You're not hurting as much as Selby is, I'd venture to bet!" he said. Lorie had never heard Rolf sound quite so cheerful nor seen his grin quite so wide.

"How masterful our young man looked last night!" Ewen's voice boomed out. He had just come onto the patio bearing a cut glass bowl filled with freshly picked fruits. He set it down mid-table where it sparkled gaily through random splashes of sunlight filtering through the wind-rustled trees.

"Lorie and I have just been discussing the important documents we managed to snatch away from The Compact by exceedingly devious means," Jeff said as their host seated himself across them. "The Compact document itself, for one. Where is it, by the way?"

"Lying in its glassine envelope on the table in the work area," Ewen said. "Placed there by Guppy, the only entity brave enough to touch it! The genius trio has been too busy looking through other stuff to give that onerous parchment even a once-over." He paused for a long moment and finally said, "I really don't want to have anything to do with it. I think everyone's kind of afraid of it! I am! I'll admit it! And I don't even believe in that kind of nonsensical stuff! Well, not entirely…"

"Have you copied it?" Lorie asked softly.

"Really didn't want to," Ewen confessed just as quietly. "I decided it was better to get pictures of all those other documents first before I tackled the big bloody one. Maybe just a distant photograph…" He picked up a peach and gazed at it, seeing something else entirely. "That bloody parchment," he went on in a grumpy tone, laying the soft smooth-skinned fruit gently on the table, "and I say that literally…well, it's bloody creepy!"

"I agree," Jeff said. "Does anyone else feel the same way?"

"Was it a kind of sensation," Bernice said querulously, "like something evil is crawling up your back headed for your neck?" She shook her head. "When I heard someone talking about it that way, I decided to stay clear of it."

Lorie agreed wholeheartedly. "Pure evil! It needs to be destroyed!" She looked at Ewen and then at Rolf. No response. They both seemed to be mulling that prospect over.

"It's kind of a historical document, isn't it?" Vince Thomas ventured. He had just wandered over to their table to chat and caught the last part of the conversation. "Would a major museum want it? For research, perhaps?"

Lorie's response was immediate and a little tense. "Who would ever want to admit that one of their ancestors signed the bloody thing! Or even worse could happen. Somebody would come along aiming to write a treatise about the poor pirates and offer motivations for their behavior! How offensive would that be to the memories of their victims? At least to me, knowing what I now know!"

Ewen said softly, "Maybe it should just be put into a vault somewhere."

"Why?" Jeff asked. He was preparing to dig into a stack of pancakes dripping with maple syrup. "Apparently, I'm the new captain. So I say, let's get rid of it! The only question left is, how?"

"Drop it into an active volcano!" Bernice suggested, half-seriously.

Ewen shook his head, chuckling. "I suspect that overflying an active volcano at a low-enough altitude to be certain the 'dropped thing' would actually go in would be a rather dodgy task. What would you think if the volcano gave a great 'whoosh' and the paper flew far away, hiding itself until someone in the distant future finds it in a desert somewhere and decides to use it again for purposes of evil?"

"How about laying it on a hot grill and watching it curl up and die?" Emily suggested. She had just retrieved Todd from Brian Talbot, who, with a huge plateful of breakfast in hand, was happily returning to his childcare chores in the playroom.

"Shred it and drop it into the Great Garbage Patch in the Pacific Ocean," Randy suggested but not too seriously. Even as he spoke, his attention was wandering to a second stack of pancakes.

Rolf laughed. "It would probably be the one and only thing that escapes the Patch and finds its way back! But," he went on with a bit more thought, "there might be something of historical value to merit keeping the damned thing. We really don't know anything about it. None of us, to my knowledge, has read anything more than a name or two— and no one's been willing to take a picture of it. Come to think of it, I don't remember Isaac ever writing a word about the specifics of what those poor men had signed up for! He just touched on it briefly. Let's just burn it up!"

Bernice let out a yelp. "Not on the grill! Compact remains on our food…?"

Randy continued that thought in a sepulchral voice. "Smoke filtering through our brains, forcing us to perform all The Compact's evil wishes for the next century and beyond!"

"Let's sauté it first," Jeff said drily, "with the hottest sauce we can find so we recognize it when it grabs us!"

Lorie felt a tug on her pant leg and looked down. Her daughter was standing there, looking up at her, a decided frown on her face. "Mama?" Saree said.

Lorie knelt beside her worried little daughter. "What are you doing out here, hon? All the little ones are over in the playroom. Come on, I'll take you back."

"Doggy," she said urgently. "Bad Doggy?" It was a quizzical expression.

A little nudge of worry crept up Lorie's spine. She said softly, "What did Doggy do, honey?"

"Doggy bited bad thing!" Saree turned, pointing toward the doorway that entered into the workroom where documents of all kinds were spread across the big tables.

Lorie looked across the area and saw the little fox trotting out through the doorway. He seemed to be carrying a curled-up paper in his mouth. He glanced toward Saree first and then toward Lorie. With a quick shake of his head, he turned abruptly and hurried away toward the edge of the woods. It seemed to Lorie that he sensed he was doing something he knew he shouldn't, but he was determined to do it, anyway! She stood up.

"Jeff," she said softly.

He looked up at her, eyebrows lifted.

"I wonder what Doggy just carried out of the workroom."

Jeff unfolded himself from his seat at the table. "What was Doggy doing in the workroom?" He looked toward the woods. His attention tracked back to the opened doorway and then returned quickly to the woods. Doggy had settled himself under the spreading branches of a thorny bush and was now busily tearing into a piece of old paper, his little head moving up and down as if he were conquering a big bug or a tasty morsel. In fact, it looked as if Doggy were actually eating the paper—voraciously!

"If that's what I think it is…," Jeff said quietly and stopped, still watching. He moved slowly across the lawn toward the little fox, his hand out. "Here, Doggy. Give me the paper, Chief! We've got to know what you have there."

Doggy rose up on his haunches, chewing mightily, growling a bit deep in his chest. Very little of the paper was left. Jeff grabbed for it and almost got it! The little fox grabbed it back, took a couple more bites, swallowed hard, and then—satisfied—settled down and began to groom his tiny paws. A long moment later, hugely satisfied with himself, he looked up at Jeff with what seemed to be a big grin on his face. He rose nonchalantly to his feet, turned, and trotted off into the depths of the woods to do his business.

A cry arose from the workroom. "It's gone! The Compact document! It's gone!" It was Brian Talbot calling out anxiously. "The kids are giggling and saying Doggy ate it, and now he's going to poop it! Have you seen him? Have you seen the paper?"

"Indeed," Lorie said softly, a grin too much like Doggy's on her face. She looked up at Jeff. The giggles came from somewhere very deep within.

Jeff tried, but when push came to shove, his laughter peeled out across the yard as well. "Problem solved!" he announced loudly when he could finally catch a breath.

That was when the real party began!

ABOUT THE AUTHOR

Marolyn Caldwell grew up in a college town called Manhattan, located in very heart of the Kansas Flint Hills, where her father was a chemistry teacher at Kansas State. She has been writing mystery stories since she could pick up a pencil. But she didn't sell her first book until she found out many years and many states later, while she was living in Washington, DC, about romance and mystery writers' conventions. When she was informed that a convention calling itself Malice Domestic was being introduced in Bethesda, Maryland, she immediately signed up. There she met an editor who was looking for romantic mysteries. *Flight into Danger* and *Whirlwind* were subsequently published by Walker & Co. Marolyn volunteered for a board position on the planning staff of the second Malice Domestic convention and was a member of that board for many years. When she retired from years of being a legal secretary, she moved back to her birthplace in the Kansas version of Manhattan, where she discovered to her delight that the Carnegie Library she had so loved when she was a child was just reaching its centennial year. She proposed a Midwest mystery convention to the board of directors, got the go-ahead, gathered up a lot of enthusiastic volunteers who had no idea what they were in for, incorporated the Great Manhattan Mystery Conclave, and for six years spent her time in bliss meeting mystery writers from both sides of the country, listening to their wit and wisdom, and learning ever so much about the craft and business of writing. The ideas behind *Battle of Wills* and its two successors predate all those conventions, drawing as they do from a family history that isn't quite spoken about but being inspired by the tales she has uncovered in researching especially her mother's family, quiet farm people who were very resourceful. They lived on the banks of the Ohio River in Kentucky and ran a very accommodating ferryboat across the river—until their town was burned to the ground by Morgan's Raiders! Which was why they ended up living in Kansas and Marolyn was born there. Full circle!